I savoured th... the men of th... Alliance real...

I could almost he... ...minds grinding to a halt. *This* is Calista St James?

I knew what *this* looked like. A cute young woman, emphasis on *young*. My standout feature was my eyes. Exotic, black, intense. I'd learned to use them. For misdirection. For fascination. For intimidation.

Apart from that, I was nothing special. It helped me get underestimated, which suited me just fine.

But now, I was known. My past with the Alliance ensured that. It was debatable whether having an overblown reputation, and having it precede me, was good or bad.

I met Sir Ashton's eyes. Former head of the Alliance. Was that a trace of anxiety I saw? Good. He should be anxious. I intended to make him pay. Make them all pay. For then...and for now.

Strong Medicine
OLIVIA GATES

MILLS & BOON®

INTRIGUE™

First published in Great Britain 2007
Harlequin Mills & Boon Limited,
Eton House, 18-24 Paradise Road, Richmond, Surrey TW9 1SR

© Olivia Gates 2005

ISBN: 978 0 263 85720 7

46-0507

Printed and bound in Spain
by Litografía Rosés S.A., Barcelona

OLIVIA GATES

As a surgeon, singer and painter, Olivia Gates is no stranger to real-life drama and high-stakes situations. It was no wonder, when she turned to writing, that she drew on her contrasting interests to help her weave the stories she loves to read and loves more to write, stories filled with hard-hitting action, danger, reality and passion.

Her artistic side insists on viewing each book as a composition, a performance, a canvas with endless possibilities. Her surgeon side relishes the adrenaline rush of jumping into her independent, highly skilled and fearless heroines' shoes.

She also loves giving those heroines heroes who measure up to them, who would do anything to deserve them, to win them. To her, there is no other kind of hero. And certainly no other kind of heroine.

To two incredible ladies, Leslie Wainger and
Natashya Wilson.
This one is for you. It wouldn't be without
your faith, vision and support.

Prologue

I laid my fingers on the baby girl's twiglike neck, checking her carotid pulse. I knew I'd find none.

The girl was stiff, long dead of literal hunger. Still her mother cooed to her, offered the baby her shriveled, bone-dry breast.

My burning eyes escaped the wrenching sight, taking refuge in the inky darkness. But there was no escape. Strewed all around me, burnt bodies languished in the sterile harshness of my emergency light, mutilated wraiths, crowding my vision, warping my mind.

Then I saw nothing. My senses blinked out, burst back to focus—on sounds. Those of renewed carnage. Their oppressors had sent reinforcements. No! These people needed more time....

"Fall back, St. James!"

My mission leader. De Luna. His order lashed across my overextended senses, imperative, final. *Preposterous*. Fall back? And leave my patients? Wasn't happening!

I'd been struggling to resuscitate the most devastated, pray-

ing for just enough stabilization to get them to stagger out of
their razed village. For two hours I'd been wading through damaging emotions I'd never imagined.

Now rage came to my rescue. I groped for it, let the tidal wave
of stress hormones engulf me, expand my suffocating senses,
boost my dwindling stamina.

I took the dead baby from her mother's insubstantial grip, laid
her to rest on the ground and yelled, "Run!" I swung to the others, urgency bursting my heart. "All of you, *run!*"

I'd depleted the Sudanese I'd learned for this mission, yet
they understood me. I knew they did. And thought I was crazy.
They stared at me out of skeletal, misshapen faces with yel-
lowed, extinguished eyes. Despair made human.

I sprang up, dragged one after the other to their wobbly feet,
steered them in the direction of the narrow stretch of jungle
about seven hundred feet away. On the other side our team
would be coming back to pick us up.

Now to convince them I could buy them the time to reach it.

I didn't know if I could. But I was damned if I'd leave them
here for the mercenaries to vent their murderous frustration on.

I got my gun out, gestured with it. They got the message. *Run,
I'm covering you.* And they trusted that I would.

Many couldn't run. So they hobbled and crawled, with the
same determination that had spurred hundreds before them today, hope and terror animating their depleted bodies.

Gunfire was coming closer, the mercenaries spreading an
advance shock wave of subjugating shots. Then the lights
went out.

"I gave you an order, St. James!" De Luna. *He'd* turned off
my light. His overwhelming presence materialized beside me,
his order a gut punch. Then my eyes adapted to the African
stars' uncanny light and I saw his silhouette. Emanating anger
blacker than our camouflage paint and gear.

I ignored him, continued helping the villagers, and his wrath became talons digging into my shoulder. "If we guard their backs as they crawl away, we're dead."

"If we don't, *they* are!" Those robbed of the basic dignity and autonomy of a functioning body *were* my mission. But his superior strength was herding me away, depriving me of any chance to do what I had to. Desperation detonated inside my head. I clung to him, tried one last time. "*Please*—we can—"

"We can't save everyone." His large hand yanked my arm again, shoved me ahead of him. "The team secured the others and are circling around to meet us at the jungle's edge—"

"Just in time to help us mobilize those remaining!"

"Engaging reinforcements isn't in our plan or capability, and these people won't make it through the jungle. Now move!"

I didn't. I *couldn't*. He shook me, hard. "You've been briefed. This is a projected outcome, an acceptable loss."

Acceptable loss. The grisly verdict crushed down on me, a jackhammer stamping out my rage, shattering my reason. Something alien, beyond rage and horror and pity, swamped me, possessed me. It screeched one thing until my skull was bursting with it.

No loss is acceptable.

My knee came up in an explosive *hiza geri*. Connected. His grunted curse was more disbelief than pain. Then agony jammed his nervous pathways, doubled him up in a knot of self-protection. I shoved him off balance and he fell, hard.

Somewhere in my fogged awareness, other voices shrieked. *This is wrong. Crazy. Crippling him like that could sentence him to death. You're sentencing* yourself *to death.*

I didn't care. Possible death was in our job description. Not so these people. Experiencing their ordeal and degradation… There was only so much horror a mind could take. This was way more.

And they'd trusted me to save them. *Trusted* me! I wasn't letting anyone write them off as acceptable loss again.

I straddled De Luna and his helpless rage flayed me as he grappled with the paralysis. He'd succeed in seconds. That was how long I had.

I stripped him of every explosive he had. He had plenty. Our—his—blitz had relied on strategy, stealth, precision and firearms. Explosives had been backup, too unpredictable in range and damage to be used as first measure with the hostages around.

As his lowly Global Crisis Alliance medical tagalong, I'd warranted only an M-9 Beretta and a few magazines of ammo. An afterthought—to defend myself if the big boys and gals of the Preemptive Anti-Terrorist Squad had better things to do than keep me safely crammed at the back of formation. After all the training and trials by fire, I'd been picked, against his will, not for my combat capabilities, just my "cool under fire" ones.

Time to put *those* to good use.

My plan was simple. Stuff my backpack with grenades, toss it at the mercenaries. One problem was, the explosives wouldn't detonate on impact. Simple answer was to trapshoot it. The explosions should wreak enough damage and chaos to buy the villagers a chance to reach the pickup site.

I zipped my backpack and heaved up to my feet. De Luna lunged at me. "You stubborn idiot, get down!"

Responses he'd honed over twenty-four grueling months propelled me in the air, clearing his pincer tackle. His enraged hiss speared my breastbone. "They're shooting blind, but draw their attention and you'll give them a bull's-eye!"

Shadows cried out in the blackness. I swung around, eyes steaming with sweat and sweltering humidity. Grotesque heaps were collapsing to the ground. Stray bullets finding targets. Could have been me. Could still be. Had to make the time I had on my feet count. I hissed back, "Get my patients to safety."

He lunged again and I exploded into a running start, just like the thousand races he'd put me through, not letting me rest until I'd broken my record and everybody else's.

I decelerated from twenty plus miles per hour to an abrupt zero about three hundred feet from the mercenaries. De Luna was right. They didn't see me. They were heading in the wrong direction. Or were they? God, no! They *weren't*.

Another three hundred feet away from them, caught in their flashlights, were their targets. Two emaciated villagers who must have been left behind. The men had found two barely alive guerillas and were holding guns to their heads, buying their kin running time. Would the guerillas negotiate for their comrades' lives?

They didn't even hesitate. Crimson burst from both captive guerillas and villagers, filling my vision, drowning what remained of my reason. And I did it.

I swung the backpack over my head, revolved around my axis over and over, built a hammer-throw momentum, let it catapult out of my hands. My hammer throw record was two hundred feet. But that was with the sixteen-pound steel ball hammer. The lighter backpack would have landed more than two hundred and fifty feet away, almost on top of the mercenaries. I didn't let it land.

I hurled myself to the ground as it began its descent and emptied my semiautomatic pistol. Every shot found its mark. *Thank you, De Luna. For that, at least.*

The explosions were deafening. Gratifying. Even at that distance, a piece of shrapnel whizzed over my head. Good. It meant the mercenaries were being shredded. Their screams were more proof.

Then darkness intensified. One of the distant flashlights flailed my way, illuminating the hot, viscous purple-black descending on my vision. Blood. Pouring from a scalp wound I still didn't feel. One frantic hand wiped it out of my eyes, the other clamped down on the spurting wound. I had to see....

Then I saw. Everything. Smeared in violence and death.

Those still standing among the mercenaries were charging.

Then De Luna knocked me down and exploded over me, bellowing, meeting them halfway, his inexhaustible machine guns echoing his intimidation. More thunder joined his in a soul-rending crescendo. His team. They'd come back. They stampeded past me, merging with him into an unconquerable unit.

I lay there, unarmed and useless, watched the carnage.

When the last explosion and roar and dying gurgle had ebbed from the air and my ears, the first rays of dawn diluted the darkness. The villagers were in the distance, no more of their number injured. The few mercenaries who remained alive were staggering toward us, bloodied and cowed. And De Luna—*De Luna!*

He was facedown on the ground, his whole left side drenched in blood—God, no—he couldn't be dead!

I ran, threw myself beside him, tasted my own blood, tried to turn him. He jerked, knocked my hands off, struggled up on trembling arms. Another burst of horror flooded me as he began to drag his torn body on the ground and I saw his destination.

The blasted bodies of three of his team.

Chapter 1

"This is all your fault!"

A grating voice hurled the accusation. It took me a second to realize it was inside my head.

Hot shivers cascaded down my body, sick sweat erupting from my every pore. God—oh, God—this *wasn't* happening!

Twenty seconds ago I was repairing our janitor's ruptured abdominal aortic aneurysm under angiographic X-ray guidance. Ten seconds ago the monitor flickered, distorted then blipped out as my newest and dumbest-yet acquisition, the so-called "like new" ceiling-mounted angiographic machine, expired in a spectacular smoke show. And it *was* all my fault. Mostly.

A guilt trip was the last thing I needed right now. I had priorities. Like grappling with an impending heart attack.

I had my balloon up Mendoza's artery and I'd lost visual. This was really happening.

Breathe, moron. This wasn't my first catastrophic intrasurgical complication. No use going all apoplectic now. Or dropping dead, either. That was the easy way out. I was in too far and I had to continue the procedure. Blindly.

Yeah. Great idea.

Problem was, it was the only idea. Another idea that appealed right now was to hurl around everything I could reach and scream manic death threats and self-abuse.

Later. I promised myself the sweet outlet. My patient needed my total focus now.

I gritted my teeth and continued, summoning in my mind's eye the last X-ray image before I'd lost visual, a map to where I was going and what I was supposed to do next.

Minutes later, relying on every iota of experience, intuition and knowledge of anatomy, I thought I bridged and sealed the rupture. Not that I was about to rely on conjectures. Time to conduct an experiment to see if I'd succeeded.

I withdrew the balloon catheter out of the top-of-the-thigh incision and turned to my assistant. "Ayesha, up fluid delivery until systolic blood pressure is 110."

Her artfully drawn black eyebrows disappeared below her cap. "That's too high!"

It was not a good time to indulge in our favorite pastime of squabbling over surgical decisions. "Ayesha—just *do* it!"

She dropped her incredulous gaze and carried out my order. I almost flinched when she did. Weird. I usually had to convince her. Sometimes she convinced me. I sure prayed I deserved her unquestioning faith this time.

Ayesha was more than my nurse. She was my partner, my left hand. My right one was Matt McDermott. They'd been the first two I'd approached with my plans of putting together extralegal medical crisis crews, setting up sanctuaries outside the system for the people who fell below its radar.

Both had left regular medical practice, spurred by a combination of personal and professional tragedies that had derailed the normality of their lives forever. Each had indelible reasons to mistrust the system, to abhor corruption, injustice, oppression and crime. And each had already been doing all they could to fight back, had relinquished all expectation of a conforming, quiet or even reasonably safe life.

Besides all that, they were formidable medical professionals, with limitless potential and kindred leanings.

Shall we say, perfect candidates for what I'd had in mind?

I'd met them both during our joint stints with Global Crisis Alliance. As sort of a colleague, I'd approached them.

Uh—truth was, I'd been their dishonorably discharged ex-colleague at the time. GCA had thrown me out on my ear two months earlier, after the Darfur "incident."

When I'd elaborated on my plans, they'd been interested. Very. They'd perked up as if I'd just handed them the answer to a maddeningly vague question that had been tormenting them.

Not that they'd said yes on the spot. They'd questioned me closely. They'd wanted to make sure it wasn't shock and bitterness at being stripped of everything I'd ever worked for talking, making me spout impossible goals and measures I didn't mean and wasn't up to.

More, they'd wanted to make sure I wasn't spiraling down the same road as Dad's.

At the time I hadn't been sure that would have been such a bad thing. I mean, Dad took care of business, when everyone else danced around what needed to be done. Luckily, I'd had more restraint—oh, okay, just less guts I guess, and less immediate impetus. They'd served me well, kept me on track, learning from his mistakes, starting the way he'd ended up, careful, organized, in control. I hoped.

Matt and Ayesha had gotten progressively more excited about the idea of putting together teams of medical people from all around the world, people who, like us, had despaired of health systems and humanitarian establishments alike, who'd been go-

ing crazy being shackled by laws, regulations and financial re-
alities that served everyone but the sick, the helpless and the oppressed.

They'd thrown in their lots with me, come what may.

We'd spread our mission statement and interviewed candidates. We'd been careful. And I mean careful. Founding an al-
most-crazy, extralegal outfit, we'd had to be to avoid the law's
notice and weirdos' interest.

It had taken some doing, sifting through the candidates, de-
ciding who was for real, who had what it took, who'd hold up
under the pressure, not only of the rigorous training, but of being in the field outside established systems' luxuries.

Proving to our recruits that we were what we said we were
hadn't been a ride in the park, either.

Ayesha's sharp inhalation brought my focus back to her.
"Systolic blood pressure ninety, and rising."

I groped for Mendoza's hand, willing him to hang on, my
throat closing. Ayesha increased his fluid drip again, threw
me a bolstering glance. Would I ever get used to my team's—
especially my core seven's—way-beyond-the-call-of-duty-and-
sanity dedication? I'd almost gotten them killed a dozen times.
Actually, I'd exceeded the dozen mark already, what with our
last skirmish with the white-slavery ring in Sarajevo.

Four years ago, those seven had been willing to train as long
and hard as it took to get ready, go as far as needed to get the
job done, including leading double lives. Or dropping their previous lives completely. Like I had.

Now we were forty-two strong, from surgeons to general
practitioners to nurses to paramedics, of all ages and sixteen na-
tionalities. Not to mention our extensive network of part-timers
and affiliates. We counted every possible job among those. From
cooks to technicians to forgers to bricklayers to bookkeepers to
computer whizzes. They handled all nonmedical aspects of our
operations, kept us underground and undetected.

And of course, there were our *benefactors*. From the very willing to the extremely unwilling. It took a lot to run our Sanctuaries, to keep our operations fluid, mobile and effective.

"BP a hundred now. Are you sure about this, Cali?"

Ayesha's agitation hit me between the eyes. She was one hell of a surgical nurse, holstering an exhaustive twenty-year experience and an astounding diagnostic skill superior to most surgeons I'd known. She'd lost her last regular job because she'd exposed the diagnostic and surgical mistakes of someone with too much power. Her concern now was right on the money.

Usually I would have given Mendoza enough fluids to correct his hypotension and shock without raising his pressure enough to increase bleeding from the rupture.

Raising his pressure above ninety now was a risk, but a calculated one. I hoped. I had to find out if the rupture was still leaking. If his blood pressure failed to rise, or rose then plummeted, I'd know it was. Then I'd be forced to switch from the minimally invasive route of angiographically guided repair to the open surgical variety. Which carried a far higher risk of complications— or death.

I nodded affirmation to her and sweat splashed into my eyes. She blotted it out for me. Tension buzzed up my rigid muscles. In a couple of minutes I could be opening up our sixty-five-year-old janitor. I doubted he'd survive that. I allowed myself a spurt of fury. That Mage, the supplier who'd conned me into buying that not-quite-a-single-use angio machine, would get his.

I broke down and started preparing for the surgery. Once he plummeted, I'd have about ten minutes in all. I forgot to breathe, expecting Ayesha to give me bad news any second. Just as oxygen deprivation was starting to get to me, she exhaled. "Pressure 115/70 and holding over the last five minutes."

I binged on a gigantic inhalation, then we raced through finishing up, placing drains in his abdomen, siphoning off the collected blood there and autoinfusing it back into him.

In minutes, I rechecked his vitals, topped off his sedation and analgesia, then Ayesha took him to Intensive Care.

Two hours later, Mendoza was doing great in I.C.

I wasn't doing so well in a claustrophobic back alley among mountains of garbage.

That this was our L.A. Sanctuary's only secure day exit didn't help my mood a bit. I added the stench to Mage's debts.

I fled into a less stomach-turning side street of the slum. Not that Los Angeles called it that. Slums around here were officially called "disinvested neighborhoods." Sure had a nice, euphemistic ring to it. Those covered twenty-five percent of L.A.'s area and fifty percent of its population. Silver lining was, these areas, being bedlams of crowding, diversity and lawlessness, were perfect for Sanctuary's undetected existence. Where else could we run an extralegal healthcare/humanitarian facility? And have direct access to society's outcasts, those who needed us most?

I took a turn down Main Street and added still more to Mage's bill. My disguise was killing me. Four-inch stiletto heels, industrial-strength makeup, skintight minidress and a waist-long blond wig qualified, in my books, as cruel and unusual punishment, me who lived in sneakers, a scrubbed face, stretch jeans and a braid. As for the neighborhood studs' vulgar comments and propositions… Man! Was it too much for a woman to ask to be verbally harassed with the tiniest bit of originality?

Yeah. Looking at the kind of miscreants doing the harassing, it sure was. They'd have to be admitted to my E.R. if they were assailed with an original thought.

It had also been too much to hope that Mage would end this peacefully. He really thought he could cross me and get away with it…

Okay. So I'd been crossed before. Being crossed was a fact of life, actually. Fully anticipated when it was illegal suppliers I depended on for every pill and syringe and piece of equipment.

I'd had the whole array of swindles—changing prices on delivery, faulty equipment, failure to deliver—the works. Not that anyone got away with any of that. We got things fixed. Always. Our methods ranged from simple to compound leverage.

Mage was begging for the latter. And then some. The bastard had taken exception to my demanding a refund through our triple-blind contacts. You see, I'd interrupted his packing for a Caribbean vacation. My bad.

His threat had been watered down by distressed go-betweens, but had retained its clarity—bother him again and the authorities would track my contacts back to me and whatever operation I was running.

If there was anything I hated more than having to wear disguises, it was threats.

I approached the edge of the sidewalk. Before I signaled for a cab, the minidress and the expanse of thighs stopped three at once. Ah, what would I do without men's predictability? Yesterday I'd stood in my nothing-special jeans and braid for fifteen minutes before giving up and resorting to on-foot transportation.

I jumped into the second cab. Liked the looks of the older driver better. I gave him the address Mage didn't think I knew. He thought he was as anonymous to me as I was to him.

He also didn't understand that asking for a refund had been offering *him* a way out. I didn't care about the money.

All right, I did. But in the scheme of things, the hundred-thousand-dollar first installment wasn't the real loss. I could ask one of our benefactors to plug the hole. Better still, I could relieve a local drug lord of a couple days' income.

My real grievance was that I could have lost my patient.

I didn't handle loss well.

Not when it was due to human factors, especially those of the premeditated variety. Even in could-have-happened-but-thank-God-it-didn't form. Mage's punishment should be in proportion to the tragic what-ifs. He had to be persuaded not to play his cons where lives might be counted among the losses.

I *could* ask again, nicely. For the refund and for the line he must draw. I expected him to refuse. I also expected him to underestimate me—as usual. Not for long, though.

Hmm. I didn't feel like beating him up. Not anymore. It wasn't the answer anyway. Profound and lasting coercion didn't work this way.

Not that Matt agreed to that. Right hand or not, it was why I'd refused to let him come. He'd left our last retribution case with three broken limbs. That sleazebag had deserved a broken neck, but still—I liked to counteract cruelty with cunning, and evil with intimidation. I liked to leave the bad guys running blind and scared. But still *capable* of running.

At least, I tried. Hard. Still—resorting to Matt's brand of justice, or even Dad's terminal methods, was tempting sometimes…

Nah. I had a better idea. I fished inside my handbag and smiled. I did every time I felt the ingenious layout. Having the Magnificent Fisk for a patient and now an affiliate had surely come in handy in preparing our arsenal. A few magic tricks didn't go amiss.

I sifted through the ultra-organized magician's bag, recognizing my drugs by touch. What would drive my point home if Mage didn't cooperate?

Oh, I knew just the thing. A hit of atropine.

Considering his age, health and size, 250 mg—no, 500 mg—should do it. With his mouth drying to ashes, his vision distorting, his every muscle fiber convulsing and his heart flailing like a butchered pigeon inside his chest, he would need a few hours to realize that I hadn't poisoned him, that he wouldn't die slow and scared. Then I'd give him another call when he'd recovered. For his sake, I hoped he'd change his ways.

The taxi turned into his street and my mind turned with it.

I was good at dodging the real issues, wasn't I?

Leaving Mage scared shitless and probably reformed was a cause unto itself. But I had more to do with this than he did. My first reaction of accusing myself had been the only moment of true honesty I'd had all day.

It had been me who'd been too impatient to get the angio, too eager to put it to use. I'd ignored basic logic and precautions. My recklessness demon was rattling her chains, wanting out, and I couldn't let the pressure to do good, the need to get things done, drive me into letting her loose. Again.

Four years wasn't long enough between sprees.

No length of time was.

I got out in front of Mage's building, scanned the row of extravagant cars. The silver sports Jaguar was his.

My lips tightened under layers of ruby lipstick. Let's face it, whatever I had to do, he had it coming. And since I would probably put an end to the damage Mage could do, I was following, to the letter, the Hippocratic oath. I was—really! *I will prevent disease whenever I can, for prevention is preferable to cure* had always been one of my favorite parts in that oath.

A man leaving Mage's building held the intercom-operated door open for me. A fake-lashed flutter rewarded him for saving me the effort of executing my penetration plan. I watched him forming the impression I'd meant to create today as clearly as watching my computer rendering a graphic. Lush. Slow. Available.

The intention to chat me up settled in his eyes, and I executed the breathless I'm-in-a-hurry-and-wish-I-wasn't routine and passed him by. I cast him one more look as he sauntered off, his eyes sweeping idle lust down my body. Predictability irons out the day again.

The moment the door closed behind me, my cell phone rang. The special ring that told me it was an unknown number. *Dad!*

At last! *At last!*

Three months. Going out of my mind with waiting. With a nauseating pendulum of soaring false hopes and plummeting, too real letdowns.

Suddenly I knew Mage would have to wait. I couldn't talk here. Had to have privacy. Air. Couldn't breathe—tears welling...

I sent up a mental promise to Mage as I burst back out onto the street. *Enjoy this time out. When I come calling next, I'll make sure you thank Dad properly for it.*

I groped for the phone as I spilled across the street and into the public park on the other side of the road, the slanting afternoon sun in my eyes.

The memorized system inside my bag felt like a maze. Alien. Numbness replaced knowledge in my fingers. They recognized nothing. And the phone kept ringing, each ring another jolt of desperation, shooting my coordination to hell.

Oh, God, he'd hang up! Wouldn't be able to get his hands on another phone for God only knew how long!

Then he did. The ringing stopped and my heart with it.

I stumbled to a bench and emptied my bag onto it. Lipstick, wallet, vials, syringes, steel wires, chains, drug darts, gun, everything fell out before the phone did.

I snatched it up, quaking, accessed its call records. Had to call him back. The number he'd phoned from was listed as unavailable.

No, no, *no!*

Call back. Call back, please!

I didn't care that the phone's clock said it was only thirty seconds before he rang again. It felt like an hour.

I had no breath left to even whimper. Missed him too much.

Needed his voice, the illusion of his nearness. The only things to fill the gaping crevice his absence had dug into my soul. I just sat there pressing the headset into my ear, my trembling fist around the mike, struggling with my ragged breathing. I wouldn't let him hear my distress. It was the last thing he needed. *Oh, Dad, say something!*

"Hello?"

The deep, cultured voice poured through my ear, penetrated my brain. Landed in an electrified rock in my stomach.

Paralyzing anticipation drained away, disappointment flooding in its wake, liquefying my legs. I staggered down on the bench and slumped, my whirling head clunking on the wrought-iron back.

Not Dad. Not Dad.

Then who?

Suddenly, another pulsing hope hit me. One I'd never thought I harbored. Not in eight long years. *Jake?*

Lord! Where did *that* crazy idea come from, anyway? Jake was long lost. Long *dead*.

Still, that voice badgered my memory only to flit just out of its grasp. The need to hear more of it got my paralyzed vocal cords to function. I croaked a wavering, "Yes?"

A moment's silence almost had me bellowing with frustration. Then the man's voice broke over me, a breaker of cool, maddening decorum. "Have I reached the number of Dr. Calista St. James?"

My name. My full, real name with Dr. attached to it.

I hadn't heard it in four years. I'd never thought I'd hear it again. Never thought it would hit me that hard to hear it.

I couldn't breathe.

I had to.

I did, hyperventilated. The crushing disappointment was enough on its own.

But hearing someone asking so rhetorically for Calista St.

James on—who was I today?—Hannah Simmons's cell phone, *that* justified freaking out.

My cover was blown!

Chapter 2

No, your cover isn't blown.

The exasperated, staid voice of reason sighed. I hated that voice. Made me feel so stupid. Then it amended, *Actually it is, but it doesn't matter. Since it's him!*

No wonder his voice had reminded me of Jake's. Modulated, cerebral, elegant. British. And once it had the benefit of a full sentence, instantly recognized.

Sir Howard Ashton. The man who'd changed my life, then had stood by and let my enemies tear it apart.

Tangled emotions skewered through me, egging me on to coo a syrupy "wrong number," jam my thumb through the disconnect button, tear out the SIM card and gnaw it to pieces.

"Calista, are you there?"

I debated my plan for one more second, then cooed that syrupy answer. The content turned out way different from "wrong number." "Why, Sir Ashton, I can honestly say I'm definitely no longer there and mean it. Calista St. James no longer exists. Thanks to you and your allies of pen pushing, cigar-smoking, penis-preoccupied, sanctimonious assholes."

Silence expanded, tautened. Then an alien sound filled the extraclear connection. Laughter! Peal after peal of it!

So this was what his laughter sounded like. As if set to tune and tempo. I'd never heard it, not once in the six years I'd served under him. Never thought he knew *how* to laugh. So, did he find me so funny that he'd just learned how?

My temperature shot up. "I *so* beg your pardon. If you're laughing, you can't be who I thought you were—a Midas-rich, back-stabbing bastard who plays philanthropist on weekdays and God on weekends. His face would crumble if he as much as smiled."

Choking sounds carried to me. Good. May he choke for real!

He didn't, brought himself under wheezing control. Shame. "Dear Lord, Calista! It has been unendurably dull without you."

"What can I say? I'm the fucking light of life." I winced. I hated four-letter words. But *he* hated them more. They gave him seizures. Sounded like a plan. "Too bad you haven't died of boredom, Sir Ashton."

A surprised bark escaped him. "Ah—it's so good to talk to you again. Although I note a marked sharpening to your temper. And an appalling deterioration of your language content."

The indulgence in his voice—how dared he? After what he'd done? Outrage numbed my lips and fingers. "Listen, *Sir* Ashton. Only my father comments on my fucking language. If you've gone senile and forgotten our last *chat,* let me refresh your memory—you're *nothing* like that to me!"

The microwaves transmitted his dimming mood. It wasn't enough. I needed it extinguished. I needed *this* terminated.

"I apologize, Calista." Boy, did he have haughty penitence down to an art! "However delighted I was with being exposed to your panache again, I shouldn't have laughed. You have every right to your acrimony, in the past and now."

Oh, no. He wasn't strumming my gullible strings. Not again. That he had tried to made me even angrier. "How fucking generous of you to grant me that!"

His sharp inhalation carried a new message now. *Enough.*

When he spoke, his voice remained suave, belying the whiplash of his words. "I value you beyond measure Calista, and it was a diverting jolt, hearing vulgarities spilling from your previously refined lips, but if you say that word once more, I will terminate this call and you will never hear from me again."

The childish urge to screech the f-word until he carried out his ultimatum was overpowering.

More so was my need to know why he was calling me. But what had defiance backlashing in my throat was his disappointment. My face tingled as if with a dozen slaps. Damn him.

No, damn *me!* Stupid, soft, susceptible. That his opinion still mattered, that *he* still did…

So—still as effective a taskmaster as ever, huh? Without a harsh word, he'd always had the most sullen rebels scampering with tails between legs to win his golden glance of approval.

But why should I feel bratty for nurturing my grudges, for flaying him with them? He was the one who'd said I'd filled the void his daughter had left behind, had had me entrusting my life to his guidance, taking solace in his fatherly substitution.

Then he'd given my enemies the means to destroy my life.

That it hadn't been destroyed had been no thanks to him!

I inhaled a bile-laden breath. "Fine. No vulgarities, as you put it. So—to what do I owe the aggravation of this call?"

Another silence-soaked moment, then he sighed. "I knew my personal overtures would have been met by your deserved rancor. That has been why I haven't directly contacted you all these years. But I've kept my eyes on you, followed your new—career…."

The hesitation before he said *career* spoke volumes. It also zapped me with resentment. "Delighted to discover you've been spying on me." I'd find out how he'd managed *that* later. "Would you mind skipping this sickening, pseudo-sentimental prologue?"

"I haven't been spying on you!" His voice rose a notch. Hallelujah. He *did* have sore spots to scrape. "I followed your actions to ascertain your safety, to offer whatever help I can…."

That was a sucker punch. I groped for air again. "You've been helping…*me*?"

"This is not an opportune time to go into particulars."

"I beg your pardon…" *Dammit. Breathe.* "But this is the *most* opportune time."

"I thought you wanted me to get to the purpose of this call."

"As far as I'm concerned, you've reached it."

"That has no bearing on why I'm contacting you today."

The man was effective, I'd give him that. Convoluted and slippery and a hell of an exhausting negotiator. He wasn't exhausting me. I had too much at stake here. I had to know what I'd been oblivious of. If he could keep such close tabs on me, who else had? Was?

"Here's an ultimatum of my own, Sir Ashton. If you don't enlighten me about the extent of your involvement in my life and work those past years then *I* will end this call, and you can resume your voyeuristic activities." And maybe I should end this anyway before I began to sound more like him.

His exhalation was long and resigned. "Very well. I've been following your every step since you walked out of Global Crisis Alliance headquarters…"

"Since you threw me out, you mean?"

"I didn't throw you out, Calista."

"Oh, no?" I tried to stop. I was taking his bait, steering us away from the details I needed to hear. I couldn't. His patient, long-suffering lies smeared my vision red. Who knew my wounds were still open? Open? Seemed they were festering! "You stood by as they threw me out. Same thing."

A new heat entered his composed tones. "Not at all. It was beyond me to stop it after you confessed to the crimes."

"I confessed to the ones I *committed.*" *And I am living to live them down,* I wanted to scream. "And those weren't *crimes.*"

"This could be debated ad infinitum, Calista."

"And I don't want to rehash this. There is no truth here, just point of view. I did what I had to do and was ready to take the consequences, death included. I understood everyone's need to resolve the incident by getting rid of its perpetrator. I accepted being indicted by PATS and getting kicked out of GCA. What I'll *never* forgive was having my medical license revoked."

A full minute passed, reverberating with the raggedness of my last sentence. Then he exhaled. "I thought you didn't want to rehash this." That maddening indulgence emerged again. If only he'd been in front of me. I bet he hadn't lost one hair of his immaculate, iron-gray mane. One good smack to mess it up…

The image of him with mussed hair and indignant crimson cheeks worked wonders. I calmed down. "I don't. And I don't need a license to be a doctor. It's what I am whether the system sanctions it or not."

"So I hear. You've been involved in increasingly risky business, Calista. Rules are not all made to be broken."

"Remember that memo about not being my father?"

His exhalation was filled with the reprimands he barely curbed. For now. That was all I needed. That he postpone any articulate objections to my methods till later. A later I'd make sure would never come. Now I wanted this conversation over. I might still catch Mage. Dad might still call. "There was a point to all this?"

"Yes, there was, and here it is. Even though I am no longer head of GCA, I am calling you on its behalf."

Incredulity erased my simulated calm. "That sense of humor you had grafted is something. As if I care what you or GCA want! A fat, final *no* to whatever you're asking. Can't say it was nice hearing from you, since it sure wasn't. Goodbye, Sir Ashton."

He brushed aside my tirade. "A number of your fellow GCA operatives long believed dead have been discovered alive and are being held hostage. We need you and your team to retrieve them."

Dammit. Two sentences and he had me ready to sign on to anything again. But I was damned if I'd give him instant gratification. Let him sweat it.

Yeah, sure. As if he had sweat glands like mere mortals. And he'd probably have *me* asking how high when he said jump. Just like when he initiated Combat Doctors Program for GCA volunteers and had me pledging my soul for a chance to enlist.

Sure enough, after a pause calculated to mess up my wiring, he drawled, placid, nonchalant, "Before you declare an irrevocable no, you should know that among the now located operatives is Dr. Jacob Constantine. What was he again? Your lover?"

Chapter 3

"That unstable criminal?" The enraged condemnation came hurtling from the other room, lodged between my eyes. "You brought Calista St. James *here?*"

I brushed it and my bangs aside, watched my denouncer's secretary. Her horror as she realized she'd left the door ajar after she'd let Sir Ashton into her employer's office was almost comical.

A you'd-better-not gesture stayed her move to correct her oversight. Might as well use Dr. Davis's defamation, play the villain. I really wanted to hear this.

She flopped down in her chair, shooting me my-God-she's-deranged-and-dangerous glances. I shot back a devilish smile. Her translucent skin blotched and she began to tremble. Jeez. She really took her boss's word to heart.

Okay. Enough. I wasn't in the business of scaring innocent bystanders. I tried a placating smile and she hyperventilated.

Whoa! This was no longer remotely funny. Man. I detested the unknown Dr. Steven Davis already.

I relieved her of my focus and she rose to unsteady feet, murmured a wavering, "I'll be right back!" and fled. Sheesh.

A phone interrupted Davis's indignation. I waited for the show to resume, patted my navy skirt over one knee. Why had I worn one? I wasn't some applicant here. *They* were after *me*.

Except, going by Davis's reaction to my presence, they weren't.

Damn. This sucked. Sir Ashton had conned me. Again. He'd recruited me against GCA's directives. Again. And he wasn't even the boss this time. He hadn't even warned the squeaking guy who was in charge before sticking me in his den.

Not that I cared. I was staging my own operation if they didn't want me along. Wouldn't be our first retrieval mission beyond enemy lines. We'd see who got Jake and the others out!

Davis ended his call, picked up his outrage without missing a beat. "I cannot contest that woman's presence here enough."

Sir Ashton's calm tones carried to me clearer than Davis's agitated ones. Had to be voice projection from his theater days. "There've been no legal charges against Dr. St. James."

"There were convictions!"

"Not where the law at large is concerned."

"But there are outstanding warrants on her alter egos. At least, there were until she hid her tracks altogether. But it's a matter of time before authorities trace old leads back to her."

"If GCA's and PATS's combined resources have failed to pick up her trace once they lost it, when they know who and what to look for, I doubt the FBI or the CIA can."

"*You* picked up her trace, if she's here."

"I'm—different."

"Indeed. But you may have done us all a favor, dragging her here. I have half a mind—"

"To report her? Then you would have half a mind. Not only

because you'd be as stupid as if you had, but because if she doesn't knock half your head off, then I will!"

"Are you threatening me, Howard? With her? For her? This crazy enforcer you want dealing with this delicate mission?"

Enforcer? Maybe. That was one way to look at part of what I did. If you're the bad guys supplying me with a steady stream of patients. Criminal could be negotiated, too, since I did break the letter of the law. If only to serve justice.

But first unstable and now crazy? To whom had that guy been talking? I exhaled, concentrated on Sir Ashton's serene qualification. "This impossible mission, you mean."

So he thought it impossible, huh? And he'd come to me. Hmm. Seemed Davis had a different evaluation. "We don't know that."

"We don't? You think retrieving our people from the depths of militant-controlled territory in the most chaotic region of the Russian Federation anything but?"

Suddenly a new voice spoke up. A familiar voice. "With PATS in the picture, nothing is impossible."

General Fitzpatrick? Preemptive Anti-Terrorist Squad's high commander? Woohoo! The whole war council was gathered in my honor! Only one was missing now. *Him.* De Luna. The bastard!

But hey! What was that about PATS being in the picture?

My hearing sharpened. This I had to record.

From the change in Sir Ashton's tone, I guessed he'd turned to Fitzpatrick. "PATS may provide tactical and combat capabilities during the release and cover during the retreat, but Calista's team is your one hope of making it that far."

"You both talk as if this is approved!" That was Davis again. The hole he was drilling in my aggravation center was getting bigger. "GCA's board is wary of the repercussions on our status as a humanitarian organization if it's ever discovered we used an aid mission as cover for a paramilitary operation. Now you want to add the anarchist presence of St. James to the mix."

Sir Ashton's tones dipped into condescension. Boy, did it bring back memories! "Are you proposing we leave our operatives rotting in captivity until legitimate channels open to secure their release? You may be GCA's current elected leader, but this catastrophe occurred on my watch. If you knew the lengths I've gone to for mere news of them, you'd know there are no such channels. Not to be trite, but beggars can't be choosers."

Fitzpatrick cleared his throat. "PATS involvement isn't debatable here, Dr. Davis. *We* discovered your operatives' whereabouts." They had? Who exactly had? Somehow I could guess who. "We're as much a part of this as GCA. But why St. James and her team, Sir Ashton? Why not one of GCA's PATS-trained teams?"

Davis jumped on that. "I can recall the Afghanistan team—"

Sir Ashton interrupted him. "I oversaw the training of every combat doctor we have, Steven. I know what they're capable of. This goes way beyond their capabilities."

Davis's silence shouted agreement. He still squirmed. "We can't entrust such a mission to one as erratic as St. James."

Sir Ashton overrode him. "Her very freedom from limitations is what qualifies her for this mission. Not to mention the difference the last four years have made in her war-readiness."

The general's grunt was eloquent. He thought Sir Ashton a soft, besotted fool. "I know she was your pet student, your pride and joy—until she brought the house down on you."

"I *stepped* down in protest of her excessive punishment."

He had?

Davis's exclamation overshadowed the momentous revelation. That guy was running a high bill! "She's still a vigilante who doesn't care who gets hurt in her crusades."

Yeah? And did that pompous ass-wipe have statistics to back those claims? Or was this about the three I'd "killed"? Again?

"How can the impulsive and seditious person you describe

have founded and directed her covert and highly effective Sanctuaries?"

Goose bumps erupted over me. Felt like the first time I skydived, hearing Sir Ashton defending me. Recognizing my work.

"So you condone her methods now?" Davis said with a sneer.

"No, I don't." Ha. What a fool. To keep falling into the same trap. Believing in him. Needing his validation. Did people ever outgrow their idiocies? "I believe in repairing the system, not in circumventing it, in reinventing the laws, not breaking them. But do you have anyone better qualified for the job?"

The silence carried to me louder than anything that had preceded it. Davis finally spoke, cornered, annoyed. "But GCA doesn't recruit outlaws. And no matter what you say, she's one."

"And so is PATS," Sir Ashton said simply.

Fitzpatrick barked, "Now wait a minute—"

Sir Ashton cut him off. "The only difference between your covert groups is that *your* parent organization, The Order for Peace, spans the world, and most governments *let* you operate outside the venues of domestic and international laws. You just have more finances, more power. In the end, you're both outlaws employing any means necessary to get your jobs done."

Now, how could I hate the guy?

Fitzpatrick grunted. Davis sighed. Sir Ashton went on. "We don't live in the same world that saw the birth of GCA, Steven. It is time GCA grew beyond its original constitution. If we don't evolve, we might as well admit we've failed."

"And our next step in evolution is the monster you've created? Is this what you're after?" Davis scoffed. "To prove that the woman who was your greatest failure is our only salvation?"

All right. Heard enough. From now on they'd just bicker. And they say women talk too much. Time to make my move.

I jumped up from the slouching, camel-colored leather couch—hated those—sauntered across the spacious waiting room. I paused at the threshold, savoring the moment when they all realized I hadn't opened the door, just pushed it wider.

Another mega-delicious moment was always to be had when men saw me for the first time after advance reports.

Davis had eyes reminiscent of his namesake, Bette. They bulged even more at my appearance. I could almost hear his mind's wheels grinding to a screeching halt. *This* is Calista St. James?

I knew what *this* looked like. A cute young woman, emphasis on young. If I wanted, I could pass for the teenager I definitely wasn't.

At 5'5", my height was unremarkable even with three-inch heels. The nonclinging suit barely hinted at the assets and totally hid the power of my honed body. My face was more distinctive if you cared to look. I made sure no one did. Bangs and a placid expression hid a lot. My unusual bone structure still made disguise tough and my honey-streaked chestnut hair, still in that braid I could sit on, was hell to shove beneath wigs. Should get it cut. Couldn't. Dad liked it.

My standout feature was my eyes. Exotic, black, intense. A jarring contrast with the rest of me, the diluted version of my stunningly angelic mother. Those were my hell-raiser Dad's. Their only hope of obscurity was colored contacts and heavy-duty makeup. They were what gave men pause, Jake had told me. He'd always talked about my eyes. Waxed poetic even. I'd learned to use them. For misdirection. For fascination. For intimidation.

Apart from that, I was nothing special. It helped me get underestimated, which suited me fine.

I met Sir Ashton's eyes. Midocean blue and just as fathomless. Astute, arrogant, amused. And was that a trace of anxiety, too? Good. He should be anxious. I intended to make him pay. Make them all pay. For then. For now.

"General Fitzpatrick." I advanced into the room toward him,

my hand extended, smile full on, the heels and skirt lending my steps that feminine prowl that made men take notice. His matte brown eyes rounded in confusion. And embarrassment. Cowboy, ex-soldier and still sort-of-a-soldier, there was no excuse for not jumping to his feet when a lady entered the room. He struggled up from another slouching couch, a hulk of a man, still in top shape at past fifty, another superior specimen of PATS's chosen.

I'd been too trivial to notice back then. He had only when I'd "killed" his agents. He'd been confused then, too, hadn't been able to reconcile the extent of the damage with this irrelevant "li'l lady." He'd pushed for maximum punishment. He'd gotten it.

I shook his impressive hand, held his eyes with an insipid glance, left him even more confused, then transferred my focus to Davis when he opened his mouth. He had nothing to say that I wanted to hear.

"Dr. Davis." I resisted the urge to squash his soft, sweaty hand. Wonder how he delivered babies with those butterfingers, how he held the reins of GCA. What a poor substitute for Sir Ashton. I could be wrong, of course. Didn't think so.

Bottle-green eyes filled with curiosity. With the relief of believing I'd pretend I hadn't heard him calling me names and accusing me of every crime under the sun. My mollifying smile led him on. His sagging, red lips parted in a flaccid smile. Dream on, bub. "So, Dr. Davis, ready to take notes?"

His lips sagged even more. "Notes?"

"I seem to have scared off your secretary. It's a good idea to take down my demands, to guard against later misunderstandings."

"Demands?"

I turned my eyes on the other two men. Fitzpatrick frowned. Sir Ashton's eyes flared with interest, his aristocratic head cocked to one side, preparing for anything. "You hear an echo? Must be the acoustics in this room. If you're not up to writing, I'll just give you the bones now, send you the contract later."

Davis's lips curled. He'd caught on. I was laughing at his expense. *And* not joking. "My terms for heading the aid mission are, one, reinstatement of my medical license with an APB dispatched to all authorities. Two, renewal of my GCA affiliation, authorizing me to use the organization's leverage to further my own operations. Three, TOP will get all investigation into my operations sealed and any old charges against my manufactured identities dropped and four, TOP will facilitate my operations, in any way, and 'in perpetuity.'"

I turned, strolled toward the door. Once there, I made a quarter pirouette, then dropped the big one. "Silly me. There's a five. A tiny financial incentive of say—ten million dollars?"

I got a hundred thousand dollars.

And a fifty-thousand dollar additional "donation."

No, not from my reluctant stuffed-shirt recruiters. I got Mage after all. Poor guy had had to abort his Caribbean vacation. The arson of his warehouse and the total destruction of his extensive inventory of "refurbished" equipment had sent him running back. I'd welcomed him home. Good thing was, he'd been reasonable. Very.

It was a debatable whether having an overblown reputation, and having it precede me, was good or bad. It usually made life harder, created unprovoked enemies and unearned vendettas. Not in that instant though. Mage had thought I'd never catch up with him, but once I did—what could I say? It was great once in a while for good to have an easy victory.

In other words, I loved seeing slimeballs shitting themselves in gibbering terror.

Now I was headed for home. Dank, decaying home.

The creaking noises the stairs made beneath my feet got lost in the cacophony blaring through the cardboard walls of my dilapidated residence. On the first floor, Luther's bone-shattering hip-hop music dominated. On the second, Lisa and Juan's usual screeching marathon as their TV blared. And so on.

My brain was a cowering mess at the bottom of my skull by the time I neared the fifth floor and my sad little condo.

Why did they do that to themselves? Themselves? To hell with them! They'd probably inflicted a hearing impairment on themselves long ago. It was those of us with respect for others' rights and intact hearing who suffered. Hadn't the crusades against noise pollution ever registered?

I fished for my sealing wax earplugs in my makeup kit. My neighbors were still warming up for the night and I needed my four-hour coma, *now.* I stuffed my ears, sighed my instant relief as the world turned off. I zipped my bag of tricks, gave it and the money it contained a loving pat. A hundred-thousand dollar check—the down payment for the faulty angio machine—and another fifty thousand cash, Mage's donation to make up for his "oversight." I'd graciously accepted it.

By the time the fraud and money-laundering lawsuits were settled he'd not only be in no position to make any contribution to our cause, he would probably be poor enough to warrant our services. I thought it a good idea to get something off him before lawyers took it all. Lucia's and Ishmael's teams had done a great job setting up the arson. I hadn't been bad myself. I grinned in the dark. All in a day's work.

I stepped into my apartment, wading into that surreal dimension of exhaustion and hearing deprivation. I decided to go for broke, complete the sensory stasis. I didn't turn on the lights as I crossed the clear path from my bare-necessities-furnished sitting room to my likewise lone bedroom. I needed darkness. Vacuum. Cessation of all stimuli.

Yeah. Good luck. No chance of that with the on-off neon lights conquering my shoddy shutters even from five levels down. My sigh was amplified in my ears as I bent to my nightstand for a sleep mask. I hated sleep masks. I lived with them anyway.

I put it on. Ah, alone for real at last.

Then I realized my mistake. Freed from the distracting feedback of visual and audio, I knew it.

I was not alone.

Chapter 4

Му heart gave my ribs one brutal kick. I almost gasped with the pain. I bit down hard on the burst of panic. No time for it.

No time to regain my vision, either. Not advisable. Snatching off the sleep mask would lose me my only edge, his security that I didn't know he was there.

Yes, *his*. It was a man. In the singular. Hard not to know that with his overpowering male aura crashing down over me. It told me a lot about him. Vigorous, big, not too young. Angry.

There was also no need to see. I knew where he was. Exactly.

I moved, forcing my body to relax, to flow in the unguarded movements of someone secure in her solitude, going through the motions of preparing for bed. I took off my skirt. Double-edged move, that. I'd free my legs. I'd trap his eyes and at least a part of his thoughts and focus there.

My mind raced with all possibilities. I had to reach into my bag for my gun. But he could shoot me first....

Stop! No time for logic. Just let it take you over. Do it.

I pretended to stretch, breathed in then out, let instinct and ingrained conditioning blank mental process, hop into the driver's seat. I had no idea what I'd do next.

I knew just what I'd do next.

From total inertia, I exploded into a forward somersault, landed in a tight ball on my bed, unfolded, launched with the completion of the motion and the hard spring of the mattress, the momentum of my violent move expending itself just where I'd directed it, in a double-footed, heels-first ram, right at crotch level. The collision force rebounded up my feet and through every bone in my body, rattling my teeth. I bit my tongue.

"Shit!"

At least, that was what I thought he'd shouted. Earplugs. I heard my harsh breathing and not much besides. He didn't fall. I would have felt his mass vibrating the whole room on impact. Judging by the concrete-like barricade I'd rammed against, it was considerable. Dammit.

I snatched off my sleep mask, tucked and rolled backward on the bed, snatching my handbag in the same explosive sweep. I hurled myself on the floor, flattened beside the bed, the only substantial cover in the room. It would take him precious seconds to pull himself together and come around it. I snatched my bag open, grabbed the gun.

He didn't come around the bed. He bounded over its six-foot width in one leap. Landed almost on top of me, kicking the gun from my hand while he was still suspended in the air.

No time to grope for it. My hand dipped in my bag, snatched the first thing I touched, one of my loaded syringes. Then I bounced up.

His arms were moving, his hands gesturing, and I heard it among the faraway droning background noise. Nah, I more like felt it, vibrating in my bones. Indistinct, deep, resonant. Enraged. His voice. He was saying something. Bellowing it.

Talk to the syringe, buster!

I lunged, stabbed his thigh with the three-inch needle. Didn't hit bone. Didn't even come near. We were talking massive muscle mass here. But I could have hit a nerve, the way he lurched. *Stay still a second, dear. That's all it'll take to pump you full of— whatever!* I hadn't had time to feel the special engraved marks I used on my syringes to recognize my drugs by touch. Not that it mattered. It was one knockout drug or another.

He didn't stay still. Had to make him, before he dislodged the needle. I clung to one thigh, arms and legs, threw all my mass into the clutch, kept him from kicking me away, kept the needle jammed deep. But couldn't get enough leverage to work the piston. Damn, *damn.* I hurled my body at his legs, bowling-ball style. He still didn't fall. Then my braid was in his grip.

I should get it cut, dammit!

He yanked it up and me with it, dragged me all the way to my feet, then higher, almost dangling me. He was an easy foot taller. Damn him.

My scalp was almost coming off. Excruciating moisture erupted behind my eyeballs. My fist jabbed at his throat, all my training and pain behind the blow. Would incapacitate him, probably crush his larynx. If it connected.

It didn't. His block was beyond effortless, more than instantaneous. Prophetic…

Predict this, bastard. My other fist followed in the next split second, connected, if not exactly. He'd ducked his head with that same uncanny intuition. I got his ear instead of his throat. He still dropped me. Whether from the force of the blow, or to regain use of both hands I didn't know. Didn't care.

This man was my match. In close quarters probably more. I wasn't testing how much more.

The hand that had had me by the braid moved toward the syringe. *Oh, no—you're not getting it out!* I pummeled him with erratic blows, distracting him. He no longer blocked me, took half a dozen blows full in the face and head, didn't even flinch, shoved me away so he could reach the needle. I rammed him, managed to pump the piston with my hip. He only snatched me off my feet as if I were a six-year-old and hurled me away.

I sailed backward through the air, feeling weightless. Then gravity reversed and I landed headfirst on the bed. Hit the backboard.

The darkness exploded in bright purple and yellow.

I hated hitting my head. Nothing was reliable after a good whack. Everything you counted on, all the things that made you yourself became suspect. Awareness distorted, consciousness flickered. Worst of all, time judgment warped. A second as I lay stunned could have been an hour.

Damn, damn, damn. I *wasn't* passing out! He was coming toward me again. It took a lot to alarm me, but here was a lot.

Get out of his range—now! Until the drug takes effect.

Before my muscles even registered the stimuli shrieking down my nerves, he came down. On top of me. Total body impact.

Still in attack mode or had he collapsed?

Didn't make much difference to my air intake issues at the moment. The collision had emptied my lungs, now that immovable-object guy was preventing my next scheduled breath. The flickering neon lights began to melt into homogeneous black.

Act. Now. Before it's too late.

I had no leverage to knee him. Yanking his head back for a good forehead ram wasn't working. His hair was too short; I couldn't get a good enough grip. Pulling his ears wasn't working.

Then he raised his head on his own and I got a great shot at his nose. I dove my head into the mattress, tensing, preparing the recoil ramming force then air rushed into my lungs as if under pressure. He'd raised his torso off my chest, took his upper body's weight on his arms, the flickering lights at his back. His silhouette loomed over me, phasing in and out.

My heart dropped a beat.

And my breasts stung. With relief from no longer being crushed and—something else? Every inch he was imprinted on sent messages, too, every breath rushing in laden with his clean, male scent, transmitted directly to my—pleasure centers?

What was going on here? Had I hit my head too hard? Or did my body know what it was talking about?

I shoved him with all I had and he rolled heavily off me, ended up on his back beside me. The trank! It was working.

I jumped to my feet, reached for my ailing bedside lamp. Nothing. Had it shorted out?

A deep droning sound reached me as I felt around the floor with my foot for my gun. He was saying something! For crying out loud! Time to resume receiving signals. I tore out the earplugs.

"…love to play with poisons. If you did poison me, you'd better have the antidote. And there are no lights in this dump."

I groaned. It was *him*.

Who else had that harsh-velvet voice that pooled in all the places where reason never visited and caution never touched?

And I suddenly remembered—I hadn't paid the electricity bill.

A quick rummage in my nightstand produced a flashlight. I turned it on and shone it over his face. He glowered, narrowing lethal, heavy-lashed and now-turbid honey eyes.

Yep. Him all right. It was all still right there. Masterpiece bones, deeper-than-the-night mane, shred-you-to-pieces-and-blow-your-mind-with-pleasure lips. Uh—just for your information, I'd only gotten a taste of the first. The second was a very educated guess.

But man and damn! He was really here. Made-one-then-broke-the-mold De Luna. Banderas/Brando-level sensual charisma and surliness and even better looks.

Damian.

My ruthless mentor. My unattainable desire.

My relentless enemy.

I shone the light in his eyes, teased his I'm-in-charge-and-everybody-knows-it nose with the tips of my braid. "Well, well! If it isn't the patron saint of physicians himself!"

He glared back at me, uncompromising, reprimanding, as he always did when he refused to give me the rise I panted for. "Making jokes, again, about my namesake and the unfortunate parallel between the atrocious career moves that led to our involvement with doctors? Now? After you've poisoned me?"

Had I? Nah, I had nothing poisonous with me today.

"So—did you or didn't you poison me?"

His tones were almost bored. Like a father asking a misbehaving daughter if she'd done her homework. I didn't bother answering him, rolled off the bed, jumped up. Had to retrieve the syringe, see what and how much I'd managed to get into him.

I found it, crushed on the floor. I liked glass syringes, autoclaved them for sterility. Had to have been his foot that packed that much crushing mass. The syringe was so much glass dust. And since I could feel no moisture around it, I'd probably pumped him with the full dose. Only way to tell which drug it was, was to take an inventory of the remaining syringes in my bag. That is if I could remember what I'd had with me!

I loaded all my syringes with mega doses. That much of whichever drug in his system for a few minutes now should be making him dizzy, confused, drowsy. Anyone else would have been out by now. But not him, huh?

I'd heard that PATS made their operatives resistant to all forms of drugs by exposing them to gradually increasing doses. A sort of immunization. Didn't sound scientifically plausible, in the case of poisons. In the case of mood-altering drugs, too, without building a powerful enough tolerance to the drug that would by necessity make them addicts. Never believed it could actually work. Evidently it did.

I felt him move and my gaze and flashlight swung to him. He'd raised himself on his elbows and was—smiling? I choked on a cough of surprise. And that was before his sensuous purr hit me somewhere beneath my sternum. "Calista—come here— come back to bed…."

Hearing my name pouring from his lips like that, dark, fathomless, *teasing,* would have been shock enough. He'd only ever called me St. James, impatient, implacable, imperious. But *come back to bed?*

I squinted at him. Could it be? I'd had one syringe of Valium mixed with GHB, a drug I'd discovered boosted Valium's knock-out effect. On its own, GHB had a reputation for inducing, among other things, uninhibited relaxation and increased sensuality. It was one of the drugs used in date rape. Problem was it hadn't been on its own in that syringe, shouldn't be affecting him this way. So what was going on here?

I walked back toward him, my mind racing. His lids swept down, his winged eyebrows knotting, protesting the flashlight. I diverted the beam and he relaxed, slumped back by degrees at my approach. He was fully on his back by the time my leg touched his, gazing at me through sleepy, steamy slits. Then he licked his lips, slow, explicit, and every nerve in my body fired a jangle of responses. Each one beyond stupid.

The guy was coming on to me under chemical influence, for Pete's sake! Seemed nothing short of tripping could induce him to do that. In his state a broomstick or a tree would do it for him.

And I *didn't* want him to come on to me, conscious or unconscious. I hated the guy's guts. And he reciprocated the loathing and then some. It didn't matter that he was the hardest hitting male I'd ever had the gross misfortune to cross paths with. He'd almost run me over four years ago. That I wasn't roadkill now was no thanks to him.

I leaned over him, intending to examine him, and he caught my hand and brought me down on him. He shouldn't still have enough power and coordination to do that. Couldn't pass out like a normal human would have, could he? Had to be idiosyncratic, didn't he? But what else was new? The guy ran on nuclear metabolism. Damian De Luna was a species of one.

My thoughts scattered, sensations and memories filling their space. Sensations that shouldn't be there, memories I had no business remembering.

Feeling him now, my naked legs opened around his unyielding mass, abraded by tough fabric and tougher maleness beneath it. Remembering lying under him, desperate, sweating, bucking. Wrestling with him, his magnificent body flexing around me, beneath me, my fingers digging into power made human, my senses drowning in an overdose of virility...

So none of it had been in an erotic context. Not intentionally anyway. On his side. But without ever meaning to, and in the throes of brutal training and exercise, he'd messed up my hormones, bad. Very bad. For two years, he'd drilled—uh—*coached* me, challenged me, pushed me beyond my limits. Tormented me. In every way. He'd remolded my body and will, plumbed abilities I'd been only partly using before fulfilling.

I should have owed him. He should have *let* me owe him. He should have been my ally. Could have been my lover...

He'd been my worst enemy.

And how I'd wanted him. But it had been impossible, for every reason there was. Thankfully. What I was feeling now had to be echoes of the frustrations and the forbidden...

All rationalizations sputtered, drowned. In his kiss.

Ah...

So this was how he tasted—how he—*we*—felt...

I sagged onto him, sank into him, his feel a narcotic seeping up my nervous pathways, numbing, intoxicating, the final straw in this roller-coaster day. I gave myself permission to take that much of him. One kiss. After six years that wasn't much. Then we'd come to our senses, hurry back to our corners...

"Calista…"

I wanted to moan his name, too. Almost did—then it hit me.

What was I doing? I'd knocked him out and was now what? Taking advantage of him? A mental slap brought me up short, cleared my hormone-hazed mind.

He wouldn't let me go, the hand behind my head detaining, begging. Then my name poured from him again, an imploring groan. "Calista…"

I could get used to this.

I sank back into his mouth. This time all the way.

It was a good thing I hadn't had a clue how he'd call my name and make it mean so much, how his tongue would feel filling my mouth, his scent permeating my lungs, his breath…

His breath! Hey—*hey!* Shouldn't he be panting? At least breathing fast? I was. He wasn't. Breathing at all. Almost.

I tore my lips away from his and my hands out of his hair, groped for the flashlight that had fallen out of my grip.

I was in time to see his eyes closing, his face going flaccid. Oh, God! Respiratory depression was among the possible side effects of any of the drugs I had with me. Not considering his mass and health condition, but why would he comply with the projected side effects when he hadn't with the expected effects?

I could have poisoned him after all!

"Damn, damn…"

I didn't know what exactly I was damning. Myself. For not taking that inventory, finding out which drug I'd hit him with, administering an antidote even if I thought he didn't need it. I just hadn't been thinking, had I? Hadn't expected him to—or expected I'd… *"Damn!"*

I exploded for my closet, dragged out my extensive emergency kit, flew back to him, already unzipping it before it landed on the bed beside him. I needed both my hands, held the flashlight in my teeth. I snatched up a bag-valve oxygen mask and swooped to clamp it on his nose and mouth, squeezed the bag, delivering 100 percent oxygen, while taking his pulse—and almost keeled over.

Twenty beats per minute! His heart was stopping. I—I… No, no it *wasn't*. He had a resting pulse rate of thirty or less. This was his normal—sorta. Still, he did usually take more than two breaths a minute! Bag valve wasn't enough—should intubate him until I made sure which drug I'd hit him with. I should also inject him with a universal antidote for respiratory depression. Yeah, yeah…

I assembled the laryngoscope in ten seconds flat, jumped to give him five more breaths, then swooped for ampoules and loaded the syringe in under ten. My jaw was almost coming out of its sockets being stretched so wide over the flashlight. I ignored the mounting pain and tension, the protocols and measures of reviving an overdose casualty streaking across my mind's eye.

I hauled up his muscle-laden, limp arm, rolled up his black shirtsleeve, snapped on a tourniquet, introduced a cannula in his ropy vein, ran to drag the clothes' hanger to hang the saline bag, injected Romazicon in it, connected the line to his cannula. Infusion should be slow, to decrease chances of sudden and very disconcerting recovery. Now to remove the mask and…

A scream rang in my ear.

Chapter 5

It took me a second to realize it was me screaming.

Damian's eyes had snapped open in perfect horror-movie tradition, his glare above the mask scarier than a reviving corpse's.

Then he was snatching the oxygen mask out of my hands.

"No, leave it on—you need to…"

I didn't have time to finish. The oxygen mask was off his face and across the room, thunking off the wall.

Oh, well, at least it was a disposable.

Damian swayed up to a sitting position, pitched forward, his upper body folding, bringing his head between his knees.

"What the hell did you hit me with?"

Wow, what a change in tone. Now *there* was the soulless, vindictive creep that he was.

"V-valium and GHB—I think…" Great. I was stammering now!

"You *think?*" He straightened, tore the cannula out of his arm, tossed it away then turned to me. Even in the indirect light, his fury pummeled me. "I know how Valium or GHB feel like and this was neither, even mixed." He snatched a look at his watch. "It's been twenty minutes since this farce started. I wouldn't revive this fast if it was either."

He was angry? Taking exception to my measures? Rich didn't even begin to describe it!

That blasted any remaining traces of agitation right off. I poked his muscle-padded shoulder with the flashlight. "Is this your way of weaseling out of begging my pardon for breaking and entering into my apartment? I had every right to pump you full of cyanide! To shoot you point-blank in self-defense, you idiot."

"Wasn't for lack of intention or trying that you didn't!" He heaved himself to his feet. The room shrank and air disappeared.

Spectacular. Not him. Though he was, that and more. Of course. But I meant the way he shook off the drug's effects. Nothing in my drug arsenal was as short acting as that!

"You have any emergency lights in this dump?"

This was the second time he'd called my dump a dump. "No. But I can still send you out of here to the emergency *room!*"

Was that a tilt upward I saw to his lips? Seemed so. There was an accompanying thread of humor in his bottomless voice. "You can try. This time I won't hold back, St. James."

So we were back to St. James, huh? As expected, really. The thrill of disappointment was what I'd call a moronic reaction. "I won't either. And yes, I was holding back, too. Seemed I sensed you weren't in the blow-his-head-off category."

His hands glided over his head, his face, his restless shifting indicating where else he was smarting. "Just the hurt-him-like-hell one, huh? And you always go for my groin first."

I laughed. I shouldn't have. It wasn't funny. Neither then nor now. But I'd missed him. Sort of. That acerbic wit of his, the no-holds-barred verbal and physical duels I'd only ever had with him. The sheer freedom of going all out, knowing he could match anything and more, getting more out of me in turn.

He prowled over to me, almost came to stand between my legs. "A symbolic emasculating gesture? An attempt even?"

"Ha. I don't consider a crippling breast blow defeminizing. Not that such a term exists. It's only robbing a man of his vaunted 'masculinity' that's such a big deal."

"Always the feminist, huh?"

"Always the chauvinist, huh?"

He raised his eyebrows. "Chauvinist? When I picked you and five other women as my top ten recruits for GCA's Combat Doctors Project? I considered your potential, not your gender."

He was right. Damn him. Not that it had been any easier admitting it then either.

During that first interview, I'd pegged him for a sexist bastard, the way he'd kept interrogating me, trying to corner me, stressing my so-called feminine limitations. My opinion was solidified when he'd suddenly caught me in a stranglehold while shaking my hand goodbye, and whispered menacingly in my ear, "Show me how you'll break free!"

I'd shown him. Left him wiping blood from his split lip, checking that no teeth had come loose from my head ram, his golden eyes blazing a dozen indecipherable emotions.

I'd been sure he'd exclude me, had been floored to find myself at the top of his list. I'd remained there, for the two years' torture—*training*—program, the one he'd driven harder than anyone, wouldn't cut any slack. I'd wanted none. I'd wanted to be all he could make me, wanted him to pulverize my limitations. He had, until for a while, I'd felt I had none.

Then he'd decided he'd made a mistake doing that and had gone all out to erase it.

I stood up, leaving bitterness behind on the bed. He didn't

budge, a head above me, his chest to my shoulder, his thighs to my hips, those eyes that shone from within brooding over me.

There'd never been sexual expressions between us. Just electric tension thick enough to suffocate me every time I saw him, to enervate me every time he touched me. But there'd been Melissa. And it had been just a year since I'd lost Jake. And Dad. And Damian had been my mentor. And then everything had blown up.

Now, standing against him, after that kiss… And he did remember it, the memory in his bunched muscles, in his hesitant glance. Hesitant? De Luna? Now that'd be the day!

But he was. Sort of undecided. Was he debating the wisdom of an encore now his faculties were back online?

Oh, yes—just one more kiss, to see if it had been real…

No, moron. The whole thing *wasn't* real. Coming up against each other this way, the darkness, the danger, the deluge of memories, today's climactic discoveries…

And I didn't even know why he was here.

I pushed him away, went for candles in my nightstand, then walked out. Better take this where there was no bed in sight.

I felt him following me, his presence a static charge at my back. Time for light to dissipate dark and disturbing nonsense.

I distributed the dozen candles on my only table, straightened to go fetch matches. He flicked a lighter at me.

"Taken up smoking?" I quipped.

One eyebrow rose. As if he'd do anything to abuse his health. He was just the ultimate in preparedness. I wouldn't be surprised if he had a spare tire on him. At least the means to fix one. It was one of the hundred skills he'd taught me.

As soon as I finished lighting the candles I knew my mistake. Damian by candlelight was even worse to be around.

I still had to sag on the couch before I managed to say, "So, to what do I owe this invasion?"

"I didn't invade you," he asserted, matter-of-fact. "I was sitting out of the way on the stairs that lead to the roof, waiting for you. I talked to you when you reached your door, walked after you inside the apartment. I thought you were ignoring me." I snorted. He shrugged. "I even shut the door behind us. Apparently you think it closes on its own."

"It does!" Malfunctioning hinges.

"Then you went for the sleep mask. Then you were out to kill me."

"I was out to defend myself against the Incredible Hulk in my bedroom. And I had earplugs in my ears."

"So I gathered—belatedly."

"So, all's well that doesn't end with someone in a body bag…" I shouldn't have said that. Should put a lid on sarcastic humor, or someone could get hurt. Probably me. He'd morphed from gorgeous to grim. *Get it over with.* "De Luna, why are you here?"

"We need to talk." Expression seeped out of him as he came to tower over me again.

"I won't be able to if my neck snaps. Sit down, will you?"

"This shouldn't take long." He still came around the table and sat down inches from me. Maybe it hadn't been such a hot idea. I'd take a crick in the neck over a stitch in the heart any day.

"We need to set some ground rules, now. This time there'll be no improvisations at ground zero, no daredevil tricks, no insubordination. Let's be clear here and now about who'll be in charge. Me. There'll be no taking things into your own hands, no matter how wrong you think I am."

Okay. He'd lost me. "De Luna, are you hallucinating under the mystery drug's effect? Just what are you talking about?"

Just as the question was out, I got it. Oh. No.

"Don't tell me you don't know I'm your mission leader!"

"I know no such thing!"

"Then know it. PATS is in charge, and I'm in charge of the PATS team."

"Then you're in charge of a different mission, buddy. The mission I'm going on, my team is in charge and I'm in charge of my team. I gave the big boys my conditions." And I knew they'd reject them. It was why I'd made them impossible to fulfill. Then I'd get my hands on their info and stage my own operation.

"I heard of your 'conditions.' You've finally realized your full sociopathic potential, haven't you, St. James? Coercion, extortion—tell me, what will you do with ten million dollars?"

"I'll redecorate this 'dump!'"

His brooding eyes left my furiously sarcastic ones, panned around the miserable reception-cum-living-cum-kitchen area. "Touché. Seriously, what will you do with them?"

"As if they'd cough them up!"

"They are." *They are?* "Why are you pretending you don't know they've agreed to all your demands?"

"Because I don't! I turned off my cell phone." After I got a message from Dad telling me he'd phone me tomorrow, there'd been no one else I'd wanted to talk to. Apparently I'd amassed a decent number of missed calls meanwhile.

I couldn't *believe* they'd agreed.

Damian extended his legs, crossed them at the ankles, threw his head back on the couch. He might be holding it all in, as usual, but he must still be disoriented. "Let me state for the record that this is all against my will and judgment." How heartwarming! "I don't know what they think they're doing, not only bowing to your demands, but to be deploying you in the first place…"

"Like a nuclear missile, huh?"

"You have comparative hazard value. Last time you caused an international incident, it was in a Third World country. This time, we're talking Russia. Someone has really flexed some bigtime muscle to get you in on this. But for the record, since it's a fait accompli, I'm willing to make the best out of it. If you are."

"And the best is me bowing to your every command?"

"Last time I checked that was what being the leader meant."

"Yes. And that's me. The doctor. Ever heard of a black-ops agent leading an aid mission?

"I'm *also* a logistician, and we lead aid missions all the time. Anyway, that's just our cover, the real mission—"

"Is *also* something I and my team can handle. I've been training for the past four years, and we got some real hands-on training like you'll never believe…"

He sat up, shadows shifting on his face, exposing the demon he shared his body with. I'd really touched a raw spot. "You're amateurs who function on a gamble and a prayer!"

"Must be hell of both then, since we've been functioning for thirty months straight. And before you say that running our Sanctuaries and putting gangs out of business is nothing like hostage retrieval, know that we got our people out of an Afghan militant camp and are keeping a steady supply of aid materials reaching segregated populations in Darfur and Colombia. But you don't know that, do you? PATS and GCA lost track of me after the first year or so, didn't you?"

He lowered his burning gaze. "*I* don't lose track of anyone. And I wanted your news like I would a terminal disease. I walked out of GCA headquarters that day intending to forget you."

Okay. That hurt. It hurt more that I couldn't hurl a similar statement in his face. Oh, well.

I yanked my braid, started undoing it. Every hair root was screaming for release. They always did when tension found no relief in action. "Seems we won't come to an agreement then."

"We must if you want this to work."

"You know I do!"

"Because of Constantine?"

Jake. Oh, dear God—*Jake*. Beautiful, brilliant, unique Jake. That he could still be alive! That I could actually see him again, help in freeing him from an eight-year-long nightmare!

A nightmare I'd been the reason for.

"I'd do anything to free anyone in the same situation." And it was true. The Jake factor only meant a painful edge of emotional involvement that need concern no one but me.

Damian's eyes swept over me, lingering on my busy fingers, my hair, my heaving breasts... Whoa! That surge of erotic imagery was a far worse idea now than it had ever been. Obscene even, when I should be thinking of Jake.

But *eight years,* most of which I'd believed he was dead, resigned myself to his loss, eight years of fresher injuries and losses taking precedence, of radical—I hoped—changes in me....

I'd almost forgotten how he looked.

God, I felt like such a sick, heartless bitch!

Damian wasn't giving me the privacy of bitter self-recriminations and poignant recollections, watching hawkeyed, analyzing my every thought no doubt.

"Let's just say that Constantine makes it all the more imperative to you. So again, St. James..." Suddenly his eyes were openly hostile. "In the interest of not having *your* lover end up dead, obey orders this time!"

His pain and rage were as mutilating as they'd been that nightmarish night four years ago. Something hot and wet burst in my chest. As if my heart had ruptured. With wanting to defend myself, rewrite history, reanimate the dead.

Memories bombarded me, somehow different, as if seen through his eyes, relived through his anguish.

Melissa. His lover. Her corpse a macabre heap in the creeping dawn, Damian dragging his bloody body on the dusty ground, his breath shearing out of him, an inhuman sound of horror and desolation calling her name.

He'd almost died then, too. Bullets had almost severed his left arm's major artery, had gone through his lung just below his heart. He'd almost bled out on one hand and drowned in his own blood as his chest filled up on the other.

My hand shot out, disobeying me, tracing a shaking map of his remembered injuries. And again, like that night, he crushed my hand and hurled it back at me. He hadn't wanted salvation if it had been me granting it.

I'd saved him in spite of himself. And it not only hadn't counted, it had only made him madder. He'd wanted to be free to hate me, no debts. If it hadn't been for me, he wouldn't have been injured in the first place, he'd raved. Wouldn't have almost lost his arm. Wouldn't have lost his lover and two of his best friends. He hadn't wanted my care then. Sure didn't want anything to do with me now.

No, wait. He did want my obedience.

No can do.

He heaved himself to his feet and walked to the door without looking back. I called after him, "I'm not the same reckless person I was four years ago."

He stopped, only his face turning to me, tossing me a glance that skewered through me. "You admit you *were* then?"

I rose, approached him slowly. "I don't want to recycle condemnations and defenses. I never denied my transgressions, just their exaggeration and the inappropriate punishment."

I could swear his eyes glowed. "You consider any punishment 'inappropriate' for causing three people's deaths?"

Oh, no. He wasn't dragging me into another vicious circle. He'd already shredded me in both GCA's and PATS's hearings.

He'd also accused Sir Ashton of hiding my real profile, of misleading him into thinking I was just an eager-to-serve young doctor and not a warped vigilante out to avenge the personal wrongs that society and the system at large had dealt me.

He'd quoted from the record his refusal to deploy me again after our only previous mission, when he'd realized I was a time bomb. They'd overridden him once with disastrous consequences.

That time, when he'd recommended I shouldn't be on an aid mission *or* let near a patient again, they'd agreed.

But I'd moved on. After months of shock and resentment, I'd taken a harsh look at myself and seen where he'd been right.

I didn't want to end up behind bars like my father before I learned, like he had, that method and restraint made us far more effective. I had that vicious blow Damian had dealt me to thank for learning my lesson with a far lower price than my father had paid. I take refresher courses in control every day on the job.

And *this* was my most important job ever. Touching deep inside me beyond ethics and duty. I had to do it right. Had to reconcile with Damian, unwilling and unwanted partner as he was.

"I don't cling to my pride, so don't you cling to your prejudices, Damian." I realized what I'd said. My lips twisted. His eyebrows dipped at my smile. Or was it at hearing his name on my lips? I'd never called him anything but De Luna.

"I have no ego here, and I hope you'll check yours." He rumbled like a lion about to lash out. "All I ever wanted was to do the best I can for as many people as possible. And I know where you're coming from now. Leadership has—tempered me, if you will." I huffed a chuckle. "Age, too, I guess. Pushing thirty is very sobering."

He turned to me then, as if against his will and obeying mine. I was willing him to understand, to make a truce. He took a step toward me, grudging. I glimpsed the man he'd never let me near, the depths I had only been able to guess at. The desire he fought and hated?

Yeah, dream on, St. James.

Then he closed his eyes and threw me out of his mind. I almost stumbled back.

"Tomorrow we assemble to coordinate roles and plans for the mission. Our window of time to have access to the refugee camp is tight. We have a week to make it there. This means we just have a day here to get our act together. Brief your team, pick only your best players. No more than eight. This is going to be hard, maybe long, too—0800 sharp, St. James."

This time he turned and walked straight out.

I let myself tremble then.

Whoo boy. Who would have thought it would affect me this way, seeing him again? That for the second time today I'd catch myself longing for approval and validation from another man who'd shaped me into who I was today?

Oh, well, a woman was entitled to her soft, stupid moments.

I walked back to my bedroom, emptied my bag, took that inventory. He'd been right. It hadn't been Valium and GHB.

The one thing missing was thiopental sodium. Pentothal. A fast-acting anesthetic. It hit the blood stream and put people out in under thirty seconds for up to thirty minutes.

Could be it hadn't been as fast or as lasting with Damian because it had been an intramuscular not an IV injection. Or thanks to his superior metabolism and PATS's conditioning. Or his physiology simply didn't resemble the human variety.

But Pentothal also relaxed inhibition and made its victim communicate his deepest desires.

That was why it was known as truth serum.

And he'd kissed me under its influence!

Chapter 6

"As you all know, the part of the Caucasus region we're concerned with lies between the Black and Caspian seas here…"

The guy's silhouette turned to tap his baton over the projected map behind him. "It's made up of Georgia, Azerbaijan, and Russia. The Caucasus Mountains form the borders of Azerbaijan, Georgia and the Russian states of Dagestan, Chechnya, Ingushetia, North Ossetia, Kabardino-Balkaria and Karachay-Cherkessia, and this is where the various militant armies of the Russian Federation take refuge…"

Bo-ring. Felt like being back in junior high, subjected to Mr. Patterson's monotonous, convoluted expositions on politico-histogeographical intricacies.

Who was that guy anyway? Yeah, yeah, something Daniels of PATS's Tactical. Why wasn't Damian doing this? He'd always made debriefing fun and memorable. Made info stick in our minds. The only thing this guy was sticking was our butts to our seats.

"The conflict between Russia and Chechnya and the situation of the Chechen refugees in Ingushetia, as you all know…"

Okay. Enough. "Excuse me…" I stood up, stretching the stitch out of my back. "But we *do* all know. So why don't you tell us something we don't?"

A ripple of laughter rose behind me. My team, of course. Damian's people, the "Dirty Dozen" as Matt had whispered in my ear on seeing them, were on the other side, not finding me particularly funny. Figured. I shared some memorable history with half of them. They probably hated having me and my team here nearly as much as Damian did.

The laughter died down only for Matt to make a sarcastic comment about PATS's pseudo-military due process. One of Damian's men volleyed a comment about our street-fighting tactics. Then the whole lecture hall jumped in. I saw Daniels turn to Damian in the dark. Damian made a movement with his hand, dismissing him.

Not good. Not Daniels relieving us from his lengthy worldview report, but our people's unleashed rancor. Made me wish both teams would go back to ignoring each other's presence as they had for the past hour after the compulsory introductions.

I had to do something about that. Starting tomorrow we'd be depending on each other for survival.

Damian stood up, beating me to it. Half a dozen long strides had him on the one-step podium. "Lights please." The lights came on immediately and there he was, in his PATS black uniform, arms extended on both sides of the dais, stance uncompromising, intention unmistakable. "Let me make this clear. Every bit of knowledge you pick up will prove crucial. And every bit of attitude you leave behind will be the only reason we, as *one* team, stay alive. You can pick up your egos and smart-assness when we're back home in one piece."

He gave his people a hard look that made them shift in their chairs. "PATS men and women know how to follow orders, how to keep personal attitudes out of dealings with colleagues, how to give an ally everything they've got. I hope *you*—uh…"

I walked toward him, mounted the podium. "Can't find a name for us? Hmm. Never bothered to name our operation something as important-sounding as TOP or PATS. How about DOCS?"

If glances could spank, I'd have one smarting backside. He fisted his hand over the mike so his words were for my ears only. "You're not helping, *Doc*. And then again, who among you is a doctor for real? You're all dropouts and outcasts."

I gave him my most serene smile. "And so are you, SEALs dropout, and wherever you got the rest of your team. You're in no position to cast stones, De Luna."

He dropped his eyes, studied his feet for a moment. I looked, too, for that extra foot that warranted such absorption.

He finally sighed. "Okay, so this out of our systems then and we can now get down to business. If you don't appreciate an indepth report on the background of the region…"

"I know all there is to know. It's where I lost Jake!"

His eyes did that weird glowing thing again. His answer, when it came one laden second later, was cool. "Point taken. But do the others? I thought a briefing might be more accessible than the brochures I had prepared. Apparently not. So—I'll distribute them after this meeting. Make sure your team studies them. Now, I'll get to the specifics of our mission."

"I'll have a word with *our* teams first." I gave the hand still choking the mike a pointed look. He unclasped it, made a gracious be-my-guest gesture, accompanied with a tiny bow. There was no mistaking it. He'd conceded my equal status in this. I could see most of his team's eyes following us, reaching the same conclusion, not liking it, but sucking it in like the good pseudo-soldiers that they were.

I wondered what had changed his mind since last night. Certainly not me. Must have gotten orders from high above. Who up there liked me that much? Sir Ashton? But he didn't have a say over Damian or PATS. So who? Not that it was important now.

I turned to the men and women who'd accompany me in the mission of our lives, whose lives I'd defend with mine, and who'd do the same for me.

I had to admit, Damian's people looked impressive. I knew they *were* impressive. Three women and eight men, superior physical specimens all. And if they were anything like their leader, it didn't stop at physical perfection and prowess.

My people, on the other hand, looked like...well, people. Average-looking men and women of all ages and ethnic origins. Ayesha, forty-seven, looked older than her age but had the resilience of three women half her age, her masses of graying hair untouched and grabbed back in a severe bun, her tall, ebony body rod straight and unyielding. Lucia, twenty-two, a beacon of enthusiasm and energy, olive-skinned, tall, lush, striking and wanted to be me when she grew up. Poor girl. Ishmael, thirty-nine, balding and soft looking, until you looked in his steely eyes.

Haiku, Fadel and Doug had their stories and their disparities. It was amazing how each had come to me from such different origins and identities, how our reasons differed yet were so much the same. It was incredible how we worked. No one but Matt, my bodybuilding blond surgical guru and the one who could take over from me if he only wanted, would ever be picked by a casting director to play the hero. But they were heroes. Each and every one of them. In his or her own way.

Crazy as it sounded, I was excited to be going up against impossible odds. Again. And just that the possibility of reaching Jake and the others existed—I couldn't wait to begin.

So I did.

"Hey, folks, excuse the lack of formalities. It's been a long time since I've been in an outfit that paid any attention to chain of command."

"And if you believe that, guys, I have a pyramid to sell you."
That was Matt, taking the initiative to spread ease as he'd taken
it on himself to initiate friction. "We may not call her boss, but
make no mistake that she is and we're never in any danger of
forgetting. She may not look it, but she's a terror."

That got a humorous murmur circulating around the hall.

"I have two bullet holes in my thigh to prove it, buddy." That
was Ed McNeil, Damian's second in command. "Damian's prac-
tically a sieve. You were one crazy dudette, St. James, if effective—I'll give you that. Hope you're over the crazy part."

Wow. I never thought the day would come when the incident
in Darfur would be brought up with anything but an overdose
of angst. Good to know not everyone who'd lost friends or been
injured that day nurtured an undying vendetta against me.

Something inside me eased. I smiled my extreme gratitude
at Ed. He winked one sparkling blue eye at me as he linked both
hands behind his almost-shaved platinum blond head. Damian
was too self-possessed to show his displeasure. I got the sublim-
inal transmission though. And how.

"And now you've heard from my highly paid PR man and Ju-
das, Matt McDermott, whom I'm firing as of now—" that got me
another ripple of chuckles "—and testimonials to my damage potential from Ed McNeil, I have an announcement. I'm not crazy
anymore." More chuckles echoed. Damian gazed into space. "Really! I must have been picked for this mission for my track record.
Postmania, that is. My team on the other hand has always been
highly disciplined. They're also capable and dedicated and are
ready for anything. I'm sure they share these qualities with you."

Then I made my real point. "I know we do things differently
but we have overlapping skills, even if your medical and our
combat training aren't as extensive as the other's. But we can
complement each other and I hope you'll swap notes. On my
part, I've worked with most of you and after my team, there's
no one I'd rather trust my fate to. I hope you can trust me, too."

Ed's smile widened. What do you know? I never expected to have an ally on Damian's side that easily. Some of the others nodded, some just relaxed.

My nerves slackened a bit more. I decided to go for broke. "One last thing before De Luna tells us what we're up against. All of you who were injured four years ago, I never got the chance to ask your forgiveness, to visit you in hospital…."

"Hey, St. James, we're soldiers—pseudo ones anyway!" Ed winked at Matt. "We know the odds each time we go out to the field. Friendly fire or teammate mistake are just more ways to go. And then it's thanks to you we *made* it to hospital."

My heart did a little tap-dance number, pumping no blood to my brain. So that was how Ed looked at it. Weird thing, it had never occurred to me to see it that way. I still couldn't.

Damian stood there, still staring into nothingness, an imposing statue exemplifying the avant-garde warrior, his face a study of insouciance. Boy, was he pissed.

I bet no one else noticed. He always was able to channel his thoughts with bull's-eye precision, transmit them only to his target. It made him a hell of an undercover agent. No one ever picked anything from him if he was bent on misleading them.

He allowed his team a minute to assimilate my speech, to buzz their responses to one another, then he stepped up to me. I vacated the podium and went back to my seat.

He began at once. "During the past eight years, we've been conducting ongoing investigations into the disappearance of GCA's nine operatives. Early on, we had allegations of their abduction by a militant group established a few months prior to their disappearance, counting their abduction as one of their first actions against 'the enemy and those who help them.'"

My blood drained to my feet. I'd been told they'd been murdered and their bodies thrown in a mass grave. My voice stifled on the accusation. "You knew that all along and never told me?"

His impassive glance glided to me. "We had conflicting reports and no claims of responsibility were ever issued. We followed each lead and ended up with thin air. *Then…*" He raised his voice, aborting the questions erupting like popcorn in my head. "A year ago, our embedded operatives in the Caucasus unearthed old evidence linking the disappearance to a militant group that is allegedly responsible for most of the terrorist acts in the Russian Federation in the past few years."

Something fizzed in my ears. My blood. Zooming back from my legs in a geyser to flood my brain.

I hated, hated, *hated* legal-military-journalism jargon. Self-serving lingo, invented to suppress and confuse the truth, make sure the talker couldn't be held accountable for anything they said. And Damian was surely laying it thick.

Allegedly had to be way up there in the list of vague, maddening crap that made me incoherent with fury.

Oh, Dad, how I sympathize. Twenty years of seeing "allegedlys" and "purportedlys" and "unsubstantiateds" letting monsters back on the street. No wonder you went out there and blew their heads off yourself.

For now I needed to hear Damian's politically correct brief. But I had something to say first. Something I'd have an apoplectic attack if I didn't get off my chest. "You waited a year to start this?"

"That evidence was four years old, so it wasn't exactly reliable. It dated from the time a branch of the militants moved their base into the mountains, where the federal Russian forces have been unable to reach them without incurring heavy losses. It took us three months to make sure that militant stronghold exists, that the GCA operatives are still alive."

"And you made *sure?*"

"Yes."

I'd already been told Jake and the others were alive. But I was too acquainted with life's cruelties, and I reserved the biggest part of me, braced for the blow, for the letdown, that the best PATS had was strong evidence but no certainties.

But if Damian answered my question with an unprecedented and simple yes, then it was a sure thing.

Jake was alive and well.

Just as the giddy thought ricocheted free in my mind, images of his elegant body emaciated, his proud spirit broken shot it down. He was alive. But well? And then Sir Ashton had said it was an impossible mission. He wasn't given to exaggerations. Knowing where they were and getting them out were two different animals. And there was another thing I still didn't get.

"What took you nine months then?" I asked. "You've been planning a retrieval mission that long?"

"Yes. And we'd reached the conclusion that there was no way to orchestrate a search-and-retrieve operation without massive losses on our side, probably the loss of the hostages, too."

"So why didn't you come to me before that? For the aid mission cover?"

"Because this became an option just last month. To understand why, I have to give you some background. The full details are in the brochure." He paused, made sure I wasn't going to cut him short again, then spoke. "Five years ago, fifty thousand refugees fled the federal troops trying to force them out of their camps and back to Chechnya. Those resettled in the only place federal forces didn't have free rein in, at the foot of the militant-controlled mountain—"

"Wait a minute!" His eyes lowered at my interruption. Hey, he was the one who'd said every bit of info would come in handy! "Why didn't the federal forces launch an aerial offensive if a ground one is so impossible?"

"It's a mountain, St. James. They could be anywhere within a sixty-mile radius. And yes—" he intercepted my question, answered it "—we don't know their exact location either. That's why I said a *search*-and-retrieval operation. Anyway, back to how the aid mission possibility opened up.

"The refugees discovered they'd jumped from the frying pan

into the fire. The militants made sure their stay became permanent so they'd use them as a human shield against the federal troops by heavily land-mining all accesses to the camp."

"But why? The federal forces weren't reaching them in the first place!"

"There were efforts every now and then, with losses on the militants' side, too. They closed that door and lived in security. But they didn't stop only the federal forces, but also humanitarian aid, and the camp became totally dependent on their mercy. Then three months ago, to soothe an outraged world, both militants and federal forces announced that they would let humanitarian aid reach the camp."

I remembered this, now he mentioned it. The federal forces had vowed not to use the mine-clear land the militants would provide to attack them. I'd thought it was big of them. For about a second. I knew there had to be an ulterior motive there. Turned out they couldn't attack if they wanted to, were just laying claim to a humanity they didn't possess. Typical.

I remembered something else. "It's been three months since relief operations reached the camp bearing supplies and logistical kits. Why didn't you move earlier?"

"Because relief operations were made to leave on the same day, the next at most. We needed enough time to find the militant stronghold, to stage a tight enough operation to get the GCA people out alive. Medical aid missions, which are by necessity longer term, were out till just a few days ago."

"We *are* planning to work in the camp while we're there, aren't we?" That was Ayesha, speaking up for the first time. I started at hearing her voice. I'd phased everyone's presence out during our Q&A volley match.

Damian turned to Ayesha, his gaze on her motherly, placid face gentle. Gentle? De Luna? Nah. "Of course. On one hand you will be helping the refugees and on the other you will make us look legitimate and validate our extended stay there."

I didn't like the sound of that. "You mean you just need us for your cover, then we'll sit in the camp while you do everything else?"

He raised one shoulder in a what-kind-of-moronic-question-is-that gesture. "That's the plan."

I shook my head in a dream-on gesture. "Don't think so."

"If you want to contest it, take it up with the people who depl…who recruited you."

"I will." I did like the idea that my team wouldn't be exposed to unnecessary hazard. But *I* was going to be in on every step of the operation. I had to be.

He continued, closing the subject. "If the idea of a projector and a map isn't too appalling, I need to show you the route we will travel. Lights out please. Slide eight."

That unseen genie he commanded snuffed out the lights, shone the map over him. He moved so it fell on the wall instead. "Our biggest handicap is our inability to stock enough weapons and ammunition. We'll have the amount that guarding the convoy can justify. We expect searches, by the federal forces, to make sure we're not smuggling arms to the militants."

"But why aren't the federal forces helping us?"

I glared at Doug. Was he out to prove to Damian we were "amateurs who functioned on a gamble and a prayer!"? I answered before Damian did. "Because *no one* must know our real purpose."

Damian didn't miss a thing, but let it go. "To avoid being hassled too much we won't land in Moscow, where our supplies would be exposed to too much scrutiny, but will come through the Black Sea. Our convoy of trucks has already been dispatched there."

Lucia, who'd been too awestruck until now to talk, asked, "What about our stuff? All the things we need to do our job?"

I picked up the line of questioning. "Yeah. I have specifications for the medical part of the mission. I need a mobile surgery unit, a diagnostic unit, an emergency and triage facility. Not to mention our own inventory of supplies and drugs, both for medical purposes and—otherwise."

"Everything you can possibly need medically and surgically is included. GCA went all out on this one. I'm sure you believe *they* know what they're doing? As for your own supplies, you can take them with you on the plane. There is no weight limit."

"So how will you solve the problem of the limited arms?" Matt asked.

"The convoy vehicles are designed to hide our weapons and ammunition. And a medical convoy will come in handy here, too. Most explosive components can be justified as medical supplies."

"Making explosives out of medical supplies is our specialty!" Matt purred smugly.

"Your boss said your specialty is medicine." Ed chuckled. "You can help mix explosives only if you're done giving shots."

"And before you can start dabbling in shots or explosives," Damian said. "We'll land in Sochi, an airport and a seaport town in Krasnodar-Kray state. You can load your stuff to the convoy there. Then we'll travel east, through Karachay-Cherkessia then Kabardino-Balkaria." He slid his baton over the map, somehow making the same thing Daniels had turned into monotony into a dynamic thing. As if we were already there and on our way, facing the unknown. "We'll be following the mountains throughout. The refugee camp is at the very south end of North Ossetia, sixty miles from the Georgian border by Mount Kazbek, where we believe the militants are."

He paused for a second, then looked at me, wearing that same inanimate expression. "Any questions?"

About a thousand and one. But I'd keep them until I had him alone. Time I started showing some leadership solidarity. Though all bets were off if he didn't back down on this thing about me being excluded from field missions.

My team started asking questions, and he raised his hands.

"I'll leave you in Ed's capable hands. These questions are right up his alley, and I have another meeting right now."

He gave a general nod, made a point of not looking at me again and strode out. I followed.

It was my first time ever in a PATS installation. Very top secret stuff. Like us really, but just with oodles more money and prestige. I could use their decorator in my Sanctuaries, too. Hell, I could use a fresh coat of paint.

"De Luna."

He'd known I was behind him. He had eyes in the back of his head and other ESP feelers. I didn't need any special perception to know how annoyed my pursuit made him. He went still at my call, turned on me and showed me how much. "Take it up with Fitzpatrick, St. James," he growled.

"Relax, will you? Sheesh. Were you always this uptight?"

There was that spanking look again. I could definitely get used to this. "I know GCA must think they have everything covered, but they're not really privy to how I work or what I'd need. So, I wanted to give you a list. If we're leaving so soon, my suppliers may not be fast enough to secure all the drugs and materials I must have on a field mission of that nature and scope. I'm anticipating anything and—"

"Just write the list and give it to Ed. He'll see to it."

He turned away. I fell into step with him.

"Now what?"

I blinked innocently. "I'm letting you show me the way."

"The way to what?"

"To our meeting."

"*Our* meeting?"

"Oh, all right. I should have said 'my.' I was just getting into the spirit of unity for the mission, being courteous."

His glare did a lot more than spank now. I chuckled. "You are going to the meeting with Davis, Fitzpatrick, Sir Ashton and those very high-ups from TOP, aren't you?"

I knew the answer without the corroboration of his frown. Was nice to have it, though. The frown.

I smirked and it deepened. "Lead the way then. For now."

Chapter 7

Now don't get me wrong. I *had* been enjoying the scenery.

Who wouldn't? Early October painted the limitless canvas of the Russian skies with miraculous cloud formations, the slanting rays of an orange sun splurging impossible hues and shadows through them, giving them mass and magic. The humbling plains and awe-inspiring mountains shared the celestial tint, if toned down. The air had texture, its very frigidity imbuing it with a cleansing effect, made being cocooned in my weatherproof GCA uniform feel safe, soothing.

Everything melded into a divine manifestation.

Made you wonder how the human race managed to even think up evil and strife with the example of such splendor and harmony right in front of their eyes.

This poetic state had been upon me for three days now, since we started our trek, a convoy of ten highly specialized trailers, with the scene changing to a different and equally mind-steal-ing masterpiece every hour as our convoy maintained its forty-mile-per-hour speed, steadily traveling east.

Besides the scenery, I'd had enough on my mind to keep me occupied. Going over our supplies, preparing contingency plans with my team, integrating those with what Damian's team had in place. Keeping out of Damian's way. Not that I had to try hard. The guy had engaged his cloaking capabilities! More and more I could appreciate his covert operations powers.

Then there'd been the two extensive searches we'd been subjected to. It had been…interesting, being stopped by tanks and having a hundred armed-to-the-teeth special forces soldiers pouring all over our vehicles and persons, poking and prodding and poring over every little detail. I'd known we looked totally innocent, yet the stress hormones danger always flooded my system with had been as usual, well, sort of like a long-lost friend, welcome, different—exciting.

Of course nothing had been found. Even to the most meticulous, suspicious investigator, we had nothing but medical instruments and supplies in every inch of our mobile facilities.

The only ones wielding weapons were the six among Damian's team who were posing as our security. One rifle and one gun each, what the federal forces in the region considered insufficient to start an uprising with but enough to defend us against a medium-sized raid. Whatever *that* meant.

No, really, what did that mean, medium-sized? Ten, twenty, fifty? And defend us how, exactly? Kill half of our attackers before they managed to kill all of us? That constituted an acceptable defense and outcome in their eyes?

Was that the penalty for being the good guys, for being bound by laws and fair play and due process? To be shackled, hampered and prohibited from arming yourself and destroyed? To be easy pickings for free-from-rules villains? To become another statistic for activists to lament for a while before being forgotten just like millions of victims before you? Like Jake…

But Jake hadn't been slaughtered. Hadn't been forgotten. PATS had kept his memory alive. To my continuing surprise.

And *I* hadn't forgotten him. I *hadn't*.

Losing him had been the catalyst that had had me crossing over in my mind, shedding every last tie to the safe and accepted, making me who I was today. Every time I reached out to someone in need or in mortal danger, I was saving him.

As the searches had progressed, I'd felt smug that we were not prey waiting to be victimized but secret weapons penetrating the system that wouldn't let us do our jobs in the open.

Then I'd felt like crap. At how deception and stealth were endless, how someone bent on destruction could breach the most intensive scrutiny to strike at the unwary and the innocent.

Right under the noses of search specialists, we smuggled arms that would decimate an army. Sure, we were on the side of good. But how many on the side of brutality and treachery were getting away with it, too? The depressing answer was, plenty.

My early point was, between the scenery, my life's most important and hazardous quest and pondering the state of a world gone mad, I had no right to be bored.

But I had been. And I'd done the unforgivable.

I'd wished for some change, some action.

And here it came.

An ominous storm of trucks and Jeeps were tearing toward us on a head-on intercept course, the thickening barrier of dust they kicked behind them obliterating the horizon, the illusion of cutting us off from the world growing by the second.

"St. James." Damian's voice flowed over our frequency-hopping private channel. As if he was sitting right beside me. So calm. "We'll handle it. Plan Delta."

Plan Delta. They'd surround us with their trailers, half remaining behind to protect the convoy on ground level, the other half running to the mountain for higher ground.

Oh, yeah? He thought I'd cower flat on my belly, count on his team and the armored vehicle to protect me? Or worse, to watch them getting hacked to pieces while awaiting my turn?

He really had forgotten more than he knew about me.

I pressed the outgoing button. "Plan Delta is out. You're only twelve. Want to bet they have you outnumbered ten to one?"

"Yeah, too bad for them, if they attack."

"If? Those guys aren't tearing toward us to smother us in kisses and welcome us to the region. Plan Kappa, De Luna. We keep the teams together, make one line of offensive-defense, my team has first strike, you follow through and keep it up."

"Do as you're told, St. James. For once." His voice sounded nearer, as if he were projecting it on cerebral as well on radio waves. And there was something almost indiscernible there. Anxiety? Worried I'd blow things up to kingdom come again?

I didn't care what he thought. "We're in this together."

"Sentiment noted—and unneeded. Plan Kappa is for diversionary-based attacks. Its time will come. There's no place for your stealth tactics here. Not in a frontal assault situation, against machine guns and rocket launchers!"

"I doubt it'll come to that." What was I doing? Debating this, now? Time to pull rank, use his self-imposed shackles and limitations. "And then I'm in charge. *Your* superiors' orders!"

"You're not in charge, St. James." This was soft, lethal.

Still raw, huh? Couldn't blame him. To annoy him more than anything, I'd demanded that he wouldn't be in charge of *me*, that I didn't have to obey any orders I didn't believe valid.

His superiors hadn't only granted me that, they'd decreed that until the retrieval and retreat part of the mission, we co-led. Unless we disagreed and then my judgment took precedence.

I still couldn't make head or tails of that decision. But I was using it, using his order-following handicap. I wasn't letting him fight alone, even if it would save me and my team. "Plan

Kappa, De Luna. You know it's *our* best chance!" I cut off the transmission. He didn't call back.

No time to wonder if he'd ignore me. Whatever he did, I'd get ready. I'd worry only about the hordes coming to slaughter us and decimate our convoy.

Uh, let me rephrase that. Slaughter us and *confiscate* our convoy.

This was no haphazard attack. Someone must have reported our existence, our visible defense capabilities and route. Someone who knew enough to know our convoy's exchange rate.

Between the vehicles and the state-of-the-art instruments, we were millions of dollars on wheels. Medical supplies were also the hottest commodity in the region after arms and food. A few doctors, caught after their guards were massacred, wouldn't come amiss either. All in all, a very drool-inducing package.

Which gave us an edge. Time to use it.

I opened the common channel. "Turn the convoy into a barricade, perpendicular to their approach. Turn right so we have access to the side entrances and more cover and ammo. They want our convoy in one piece, so they won't open fire. They have to come around our barricade to get us. We'll get them first."

Damian and his men were already doing just that. Following my order, or just reached the same conclusion? No matter. We were on the same wavelength. May we continue to be. If we didn't…

I'd have to override him. Again. But this time, he would be guilty of insubordination.

Ayesha was taking her turn at the wheel of the STS. She caught my eye as she followed Matt's truck, her usually open, kind face hardening with tension and aggression.

In a minute we had our trailers in a six-hundred-plus-foot barricade, with just enough space between vehicles to afford us maximum security and optimum keyhole firing windows, while making them unable to shoot at us with any accuracy. Marauders were never sharpshooters anyway. Never a need to be, with machine guns and indiscriminate fatalities in mind.

On our side, sharpshooting didn't even begin to cut it. A new word had to be invented for that kind of marksmanship. Some of our number definitely warranted the label of marks-*inhu*man.

At their speed, I estimated our enemies would be on top of us in five minutes. Had to have everything ready by then.

Piece of cake.

I unzipped two "disaster bags," snatched out trauma kits and trauma holsters. They seemed to contain the supplies needed for a code-red emergency. And they did—just not a medical one. With the only lives at risk being ours, our readiness was not geared toward saving lives, but taking them.

I retrieved the air gun and blowgun components I had disguised in various places on my own person and in the disaster bags, reassembled two of each, the much-practiced procedures melting to completion in my hands in under forty seconds.

Ammo for the air guns was preloaded, special-made hypodermic darts with large-bore, three-inch needles. Too bad they could only take one dart at a time. Good news was, reloading time had contracted under duress practice to less than three seconds. The blowguns were an upgrade on the most lethal military-issue ones, capable of delivering a dart at two thousand feet with a speed of more than one thousand feet per second.

Ayesha donned two holsters, emptying the kits in them, her actions quick, fluent. God knew we'd had enough practice, grabbing our gear, setting and psyching up on the fly in emergencies and raids alike.

I tossed Ayesha her weapons and she ground her teeth. Among us, we had enough poisonous drugs to kill ten herds of elephants. Not that we'd hurt an elephant. Ayesha wouldn't even if it were about to trample her into a sticky mess.

She wouldn't bat an eyelid with our aggressors.

I tightened my holsters to my sides, snapped on the chest harness with the radio and the extra supplies, and jumped out after Ayesha, my heart riding the lurching waves of apprehension, bounding to the proddings of healthy fear. And not-so-healthy exhilaration. Boy, I was a weird one.

I caught Damian's eyes over the heads of our crouching teammates as soon as I took my position in the slot between our trailer and Matt's. A ray of setting sun caught the side of Damian's face. Amber fire shot off one implacable eye.

I know what I'm doing this time, I tried to tell him.

I'd lay good money his answer was, *We'll see!* If *we survive whatever you have in mind.*

We disengaged each other's focus at the same moment, turned to our teams with final orders and instructions.

I barked my orders over the radio. I had a little amendment I couldn't afford anyone to miss. "Stick with strychnine. Go for curare and cyanide *only* if you deplete it. Take your time. Wait until they are at a maximum of one hundred feet. They're moving targets and we can't afford to miss. Neck shots if possible. If your target isn't smothered in layers of clothes, the heart is your second choice."

I knew what they were all thinking. Curare and cyanide acted faster. No time to elaborate why I'd chosen strychnine as the poison of choice. I hoped I was right, that what I was aiming for would happen. Whether my team agreed or not, they all implemented my order. I felt it rather than saw it. Had no eyes but for our attackers now, my heart slowing, each beat a thunderclap, pumping honing adrenaline through my system.

The enemy was about five hundred feet away now and closing in. No doubt now. If there ever was one.

This was to the death.

At the moment, they were just confused about *whose* death.

Couldn't blame them. They'd grown to expect others to accommodate them, play good, cowering targets and die.

They were even vociferously furious at our show of so-far passive resistance, roaring as they shot up a storm. In the air. Mustn't scratch the paint job, huh?

They finally stopped about three hundred feet away and came pouring out of their vehicles, their roars unbroken.

Had to make sure De Luna played by the rules. "Hold your fire. We go first. Go team…"

Anna, from Damian's team, yelped and fell back.

God! A stray bullet. Or a marksman after all.

I heard Damian shout for everyone to stay out of sight, his eyes slamming me with his fury against my restraining order in the split second mine darted to check out Anna. I was in time to see the side of Pierro's head exploding in a shower of blood.

Compulsion burst hot and wet inside my head. *Run to them, examine them,* save *them.*

No time. This time I'd seen him. The marksman. Not charging with the others, standing aside, taking leisurely shots. He was mine.

I fired. A dart tore through the air, silent, treacherous, found his neck, lodged deep, pumped its lethal load. De Luna had trained me well. I never missed. So far. I got his external carotid artery, at worst his internal jugular vein, the dart's load pumping directly into his blood stream, the drug taking effect with his very next heartbeat. Lethal dose for a big, adult male was 350 mg of the usual variety; 500 mg of our special strychnine was overkill really. Overkill was good. Needed him dead, instantly. Before he could do more damage.

I knew my team each got their target, to one degree of efficiency or another. I counted to three, waited for the show.

It came. My victim fell first, followed by seven more. Eight men going into sudden, violent seizures, writhing on the ground as if with a phantom possession, ending bowed upward, only the top of their head and heels on the ground, as if trying to break their own backs to exorcise the demon that rode them.

It was a hellish way to go. A merciless hypertransmission of nervous signals, a bonfire exploding in every nerve ending, the tiniest stimulus leading to exponential overstimulation, the resulting violent convulsions beyond excruciating. They wouldn't even be able to scream their agony as their respiratory muscles locked, suffocating one cell at a time, their minds clear all through the atrocious expiration.

But my objective, the best thing about death by strychnine, was what it did to the ones still alive. I enjoyed that part.

All criminals were deadened to the sight of bodies bursting in a hail of bullets or being hacked or blown to pieces. That was why I counted on our strike being more effective than De Luna's. Witnessing the poltergeist-like contortions of a strychnine victim scared the most hardened villain shitless.

But it was the face of a strychnine victim that I bet woke up those who witnessed it from wetting-themselves-and-shrieking-for-momma nightmares. A fixed, bloodcurdling grin in the tradition of the spine-wrenching Joker. *Risus sardonicus* was mega-phobic, unerasable, manic terror. It was what I was after. The manic part.

It worked. Criminals really were a superstitious, cowardly lot. Their retreat was as mindless as if they were paid extras in a horror-movie set.

Their gunfire hadn't stopped during their retreat, but now more joined it. Damian and his team, following up our strike. The exact amount of bullets from our side corresponded to our attackers' heads bursting in fountains of crimson. Twelve, thirteen, fifteen down. How many left?

"About ninety left." Ayesha's shout was loud enough for me to hear over the din. Never ceased to startle me, that uncanny detail-processing power of hers. "Plus twelve drivers and whatever higher ranks back safe in their vehicles."

Damian and his men got two dozen more in half as many seconds. God, how easy slaughter was.

Had to make sure it was total, too.

I shouted on the common channel. "Whatever happens, no one escapes. Everyone dies." Now our attackers knew we weren't just another aid convoy. If even one was left alive to report us, we'd be exposed. It would be all over. Wasn't even an option.

I alternated between air gun and blowgun, firing one dart after another. They joined my team's fire and Damian's team's gunfire, pursuing our receding attackers. Two dozen more fell by the time the rest were back in the protection of their vehicles.

Ayesha pounced for a real emergency kit, threw it in the air at Ishmael, the one near both Anna and Pierro.

"Ed, Suz, José, Shad," Damian shouted. "Hop into the front and rear vehicles, turn our barricade into a circle." His people exploded to do his bidding even before he finished talking, hopping in the driver's seats in two seconds flat. "They'll try to get us in a pincer. They're willing to do anything now to get us. No more counting on their desire to preserve their booty."

Next moment proved how right he was.

A marrow-liquefying shriek speared through my ears. Antitank rocket!

Next second the trailer making up the exact midpoint of our barricade exploded, the compression wave knocking everyone on both sides. I tucked and rolled with the blow, saw the trailer crashing back on two wheels for a second, then toppling on its side with a bone-splitting thud.

There had been four people behind that truck on both sides. I could see three. Only one missing. *Damian.*

The frenzied shout for him backlashed in my throat. Couldn't distract the others. They were scrambling back to their positions, getting ready for the second wave of attack now that our attackers considered us breached, softened. I didn't get back to mine. Couldn't. Had to find him, get him out. *Save him.*

Wrong move, an angry, tactical voice inside me shouted,

drowning out the cacophony of the escalating miniwar. *Your team can't afford to lose their remaining leader.*

Didn't care. They no longer needed a leader. This was on autopilot now. To the grisly end. *Damian. Just find him.*

Something still stopped me from taking the shortest cut to the other side of the fallen behemoth, streaking over its smoldering body in full sight of our now-rabid attackers, daring fate and teasing their bullets with my tender flesh. Must have learned something gut-real since Darfur then.

I ran behind the truck's cover as more rockets pounded it, shearing it in two, widening the gap in our defenses.

Two voices inside my head drowned out the uproar.

One wailed, *Stop! Damian is under this thing.* The other, maddening, logical, droned, *Hmm. Not blowing up more vehicles. Not willing to do their spoils more damage than necessary. Must think there is more per person now their numbers are diminished.*

Then everything went silent as the compression waves buffeted me, felt like huge vicious feet battering me even with the trailer taking most of the brunt. The last blast spun me around my axis, slamming me flat on my back, headfirst.

Always headfirst. Had to be the heaviest part of me. Good. It was the toughest, too. Not tough enough to ward off the avalanche of noise and pain and near-terror though. I crushed down on the debilitating sensations. *Get to Damian.*

I crawled on the ground, lizardlike, my awareness wide open, bombarded by everything. My team, Damian's, even Anna and Pierro partially patched up, fighting back. The enemy was almost on top of us. Then I found a—body. *Damian!*

Flat on his face. Clear of the trailer by an inch. Just knocked out, or more? I lunged for him, reached for his carotid.

Thick pulsations pushed hard against my fingertips. My forehead touched the ground in a nanosecond prayer of thanks.

His pulse quickened against my fingers as I poked him, accelerating his revival. His eyes snapped open, bore into me, instantly alert, the same sweep of eyelids seamlessly segueing into a lightning-quick succession of movements. Rolling on his back, finding his rifle, readying it, lunging for me, covering me with his massive bulk as another explosion knocked us flat on the ground again. Coming from the opposite direction.

They'd circled us and were blasting an access through our vehicular fortress, pouring at us from both sides now.

Weird details invaded my awareness. The clash of multilingual roars, a profound world statement. Ayesha had a gun now, was using it, stony-eyed. Matt snapped someone's neck, predatory growls issuing from him. Ed blew away another, an elated radiance to his cruelly handsome face. And Damian…

How fierce and beautiful he was. How damned heavy. His mass impacted me, stopped my attempt to rise. Then his roar resounded in my head as he pushed me down harder, firing.

Hot viscosity spattered my face, froze as I registered the bodies falling a foot from us. Everything stretched as I twisted, fired my dart above Damian's shoulder, returning the favor, getting his attacker in the thigh. My victim still had time to shoot Damian. It took a millisecond to pull a trigger.

It was how long it took me to yank Damian's arm around, impulses arcing through my nerves to his, his inhuman reflexes completing the circuit, boosting the reaction, getting his would-be killer between the eyes. Doing him a favor, really.

Then a gun was shoved in my hand and I was yanked up. The remaining marauders were on top of us, and I was on my knees and plastered against Damian, braced against his immovable support.

We were going to make our final stand back to back.

Chapter 8

A total bloodbath.

That was what it was. And it was about to get far worse.

For the few left alive that was. And for us, too.

We'd pulverized our enemies. The whole thing had taken less than twenty minutes. Twenty-one people taking out 136. Talk about destructive capability.

This was as bad as Darfur.

That night four years ago, I alone had killed more than sixty people. Hard to even imagine that. The number. The enormity. Impossible to grasp the concept. People with lives and problems and dreams. Snuffed by me in a few explosive seconds.

But those people I'd killed, in the past and today, had chosen to kill others for a living. They'd irrevocably relinquished the rights of the living.

Still, killing them, killing period, was ugly and damaging. Most people I knew reduced the act to something unreal, like slaying virtual monsters in video games, to make it easier. Then it even had an element of excitement, of achievement. Of superiority. Killing had become all that for Dad, until it had almost cost him his mind and soul. It had consumed a hefty chunk of both. I knew.

It could consume me whole far more easily. I knew that, too. I was more volatile, my basic nature far closer to the surface, my motives far more personal. I couldn't afford that. Couldn't take the least satisfaction in killing. In relieving victims, saving lives, stopping brutality, yes. In the act itself, never.

It didn't mean I wasn't good at it, though.

I was. Very.

Today I'd killed nine. Lifetime body count had risen above ninety. I should be numb to it all by now. How I needed to be.

I couldn't afford numbness. Monsters or no, I had to regret it, to let it—to *make* it—hurt like hell.

My hand fisted around the scalpel with which I'd made an opening in Pierro's chest, welcoming the pain as it cut into my gloved palm, summoning nausea, proof of my sanity and humanity.

I stared at the trickle of blood, then at the fresh glove Haiku extended to me. I snapped off the soiled one, put on the new one and reached for a thoracostomy tube. I turned to my patient, started the procedure of introducing the tube into his chest.

It was the one way this was better than Darfur. Our fallen three were just injured, not dead, and only Pierro had a significant injury. It wasn't fatal. *If* I did my job right.

But this was also far worse than Darfur. We'd taken prisoners then. We were about to…

"…kill me, Doc?"

The strident gasp went through my brain. *Concentrate, Doc!*

I smiled down at Pierro. Big and powerful like the rest of his team, narrow face inlaid with slashed Roman features denying his pain, naturally bronzed skin obscuring the blood loss and shock. His lips betrayed him, blue with oxygen deprivation and cold, cracking with dehydration. His eyes did, too, translucent blue turning murky with depletion. I flicked the sliding control of the giving set, increased his fluid delivery.

"No, Pierro," I quipped. "I'm just skewering you to see how much blood is left inside you after that scalp fountain."

His grimace was an attempt at a smile. Figured he'd appreciate the morbid joke. We doctors had ghoulish humor in common with soldiers.

I had another purpose for the joke. His blood pressure had been low for a long time and "getting" humor now was a good diagnostic sign that there was no brain insult. There would be if I didn't correct his hypotension. Hypoxia, lack of oxygen, was even more dangerous. Should I intubate him?

Nope. His breathing problems were a symptom. Empty the blood around his lung and it would go away. The bullet had penetrated his right lung and come out of his back, shattering the tip of the scapula. Blood collapsed one lung, was pressuring the other lung and heart, leaving him no space to breathe, his heart no place to beat. Adding to that a liter of blood loss, his right ear nearly being blown off along with part of his scalp.

Pierro groaned again as I advanced the thoracostomy tube into his pleural space. I turned to Haiku. "You did inject the incision site with 2 cc's of lidocaine, didn't you?"

Haiku's slanted eyes attempted to round in self-defense. "I injected three! He can't be in pain. You in pain, Pierro?"

Pierro's long grunt was answer enough. So the local anesthetic wasn't working. I'd had it up to here with PATS drug-resistance conditioning!

I secured the tube with a suture and tape, attached it to an underwater-seal bottle. Blood gushed into the bottle under pressure, didn't stop until there was almost a liter. It still came, slower, but steady. This wasn't looking good. I'd need to go in and stop the bleeding surgically.

Haiku listened to his chest. She removed the stethoscope and chewed her lip. "Breath still sounds unequal. Clearing on the lung base, but no breath sounds at the apex."

So his collapsed lung wasn't reexpanding fully on its own either. If it didn't in about fifteen minutes, and if blood still came, I'd have to operate. I closed my eyes, praying it wouldn't come to that, opened them, motioned for Doug and Ishmael to take him to the Surgical Trailer Suite.

"Have something better than a bullet to the head on you?"

I almost fell face-first in my open emergency bag. Damian. Behind me. Man, I was beyond wrecked. Sick electricity buzzed though my muscles and right to my heaving soul.

"You okay?" His large hand clamped my arm, pulled me back against him. I almost leaned back, sought his refuge. God, I needed it. A moment. Of life and warmth and contact. Just to defuse my discharging mind, to neutralize all this death.

What the hell! Why was I fighting it for? I deserved this, succor from a partner in crime, halving the guilt and ugliness.

I sagged back, augmented his tug with my yielding, ended up with my back against his chest. I went for broke, turned my face into his neck. He smelled of danger and mystery and man and life. Of death, too. He'd killed far more than me today. I bet he made my record seem measly. Wondered how many he'd shot, blown apart, shredded with his bare hands…

"Calista…"

Not a good time for him to say my name, whisper it this way, ragged, mind-and-hormone messing. It jerked me out of the moment's solace. With a deluge of could-have-beens and could-never-bes. Of faces, dead, thought dead, alive but lost…

Nauseating pressure pushed behind my eyeballs. I waited for it to dissipate into tears. It didn't, built inside my skull, turning the twilight into night.

I pushed away from the shared penitence. *If* he indulged in that. Nah. Remorse wasn't one of Damian's permissible weaknesses. Not in the black-and-white universe he inhabited.

But without remorse, how could someone retain their soul? Really, how much soul did he have left?

He didn't think *I* had much left. I never had much to start with, in his opinion. Which was something really. I could understand that from Sir Ashton with his activism and puritanical views. But from Damian, the archangel of retribution and destruction? Did he really think I was worse than him?

I probably was. Damian had no moral dilemma, bore no guilt, committed no transgression. He was an undisputed tiger whose predatory nature was not only a God-given right, a brand of status and superiority, but a necessity for maintaining the balance of nature. I was the one who was the unnatural freak messing with the balance, the one who'd enlisted as an angel, who'd become a hellhound out of choice, who no longer knew where one side stopped and the other began. I was the one who'd taken an oath to help anyone in need, even an enemy.

I was going to kill my enemies now.

Suddenly what Damian had asked me took on a different slant, a taunting, salt-rubbing intention.

Could be just guilty conscience. Made no difference now. I blinked back nonexistent tears, vision fogging with aggression. To think I had any left after the last hellish hour. Seemed there was an unending fount of the stuff in my system.

I snapped off my gloves and turned on him. "So you think I'm more effective than a bullet to the head now, huh?"

We were by the open STS. Cold fluorescent light doused us, illuminating Damian's face. His expression shifted. It was only then I noticed the softness I'd just erased. The softness I'd never seen before.

The pressure between my ears soared, desperate to rewind and replay that unprecedented and I'd bet unrepeatable warmth.

Oh, for crying out loud. Warmth? What next? Holding hands as you go blow seven men's heads off?

I ground my teeth. "Am I okay? Physically, not even a scratch.

Otherwise, I don't know. Are you? With what we're going to do?"

"I don't have to be."

I tried to read him. Was he disturbed by this, too, but doing what must be done? Or had the line long blurred and everything had become one extreme realm where only the cause existed? Had it become the excuse for crossing all lines?

Better luck reading a blank board. No—a board overlaid with a dozen pages in a dozen languages. Everyone would find what would validate their own wishes reflected in his expressions.

And I'd bet everyone would be wrong.

I tore my eyes away from his. This doctor didn't prescribe more emotional turmoil. "So we'll do it?"

"Do you have any other ideas?"

None. And he knew it. I'd already ordered everyone dead.

But at the time I hadn't factored in the possibility that not everyone would be killed in the battle! Not everyone had.

We couldn't spare them. They belonged to a militant faction that occasionally did business with the militants we were after. One left alive would flee back to his people to report us.

It was a choice between our lives and our mission, with all the refugees we were going to help and the hostages we were going to free, or them. No choice, really.

God, if only they hadn't surrendered!

"I thought an overdose of some sort might be more—humane…" He suddenly huffed a short laugh. I swung around to glare at him. He shrugged. "Some things are so ugly nothing but a laugh can do them justice, deliver a more comprehensive statement."

So *did* he think this was monstrous, no matter who they were or what the stakes were? The act itself carried the same horror for him? I had no idea. Funny how I thought I knew him one second, and realized I don't know anything about him the next.

I mimicked his laugh. His eyes widened, questioning. "A

laugh is the only thing to do you justice, too, De Luna. You saw how the ones I killed died. I bet any of them, given the choice, would have taken a bullet to the head anytime!"

"Yeah, I bet." His eyes took on a shrewd cast. "You really are ruthless, aren't you? You decide what needs to be done, then you go for the maximum pain and damage way of doing it."

So he *was* driving his eternal point home, huh? The creep!

He drove it deeper. "I know what strychnine does—hell, we've used it, knocking off sentries here and there. But I never thought it a possibility in direct combat. Your equipment and targeted delivery made it as instant as a bullet. Combatants the world over would literally kill for your patents and drug potency. And the most savage Amazon Basin or Ninja warriors can only dream of your anatomical knowledge and precision."

Yeah, yeah. So that was what it meant to be damned by praise, huh? If that *was* praise. It sounded like… I didn't know what it sounded like or what it really was.

Get this—whatever this is—over with already! "Listen, De Luna. My team is setting up for surgery. We need to wrap up our prisoners issue pronto so I can take care of Pierro. I may have to do a thoracotomy—y'know, open up his chest to find the bleeding source and stem it. Then I'll reconstruct his scalp and ear. So whatever your point is, will you cough it up already?"

His nod was slow, his eyes still sweeping me. "Hmm. I had projected our victory but with more losses, at least injuries. It was thanks to the psychological damage you dealt the enemy that we're more or less in one piece. They could have retreated to regroup. They should have turned around and waited to ambush us with reinforcements a hundred miles from here. But you both spooked and incensed them into mass hysteria. They attacked with no plan, with the same uncoordinated terror and suicidal desperation the doomed fight an unseen demon with."

I huffed out my confusion and oppression. "So this is your roundabout way of admitting I'm effective, huh?"

"I never thought you anything else. I only questioned your damage potential to allies. I draw the line at Samson tactics."

"I didn't pull any this time. You already admitted we're all in one piece thanks to me."

"Yeah." He gave me one of those looks that left me wanting to cover myself up. Figuratively speaking. "You know people, don't you? You're not only intimate with the way their bodies work but with their psyches, too. And to think I thought you never paid attention during psychological offensive sessions."

Was he for real? I'd hung on his every word, every damn libido-provoking move. Oh, for Pete's sake!

"But you never needed me to teach you such stuff, did you? It's innate, the way you're intimate with the criminal mind."

"It takes one, you mean?"

He didn't even attempt to deny it. Creep just wasn't enough! "You do share the same anarchist tendencies. You understand them far better than someone like me, who only gets anarchy on a mental level."

"While I do on a gut level, huh?"

His head tilted, his lips pursed. "It's what makes you a menace, in my opinion. And then you've got the knowledge and the passion to make your unpredictability lethal."

Why was he doing this now? After we'd fought back to back, when I felt we'd finally connected, been on the same side. I couldn't bear his shoving a mirror at me now, going back to square one. Or was that what he was doing?

"That unpredictable lethalness was what saved lives today," I spit. "Or at the very least limbs. *Your* admission."

In answer to that, he just…smiled. Dammit all to hell. And what a smile! An eyes smile. Real. Reaching deep into him. And into me. Metamorphosing, approving, even teasing. "Don't let it go to your head," he finally murmured.

That smile went straight there. To other places, too. Now I knew why he never really smiled. Sobering casualty counts!

Change the subject. Dwell on death and destruction.

I looked around us. Plenty of distractions there. Our teams were rushing about, checking the dead, ascertaining their deaths, gathering their weapons, guarding our prisoners, securing the perimeters. I gestured toward them. "You have to admit, we did a good job together. Our teams meshed."

"Yeah, and I'm still surprised. Hearing about your drug-based weapons, I thought you'd kill us all at the first hurdle."

"Big*oted* of you!"

"I'm admitting I was wrong here. Don't I get leniency points for that?"

Was that man choosing his words for maximum distress value? Did he have to say leniency when we were about to execute seven men? "You're really okay with this, aren't you? You're one fine, causal killer, De Luna!"

His smile twisted and—heated? No, no, I didn't want it to. I wanted him to remain my old mentor and tormentor. My new beleaguering co-leader. I couldn't handle anything else.

Even if you're dying for everything else?

Oh, shut up!

"So are you, St. James." He was enjoying being proved right, wasn't he? "This is the first time I've seen you actually premeditatedly kill, and you know what? You were born to it. It really takes a healer to be the best killer, doesn't it?"

That hurt. For being so true. I did spend equal time perfecting my healing and murdering techniques. Rationalizations for the latter didn't seem to matter now. Didn't seem enough.

He probed deeper. "So why are you pretending to find it so hard to kill those who, if the situation were reversed, wouldn't have only killed you but raped and mutilated you first?"

I looked at our vicious-looking but now cowering prisoners. They wouldn't have been that kind. I said so. "They probably would have kept me as a medical-sexual slave."

"So why are you balking?"

"Because the situation isn't reversed and I have the upper hand. Because the heat of the battle has cooled and self- and others' defense is no longer an issue. Because I'm going to kill someone who's surrendered to me, counting on my integrity and mercy. And let me tell you something, if one day I don't find it hard, I'd advise you to be very, very worried."

The world went on around us. The setting that an hour ago had been a shard of heaven was now a dimension of hell. Our colleagues raced around us, casting us curious glances, not missing a beat of their gruesome work. I hung in stasis, lost in the thousand things I could and couldn't read in his eyes.

He finally drew in a sharp inhalation, let it out. "You don't have to do anything. I'll take care of everything."

He was offering me a way out. A chance to look the other way and pretend I had no part in it. I probably should take it, in the interest of my mental intactness.

I didn't.

I jumped up to my feet. "I can give them a lethal injection. Y'know, just like in capital punishment."

"You have those drugs with you?"

"They're all drugs that I'll be using in their medical capacity. Sodium pentothal for unconsciousness…" Was that a flare of realization? Acknowledgment? That it was what I'd hit him with that night in my apartment? If so, he wasn't going into it. Good. *Great.* I gulped, went on, "Tubocurarine chloride for paralysis and potassium chloride for cardiac arrest."

He shook his head. "All these drugs would have to be administered one after the other, since they can't be mixed outside the body or else they'd precipitate." He knew this execution business as well as I did. Strange that I kept forgetting that. Good thing, too. What I'd just proposed was more torture than a firing squad. Never ceased to wonder why anyone thought it more humane than a bullet to the back of the head.

Seemed Damian agreed with my opinion on that, too. "We

don't want to turn this into a struggle and an even uglier mess. We need something quick. Just not as excruciating as strychnine. Doesn't have to be lethal, just something to knock them out."

"Okay. I'll go for a tranquilizer."

I rose to my feet, heartsick. Darkness was swooping down like a vulture, numbing cold following on its wings. It wasn't why every cell in my body knocked against the other.

His heavy-lidded gaze wrapped around me, hot, welcome, enfolding. I turned away and he caught me, my back to his front.

Standing up, I got to lean all over him. My teeth clattered together and his arm went over me, just below my breasts, pressed me hard into his solid power. "Don't." His whisper penetrated me. "Just give me the drugs and I'll see to it."

I shook my head. It rolled against his massive shoulder, reducing me in size. I felt small and forlorn. Needed to hide, to run. To just let him take care of it. Of me. I couldn't.

"That's my job," I insisted.

"No, it isn't. I'm the professional assassin here. You kill only to guard your patients and protect yourself and your team. And don't you dare pull rank on me, St. James. To hell with this 'who's leader' shit! I'm not letting you kill any more than you absolutely have to. I won't let you break your Hippocratic oath and code of medical ethics."

Incredulity burst out of me on a demented giggle. "You're far, far too late, buddy!" I hiccuped and the tears I'd been desperate to hide finally welled up from my depths.

He pressed me harder into him, the building pressure mounting relief. So weird. To find comfort in his arms. To be offered it there. "No, I'm not. Self- and others' defense is always defensible, acceptable. This, now, is where I come in."

"You were there all through."

"Yes, and now I'm finishing it."

"I have to—"

He pushed me away, circled me in a brooding prowl, making my insides quiver with the need to throw myself back into his assuaging vice. "If corpses are found without a mark on them," he said at last, slow, distinct—cruel, "it won't be too far behind for them to suspect poison. Behind poison, drugs and doctors aren't far behind. We have to make this look consistent with a regular guerrilla battle. So, *do* you want to go out there, shoot the corpses of the men you and your team killed?"

Oh, *God!*

I guess I just found my limit. He'd found it for me. I closed my eyes, moaned, "Damn you, De Luna!"

"Yeah, that's me. 'Dam' De Luna. Give me the drugs, St. James. Go do your real job. Tend the living."

Chapter 9

The suction machine was whirring and slurping. Matt's lips were pursing and releasing as we worked in tandem, whistling softly as usual. Ishmael cracked a finger at a time in between monitoring Pierro and adjusting his anesthesia.

I heard none of it.

Not even the bullets and explosions that had been blasting outside for the past hour. I registered those only when each discharge resonated in my bones. Damian and his team had been shooting the dead and blowing up their convoy, setting up an authentic postguerrilla war stage.

I almost didn't hear myself as I talked to Pierro like I always talked to my patients when they we were under, encouraging, soothing, cheering on.

It was Damian's last words. They looped in my mind, a broken record phasing out everything else.

Tend the living.

How weird that the same words could mean so many things. Our prisoners had still been the living when Damian had said that, and he'd been about to tend them, too. Felt so strange, to have been in here fighting for one human being's life, while Damian had been out there ending so many others.

I cauterized the last bleeding artery lining Pierro's ribs, that always disconcerting barbecue scent filling my sinuses. It would remain there for days, I knew. It never really left.

Matt removed the rib spreader and I moved aside for him to close Pierro's chest. I transferred to his head to start working on his ear. Ayesha removed the bandage, and again my long-empty stomach heaved in protest.

On its way to avulsing his scalp to the base of his skull, the bullet had blasted the middle third of his ear. Good thing the severed part hadn't been lost, was still hanging by a thread of tissue. We'd agreed that reattaching it had a good chance of success, due to the rich blood supply in the area.

"Dammit! He's fibrillating!"

Ishmael's shout pummeled through my deafness. The erratic monitor sounds transmitting Pierro's haywire heart activity followed, screaming its ominous verdict.

I stared dumbly at Pierro.

Then I heard my voice, loud and clear now, vibrating with shock and anger. "You've been stable all through! We're *finished* with the hard part! You're *not* fibrillating, Pierro!"

On some detached level, I noted how crazy I was, scolding Pierro as if it would stop him being a bad boy and flatlining.

But Clara shouldn't be fibrillating, her heart shouldn't be stopping! There is no reason! She's young and healthy and—and…

Focus. It's Pierro here. Pierro!

But he shouldn't fibrillate either. He couldn't! Oh, God, please no….

Steam scorched my lungs, fogged my eyes, burned my heart and reason—

"Cali, snap out of it!"

Matt's growl lashed across my senses. I felt my body respond to his scolding, falling into the practiced motions of resuscitation on its own accord right along with him and Ayesha. Between us the external defibrillator was readied, charged and the shock delivered in seconds.

Sinus rhythm resumed at once.

I stared at the monitor, the healthy, steady spikes, at the intubated Pierro. He was back!

Oh, Clara.

Tasting blood and bile, I turned to Matt, Ishmael and Ayesha, groping for the moment we all needed to touch base, seek comfort and confirmation after such a scare.

Then gave it, received it and we each turned back to our own parts of the job. I touched shoulders with Ayesha. She pushed against me, knowing what I was seeking. Her support was what kept me on my feet now. We went to work, putting Pierro's scalp and ear back together.

Anger and anguish still roiled inside me, poured out of me, muffled by my mask. "Were you trying to force us to finish, Pierro? We can, y'know? You're out of danger. You're going to be fine. We can take you to Intensive Care this minute if you like. We just want to give you a matching set of ears again. If you want that, too, you'd better not scare me like that again! I'm not losing you, do you hear? I'm not going out there to tell your friends I have no idea why your heart stopped!"

"Take it easy on the guy, Cali," Matt murmured, putting the last sutures into Pierro's skin, closing his chest and placing drains. "He fought with us with a lung filling up with blood, lost liters of blood, then we opened up his chest and mucked around. That he fibrillated only once and responded this quickly is the miracle here." For once Matt was taking it easy on me. He knew my phobias and nightmares. A patient fibrillating on the table was foremost among those. "This isn't out of the blue."

Like Clara. The words he left unsaid boomed in my head.

Yeah, this wasn't like Clara.

I nodded my gratitude for his defusing insight, the tears blocking my sight and breathing easing back. I took the scalpel from Ayesha and started to debride Pierro's ear.

Another explosion vibrated the whole trailer, rocked my already shaky focus. I gritted my teeth and carried on.

"Why are you like that?"

I turned on Ed as he jumped out of our Intensive Care trailer after me. The transition from the trailer's central conditioned warmth to the cold outside air was a rude slap, augmenting my irritation and goose bumps to the point of pain.

"I'm like that, because you were in Intensive Care without permission from any of my team. *And* making Anna laugh so hard she was in danger of busting a stitch."

"Yeah, yeah." He sighed, rubbed his large hand over his eyes. "I deserve to be punched out for that. I was just—you know how it is, Cali!" I started at hearing him say my nickname. He'd never called me anything but St. James, like his superior officer. "Anna and I, we're—special. On our way to being so, at least, I hope. Seeing her hit, waiting outside, taking care of business while you took care of her… I couldn't wait anymore."

His motives for invading I.C. hadn't even occurred to me. I'd found him there and I'd just pounced on him and dragged him out.

My shoulders slumped. "Jeez. Sorry I hauled you out like that. Guess I'm in hyper-knee-jerk mode, too. Anna's going to be just fine, Ed."

Anxiety still tinged his gaze, and the need to wipe it away almost had me reaching out to him.

Not a good idea. Reaching out. Getting involved. It was none of my business. I was involved with my team enough as it was. Didn't need more distractions. More ties.

But man, why was he doing that to himself? How did supposedly rational people fall for colleagues who could be blown to pieces in front of their very eyes at any time? How had Damian done it? Loving Melissa, keeping her by his side, knowing full well that one of them would likely end up maimed or dead with the other looking on?

Ed's eyes emptied of agitation only to fill with that curiosity he'd always regarded me with. "Yeah, I guess. In my mind I know she will be. Thanks to you guys. We're trained to treat our fallen colleagues, but what you did for all of them was way beyond anything we could have done."

I nodded and was about to walk away when he added, "But it wasn't what I asked. I always wanted to know why you're like *this*—y'know…" He made an encompassing gesture. "*Doing* all this."

I huffed in surprise. "Wow. What a simple—and let me add, timely—question, Ed! Don't you think moving out asap and saving our butts takes precedence over analyzing me right now?"

It was two hours since the attack. Our enemies must have been in contact with their people when they attacked us. God only knew what they'd transmitted before we decimated them. We had to assume reinforcements were on the way.

But we couldn't have moved on earlier. On our side, we couldn't have operated, on Pierro especially, with the convoy on the move. On Damian's side…

My eyes swept the scene, inspecting his handiwork.

In the moonless night, the postapocalyptic scene flickered by the dying flames of our enemies' burning convoy. The eerie lights seeping from our vehicles tinged it in an otherworldly chill. Damian had pulverized everything, especially the two trailers we'd lost, into an indistinguishable wreck.

Our convoy was in order again, crouching aloof from the devastation, a huge serpent-dragon that had mangled and scorched its prey, even the parts of itself that had been damaged.

As for our enemies themselves—their bodies were scattered

consistently with the kind of blitz he wanted to paint. The guy knew his mass murder stuff well.

And there he was. In the distance, in silhouette. I'd recognize him anywhere.

He and the rest were still dealing with the enemy's arsenal, making it look like someone had attacked them before they could attack us, had confiscated their weapons. We were taking some choice weapons, anything that could be hidden or camouflaged. Damian was burying what we couldn't take.

God, how convoluted and devious it all was! Playing our enemies at their own game made us so much like them. No. With our training and abilities, we were so much better.

So much worse.

Ed was watching when I turned my eyes on him. "Hey, I did my quota. And we're not moving on before Damian says so."

I considered telling him I could override his precious Damian, tell him to take the stuff to bury elsewhere and move out now. I didn't. Damian must know what he was doing. No need to flaunt my authority.

"So we have time," Ed said. "I mean—I know why *I'm* doing this, why my team is."

Did he? Did he really know what made Damian tick? Beyond the obvious? Now that would be something I'd want to hear.

"So why are you?" I challenged.

Blue devil eyes sparkled at me in the dimness. "Me first? Sure. It's clear and simple. We're professional soldiers. We left one army, enlisted in another where we thought we could do more good, where our specific abilities were most needed."

I doubted that was all. Not for Damian at least. Nothing about him was either clear or simple. Not that I could come up with a better explanation. But would I ever find out? He knew all there was to know about me. I bet he had my DNA map. But I knew nothing about him. No hard facts. Presumptions, deductions, beliefs. I could be wrong about the very ABCs.

"Your turn." Ed grinned, one blond eyebrow challenging.

I pulled a mocking face. "Yeah? You tell me less than nothing and what do you expect in return? A detailed biography?"

And no I wasn't being evasive. I was stunned. I suddenly realized I didn't know the answer to his question.

Did I know why I was like this? I mean, really? I'd always had heretical leanings, out-of-the-box traits. At least, that was what my teachers and acquaintances said. I'd inherited my father's drive and stamina and precarious temper. And because they'd appealed to my basic self, I'd adopted his extreme views of justice. Then I'd stood at Clara's grave. Then at Jake's empty one. Stood by as Dad was taken away for life.

But what had happened inside me ever since the wheels started turning wasn't something I could explain. I'd sure had no clue then I'd ever come this far. Still found it a bit surreal.

Ed was still waiting for some kind of answer. I raised one eyebrow at him. "Got a couple of days while I recount my life story? I should give you the whole bundle and let you sort out why I'm like that. Then *you* can tell *me*."

Then something clicked. I frowned. "Wait a minute. Why are you asking? You've got me on file in PATS, with a full psyche profile attached. You probably have more insight into what makes me tick than I'll ever have."

He grinned. "What can I say, babe? You're classified material. I haven't made it high enough in PATS to have access to your files."

He hadn't? Now *that* was surprising. Ed was Damian's number two on this mission. He wasn't far beneath Damian in overall rank. We were talking some high reaching power here. Which, come to think of it—and I had no idea how I hadn't thought of it before—made it capital *W* weird that PATS would risk sending two of their top men on the same mission. Or on a mission at all.

If I understood right, Damian had risen very high in the ranks of PATS, with only Fitzpatrick and the two I'd met at PATS head-quarters outranking him. Tactical commanders stayed home be-hind huge desks in war rooms orchestrating stuff, not running around the world's hotbeds risking their invaluable experience and irreplaceable hides in extreme-risk field operations.

Hmm. Was Damian being punished then? Had he been de-moted? Was that why they'd put me sort of in charge? To rub his nose in it?

I could see a lot of questions heading Damian's way. And slamming back in my face unanswered.

But Ed was in the dark about me. Hmm, again. So Damian had withheld the lowdown on me and my case. I wondered why.

And there came the man in question, formidable body flow-ing toward us in the dark. Now that was what I called sheer po-etry of motion. Whoo boy! I was getting fancy in my exhaustion. But what could I say. The guy was a world-class hunk. And then some.

He came to a deceptively relaxed halt three feet away, that space-shrinking aura of his at full blast. His eyes moved from Ed to me, cooling in the transition. I smirked at him. "Hey, De Luna! Do you know what makes me tick? Ed was asking."

He ignored my question, delivered his intended communica-tion. "We found a silent SINCGARS unit in one of their vehi-cles before we destroyed them." SINCGARS, or Single Channel Ground and Airborne Radio Systems, had a maximum range of thirty-two miles. Extensive radio communication knowledge was one of the skills he'd hammered into me. "So we knew their base had to be farther than its longest range. That wasn't too re-assuring until we found another silent 200 W SSB vehicular ra-dio." And since that had a range of eighty miles it meant that their base was farther than that. "Twenty minutes ago a man started yelling on the other end on the short-range frequency for status report."

Which meant they'd just come in range then. They'd probably allowed for two hours after radio silence for their attack force to decimate us and come back in radio range to report. They must have gotten suspicious when almost three hours passed and no word was transmitted. Hmm, around eighty miles—at sixty miles per hour—surely the most anyone can manage on this kind of road—meant about an hour and twenty minutes until they were here.

"I think I managed to solidify our scenario." Damian went on. "I told him we, their target, must have detoured, and that instead they were under attack and that everyone was being massacred. We gave him an audio show to make it convincing."

"You speak Russian?" I blurted out.

His look said the question wasn't even worth the breath it would take to exhale in exasperation.

Hey, it was a valid question. Never thought Damian spoke anything but good ol' American. And Spanish, of course. Must be another undercover power, knowing far more than he appeared to know. Hmm—I definitely had a thing for a guy with a versatile tongue. Uh—pun not intended. Come to think of it, definitely so. I'd had a sample of his tongue's versatility that night in my place. Wondered what he could do with it if he wasn't drugged…

Whoa! Mind shooting off on crazy tangents here!

Then another tangent followed, something I'd forgotten.

Jake spoke Russian. And ten other languages besides. All fluently. It had been among the things that had impressed me most about him. His genius, the humbling effortlessness of uptake and retention. Compounded by his freedom from rules, his remorseless wit—let's just say the word "soul mate" had been used copiously during the year we'd been lovers. The counted-on-two-fingers sex I'd known after him, when I'd finally buried him in my mind and forced myself to move on, had sent me into contented celibacy.

Okay, so not so contented. With Damian unavailable, I'd just barked up the wrong tree in my bid for intimacy.

The man in question was still talking. "We're done here and we're on our way in five minutes. The rocky terrain won't leave trails for them to follow. We'll still have to make a large detour to Malka to get out of their way. And to get ourselves seen for an alibi, too." He looked at me. "Pierro, Anna and Joe?"

It was Ed who answered him. "They're doing great. A regular miracle worker is our Cali, isn't she, Dam?"

"Yeah, isn't she?" Damian said, without opening his mouth. Did he have ventriloquist abilities, too? Wouldn't surprise me.

He must also be into pyrokinetics. He was fuming. What now?

Was he remembering the night in Darfur? When it had been him I'd struggled to save, with Melissa's and Ben's and Idi's hacked bodies back in the truck as we raced out of there?

Anger wasn't good for the soul. I'd make him vent it. On the object of his rage. I cocked my head at him. "Five minutes are long enough to sum me up, don't you think, *Dam?*" I wanted to hear how he would. Would give me a lot of insight.

He gave me a protracted look, simmering, disturbing. Disturbed? I sure hoped I messed him up a fraction as much as he did me. If I wanted him before, now I was crazy for him.

Must be posttraumatic stress. It always made me hungry. I usually fed my PTS massive amounts of food. Now I wanted Damian on my menu, too, to glut all other appetites.

He turned his eyes to Ed. "At seventeen, St. James's sister Clara went in bouncing and excited for elective mole removal and esthetic repair and came out a corpse."

My lungs emptied with the sucker punch.

Going for maximum damage right off the bat, huh? I forced my clouding vision clear. Fine. *Give me you worst, De Luna.*

He met my challenging eyes, my consent for him to go all out received and acknowledged. Everyone was boarding their trailers. We'd follow in a minute. He'd make it enough.

"Clara's doctors followed with apologies and no explanations." His words were still directed to a now somber Ed. Each hacked into my nine-year-fresh wound. "She just fibrillated, didn't respond to resuscitation efforts. An autopsy revealed nothing. Verdict was, it happens. They used the system to bury their mistake fast. Bury Clara with no trace or price.

"That day, at just twenty and with one year left of med school, having jumped grades, St. James lost her beloved sister to the system and the kind of medical practitioner it spawned. She was already ripe for rebellion, but that was the trigger."

He kept his eyes on Ed. Strange. Would have thought he'd have a ball seeing me shrivel up. "She swore she'd never be another doctor serving and being served by the system," he said. "Never give it the chance to corrupt her into someone looking out for her interests and safety over her patients'."

I'd always known he knew. Since he'd gone digging up all the ammo he needed to expel me from GCA and medical practice.

But oh, God, he more than knew—he understood!

But that didn't say whether he excused or sympathized.

His next words offered no insight. "So she sought GCA's unorthodox medical licensing program. Sir Ashton broke all rules, accepting her when she didn't have the required credits, lavishing privileges and special training on her, putting her to work before she obtained her degree. She threw herself into the on-the-job training, did so well he started the Combat Doctors Program to give her the final edge. He even falsified her records when he handed her over to me. The rest you know."

He made it sound as if Sir Ashton had started the CDP for me! Was that what he thought? And he made no mention of Jake. Or Dad. Did he consider Clara's death to be what had shaped me? Or just another catalyst in the chain reaction?

He could be right. I'd stood with my parents at Clara's grave, wondering how much of *their* souls were being buried, how much rage and outrage would forever eat at the remainder.

A staticky voice erupted from the one Jeep left intact. We ran toward it, listened. I knew some Russian. None of it included in that torrent. Damian's knowledge clearly outstripped mine. He pressed a button and answered.

Cold air rushed into me through my open mouth.

A high-pitched voice, issued from somewhere inside him. Like a horror movie, when an alien voice issued from someone's lips. The person inside Damian choked on a bleeding whisper, someone with seconds left of life power and total body injuries like the man he had arranged at the wheel. He signed off on an ultraconvincing gurgle.

"We have thirty minutes tops. Should be enough."

Ooh, Mama. The way his voice switched back to his authoritarian tones! Versatile didn't even begin to cover it.

He looked straight at me and said, "Let's get on with it."

Yeah. Wouldn't I just love to.

Chapter 10

"Are we there yet?"

Ayesha guffawed, took her eyes off the road to look down on me. I had my head cushioned in her lap. "I swear, Cali, you're like a bored, whiny kid. You ask that every five minutes."

I looked at my watch. "It's been *thirteen* minutes since I last asked!" I whined ever louder, playing along.

"Asking won't make us go faster and you know it. Not that I think I'll convince you any more than I ever convinced Fatima."

Fatima. Her daughter. She'd disappeared without a trace at fourteen, fourteen years ago. Police and private investigators had had theories, each more gruesome than the last. From rape and murder to kidnapping and slavery. Their optimistic possibilities had pegged her as a runaway drug addict. Everything ended in her being lost beyond hope of retrieval.

When Ayesha had thrown her lot with me, she'd enlisted my help in finding Fatima. It had been a major reason why she had joined. Three months later, following her suspicions and vague information and mother's instincts, we'd found Fatima's trail. Fatima had been kidnapped by an organ-harvesting operation.

They'd been our first bust. Our first executions. We'd tried breaking up their grisly operation first. But they'd slipped through the loopholes of the law, had gone on "filling their clients' needs." They'd even come after Ayesha herself. She'd executed her would-be murderer and her daughter's herself.

Afterward, she'd always talked about Fatima as if she were there, safe and growing up right under her eye. Matt freaked out when she did that. An eternal widower himself, constantly talking of the wife he'd lost to a gang rape, he lived with her same unimaginable pain and wrath, vented his agony in aggression against all sorts of rapists. But her inability to tell fantasy from reality made him fear she might be a time bomb. Remembering Damian's denunciation, my stock reply was, "What's another time bomb in this outfit?"

I *had* worried for a while at first. A very short while. Modern psychology diagnosed her as delusional, but I'd long ago stopped putting much faith in its tenets. Ayesha had found closure when she'd watched the man who'd hacked up her daughter and sold her a piece at a time, and all those who'd helped him, die.

I believed sinking into depression, as any other bereaved parent would have done, was the morbid reaction. Channeling her outrage and pain outward, turning it into a fearless, selfless struggle so that others wouldn't meet the same fate as her and her daughter, was mighty healthy in my opinion. And that was before she'd told me she was fully aware that Fatima wasn't there, but saw no reason to deny herself the make-believe comfort.

Apart from that indulgence, she was probably *too* rational. Ayesha was neither violent nor unstable. She was methodical, analytical. She was no time bomb. She was at peace. And boy, therein lay her danger. Villains beware.

She now chuckled, held one of those sesame candy bars she'd gotten me hooked on over me and let it drop. "Go ahead, you baby. Make it all better with an overdose of sugar."

The bar landed on my tummy and I pulled myself up. "I want two!" I complained over the drone of the motor.

Mock-malicious pleasure lit up her dark-chocolate beauty. "You ate your quota for today. For the next week, you glutton. Wonder where it all goes."

I pouted, crunched the delicious, toasted, sticky calorie bomb. "I can *feel* it settling straight into my thighs, sitting in this trailer doing nothing for days on end."

"It's only been six hours since we left Nal'chik. And it won't be long now. According to Damian it's two more hours until we reach Zovodskoy, then another three until we find our way to the camp up the Terek River. So settle down, will ya?"

I scooted on the seat, huddled against the door, nibbled the bar, watched more magnificent mountains on one side and rolling plains on the other, and sulked.

Let's face it. If Mount Elbrus, rising almost nineteen thousand feet into the sky, snowcapped and daunting as we passed Kislovodsk on our way to Malka, hadn't brought me out of my funk, nothing could. Everything, pun intended, was downhill from that!

I was going out of my mind with this field trip. So sue me. The detour to Malka had stretched our road time by just forty-eight hours. But we must have entered a time warp or something. The damned pale, warmth-free sun had been winking coldly on an off between cumulus clouds, hanging in the same spot, for hours.

I should be grateful that time was passing so uneventfully. We'd passed through villages and towns with smiling people and pursuing, shrieking-in-glee children. Seemed we'd covered our tracks, gotten away with it.

No way to be totally secure though. Stuff could still surface, literally. Readiness must be in the red at all times.

Sure. That was why I'd been deep in hibernation most of the past two days. Escaping I guess. The memory of the massacre.

And Damian. Mostly Damian. And what he made me feel. Hell, he didn't *make* me feel anything. I was seething on my own.

His total trust as we'd fought back to back, the way he'd spared me from killing our prisoners, had a lot to answer for.

I'd gotten used to—hell, I'd become *secure* in his antagonism. I couldn't handle that glimpse into his unexpected humanity, his against-his-will compassion. I'd been safe in the knowledge that I was forever exiled from his approval and validation. Then, no matter how grudging, he'd gone and given them to me. Being grudging made them even more hard-hitting.

Pitiful, wasn't it? Needing either? Stupid fact was, I did. Always had. But when he'd been out of reach, pragmatism had been a refuge. Now, Sir Ashton and his cronies had chained us together and thrown us in shark-infested waters to sink or swim.

Didn't the old, dried sticks know what they'd done? Forced proximity, desperate conditions, extreme stakes. Throw in enough sexual tension to power a city, at least on my side, conflicted history to fill a library, and a years-old frustration, and we were talking critical mass and impending meltdown.

Even without all that, the guy was more than a one-of-a-kind body running on an unlimited supply of refined testosterone. He'd been sort of my Pygmalion. I'd been a potential, a possibility, and he'd made me a reality. Whether I should thank or damn him for it remained open to debate. But like an unlikely Galatea, I'd never gotten over losing the empowering glint in his eyes when I met and surpassed his expectations.

As for the glint in his eyes now… I could be imagining it, but my hormones sure didn't think so. Silent admissions, pent-up rage against equally helpless hunger—the works.

Truth was, I was *this* close to pouncing on him and getting it out of our system, for everyone's sake. Not wise to have the mission's leaders writhing in frustration with nothing but long, hot, hard sex on the brain.

But it could fizzle out to nothing. Or worse. My body had demanded a sexual outlet, a proof of life, before, and afterward I'd wished I'd used the energy cleaning toilets instead. A fumbling dud with Damian would only leave us even more at each other's throats, the mission more at risk.

So okay, only in my dreams could "fumbling" and "dud" be associated with Damian, but it was just another thing to keep me biting down on the insane urges. The main thing was…Jake.

Jake. I could see him again. I *was* going to see him again. But—oh, I'd changed. And what could have happened to him? What if what I remembered feeling for him was amplified by the way I'd lost him, by time and distance and guilt? I no longer longed for him. Thought of him even. But what if everything was resurrected the moment I laid eyes on him again?

I only knew it felt wrong to have Damian occupying my focus and senses this way when Jake could reenter my life at any time now. When he'd left it through no fault of his own.

Through *my* fault.

I was the one who'd made him join GCA. I was the one who'd cost him almost one-fourth of his life.

So I slept. I escaped the hunger and the confusion and the guilt. I pretended to be charging up for whatever was coming.

And Ayesha spoiled me, driving most of the time, feeding me, singing gospel songs, lulling me to sleep.

I brought out her motherly side. She'd been a mother at nineteen, so a couple of years earlier and she could have had a child as old as me. But I wasn't a replacement for her daughter. I mothered her, too, enjoyed doing it. And enjoyed it when she brought out the little-girl side of me. It wasn't the first time that I'd snuggled up to her like I used to with my mother. Before she left. Oh, Mom…

I never blamed you for leaving.

Who was I kidding? I blamed me. After Clara, and between Dad and me, especially me, we'd driven her beyond endurance. I only hoped she'd managed to find peace away from us. To one day see her again. I doubted I would. The day she'd left me our house and disappeared, she'd vowed—no more.

I'd sold the house and put half the money in the bank in her name. The rest, I'd used to buy equipment.

She'd been right. I was lost to her, to the life she—

Something jolted me clear out of recriminations and memories—a succession of things. Coming at my fogged awareness like a hurtling train in the dark. Ayesha's shout. The wrenching braking. The bone-rattling ram into Matt's trailer. And before all that, during and after, the detonations. Then the big blast.

My unrestrained body slammed into the dashboard, the only thing stopping my crash through the windshield our low speed.

It took me three frantic heartbeats. Then I realized.

Land mines!

I heard my furious shout. "They *lied!*"

Weird what my mind came up with in extremes. As if *that* was a shock. Or relevant. So they hadn't cleared the mines. Or had they just put in more? Nothing easier after all. The filthy cockroaches! And I'd felt bad about exterminating a few of them!

But which truck had detonated the mine? Had to be one of those in the lead. *The* one in the lead? Damian, oh God…

"St. James! Stay where you are! You will let me handle this if I have to shoot you with one of your tranquilizer guns!"

His voice boomed in my heart. *Not him—not him!*

Not Matt either—his trailer was intact and right ahead of us. So who then? Had they been hurt?

My fingers missed the button as I fumbled to answer him. He gave me no chance, switching to the general channel and barking his orders. "Everyone stay put. UXO situation and protocols. That's Unexploded Ordnance for you docs. Land mines. Ed—report." This last order held an edge of agitation to it.

So it had been Ed. He had Shad and Suzanne with him.

Silence answered Damian, descended on me like a suffocating shroud. Oh, God! Too injured to respond?

Logic and horror shut off, autofunctions taking over. I
dragged out the real disaster bags, opened the door of our
trailer's truck unit. Damian went into a fit. Must have seen me
opening the door in his side mirror.

"Stay the *hell* put, St. James or I'm coming to knock you out
with a fist to your jaw!"

"Save your aggression for the ones who planted those mines,
De Luna. My weight won't detonate the antitank mines and
I—"

"Will just trigger off one of the antipersonnel mines littering
antitank mine zones to discourage demining efforts!"

Actually I was going to say I'd learned very well when he'd
taught me all there was to know about manual demining methods.

With a face shield and my telescoping baton I'd probe the surface at a shallow angle to avoid pressing on a detonator or tripping a trip wire. Upon contact, I'd probe more to establish size
and nature of the mine, then I'd excavate and disarm it.

Yeah, sure. There was a minimum of three hundred feet to
Ed's truck. I'd take all day to probe a foot-width of that distance.
If I had all day. I didn't. Had to reach Ed and the others now.
Seconds could count.

No one said I had to set foot on the ground to reach them.

I stood on the wide stepping ledge and saw Damian in the
distance, doing the same. I heard him well now without the benefit of a radio, still bellowing for me to get back inside.

Just that he thought I was moronic enough to run over mine-
infested land—ooh!

I wound down my window and put one foot on it. I braced
the other one on the seat's back and the door swung wider under my weight. I stood there, legs split, thanking the past six

years of daily, intensive physical conditioning that made keeping this position possible. I looked down on Ayesha who'd scooted to my end. "Hand me the stuff when I say so!"

I hooked the door back, narrowing the opening, bracing it in place, reached up and tried to get a grip on the top of the truck. Youch. Freezing metal. But putting on gloves wasn't an option. They'd weaken my grip, probably make me slip off. I had little traction as it was with the damned modern, sloping design of the truck.

Gritting my teeth against the burning cold, I adjusted my center of gravity, transferred my inside foot to the truck's vertical four-foot chrome handle just beside the door. I had about two inches of support there, curved, highly polished support. Not a footing I'd trust being fifteen feet up and in danger of falling onto a mine. Had to. No other option.

I stood on tiptoe, gaining extra inches to make it possible for me to place my open palms onto the back of the truck. One palm was on the aerodynamic edge. They surely hadn't designed the thing with climbing on its roof in mind. Had to contact the manufacturer for side ladders on their next model.

No leverage, no footing, curving, slippery surfaces, land mines snapping their jaws beneath. Put a spin on the expression *having a blast.*

My flesh stuck to the metal. I gave thanks. In warmer conditions, I would have slipped right off. With that adhesive effect, I pumped my body up in one slow motion. When my arms were almost extended on top of the truck, my right knee tried to come up between them, seeking support. Didn't make it high enough, hit the rim of the truck full force. I lost my grip, my balance, spilling downward, breaking my momentum on the side mirror. My heart made one resounding detonation in my chest.

Don't break it!

Hel-lo! I could break every bone in my body falling off and I was worried about the *mirror?* Nuttiness galore here. Should be used to it, my mind leaping into the ludicrous in extremes.

My heart still booming, helping to drown Damian's fury, I began all over, a new strategy, changing the angle of pressure on my hands, bringing both feet on the mirror for equilibrium, giving a controlled shove, tucking my body into an L-shape. Then, pouring everything I had through my arms to my whole body, I unfolded upward in a two-second handstand. I ended the impressive gymnastic maneuver with an ungainly crash on my back, almost falling off after all.

Groping and scrambling from the edge, I rose to my knees, trembling with the effort and the close call, my numb hands beginning to sting. Real pain would follow, after the deep anesthesia of extreme cold wore off. Hoped they weren't damaged. No surgeon would dream of abusing their hands this way. Which made me—what? Reckless, unstable, irrational… Yeah, yeah.

I immediately flattened on my stomach, dangled off the truck's roof for the bag. Ayesha was lifting it up, standing where I'd been seconds ago. Intent on following me? Uh-uh. There was no way she'd make it up here in one piece.

"Stay here." I told her, uncompromising, cutting off any intention to debate my decree. "Prepare me another bag. I'll come back for it if I need it."

I jumped to my feet, maneuvered the bag's straps backpack-style, got a bird's-eye view of the whole scene. The first thing I saw was Damian, standing on top of his truck, laden with equipment. Had the same idea, huh? Of course he had.

Just ahead of him was the bombed trailer, its rear half blown to a metal mess. Had to have been one hell of a huge mine. But the truck itself hadn't exploded, thanks to our almost empty gas tanks. We'd been scheduled for a refill just about now. Thank God it hadn't been the supply trailer, or we would have all gone up in smoke.

The trailer's current position told its own tale. They'd moved out of line with the rest of the convoy. Just a few feet. That meant there was no telling what a few inches off our current course, even if we tried retracing our steps, would entail. We were probably smack dab in the middle of a minefield.

We were trapped.

My heart fired again. Ed's driver's window burst out in a shower of glass, then there he was, sticking a blood-drenched head out of it. Ed!

"We're alive!" he called out and I almost sagged in relief. "The radio was knocked out and me, too, I guess. Then it took me a while to check on Suz and Shad."

"How are you all?" I heard Damian's anxious question though he was talking at less than normal level. The silence was eerie.

"I cut my scalp. Suz fractured her arm. But it's Shad I'm worried about. He was in the body of the trailer. He's knocked out, lying in an awkward position. I'll go back to examine him…."

"Don't!" I cried out. "You may exacerbate his injuries. I'm coming."

Damian bellowed again. "You stay where you are and I'm *not* repeating this!"

I glared at him. He didn't really think I'd let him stand in my way, did he?

Not that that was an issue now. *I* was well and truly out of *his* way. All he had to do to reach Ed's truck was take one of those long-legged leaps of his, from a standstill, too. Me, I was in a whole different situation.

I jumped easily from my truck to Matt's. There was just the gap made up by my truck's sloping nose between us. The next truck, Ishmael's, the supply one, was another matter. It hovered ten feet or more away. I could guide him through a reversal along their exact tracks, but if he messed up—let's just say my solution was far less costly.

Okay. One long jump coming up. Mine and Matt's trailers' one hundred thirty feet of combined length would have to do for a running start.

"Don't you even dare think it, St. James!" Damian shouted at me without turning from his on-his-belly position as he pulled Ed out. Those feelers in his back.

"It's just ten feet," I protested.

"Thirteen to fifteen if I know anything." He cut me off. "And you're fifteen feet up in the air above a minefield! Throw me the bag and I'll take care of Shad."

"With all due respect to your paramedical expertise, De Luna, I'm the one Shad needs now."

"I'll stabilize him and get him out for you to examine, when we solve this mess."

"I have to examine him before you move him. And fifteen feet are no big deal. My long-jump record is twenty-two feet seven inches!" As I was sure he remembered well in that archiving mind of his.

His dismissal hit me across the distance. "On the ground, with a four-hundred-foot running start."

"My standing long-jump record is ten feet. Here I even have a hundred-and-thirty-foot running start."

"You call slippery, uneven roofs a running start?"

Why was I debating with him? I knew I could do this. Okay, I didn't know. I had to try. No, correct that. I had to do it.

I turned on my heels to more of his bellows, jumped back to my truck, ran over the trailer's sixty-five-foot body to its end. Then I paused, took position, rocked back and forth on my heels and tiptoes, once, twice, then I shot forward.

The slick surface became every treacherous terrain that Damian had made me race and dodge on, oil and mud and ice, the chasm between the vehicles his fire pits, the helicopter-transportation rungs on the trailers' roofs the barbed hurdles he'd strewn in my path—everything an incentive to allow for nothing but perfection on the first go.

I reached the edge of Matt's truck and launched in the air. I arced, folding my body forward in the accustomed position, legs and arms reaching, my focus not on the chasm beneath me but on Damian. He'd risen to his feet, watched me flying, his face seized, his body clenched. A portrait of enraged horror.

I landed. Feetfirst. Well inside the truck's body. Phew.

Relief didn't have a chance to sink in. The trailer was moving! Ishmael must have decided to bridge the gap for me, not realizing I'd already jumped, not thinking of the consequences.

I heard my screamed, *"Stop!"* echoed back to me on Damian's voice. Ishmael braked. Too late. For me.

The backpack's weight, my landing angle, the braking countermomentum beneath my feet lost me my balance, dragged me down to my butt. That had nothing but thin air to land on.

Panic flashed at the weightless sensation, at knowing landing was going to hurt, to damage. Logic pursed its lips, hoped for nothing more than that. Then both panic and logic disappeared.

I went over the edge of the one-and-a-half-story-high trailer. Into limbo.

Really annoying this habit, falling headfirst.

Chapter 11

Something went wrong.

Or maybe right. *Definitely* right.

I wasn't falling.

A vise snagged my ankles, aborting my plummeting momentum. That had to expend itself, gripped my whole body up to my knees and slammed it against the rear of the trailer. The backpack took the brunt, transmitted it into every bone in my back. Pain shut me down.

Damian. His name flickered in my mind, the first thing to register as it came back online.

He'd caught me. Had to be him. Greased lightning had nothing on him.

Impossible strength dragged me up. I completed the movement with my life's hardest sit-up, rebounded right into Damian, banged my nose on his forehead.

He surged right back, his face shoving into mine, his anger

and agitation flaying my burnt-frozen cheek. "Why do I bother? Why don't I just let you kill yourself?"

I grabbed hold of reality and stability, his arms, stress hormones enough to power me for a decade flooding my system, making my fingers dough and my nerves exposed wires. "All your troubles would come to end then, huh?" I choked.

The gold of his eyes shattered on green spikes, his open lips hovered over mine, pouring his breath and distress into my lungs. "They'd really start, you lunatic."

Okay. All right. That was one hefty statement. And no chance to probe deeper. No probing advised anyway. Contraindicated even. One thing mattered now. Shad!

I pushed to my feet, ignoring the screaming in my hands and back, the hitch in my heart. Damian followed, hovering over me. Then we ran to our injured teammates.

We worked in tandem again, him on his stomach dangling me down as I backed off the edge of the truck and inside. I entered the battered vehicle with a helping from Suz's good hand. She looked okay. "Get Suz, Damian," I called out.

He did just as I saw Shad through the distorted hatch communicating the passenger compartment with the trailer body. My breath vanished.

Not now. Get to him. I threw my bag ahead, slithered through the hatch, realizing halfway through that I should have widened it first. I'd have a new scar. All the way down my back.

I crawled toward him among the debris, the destabilized compartment creaking beneath my weight. I conducted a lightning exam and my breath stalled again. Did I ever mention how I hate multiple trauma? Especially blast injuries?

I needed help. I pushed my radio's button. "De Luna, I need a backboard, semirigid collar, total body harness and foam blocks. And *don't* rock the trailer."

I started my measures, was done with the most critical when Damian entered the truck through the window in one weightless motion from the best panels of a Batman classic. He turned, reached out as Ed handed him the stuff I'd asked for.

I outlined our problems as he joined me through the hatch without widening it. The guy had contortionist talents, too! "He has extensive primary blast injuries," I said. "Pneumothorax, ruptured intestines, worst of all arterial gas embolism."

Most people thought explosions killed with shrapnel. But those caused only secondary injuries. The primary ones resulted from the concussive blast itself, compressing an air front that ruptured air-filled organs, producing more insidious, harder to diagnose and treat injuries. It made me want to gnaw those who planted the mines to death.

Damian gritted his teeth, clenched his fists, echoing my impotent rage. "What do you want me to do?"

I bit my lip, stifling the rage, focusing. "We must put him in the coma position for the AGE, to protect against coronary and cerebral embolism."

He moved immediately to implement my words. I stopped him. "Not so fast. I think he has a neck fracture."

He started, rasped, "You think, or you know?"

"I'll need CTs and X rays, but—yeah, I know." His shoulders slumped. I squeezed his hand. Something inside me melted when he clung back. "His spinal cord is intact. All this gear is for keeping it that way."

He closed his eyes for a long moment. I knew what he must be feeling. One wrong move could make Shad a quadriplegic. But neither of us intended to make any.

We started working then, as if we'd always done so, with him giving my expertise undisputed deference. Felt strange, like holding my face up to a trickle of cool water in an inferno.

Let's say it was tricky stabilizing Shad's cervical spine, intubating him then getting him on the backboard with his left side down and his elbow and knee supporting his body. After we managed it, I anxiously rechecked his neurological status. I nodded assurance to Damian and his pent breath escaped. "I see you've decompressed his chest. What about internal hemorrhage?"

"I started fluid replacement. But what I pump into him will just leak out through the ruptures. I need him in O.R. asap."

"Can't you do something here, until we demine the area from here to the surgery trailer?"

"That'll take a day, Damian. At least."

He muttered something in Spanish. Sounded obscene and murderous. He barked in his radio. "Ed, get all who can manage it up there. We have to get Shad out of here and into surgery without touching ground."

We kept busy as we waited. I felt Damian's eyes on me at one point. I raised mine, asked, "How many of us do you think will fall before this goddamned mission even *starts,* De Luna?"

He raised one nonchalant eyebrow. "Considering we're in the middle of a minefield, supposedly every last one, St. James."

"You being funny? You're going to let a few hundred mines and the bastards who put them there get the best of you?"

A vicious lip tilt answered me. Then he did. "I said supposedly. As in, not going to happen."

The daredevil inside me leaped in answer. "Good!" I smiled back, fierce, defiant. "Let's start thinking how we're going to take on a minefield and win."

Well, we won.

All right. Not exactly. Not yet. We'd won half the battle. Oh, I shouldn't be bandying percentages. No way to guesstimate our chances by the remaining distance to the camp. One more mile could still mean hours. Or more vehicles. Or lives.

One thing I knew for sure. We were *crazy.*

But hey, crazy or not, we'd made it so far. *So far.* No tempting fate, thank you.

It had taken us an hour to get Shad out and into O.R. Then we'd worked on him for another three. Once he was stable and on the gyroscope-mounted table in I.C., I'd joined the rest in demining our immediate maneuvering vicinity. It had taken us the rest of the day and night. We'd been smack-dab in a beehive.

Damian had clamped my arm and pointed at just where I could have fallen onto clusters of antipersonnel mines and been blown up. He made sure I got a good look, then threw my arm back at me.

But it hadn't been anger at my disobeying his orders. It had been unappeased anxiety. For what could have been. Knowing that had gotten me hotter than anything ever had. Throw in the all-present danger and you had one explosively—uh, all things considered, make it one *overwhelmingly* tense situation.

Once free to move, I'd taken myself out of Damian's range, accessed my less basic self and dreamed up ways out. One way took hold of me. I'd let Damian in on it, expecting him to blow me off with ridicule. What blew me away was the way he'd latched on to it, expanding on it, debugging it.

Contrary to humanitarian demining efforts, where every inch of land had to be made safe, we needed only to clear our immediate path, military method-like. That was *still* impossible using the accepted methods, considering we still had about sixty miles to go. We would have taken weeks—months!

There had been two ways out. Retracing our steps, hoping not to trigger the mines we'd been lucky to sidestep going in, and ending our mission. Or detonating our way out of there.

Being crazy, we opted for the second option, unanimously, no hesitation. My plan was simple. To use our already bombed trailer for detonator and shield.

"We attach one of our snowplows to it, let it dig out and detonate all mines in our path," I had elaborated. "Steering will be our main problem without anyone at the wheel. So we need to devise a remote steering mechanism."

Damian's eyes had gleamed. "We have hooks and steel cables for setting up the field hospital and unbreakable chains for towing the vehicles in breakdowns and extreme weather. We can make a harness for the wheel. Then we can maneuver from my trailer as I shove it ahead of me."

"We'll also need navigators on top of your truck, keeping in contact with you by radio, being your eyes since your view of the road ahead of the bombed trailer will be limited."

Once problems had been ironed out, we'd been on our way.

It was my turn as navigator now. And I was shuddering apart. Good sign really. You only needed to worry about hypothermia being irreversible if you stopped shivering.

"Ten degrees left." I bit off into the radio before Damian drove us into that not-so-nice-looking ditch.

Damian adjusted his direction until I gave him the clear. Progress was snail-slow and torturous, especially since we'd gotten off the road to avoid the high concentration of mines there. It was still far quicker and safer than any other way.

Next thing I knew I was facedown on the freezing roof.

The truck had triggered another antitank mine, a biggie, enough of a shock wave to blow me off my feet at this distance.

I was getting used to being knocked about by explosions. Would kinda miss it when it was over.

Problem was, the truck had had enough, was now an unmanageable heap of junk.

Time to sacrifice another truck for the demining effort.

I couldn't feel my fingers as I pressed the outgoing radio button. "D-De L-Luna, your t-truck's t-turn."

"Is this static or are you stuttering?" His bark battered my cold-brittle eardrum.

"The t-temperature took a d-dive in the last c-couple of hours-s."

"And you're waiting to start hallucinating with hypothermia and take a dive yourself? Get down, St. James! Now!"

I did. My mind *was* fogging. What else would make me get down without making a comeback?

They started the harnessing protocols all over again as the girls fussed over me with hot drinks and packs. Then we were on our way again. After twenty minutes, another explosion boomed.

There went another trailer. I hoped we'd have some left by the time we reached the camp.

We reached the camp. Were in sight of it. And we did have trailers left. The most important six. Five days later, four trucks and about ten-million dollars' worth of equipment poorer, but we'd made it to our destination in one piece. More or less.

Shad would be out of action for the rest of the mission. It would take at least two months for his neck fracture to heal even with internal fixation. But his blast injuries were resolving and he was out of danger. Pierro was almost back to normal, and so were the others.

Not bad after a massive raid and a hundred and twenty miles of mines. Gotta hand it to us. We were good!

We were also clueless. We had no idea whether the minefield had ended or not, or if it went up to the first tent.

Then there came proof that it didn't. A convoy of 4x4s was coming toward us from the camp.

Ayesha and I exchanged raised eyebrows. She shook her head. "You'd think 4x4s are the camp's standard-issue transportation. Or that this is a welcome mat."

My lips twisted. "They're not firing, so it sure is. They must be the militants controlling the region, our hosts so to speak, here to look us over."

"St. James." Damian's voice poured from the radio in my lap. I jerked. I was in a bad way! "Let them come right up to us, to make sure there are no more mines."

I agreed. I just didn't appreciate his insistence on considering me a harebrained idiot. "No, De Luna, I'll go test the ground's safety at the cost of my only pair of legs."

He got off our private channel without a word in answer. Loved it when I drove him to silence.

It took our inspection committee another fifteen minutes to arrive at their leisurely pace. They fanned out around us, confirming the land's safety. Then they jumped out of their Jeeps and walked up to us, inspecting our sacrificial trailer. They laughed and called out to one another, pointing at it.

The maggots found our efforts to trudge through their mine-infested territory funny? No—they actually looked impressed.

The one who walked with the assurance of the pack's leader walked up to Damian's truck, his gun swinging at his back. I grabbed our documentations and jumped out of my truck. Damian stepped out of his. A pack of militants flocked around me, escorting me up to their leader, their eyes restless, looking me up and down. No insight needed to read their filthy minds.

The leader was shaking his head and letting rip a torrent of merry Russian. All amusement came to a sudden halt when Damian spoke up, his accent indistinguishable from theirs.

Dammit. He spoke too quickly. What had he said?

Whatever, he'd surprised the hell out of them, robbed them of the advantage of saying what they wished in our uncomprehending presence.

The leader's pale blue eyes narrowed, a new consideration creeping there. He spoke slower this time, asking Damian if he was Russian. Yeah, sure. Everyone knew Russians had well-known and pure Latin lineage!

A Ping-Pong match of Q&A followed, my Russian unable to keep up, leaving me in the dark. Raising my temperature. Damian was flexing his multilingual muscles, showing me who had more of a literal say now. Fine, let him be our spokesman. I was the *aid*-mission leader, no co-leading involved there.

Seemed he wasn't about to contest that. He turned his impassive eyes on me and made introductions. The leader actually made a bow, then mutilated a few English sentences. "Welcome to our beautiful and conflicted region. It's so noble of you to want to help our poor people. We will forever be in your debt."

Huh? Our poor people? Those they used as human shields and held hostage inside an invisible prison of endless mine-fields? Man, I could just see my fist driving through his thin, shrewd face, imagine in 3-D, X-ray detail the exact anatomical damage.

It wasn't common sense that interfered with the urge to punch his face in. It was the chill that welcome speech gave me.

Someone who pronounced English that bad couldn't have come up with that piece of consummate propaganda. Someone must have taught him those words. One of their hostages?

Jake?

I didn't want to think what else they made them do.

What was this all about anyway? Why were they trying to paint us a noble picture of themselves, after they'd reneged on their word of clearing the mines? Did they or didn't they want us here? Seemed they did. So could it be it hadn't been them who'd sowed those mines? Who else could have?

The answer shouldn't matter now. Didn't. I had too little information to even begin forming theories. No rush. The truth had a way of revealing itself. I'd be right there when it did.

Damian extended his hand with our papers, avoiding eye contact. Wise. No reason to give the militants any insight into the dynamics governing our team. Best protection was being faces and names with no identities or personalities or connections.

The leader's inanimate eyes ran over our extensive GCA documentation, issued in both English and Russian, before he turned to our individual passports. He left mine and Damian's for last. He dismissed mine sooner, lingered over Damian's as if poring over his meager personal info and looking back and forth from picture to real thing would give him more insight into an entity that intrigued him. Not good, that interest.

I moved my gaze about vaguely, caught a glimpse of Damian's reaction. And let me tell you something. It took a *lot* to stun me. And here it was.

The gracious terrorist I took in my stride, but an *affable* Damian? Then he said something that made every militant within earshot burst out laughing.

My mental mouth hung wide open as the leader patted him on the back and they plunged into a nonstop overlapping exchange that I doubt even they fully understood.

Then the militants detached the destroyed trailer from Damian's and towed it out of our way. The leader stood with us, watching the proceedings. When it was done, he turned to me, handed me our papers, shook our hands with great cordiality, turned on his heels and signaled for us to follow.

"That was *so* sweet," I mumbled, keeping my face and body expressionless as we moved back toward our respective trucks.

"Yeah, wasn't it just?" Damian answered, doing his ventriloquist thing again. "But what was really sweet, and surprising as hell, was you keeping your mouth shut."

I let my voice make a face. "The fluency barrier, you understand. And then you yapped enough for the whole team."

"They were impressed with our method of getting through the minefields to the point of suspicion. Any other aid operation would have just turned back and filed a complaint with the UN or something. I had to allay their suspicions."

"And you did that—how?" I asked, dying to know what he'd said in detail, especially what made them dissolve in laughter.

"With the best kind of lie, the truth-mixed variety."

"Whoa—enlightening!"

He gave a tiny sigh. "I said we were deep in the minefield by the time we detonated the first mine, tried to go back and got hit again, tried to call for help and no one answered, so we had no choice. I made a few jokes about desperation being the mother and father of ingenuity."

Something dripping with sexual innuendo I bet. Probably the offensive kind. The way they'd laughed it had to be. Hmm. Hard to imagine the Damian I knew practicing common male vulgarities. He seemed to have a different personality for each occasion. So which was the real him? *Was* there a real him?

We'd reached his truck now. He jumped up and I continued on my way. There'd be no radio communication, even on the secure channel-hopping mode, until we made sure no busy ears were eavesdropping. Hoped we didn't need to communicate till then.

I took the wheel now, started the motor and looked around. It was the first time in five days that I wasn't glued to Matt's trailer with my eyes compulsively glued to the ground. We'd stopped only at night when looking around hadn't been any use.

"Holy moley, Cali!" Ayesha whistled, echoing my thoughts. "That's one stunning sight!"

Stunning was too mild to describe our surroundings. A daunting peak presided over atmospheric plains. Moody, cruelly beautiful, the snowcapped Mount Kazbek was actually a more than fifteen-thousand-foot-high volcano. It loomed majestically from Georgian soil, its extensive Russian side cascading toward us, rugged and verdant and poetic, ending in the sloping meadow the refugees had settled in. The camp languished by the Terek River, which flowed from the mountain.

"Are the borders close?" Ayesha asked.

"Yeah. And so is the ancient Georgian Military Highway."

"What's that?"

"Ayesha! You didn't read the brochures!"

She chuckled. "Now when would I have done that?"

I pursed my lips in mock severity. "*Plenty* of reading time between searches and incursions and explosions." Ayesha laughed.

"And just because you're my favorite person," I said, "I'll give you a free guided tour. The Georgian Military Highway is a road running 140 miles from the Georgian town of Tbilisi to Vladikavkaz in North Ossetia, Russia, you remember? That little town we passed before we entered the minefields? Anyway, the highway was so named by Czar Alexander I, but the route dates from way before the first century B.C. From time immemorial really. It's still important as one of the only links to Russia through the Caucasus Mountains."

"You think that's where the militants' base is?" she asked.

I shrugged. "Probably. Not that knowing that helps anyone in finding them. It's a perfect hideaway. Certainly dangerous enough. It winds its way through towering mountains, climbing to more than seven thousand six hundred feet at the Krestovy Pass. Plenty of treacherous hairpin bends and sheer drops to strike terror in the hearts of any army, ancient or modern. It isn't coincidence the route is featured in grim stories by Tolstoy and Alexandre Dumas."

And before anyone asks, no, I didn't know all that from Damian's brochure. Since Jake had disappeared somewhere in the Caucasus, I'd studied the area. I was brimming with endless data about the region, data I thought would be forever useless.

Ayesha whistled. "Hot damn, Cali. Shades of *National Geographic!* All this knowledge should come in mighty handy."

Didn't know about that. Wouldn't hurt though. My firm visualization of the region was becoming multidimensional now that I was here. Maybe it would count for something. I hoped.

My eyes strayed to the mountain-dominated horizon. Ayesha's eyes were glued there, too. I continued my guided tour. "For a really humbling view you need to be at Kazbegi on the Russian border. And I'll have you know that Mount Kazbek isn't just a pretty face. It's a holy mountain, according to the Georgians, where Amirani, the Georgian Prometheus, was chained in a cave as punishment for giving mankind fire. Some say it was where Christ was buried, or even where he was actually born."

Something occurred to me as I said those words. *Had* this

mountain been chosen by the militants for more than convenience, for its historic and theological claims? Were the militants playing a modern-day Prometheus, hunted and self-banished for their holy cause? Were stories of their being God-chosen circulating among the simple people?

Whatever, Damian had been right. It would be impossible to find them in the extensive and inaccessible mountains by intelligence alone. This was a hands-on investigation.

Before we could start, we had to establish ourselves, have the militants cooperating and unsuspecting. Damian had started us on the right track, painting us as a bunch of harmless, fumbling bleeding hearts who'd lucked out.

All mental debates froze as the camp crept nearer, huddled in the lap of all that beauty, quivering by the gushing Terek, a materialization of human suffering, a testament to human depravity. And that was from afar.

On a now grassless meadow, as far as I could see, ragged rows of flimsy tents flailed in the brutal October wind. People in colorful tatters huddled in endless lines, waiting in turn for food or latrines.

Then the masses began taking individual shape and form.

True heartache began right here. When faces started leaping at you, when personal desperation bombarded you, when snatches of the aborted lives started seeping into your consciousness…

My heart fisted on rending pity. The ache to run to them, to contain them in a collective hug spread in my gut… No!

No pity or useless sentiment. I wasn't here for this.

I was here to set things right.

Chapter 12

"Cali—for God's sake!"

Ayesha's cry drew my attention to a simple fact. Matt was double-flashing me, stopping. I wasn't. Seemed I'd gotten used to kissing his bumper. Not a good idea, coming so far to die in a motor vehicle crash. I braked. Hard.

Get a grip, moron. Starting with an emotional overload was against all we wanted to establish. If I marched down and started antagonizing our hosts, we'd be cast into another sort of minefield. No time to let my demon out.

She still rattled her chains. *Soon,* I told her. *Promise.*

We came to a halt at the camp's edge. There were no fences, barbed wire or otherwise. Figured. Why put up a fence when you had an invisible force field of land mines?

Not that a fence here would have served the usual purpose as in other refugee camps, where it was mostly for protection against aggressors and opportunists. Here one was needed to keep everyone from wandering out and getting blown to pieces.

I jumped out of my truck and strode toward the militant leader, falling into step with Damian.

The lanky man was waiting by a large tent at the camp's entrance. Had to be some sort of reception center. In normal refugee camps, those were vital. When new refugees arrived, they rested there while waiting to be registered. Registration was a priority. Keeping track of demographics was the only way aid workers could assess the needs of the population. Registration documents served as refugees' entitlement to food rations, shelter and other relief items such as blankets, clothing and cooking utensils if they'd arrived without their own.

None of that applied here. If there'd been registration, I'd bet it had been for the militants to keep track of the ones already here, not of new arrivals. They expected none.

So it probably was a base for the militants' presence here. Maybe we'd get an orientation of the camp, meet the camp leaders, get a list of priority cases.

One thing we needed was insight into the dynamics of the militants' rule.

I knew I shouldn't stare, but my eyes knew no such thing. They kept succumbing to the pull of hundreds of other eyes. Mostly women's and children's. Drawn in through innocent confusion only to drown in inescapable despondency.

Desolation and degradation were destinations I'd frequented in the last years. I should be used to them. I wasn't.

I escaped the eyes, promising a continuation, entered the tent ahead of Damian. A dozen men and women were there, nothing in common but that spark of versatility. No doubt, they were those elected or assigned from among the refugees to be camp leaders.

They came forward, expressed their gratitude for our presence. Cowed, beyond trying to hide it. Damian accepted their welcome, made a little speech, then looked to me.

It took all I had to empty my vibes of hostility as I turned to the militant leader. "Thank you for escorting us," I carefully articulated my prepared speech. "Now we'd like to get to work. There's so much to do and the sooner we start the better."

He barked a surprised laugh. "Do you *all* speak Russian?"

"I speak it very badly, compared to Mr. De Luna." I flashed him a smile, devoid of anything feminine or suggestive, just friendly and accommodating enough. "Enough, I hope, to get by."

"We'll leave you to your job, then." He made a gesture to his men to get out. "If you need anything to make your stay here more comfortable and your job easier, a patrol comes here twice a week. Report any needs to that day's leader."

So he wasn't *the* leader, huh? Just today's. Interesting. And logical. Overall leaders kept themselves hidden, safe. Wonder who theirs was, and where he kept himself.

The moment they left I turned to the camp's leaders. I was surprised to see no change in them now that their oppressors were gone. Could be this subdued state had become their natural condition. Or the militants' presence lingered, through insiders reporting every move and word. Could be something even worse, though I couldn't guess what.

During the next hour, we got a comprehensive assessment of the humanitarian catastrophe. It was even worse than what my eyes and senses had initially told me.

There were twelve people in each three-person tent, one rations outlet for every two thousand, one tap of purified water for every thousand and one pit latrine for every hundred. That was four to five times more people than the minimum requirements for health and sanitation.

As usual, problems spawned more festering ones. To get around the dearth of facilities the refugees engaged in practices that only increased their plights. With latrines and clean water being so inadequate, most people wandered to the river to meet their needs, polluting the water source. The only thing limiting the damage from either practice was their apparent fear of straying from the camp for any distance on their own.

Heart-itching eagerness to start, to do something *right now* propelled me out of the tent. Damian and the others followed.

I surveyed the camp, my mind filling with countermeasures to fix the diseased entity, not only while we were here, but until their plight was permanently resolved.

I turned to Damian with an impatient hand on his arm, forcing him to conclude his exchange with the refugees.

"Let's set up." His eyebrows rose at my tone. Oh, give me a break. *He* sounded imperative *all* the time! He'd better get used to it, now that I was the boss for real. "I want to set up our field hospital where we parked, with full access to the STS. Two hundred feet away, I want a cholera camp, for segregation of cases. With them drinking polluted river water, the cases of severe diarrhea they reported is probably that. Over there…" I pointed to the middle of the camp. "I want vaccination tents as well. I bet every one of the eight thousand children below five needs a full schedule of vaccinations."

His eyes narrowed on me for a moment, their expression unfathomable. Then he turned to Ed and Matt. "You got that?" Both men nodded. "Get on it then. Assign six to setting up our living quarters, too. Engage full safety protocols."

"One more thing," I called out, stopping Ed and Matt. "I want ten health posts interspersed throughout the camp. Each will serve five thousand refugees, who'll go there instead of walking all the way to the hospital. One paramedic will do in each, handling everything that doesn't require a doctor's attention, and referring only those who do."

That got me a readable reaction from Damian. A spectacular frown. "That's my people and I want them free so I can round up a team whenever I see fit for reconnaissance. If they have a post, it would make them visible, would tie them up, make their disappearance from it obvious and questionable."

I answered frown with glare. "I don't care if I'm compromising your team's free movement, De Luna. Helping the refugees comes first, everything else takes second-row seat."

"Commendable of you to feel this way. As I predicted you would." Seemed he knew me more than I knew myself. I thought I'd be able to use the aid mission as just cover. Something tender flitted in his eyes. *Tender?* Damian? "That was why I said you should get on with your job, while we get on with ours."

I shook my head, more to rattle some much-needed reality checks into place than to stress my point. "To do my job, I need paramedics at those posts. It was you who limited the number of my team and I need each one of them by my side. Your people, dispersed throughout the camp, is the only way to set up an effective and rapid health scanning operation. If refugees inundate the hospital it will be chaos. Your job can wait."

"It's *my* job then?"

Oops. Slip of tongue. Or concession? Oh, fine! "So it is more your job, the covert stuff. I'm not interested in debating percentages here. Logic says if we rush with our retrieval job, accomplish it, there'll be no turning back to the aid mission. The other way around is the only possible way.

"And how long can my job wait? You expect to settle things first, if ever? If either part of the mission is to succeed, both missions must run simultaneously."

"They can't. Our best security, the most cooperation we'll get from both sides here, is if we establish ourselves as a formidable aid effort. I don't have enough people to do that on my own."

"Aren't you anxious to release Jake? Or is this your over-the-top way of showing me you've got your personal feelings vanquished?"

His lie-detector eyes penetrated me, shrunk me. Why did he keep doing this to me? Wasn't it enough he existed and made me forget everything, including Jake? Did he have to spell it out now, make me feel inhuman for not thinking of Jake first?

But I couldn't think of Jake first. Even if I did. Even if logic argued that I wasn't here in a bid for the refugees' relief or free-dom, but for Jake's and the others'.

Logic had no chance. Being exposed to mass suffering had a way of dissolving my plans. As emotionally fraught as it was for me to free Jake, it still felt so small a cause in comparison, reeking of self-interest.

I cleared jagged emotions from my throat. "Our lost people are nine. There are fifty thousand lost people here. And I have the unprecedented chance to do something for them."

"Be realistic, St. James. Whatever you—*we*—do, it's tempo-rary, leaving no lasting effect."

"You're wrong, Damian." Why did his name slip out when my emotions lay bare? "Those people need hope beyond all else, the knowledge that they're not forsaken. We may not lift their oppression or cure all their ills, but we will cure a few, and that *is* a big thing. A lasting thing. I have to know we've given them our best. Jake is my heart's concern, but what is my heart com-pared to all that?"

A flare of supernova proportions lit his eyes, burning away something that had been between us since the day we met. A bar-rier, some limit. Felt like a crossing over. Into what?

Another thing I'd have to wait and find out.

His eyes returned to their infuriating coolness. "Okay, St. James. You get a week as total boss. Let's set this operation up, show them what we're capable of. Any more orders?"

Nothing I could think of. Nothing non-X-rated at least.

Work. Get busy. God knew there was far more than enough to exhaust me out of this crazy lust.

There were endless things to be done.

I couldn't wait to begin.

When would it end?

Right now, *please,* would be a really good time. Yesterday would have been better. Where were gunfire and land mines?

Where was anticipating being riddled or blown to bits at any moment when I needed it? Give me danger, give me terror, give me pain. Hell, give me another bullet through my colon and another in my thigh. They'd been nothing compared to this torment.

I tried again to put an end to it. "Help? Please?"

What I really needed to yell was, "Lady, do something to shut your kid the hell up!"

No chance of that. You didn't speak to your patients that way, even if you were teetering on the edge of berserkdom.

This was my eleventh hour, and not only on a metaphorical level, of being exposed to bone-splintering screams. One hundred and thirty kids, one handing the flagellating baton to the next.

A shrieking kid below the age of five was a form of agony overlooked by all torture connoisseurs. You want to drive a tyrant to repent his atrocities before killing himself an inch at a time? Put him in a roomful of screeching kids.

Little four-year-old Misha here had an edge, the frequency of his shrill screeching enough to liquefy metal. He'd already been in pain when he'd come in.

I'd exhausted all my cajoling powers. They'd only worked anyway with each kid until I'd given him or her the first MMR shot. Then all gloves had come off.

I tried to approach Misha again and the little boy did the impossible. He raised the pitch of his scream another octave. I almost crumpled to the floor like a dog bombarded by a supersonic barrage.

I watched him break out of his mother's ineffective hold, sagged to my chair, my sigh almost deflating me. I glared at the uncooperative woman and swung my pulsating head around. "Haiku, will you do the honors?"

Sedation was in order. I had no hope of convincing little Misha that the rest of the vaccinations, followed by a local anesthesia injection and scalpels to open and drain his abscess, weren't a torture-murder scheme.

Haiku, knowing there was no use sweet-talking the boy, pounced on him with a mask of nitrous oxide. The boy grew groggy after the first gigantic breath between screams.

We, too, pounced on him the moment he stopped thrashing. Ishmael injected him with the remaining vaccines while Lucia handed me instruments as I incised the abscess in the heel of his right palm, draining it and extracting the offending foreign body, a splinter embedded deep in his flesh.

I stuffed the abscess space with antiseptic-dipped gauze, left it unstitched to drain, bandaged his hand, leaving his fingers free to move, injected him with broad-spectrum antibiotics, and felt like shit all through!

I should be used to kids being scared witless at the sight of medical instruments, not to mention after taking an injection for the first time, no matter how light my touch was. I wasn't.

Then again, I was. At least, I handled it. *This* had just been too much. I'd never faced that level of hysteria. And after they'd almost all exhibited the same inconsolable fear, with their custodians or parents useless in explaining the fear or in curbing it… Let me tell you, screaming and drumming my heels myself sounded good right about now.

To add to my aggravation, at one point Damian had burst into our minor surgery compartment, rushing in from his head paramedic station at admittance. He'd stood there, taking in the scene, his now perpetually simmering gaze skimming me and Haiku as we restrained our kicking and screaming patient, making sure nothing serious was going on. Then he'd drawled, his voice throbbing with dark amusement, hitting all my raw and inflamed spots, "Always knew you had a sadistic streak, St. James."

The huge rat had actually chuckled. Then he'd left me stewing, hadn't tried to use his vaunted colloquial Russian to soothe the kid or prod his apathetic custodian into a more active role.

The crowning provocation had come when I'd moaned to Ishmael, "Is it me? Am I that scary?" and the jerk had actually had the nerve to give my question serious thought. And to come up with a "We-ell…" sort of answer.

I sent the now knocked-out Misha away with his sluggish mother. Then I took care of business, filled in his vaccination card and a brief history of his general and malnutritioned condition from the mostly aborted exam. The rest disposed of used instruments and sterilized multiuse ones.

Bless them, they moved soundlessly. Or maybe I was deaf by now. Whatever. Silence, after two days of constant cacophony, swooped down, an equally painful whooshing vacuum. But at least I could hear myself think. And now that I could, suspicions trickled in with every forming thought.

All this fear—had it been directed toward me—us? Or had the kids come into the exam room with an ingrained reaction waiting to be triggered by the sight of any stranger? Were the militants abusing them then, and were they now terrified of any unknown grown-up?

I needed no more reasons to abhor the militants, but this possibility almost had me going after them right there and then. Their representatives were out there now, on one of their biweekly patrols.

They were also bringing the refugees' rations and fuel, those they'd confiscated from the relief efforts, and were now dispensing at their discretion. Now the mines were back in place, there'd be no more operations. Wondered how that fitted in their bid for popularity. And with only the meager plots of land the refugees farmed, the sheep they kept and what they'd originally set up the camp with, they were back to depending on the militants for everything they needed to survive.

They were keeping them like caged animals, or worse, like a sort of reverse bait, a repellant, feeding them just enough to keep them barely alive and their human shield effective.

But was that all? If the children were so scared, what else where they doing to them?

"Are we done here?"

My eyes swung to Lucia. Sallow, swaying on her feet, her eyes ringed and bloodshot. I'd driven her, and everyone else on our team, beyond capacity in the last six days. And tomorrow I would push harder still. Our worst projections had paled in comparison to the horrifying reality. We had to pack several days' work into each one we could snatch here. It would be over all too soon. It was over for tonight.

"Yeah, we are." I nodded, stood up and herded them outside. "Go get unconscious fast. Tomorrow we start surgeries, and we need twenty hours minimum to get through our day-one list."

To their credit and to my continuing amazed admiration, their expressions betrayed only anticipation among accusations and moans of "Slave driver!" and "Sadist!" and "Damian is *so* right!"

These were good people. The best.

And palliative measures or placebos, as Damian had dubbed us, or not, we were making a difference. Sometimes placebos had the effect the hardest-hitting medicine couldn't have.

I walked out, alarmed to feel a drag to my feet, a droop to my lids. Being unable to defeat gravity was not a good sign. No problem. In four hours I'd be fully charged again...

Uh, all right, make that four seconds. Estrogen-rush here. All-systems, red-blooded-male alert.

Damian was stepping out of the nearest Health Post, his eyes slamming into me across the hundred-foot distance. Should be too far—too *dark* to see that gold flash by the feeble lights of our field hospital and the camp's. Had to be short-circuiting imagination.

I stopped, let him come to me. A woman had to get her distractions where she could, y'know? And watching Damian De

Luna undulate toward me like the sleek jaguar that he was, was one of life's gourmet moments. Made me thankful to be female, to fully appreciate what he was. Pure erotica on legs. Worst thing was, he didn't seem aware of it.

He stopped a foot from me, drawled, "Your interrogation tactics are appalling, St. James."

No imagination involved now. There was that flare. Humor too, whimsical and scalding, flitting on those lips.

Uh—why was it again that I wasn't devouring that smile off them right now?

The mission. Jake. Melissa. And just about everything else.

Right. *Keep it light.* "And ineffective, too. Not one kid broke down and spilled even their own name!"

And that applied to their parents, too. We'd been trying to get refugees to talk. We needed in-depth info on our enemy, their movements, their numbers, their arsenal, their chain of command. All we'd gotten was a head-on collision with a new face of hopelessness.

People moved around like zombies, came in for exams, tense, wary, morose, left the same way. Those people were even worse than the ones in Darfur. They'd given up on their people's help, their enemies' mercy and the world's intervention. They were past grabbing at a rescuing hand.

Thoughts crashed in a pileup. Damian… His hand was gliding from the curve of my shoulder down to my waist, languorous and I was a pumpkin if not intentionally sensuous, steering me toward our surgical trailer.

Hey. *Hey!* What was going on here?

Had he decided to act on the not-so-dormant volcano between us?

Sure. My hormones would say that. They were accumulating in hope, after all. He'd probably just had enough of my phasing out on him, was anxious to get on with our daily wrap-up.

At the end of every day we met to report details of both

teams' progress. Patients screened and treated, lab work done and needed, sanitation measures installed, high-energy biscuits and dietary supplements distributed. We'd lost a lot of our provisions, instruments and all the in-trailer sleeping arrangements with the four lost vehicles. Thank God we hadn't lost our latrine and showers. And that Damian had turned out to be one hell of a logistician. I should have known he would be.

Each night I told him what I needed the next day, and he somehow made the supplies we had left do, kept track of everything, dispensed the needed stuff at the right moment, made us feel everything was at our fingertips. He even sorted out our stuff, not only GCA and PATS supplies. I could see now how my team, as organized as we were, wouldn't have been as efficient.

As if I needed more reasons to I took a step ahead, severing the contact. If this was business, let's keep it strictly so. "I left the report back at the hospital."

He caught up, bent and put his lips to my ear, literally, whispered, "I just want some—time together."

Oh. Oh? Real "time together" would be back in my tent...

Down, moron. So he was offering...something. Uninfluenced by mind-altering drugs this time. Didn't mean I had to snatch at it, and at him. As if I was dying to. Even if I was, *I* got to say when we had time together. When I thought the time was right. If I ever did. I turned my brightest smile on him. "Okay. So—you get any luckier with your hypnotic interrogation methods?"

Lightness seeped out of his face. Good. Would only be fair if I messed with his testosterone levels, too.

He handed me into the truck. Needlessly. Kept his hands on me, until I felt his imprint all over my genetic map.

Then he was coming *over* me. Well, he would have if I hadn't slid across the seat. No doubt now. He *wanted* to be all over me.

What the hell. Time was right. Time was up. At last.
Watch out, De Luna. Coming right up, for real this time.
Time together.

Chapter 13

I slid back over him. One knee rubbed over his hard thighs, pulled, gathered them between mine. Then I straddled him.

My hands tangled in his night mane. Hmm—much longer than the last time I tried to do this… I tugged, hard, dragged his face up to mine for a fierce nuzzle. He tugged on my braid, his wine-dark groan echoing mine. Yeah. Ooh, yeah, yeah. Me, too.

So *good.* Such relief. The contact. Letting go.

Then it wasn't enough. Would anything be after six years? Doubted it. Felt like a duty to find out.

I sank into him, lips and embrace, took his brunt. Aroused aroma, all-Damian feel and taste, frosty mountain air clinging to polished skin, a dam of hunger bunching steel muscles.

My thermal-layered uniform constricted, shackles cutting off my breathing. My swelling flesh quivered for release, for his hands to demolish our barriers, silence the hunger.

I yanked down my front zippers, dragged his hands to me.

He completed the motion, reaching through the layers, finding my bra-imprisoned breasts, kneaded, pinched, possessive, savage.

I ground my flesh harder into his palms, bit into his gasping-my-name lips. His growled Calistas told me *I want to thrust inside you* now! I poured his name down his throat, my message as clear, as ferocious, *first move gets me first ride.*

Then suddenly I was hauled off his lap and shoved away across the seat.

"They're…gone," he panted, staring across me through my window and into the night. The words sank in slowly. Hit bottom.

The patrol. It had been for their benefit, to—to what? Whatever. I didn't appreciate being pawed for a diversion. It had better be for a critical cause.

"So—did we put on a convincing show?" I swept my bangs off my steaming forehead. Gotta trim the damned things. Getting in my eyes, misting them up…

"Outstanding." He huffed, wryly eyeing his bulge, shifting in his seat, a grunt escaping him. Outstanding was right.

And for it to have been faked, after all these years, all these yearnings…

Well, one thing hadn't been faked. His erection. I could have bruised my knee hitting it. Could still do. Hoped it hurt him as bad. Worse. I had half a mind to rub him, bury hot lips and moans and nibbles into him, really make him blow his prostate!

He explained, probably saving his potency. "The militants were becoming fixated on us. They didn't buy it that as chief logistician and paramedic I had lots to discuss with you. I felt they wanted me to admit we were—involved. So I sort of did. I saw them circling in the background and decided to satisfy them. If we're cut and dried, it will take their focus off us."

Hmm. Okay. Maybe. "But if we're involved, how come we're not in one tent, taking our amorous workouts away from prying eyes?"

He ran his fingers through the hair I'd made a feast of mussing. "I intimated that we weren't that far along yet, that I was still working on you."

I snorted. "You should have told me. I just went and made a liar out of you, pouncing on you that way!"

His eyes did that glowing thing. "They'll just think my keep-it-cool strategy got you so hot you jumped my bones first."

Sounded too much like an account of our situation.

Was this how men ended up dead in crimes of passion?

"I was about to ask you to play along," he continued. "Then you just did it, so I thought you'd realized it on your own."

"How was I to know what to play along with?"

"Yeah, that did occur to me at one point before everything but you ceased to exist."

"Sure. For about two minutes before you flung me off you. And you sure kept a hawk's eye on them in between gropes."

The big lout didn't even leave me the last violent thought, the appeasing image of me neutering him! He turned to me, his voice dipping into an unknown range of sincerity. "Do you think I wanted to stop? I only did because now would have only been followed by confusion and regrets."

Now? Meaning what? That it *would* happen between us, when there was no more confusion and no possibility of regrets? How was that for Catch-22? Goddammitall!

I did up my zippers, squeezed the still-pounding ache between my thighs and damned him and everything else stopping me from assuaging it to hell.

Think about work. That'll freeze your libido solid. Hopefully.

"Let's talk important stuff." His eyes lowered. Good. My barb had connected. Assigning him and what had just happened to irrelevance, returned the balance and the facade of detachment I'd lost. No need for him to know it was just a facade. "I'll go first. This morning, I finally met three more cooperative refugees, all younger men…"

"Sure they are!"

He thought they'd buckled under my irresistibility, not the insidious psycho-manipulation I employed? Not a bad concept. I'd take my ego supplements wherever. I puffed out my chest, plowed on. "Younger men with no family, no emotional attachments, no one to fear for. They know some English and jumped at the chance to exercise it."

He gave me a disbelieving smirk, but shrugged. "So what info did they give you?"

"Zilch, where our original questions are concerned." Those untraceably probed into the workings of the militants' outfit, the presence of dissension, friction. I'd gotten info I wasn't looking for instead. "They started out much more open, gave me a lot of insight into the camp life, and along the line each mentioned loathing digging duty. Seems the cemetery outside the camp is overflowing. When I tried to understand if they meant all these deaths occurred in the last year or five, each began to babble, saying his English was very bad. I reverted to Russian and each insisted he didn't understand me."

"I met the same opacity. About anything." He had, huh? With his superior Russian and no chance of his being misunderstood?

"It's a pact of silence, then."

He nodded. "They're scared. They can't afford to blab to us about their captors."

"Understandable. If only on a cerebral level, as you once said. Only they can know what living with all hope gone is like. And as bad as the militants are, their best interests lie with them. We will soon leave them to their fate. But what would they accuse the militants of if they weren't too scared to talk?" I told him about the children's overreaction and my suspicions.

He pursed his lips. "We can only speculate. Could be nothing. Could be they're just paranoid and the children hypersensitive. Justifiably so."

"Could be. But you know what, De Luna? They have every

right to be contemptuous of our efforts. Giving them hope only to abandon them again feels even worse than never coming here in the first place. At least the militants are consistent."

"Cut the melodrama, St. James. You were the one who insisted on going all out in our aid efforts."

"Yeah, I know. Even if we are a cruel and fleeting glimpse of relief, I am doing everything I can for them, while I can."

"Yeah, me, too."

That was right. To my surprise—a surprise I was becoming more ashamed of as time passed—Damian was totally passionate about our work. It jumbled my image of him as a relentless black-ops agent, reminded me again that I had no idea why he was in this line of business in the first place. He'd turned out to be a world-class aid worker, that was for sure. It took a lot to be one, even on a temporary basis.

I had to give him his due. "I know you are. I couldn't have come this far, done all this without you."

He didn't look me in the eye, stared for a long moment at my throat. Then he just said, "Ditto." Simple. Devastating.

My turmoil found expression. "It doesn't stop me feeling that inhuman filth like the militants are the lesser evil."

He looked into my eyes now. "You're indulging in self-doubt and pity. Are you one of the people who find their pleasure in whining? Does it turn you on?"

"No. Only *you* do. Damn you." There. Out in the open. Declared. How would he respond to that?

The last thing I could have expected, of course. He turned on me, dragged me over his body, opened his lips on mine. Just the exact taste and heat and level of seeking, of license, of violence. That was a kiss then. A fusion, a stab right through my heart and loins. I clutched at him, pure power and passion pulsing in my grip, drove my tongue inside the fount of his maddening taste, met his, needing more of this, more of him.

Then I was bereft. He'd wrenched his mouth away, his arms

trembling as he lifted me in the air and off him. I hung there, suspended, looking into raw eyes.

"And you turn me on…" His rasp abraded my exposed nerve endings. He let me down, grabbed my hand, pressed it to his erection. Some adjective other than outstanding was in order. "*And* on." He threw my hand back at me. "Damn *you!*"

All right. Okay. So now we knew where we stood.

Something eased inside me. Among eruptions of molten readiness and quakes of cramping emptiness, of course. So I *had* been going crazy not knowing for sure, huh?

I handled climbing-the-walls frustration better when it wasn't accompanied by will-I-ever-know uncertainty. Not really well though. My body was still primed, no idea it was out of luck, my mind still played us going on, saw him between my legs… Only good thing here was feeling his equal suffering. Loved knowing it.

I fumbled for my professional switch, for my breathing regulator. "So we're even. Business then… Search plans in place? You got the satellite-transmitted maps into a coherent on the ground path for us? The week you gave me is over tomorrow."

He stared at me, his eyes turbid, startled amber. Unguarded. Tonight was one for firsts. Then he whispered, "I get so sucked up in our work I keep forgetting the reason I'm here. I have to keep reminding myself."

Same here. But coming from him, that was some admission.

I'd thought he couldn't get involved in anything but his job. I'd thought him a self-made prisoner of his subservience to his job, his cause, his self-imposed rules. I also thought everyone around me inmates in one prison or another, obvious or concealed, all equally inescapable. Prisons of bars, guards and minefields, of pain, fear, of others or for others, of chemical dependence, moral degradation or physical incapacity. Sometimes it felt I was the only free one I knew.

But was I? Could anyone be totally free? Limits and

boundaries, recognizing them, abiding by them made us human. Prison walls weren't all built of negatives. Loves and desires and beliefs tethered me, manipulated me. Imprisoned me. I was still the freest person I knew, my prisons ones of luxury. I owed it to the world to use this most powerful of weapons.

Damian drove his hands in his hair, grabbed the back of his neck. That had to leave one beaut of a bruise! "But yeah, the paths the militants travel till they enter or leave dense mountains are ready. So are their schedules down to the minute, the alternating patrols, the number of men, names, habits, characteristics. Good thing they're punctual and systematic."

"Must have a slave-driver leader. And not so sucked up in work after all, are you? So—we're ready to make our move?"

He opened his door, paused before he got out. "Get your surgeries done tomorrow. If you're still awake by then, you can come with us. Reconnaissance sweep at 2100 sharp."

"I'll be there." He swung his long legs onto the stepping ledge. "And De Luna…"

He swung back to me, a man at the end of his tether. I surged into him, gave him one brief, all-the-way kiss.

I pulled back, my own pain attenuated at the sight of his. I grinned, feeling powerful and reckless and aroused out of every inhibition, kissed him again, murmured into his mouth, "Just in case someone's still taking notes."

All good things came to an end.

Well, all things end, period. We just noticed it, hated it, when good ones did. And there was one good thing ending right there.

In catastrophe.

As usual, in moments of extreme peril, my mind played this whistling-as-if-nothing-important-is-going-on thing. It replayed the previous four nights in detail, leading up to this moment.

Each night at 9:00 p.m., when all the inmates who rose at first light had succumbed to oblivion, we stole out. We wasted up to three hours on the way and back. The farther we reached the longer it took, and we couldn't have been more than eight hours. We had to get back before the first refugees woke up.

Let me tell you, a lot of running was involved. Damian's team was tireless. Good thing I was as fit to start with. My fitness level zoomed up with the ultra-rigorous exercise. Only downside was we went through rations like locusts afterward.

Besides the distance, another obstacle had been the loss of our night-vision goggles. They'd been hidden in the two trucks that got picked for target practice. Good thing I'd disguised two specially made ones among the head-harness binocular microscopes and ophthalmic lasers. Guess who got them?

Still, it wasn't imperative to have them since there was a healthy moon. When cloud cover allowed its emergence.

We'd already found out a lot of vital stuff. The militants' garage and warehouse, where they kept their vehicles for pick up when they descended to navigable terrain, and the supplies they'd confiscated from the aid efforts. The route where they smuggled their supplies and weapons from Dagestan through Georgia. Several paths continuing from the path we'd mapped, hopefully one ending in the route to their hideout. And all through we'd avoided detection. Yeah, things had gone really well. Couldn't have gone better.

But we had to maximize our search now, while the going was good, while they treated us with the same level of suspicion they treated the refugees. We had to consider a change of tide, a heightening of intolerance, if not suspicion, leading to tighter surveillance and more frequent patrols.

After four spectacular covert-ops successes, tonight had started out even more ambitiously.

It was supplies day. With one of the militants' trucks going back empty, I'd seen an opening to hitch a ride, gaining us hours of search time and the possibility of going farther than ever before. It would have to be a much smaller team, three or even two. Maybe only one. I said I'd go.

Damian had vetoed my plan as too risky. We'd leave earlier, explore longer, he'd said, the others would make a diversion obscuring our departure and return.

I was considering my options, adopting his method or overriding him, when the militants demanded our presence during rations handover, making it impossible to slip away earlier as he'd projected. It was almost midnight when they were finally ready to leave, making it pointless to make the trip, only to have a rushed couple of hours search. Staying out later wasn't much of an option then. There was a limit to the diversionary tactics the others would employ if we arrived back in broad daylight.

He'd relented then. We couldn't afford not to follow up, to lose a day's worth of investigations. And he also didn't like the way the militants had clung to us, involved us in their jobs and kept us around. If they were starting to suspect us, we needed solid info fast, the exact location of their base, for a possible emergency evacuation and incursion.

So we'd hitched that ride. Only me and him and Ed.

And no, that wasn't when catastrophe hit.

We hid behind bushes in the trucks' path, ran after the second one, jumped and clung to its rear with suction grips. We held on for the forty-mile trip, jumped off a few hundred feet from where they parked, hid to watch them starting on their way home. This was our big chance. All search could end today.

We gave them a head start then sprang after them. They took one of the paths we would have investigated last.

We went higher along the mountain, jogging up increasingly perilous terrain. There were endless grottoes along the Georgian Military Highway. Soon, a shortcut had us at what must be the infamous Daryal Gorge, a treacherous ten-mile winding road on a narrow shelf beneath and above granite cliffs one mile high. Quite a drop, huh?

To make things more interesting, we frequently passed the graves of earlier travelers. No one who'd found them had been about to drag them all the way down for a decent burial. Each time we found one, I bet each of my two companions had flashes like those I had. Questions like, *What was I doing traveling in those fools' doomed footsteps?*

In the moonbeams struggling for a chance to shine through bloated and furious-about-it cumulus clouds, the Terek waters glinted in equal savagery, gushing in the ravine below us, hungry for lives to engulf.

If someone fell into it, the river would sweep him or her through North Ossetian, Ingush and Chechen territory on its way to dump all its secrets and flotsam in the Caspian Sea. Yep. One hell of a flush.

And no, none of us slipped and fell to their doom in it. That wasn't the catastrophe. Not yet.

Could happen any time now though.

The militants were coming right at us!

Yes, *that* was the catastrophe. They were doubling back on a twelve-foot-wide stretch of road where we were on an unavoidable intercept course.

Falling off wasn't an option, of course. Sending the dozen militants to their watery graves was. Very tempting. Very easy, too. Between the three of us, we'd take double their number, no problem. But it would mean a very premature exposure and an abortion of all our efforts so far.

I hadn't come that far to be thwarted by a bunch of unbathed and unwitting hooligans.

That was the infuriating part. Their detecting us and coming back for a confrontation I'd respect. I'd appreciate a face-off for something intelligent and premeditated on their part. But from the way they were lumbering back, seemed they'd just forgotten something in the trucks and were going back for it.

They were just going to stumble on us.

But they hadn't seen us yet. My goggles had picked up their body heat emissions far before a visual could be obtained.

It had only been a dozen heartbeats since I spotted them. I was operating on a zillion gigahertz. Before I alerted my companions, everything zoomed across my logic circuits, processing our options.

We had three of those.

Option one, get out of their way, run back.

Problem with option one was, once we reached open ground they'd spot us after all.

Option two, slaughter them.

Problems here were self-evident and above-mentioned.

Option three, hide until they passed.

Two problems here: One, we'd have to hide until they were back and gone, continue behind them or go back after all. Two, we were on a sheer cliff a mile up, no grottoes, only place to hide up or down the jagged granite mountain face.

Two shouldn't be a problem, though. Rock climbing and building scaling were among our engrained skills. With our gear and probably without it, we could pull a Spider-Man for as long as needed until they passed.

If we had time. We didn't.

Time to buy us some.

I reached in my backpack like an archer for her quiver, fingered my drug-dart kit, pulled a blowgun dart, the one ready loaded with eight darts filled with a mixture of diazepam and succinylcholine, a double whammy tranquilizer and muscle relaxant. My target would collapse in under twenty seconds.

Damian became aware of what was going on the moment I reached for the blowgun dart. I knew because he engaged his cloaking powers, all vibes emanating from him ceasing. Ed followed suit. I took aim at the first incoming faint green luminescent shape's head, blew. Then again and again.

The shape crumpled to the ground, followed by the diversion

we needed. The militants stopped, scattered then gathered again, bending over their comrade to check him, crying out their surprise and irritation at his fainting fit.

Now!

I turned to Damian. At least I tried to. His arms took me from the back, stopping my whirling motion. Then he was lifting me up, making me feel weightless, making me reach the rocky protrusion leading to a miniature ledge fifteen feet up. My gloved hand clamped on the icy rock, anchoring me. Adjusting my center of gravity, I swung my weight up, braced my legs on his shoulders, then sprung from their immovable support to the protrusion then up onto the ledge.

The moment I gained a footing I wound a rope over and over an outcrop, then around my own body, wedging my back to the cliff and my feet to it, then threw it down. Between the rock's anchor and my leveraged weight, a man of Damian's size could easily climb it up.

The one who tested and proved this theory, climbing up in under two seconds, was Ed. Damian was taking care of his people first.

Get up here already, you macho pain!

The militants, rattled by their colleagues' collapse and needing to conclude the mission they'd originally embarked on even more it seemed, were now rushing toward us.

They'd see Damian in a second!

In a second, even I didn't see him.

He'd fallen off the cliff!

Chapter 14

I knew only one thing. I was jumping after him.

His fierce whisper stopped me. "He's hanging from a rope."
Large hands, clamped around my wrist and mouth. Ed. *No!
Damian!* He could still be hanging over the edge. I could still
reach him….

The militants were almost beneath us now. I'd blow our cover,
end the mission, give up on saving Jake.

So? I wasn't saving Jake at Damian's cost.

Damian! Hanging by his fingertips, scalpel-sharp rocks
shredding his flesh, pain fogging his mind, gravity snatching at
him, the void clamoring for his flesh, for his life force… A fraction of a second counted.

"He's hanging from a rope!"

His fierce whisper stopped me.

"You're sure?" He had to be. He'd jump after Damian,
too, if he thought him in danger. I guess. If he wasn't under

orders not to preserve the mission at any cost. No. Knowing Ed, he'd brave disobeying Damian to save him. He'd told me the truth.

It was okay. Damian was safe.

I peeked over the ledge.

The militants were busy running in both directions, six heading to complete their errand, five carrying their unconscious comrade and retracing their steps.

Not that I cared.

Where was Damian? God, what if Ed had been wrong…?

He wasn't. Damian was swinging up the cliff's edge, unhooking the rope he'd managed to secure before jumping off the cliff. I shuddered, relief and what-ifs attacking my balance and power, slumping my body. He could have messed up in his haste. The rope could have snapped off under his plunging weight. And he called *me* reckless!

I perched on the ridge to undo the lasso around my waist, then swung down the rope. I landed on bent knees, felt Ed following then unhooking the rope.

I just wanted to run to Damian, knock him to the ground and scorch his skin off in anger and kisses.

"That was all for ultimately nothing," was all the lout said, his resonant voice low, matter-of-fact.

I don't know how I murmured back, equally cool, "There's a why attached to such a profound statement?"

"When they find your darts all over him—"

I cut him off. "They won't. My darts dissolve." His expression blipped, caught off guard in a rogue moonbeam. "Don't be so skeptical. Knocking someone out only for the culprit darts to be found and the drug analyzed defeats the whole stealth purpose. So I made those darts, a rigid, needle-sharp variation on absorbable catgut just with a much faster absorption rate. The part inside the body at least. The part outside falls off."

Damian just stared back at me. It was Ed who whistled almost soundlessly. "Impressive. But shouldn't we be following the ambulance quintet? They'd lead us to their base."

Damian shook his head. "And have the other sextet coming up behind us? Only way is to follow them. But who knows how far their base is, or when they'd come back? We can't risk being out there in full daylight. No. We know enough for now. Let's go back. We have a hell of a roundabout route to avoid bumping into them as it is."

I didn't move. "I'm with Ed. I think we should get this done once and for all." I could almost taste our target.

"Live to fight another day, St. James. The first rule of engagement."

I stopped arguing. My mind might be egging me on, but my guts were with Damian. They were screaming *go back*.

They had a mighty bad feeling about it all.

It couldn't be worse.

God, when would I ever stop tempting fate? When would I ever learn there was always, *always* something worse?

And no, it wasn't worse for us. Served to remind me our troubles and dangers aren't the center of the world.

All the way back to the camp, I'd been sweat-frozen, pissed and just about done in, promising myself two solid hours of sleep even if I had to dig a six-foot-deep hole to lie in.

Making our way back to the camp had been hair-raising. We'd missed being seen by a hairbreadth on three separate occasions. Our circumventing route had brought us only in sight distance of sentinel posts. It had taken us five hours of wrestling with maximum risk terrain to circumvent them.

Just when I'd been thinking it could only get worse if we were forced to engage the enemy, we'd reached the camp at a glaringly sunny if freezing 9:00 a.m.—to absolute chaos.

We'd gone to great trouble to approach the camp from the

most concealed route. We shouldn't have worried. No one was paying us any attention.

The refugees, thousands of them, had better—or worse— things on their minds, huddled and focused where the real drama was unfolding far in the distance.

Ishmael and Lucia ran to meet us carrying disaster bags.

"A few children ran out to the minefields," Lucia panted. "Seems they wouldn't come back when their parents called them. They triggered half a dozen fragmenting mines by the time their parents reached them. They got blown up, too."

"The filthy monsters! The sons of bitches. The cowards!" Venom and hatred filled my parched throat, choked me. I snatched the disaster bags from Lucia, told her to go for more. A paroxysm I hadn't been prey to since Clara shook me apart, gray and garish crimson blanked my vision. Yet I ran. I saw it all.

The mass casualty situation that shouldn't be.

Children should be left out of it!

Why were they the ones that ended up suffering? How could people sleep at night knowing it was happening? Why wasn't everyone out here with us, running to save them? Didn't every- one understand these people were once just like them, until madness and terror forced them to flee for their lives, only to torment and torture them for the rest of it? Didn't they under- stand it could be *anyone's* turn soon?

Every member of our teams was out there in the distance, probing the ground beyond the known safe boundaries, demi- ning before they could chance treading the infested ground to reach our casualties. They couldn't even throw them ropes and tow them out of the field. They could only trigger more mines.

My blood frothed, almost bursting my head, my vessels.

To see your casualties lying there, their life ebbing with each blood-pulsing beat, to know you could save them if you could only reach them, and not being able to....

Rage pumped more power to my legs, overtaking the rest.

Damian increased his speed, caught up with me. "No daredevil tricks, St. James!"

I wanted to sock him. It was my body, my life. I was free to risk it to get to my patients. He should know I wouldn't.

"Stuff it, De Luna. Whatever you think of my IQ, you should know that *I* know I'm no good to them if I join them in a mutilated mass on the ground."

Something terrible came off him in a battering wave. "Wouldn't be the first time you pulled a suicidal trick when an atrocity blinded you enough."

I snatched my eyes away as we reached the others. "I learned my lesson. I'm not spending my life apologizing to you!"

"It's not me you should apologize to."

Ignore him. Get this done.

We were there. I crashed to my knees, threw open the bag and produced my probes. The others had already mapped out the land to our victims in a grid of ropes, each taking care of demining their own unit of the grid.

I tried to keep my eyes away. I didn't need this. The soul-deep scar of seeing the crumpled torn bodies, their final degradation, the agonized terror in the eyes of those whose consciousness hadn't faded, sparing them the ordeal.

It took us an hour to clear the forty feet to them. Twenty-three improvised antipersonnel mines found. Fragmenting type, designed for maximum, widespread damage. Cost a couple of dollars to construct, a couple of minutes to plant and incalculable limbs and lives.

My blood had charred by the time we'd finally, finally gotten them out. There were fifteen of them, six children, six women and three men. Couldn't rush them to surgery right away. Had to assess injuries first, perform the ABCs of stabilization and resuscitation. It took half of us another thirty minutes to do that while the other half expanded and prepared the STS. Then we rushed them there.

And the real struggle began.

* * *

"When I say suction," I barked at Ayesha. "I mean *suction!* I can't see a thing!"

Ayesha made a terrible sound. She increased the suction power, barely beating the blood accumulation rate in the little boy's abdomen, clearing my operative field.

I saw my fingers again, deep in the bloody tissues. God, oh, God, what a mess. What a mess!

I finally cross-clamped the aorta, cut and stapled the torn intestines, sewed the liver injuries, flushed the abdominal cavity with three liters of saline and started packing it with sterile abdominal packs, stemming the last of the bleeding.

"Pulse 190," Ishmael said, his voice grating. "Ectopics all over the place. Blood pressure 60 over 30."

"Lucia, increase blood and fluid delivery rate."

Lucia's eyes reflected my agitation back at me. "It's the last 100 cc's!"

"Where are the cross-matching results?" I hissed. Then swore. "We can't wait any longer. Get me six units O-neg blood, *now!* You know who has it. Force donations if you have to!"

Lucia rushed to carry out my orders, her startled glance telling me what I already knew. I was losing it.

And I was losing the boy. God—why now?

The explosive fragments had torn through his fragile body, shredding his legs, penetrating his abdomen. When I'd first stabilized him, all I could think was, how did such a small body contain all that blood? How had he bled so much yet hung on the hour and a half we'd needed to get him here? But he had.

Why wasn't he hanging on anymore now?

Matt had taken on the leg injuries as I'd worked on the abdominal ones. Just as I started the laparotomy, Matt had pronounced his defeat, his gruesome verdict. The boy's legs were unsalvageable. To stop the unstoppable hemorrhage, the inevitable gangrene, he had to amputate both devitalized limbs to midthigh level.

I'd stood beside him as he'd sawn off the little, mangled limbs, my hands deep in his massive intra-abdominal hemorrhage, my mind thrashing inside of me, screaming. *Detach yourself. Get it done. You can still save his life.*

But I wasn't doing any good. I'd stemmed his bleeding, decontaminated his abdomen, pumped back blood and fluids into his system. Why wasn't he responding?

Oh, God, please, just a few more minutes. A response to build on. Something to hold on to, to drag him back with.

"He's gone, Cali."

Ishmael's whisper fell on the last of my control like a scythe. "No!" My shout splintered my ears, jarred me. I wasn't accepting that. I swung to Ayesha, dragged down my mask, suffocating, panting, "Defibrillator!"

She just shook her head. "Let him go, Cali."

"I can't!" I was doing this. I didn't need their help.

I snapped up the defibrillator. Matt turned from the other surgical station, tried to take it out of my shaking hands. I clung to it.

"It's no use—mercifully for him." I still resisted. He gave the defibrillator one good tug. I let it go. "Now get a hold of yourself and let's tend the other casualties."

"You don't know it's no use…."

Matt's eyes gentled, his tone hardening. "*You* do. You've known it all along."

I sagged, inside and out. Yes. I'd known. Just had to try. To add another defeat, another horror. Another scar.

And it was far from over.

It was all over. For today.

Dense night and biting cold bore down on me the minute I staggered out of the surgical trailer. I'd been in surgery for twelve hours. Among us, we'd saved thirteen out of the fifteen casualties. We'd lost the boy's mother, too. Wondered if she'd let go when she'd known her kid was gone. Wondered if it was better that way. For her.

I wanted to go home.

Was it some sort of answer to my prayer that Damian materialized beside me now?

I had to be beyond finished, if I was equating Damian with home. I *had* no home. As for Damian...

He made me wish I had one.

Okay. That was it. I was hallucinating.

Wishing I had a home, was I? Complete with picket fence, two and a half kids and a dog? With Damian in it? Yeah, sure. Twilight zone material and alternate reality setting for sure. There were no two with more unhomelike potential than us. As for our very combination...

What more perfect combination was there?

Nuts. I was going nuts. Going to pieces. I could actually feel stuff crumbling inside my skull, my heart...

I didn't do crumbling, didn't go to pieces. Sleep. All I needed was to sleep... With Damian... Oh, shoot!

And what was he doing now? Another show for the patrols? They'd come outside their schedule, stayed longer, considering what had happened today.

I didn't look. I didn't want to see them or Damian's eyes as his hand glided up my arm, round my back, the movement rich, sinking soothing talons in my rawness. Then his arm was around my shoulders, snaring me, cushioning me into my body's protection, stripping the last remaining layer of armor.

I twisted, pushed, turned on him. "Go away!"

"No."

Just no? Oh, there was nothing *just* about it. What he did to me when he didn't even try. When he didn't want to do it.

There was only one way to make him go away, leave me alone. To make the pain subside, the suffering stop. I punched him.

Not a good idea, punching the man of steel in his abs. A slight intake of breath was my only effect, his intention to draw this out hardening with his instinctive guarding.

Sorry, not playing. *His groin. Be predictable. Go for it.*

I did. He sidestepped. Then he turned me, my back to his front, had me in a headlock. And the gentlest damned embrace. Then his whisper filled my head. "You did all you could—and they knew it. You lavished your heart and caring and genius on them. No one can give more, Calista. They died in the hands of someone who was fighting for them, honoring them. They're at peace now. Be at peace, too."

Tears burst out of me under pressure. An image from a Bugs Bunny cartoon with his tears arcing out in the air filled my head. I giggled. Sobbed. "Oh, God, Damian, have mercy. I can't deal with compassion and support right now. Not from you!"

He tugged tighter on my hands, squeezing my breasts against my crisscrossed arms. "Shut up, Calista." His indulgence poured over me like hot caramel when I was freezing and hypoglycemic. "You need my comfort, so take it. You just walked through hell, and your soul is bleeding out of you."

"So you think I have any left?"

He pressed me harder. "You always had too much. That's your danger, your curse. You're overloaded with caring and compassion. Hell can't rival your righteous wrath, and your passion—God, Calista, your passion…"

I twisted around and pounced on him. Mouth and teeth and arms and legs, climbing him, bruising his lips and jaw and neck, clamping his head, his buttocks, needing, kneading, devouring, now. *Now!*

His arms crushed me back, his tongue and teeth and loins returning my onslaught. I fought with him, in panting silence, the power of a bursting dam, six years' worth of pent-up denial behind every touch. He tore back at me, our long-standing cold war blazing out of control in a showdown for harder, deeper, more, more. All!

"Damian—my tent…"

"No—mine." I started to argue and he grunted, "Condoms."

Oh. Ready, was he? And condoms? Wondered how many he had. How many we'd use. Before we came to our senses.

Not now. No way. Had to have him. *Have* him.

I dismounted him and we stumbled, unable to stop rubbing and tasting and groping, our eyes and legs and tongues and breaths tangling. His tent was the nearest one to the STS. Would have opted for it just for that huge advantage anyway.

He tore the tent open, dragged me inside just as I shoved him through it, reveling in the power bouncing off my hands everywhere I pushed and wrestled. We staggered together, spilled on the tent's insulated floor. He twisted midfall, taking me on top. We didn't even make it to the mattress. Didn't matter.

My vision fogged, my brain heated, pushing against my skull. The ache between my legs, the emptiness, spread. I felt it imploding me. I writhed over him, kicking out of my uniform's pants as he heaved beneath me, reaching for condoms in his toolbox. His *tool*box…

A manic giggle gurgled out of me at the double entendre as I pounced to free him. Out with it. *Out!*

The zipper snagged on the enormous obstacle pushing against it. He huffed an agonized chuckle, his hand crushing mine, stopping my yanking motion. "Not in your best interest, causing me irrevocable damage now."

I pushed him on his back, let him fumble himself free and ready for me. *So* ready for me. I rose to my knees, then higher to scale his length, opening myself on him, grabbing his hardness, ramming it against my swollen, weeping entrance. So long, so damned far away and barren. So tight.

I bore down on him, using his hot girth to forge a path inside me, to fill the void. Pain seared me. His passive invasion split me wide open. Beyond my capacity. Too much.

"Yes!"

The scream burned me on its way out. Everything collapsed inside me, around him, my insides compacting, a pinpoint of monstrous gravity, an unbearable pressure. Excruciating. Exquisite. *Enough!* Had to—had to… An outlet, an escape…

Sobbing, desperate, I rose. Crashed back on him. My shattering, melting flesh engulfed him whole this time. Felt like a comet crashed in my core. Detonated. Released all agony in an agony of release. Squeezing all of me around all of him. Wringing me dry of sensation, of essence.

I think I ceased to exist.

Chapter 15

I'd only been asleep, I realized.

Okay. I'd been more than asleep. I'd been knocked out cold. More like comatose.

Interesting part here was my bed. Damian. Sprawled under me, big enough to sleep on comfortably. And just if I needed confirmation that my memories of ravishing him were true, still inside me. Big enough to be uncomfortable. A very good discomfort. And getting bigger with my every quickening breath.

His "good morning" reverberated in the perfect acoustic resonance of his chest under my ear.

I raised a head that weighed half a ton, squinted down on him, struggling to keep lids weighing no less open, to adjust to the lowest light level of the dual-fuel lantern. "Good? For me, whoo boy, certainly was. For you, I doubt it." I let my head flop down, rubbed my face into his warm neck, caught his scent and trapped it into my lungs. "Sorry for the premature orgasm."

He stroked his rough hands down my back, through my hair. Hey, when did I get completely naked? When did my braid come undone? "You needed it," he said simply.

I *had* needed it. Still needed it. Him. Us. His hands settled on my buttocks beneath the heavy thermal covers that must have materialized sometime during my coma, spreading me wider for him to drive up into me fuller. I gasped. He whispered, "And if you're worried about me, I have proof it was good for me, too."

Proof? Oh! Oh. Okay. Good to hear it. Great. "So you enjoy it rough, huh?"

"Seems so. Never tested it before. No woman had ever pushed me down, had her way with me then collapsed asleep without as much as a 'thank you, sir.'"

I chuckled. Who could have thought? Damian taking it so lightly that I'd reversed the sexual roles. Not a lot of men would have. But then it took someone supremely assured in his sexuality to have a sense of humor about it. And Damian was sexual supremacy incarnate. Wondered how many women, how often…

None of your business. Outside this tent, these hours, you don't get to even think what he does with the rest of his life— with his body…

I adopted his teasing attitude, let a curtain of my hair fall over him, quipped, "Not that my lack of proper gratitude put you out or anything, huh?"

He rubbed his face into my hair. What was he sniffing so appreciatively? It must stink after yesterday! "It sure didn't." Smugness purred out of him. "Just seeing you come, hearing you, feeling you explode around me—I could have blown an artery."

"Oh, no, you don't. I'm so not taking you as a patient. Good thing you had a safety valve!"

His virile laughter drenched me in pleasure and joy.

Uh—pleasure was obvious really, but *joy?*

This was surreal. Me and Damian, joined, caressing, indulging in lighthearted pillow talk. About to have sex again.

I knew we would. If the clumsy prelude was anything to go by, there had to be an encore. Many encores.

I rubbed my stinging breasts over him and met only clothes. Apart from his open fly, he was still fully dressed. An emergency if I ever heard one.

I spilled off him and regretted it. I wanted to impale myself on him again, right this second. He moved out of my groping reach, flowed up to his knees in the three-quarters darkness, turned away. "Gotta take care of something first," he said over his shoulder.

Oh. Protection. Dammit. And thank God for it.

It was only a second's deprivation anyway, as he got rid of the used condom and fetched another, then he was back and snaring me in his strip show. I fumbled on my hands and knees for the lantern, turned it up. Gotta see this well. And what I saw had another rush of desire gushing inside me.

It wasn't his *Playgirl* centerfoldness. I'd seen him just about naked before, in painted-on swimming suits, knew his every line and motion in obsessive detail. Neither was it his blatant lust. He'd already said I turned him on, showed me just how much. Oh, all of the above helped. A lot. But what got me was the intimacy and the other stuff crowding his expression.

I had to be seeing things. What I wanted to see?

Why would I want to see tenderness or possessiveness in Damian's eyes? I didn't want either.

Didn't I?

He reached for me, gathered me to him, stifling my inner debate. Ahh…

The long, still moment, the feel of him, the full body contact. The peace. Beyond description. I'd fantasized. When he'd challenged and changed me, when he'd hated and fought me. Then ever since he'd exploded back into my life. My reluctant ally, my indispensable support and occasional savior.

For once, fantasy fell far short of reality.

Then I needed more. As if I'd demanded it out loud, he gave it. He sank with me to the mattress, in luxurious tongue mating, in generous, greedy all-body stroking and kneading.

Exquisite. The warmth and closeness. Experiencing his perfectly packaged and leashed power. Such lethality housing such protectiveness. Heady stuff that. I'd always teased him during CDP's survival course that he lived up to his namesake, St. Damian, the patron saint of physicians. But Damian was a patron saint of the oppressed, too, not just the harbinger of death to the oppressors. I'd never been sure. I was now.

I was impatient now. All the promises his tongue and body and eyes were making—he'd better deliver on them. Fast. I'd hurry him up. I bit an anchor into his pectoralis, took hold of him, stroked him, and his chuckling growl detailed his approval of my eagerness, of what I did about it.

"God, Calista, I thought I knew how hot it would be between us, thought I've been blowing it out of all proportion."

Him, too? Good thing we hadn't known then. Imagine the frustration level if we had. The frustration level from now on…

Take now. I surged onto him, taking all I could, hoarding the freedoms. I pushed him back, rolled on top of him, rubbed myself all over him, reveling in the equality we'd developed. In the spirit of equality, he didn't take it on his back this time. He wrestled me around, sustaining the fusion of our lips.

"Damian!" I sucked his name through his lips, breathing in his breath. My legs opened, clamped him, my hips rising for his completion. He raised himself away—to put on the condom? No—he took masses of my hair with him, wrapping it around his nape and back and groaning as it cascaded over his skin.

"Do you know what this braid of yours has done to me all those years? What I went through imagining undoing it, bathing in your hair this way?" He left the speculations up to me.

I owed Dad for not letting me cut it then. If it influenced Damian this way, I was all for putting up with the hassle.

He was exercising influence of his own, doing things to every inch of me. Then he moved to my tense breasts. I almost pushed him away. I'd never been sensitive there. Not to pleasure. I'd never had him there, either. Now I did.

He licked and stroked around my nipple until I felt my breast would burst. Then he started feathering it with his fingers and tongue and breath and words, each phantom touch a bolt of pleasure forking to my loins. I jerked off the mattress each time. Enough! I thumped my fists on his back. He got the message, closed his lips on it. And suckled. I convulsed. My breasts had selective receptors with his name on them then.

I gave myself up to the alien sensations, beyond even trying to stifle my very vocal reaction. He gave me his hand to bite down on. Afraid of waking up the whole camp? Good idea. I sank my teeth in him.

He took every liberty. I gave them to him, pummeled him for every one. He growled and his suckling grew frenzied.

And I screamed.

I didn't care who heard. I'd been stifling it all ever since Clara died. Since they took Dad away and Mom left and Jake was lost. I screamed now, all the screams I'd missed, suffocated on. Liberated. Released.

He came up, stifled the frenzied sounds in his mouth, my catharsis, my tribute to his pleasuring. He reached between my legs and stabbed me with more, opening my folds, finding the focus of my agony, stroked and stoked. I bucked, squashing myself against his hand. *More.* He gave it to me, drove two then three fingers inside my cramping flesh, knowing just what to do, how hard to do it. I exploded around them.

It had to have been an hour later and I still quivered with aftershocks. "Oops." My voice creaked against his lips. I'd really abused it in my abandon. "*This* premature orgasm is all your fault though."

"My pleasure." I felt his smile spreading on my quivering lips, his hand cupping me, drawing out my pleasure, desensitizing my flesh.

I was done. I had to be. This last climax had been way up there on the megaton scale. Wondered what form of relief I'd offer him in return.

He slid down my body again, laved my breasts, soothing away the soreness I'd made him inflict on me and—let's say I shouldn't have worried about being an active participant in his relief. Seemed my body was just hitting its stride. And ready for a long, hard, jarring ride. But first...

I bent to his erection, my mouth watering. Man, I was drooling for real over him. Figured. He was incredible. Bulky and hard, sleek and polished, just like the rest of him.

I took what I could of him in my mouth, bingeing on his taste and texture. He let me, accepting the pleasure.

I held his eyes, greedy for every nuance on his magnificent face. He didn't hold back, generous with his demonstration. Something I thought he'd never be. My heart expanded, filled my whole chest.

"Calista, don't get me wrong," he wheezed in between grunts. "I dreamed of you doing this—*everything* to me, with me, but..." He stopped, heaved himself up and hauled me over him, taking my tingling lips in another exercise of profound intimacy. "But I want *you.*" He was panting now, the man who ran ten miles before his breath sped up. "I want to be inside you, feeling your flesh clinging to mine, crazy for what I do to you. I want to scent your pleasure and see your incredible obsidians abandoning all tension and worry and pain. I want to lose myself in you, make you lose yourself to the pleasure of me."

"Damian, if you don't shut up and do it, I swear the only thing I'll lose is my temper!"

He laughed. God, I loved his laugh. "And we know what happens when you lose your temper, eh?"

International incidents. Casualties in the hundreds. Dead

loved ones. What happened to make him bring this up without a gallon of venom and bile? Lightly even? Sex? The expectation of it? Was he testosterone-operated like all men after all?

With him at full mast and panting for me, being so indulgent with me that I almost didn't recognize him, it sure seemed so. Somehow I didn't think it was that simple.

But that implied I could think. Beyond thinking of putting that condom on him and jumping him for a repeat performance.

I tried, but it was harder than it looked. Or maybe I was just coming apart. Or just too inexperienced to live.

Ironic, wasn't it? The bitch-monster Calista St. James had a sexual résumé to fit on the back of an inch-by-inch price tag! Jake had been so long ago, had been careful and worshipful and slow. None of our encounters had extended to condom-fitting while shaking with the ferocity of my body's demands like that.

Damian pushed my hands away, completed the simple task with all the finesse of a fifteen-year-old on his first, fumbling back-seat time. Good. I weakened him, too.

Then he drove up into me, hot and thick and so long craved. Felt like the first time. Was. The other time didn't count. I hadn't really felt him then, bent on my release. I felt him now, shuddered, fell on him, biting his shoulder in my extreme.

"Don't you dare come on the second thrust!" His distressed humor made me hotter. This side to him was like finding a feast where you never hoped for a crumb. I showed my extreme appreciation, bit him harder and he gave it to me, the second thrust, then the third. Then I lost count.

Everything we'd ever shared, all the ferocious, tangled feelings, the crazy, convoluted history unraveled. Then I did.

No! I wanted him with me this time.

No use. Beyond the physical reality, the grind of flesh in flesh, the *idea* of him inside me, doing this with me, to me...

Every heartache and frustration looming in my life's horizon crashed on me. Shock waves of pleasure, damaging in intensity, needed some outlet besides screams. Tears, suddenly easy, vented the critical surplus.

He bore my storm, rode it, lapped my tears until I was whimpering "No more." Sated, sensitive, raw.

He only began moving again. "Again, Calista."

Again? Had he lost it? I was depleted never to recharge. So how could I tell him to just go on and help himself?

"Want a live body, you'll have to get another one," I gasped. Then winced. This had come out far worse than anything I'd been worried to say.

"I'll *give* you another one." His smile was threatening. He flopped me on the mattress, took my legs over his shoulder, held my eyes and plumbed new depths inside me. Then he made me watch as his fingers did things to me that I didn't know was there to do. And the tide rose again in me, as if it had never ebbed.

How did he know? How did he *always* know I had more, how to mine it, exploit it, wring it dry of potential? I lay back this time, open, accepting, taking him and all he gave, letting him show me just what my body was capable of. He gave more than I should have been able to stand. I stood it fine.

Then it was happening again, stimulation reaching critical mass inside me. I bit down hard on the heel of his much-abused palm stifling a scream that would have brought our teams rushing to investigate. I didn't want to come without him again.

He still held back, damn his stamina, kept watching me bucking and convulsing. Then he grunted, "Look at me, Calista."

My drooping eyes opened wider and understood the gift he'd bestowed on me, insisting that I watched. There could be nothing more incredible than Damian in the throes of orgasm.

Then he collapsed, melted into me. Such mass should be suffocating. It was just completing, anchoring. His arms went beneath me, lifting me into him, clinging. I clung back, full of him, of the harmony we generated.

He buried reverent lips in my neck. I arched and lapped up his homage, the way he kept saying "Calista" as if in humblest prayer. Once, then silence. Then again. "Calista."

At one point I found myself on top, draped over him like a sated blanket. And it was full daylight out there.

He still chanted my name and curiosity and then unease rose to an irrepressible level. I had to ask.

"Are you trying to get used to saying my name? Or will I revert to being St. James the moment we leave this tent?"

He didn't answer that. I could take his evasion as I pleased. Instead he said, deep, deep and gravelly, "You take your pleasure the same way you do everything—fiery, unpredictable, extreme. And it's so arousing. Everything you do is *damn* arousing."

And that was bad, why? He sure didn't sound happy about it. But *everything* I did? Now that was a staggering piece of news. "I thought everything I do only aggravates you."

The gold in his eyes grew thicker, brighter, like lava. "Aggravation is arousing. Coming from you."

I felt all-powerful with his admission. As all-feminine as the earth goddess. Weird feeling, when I didn't dwell on my femininity much. My femininity dwelled on me though, whenever he was around. "Never took you for an articulate lover, Damian. That's so damned arousing. Overkill in your case, really."

He took a heavy lock of my hair and wrapped it around his forearm, let it slither over his face, catching at it with his lips, groaning in what had to be some kind of suffering. "Overkill should be your middle name. You stimulate me to the point of pain, Calista. You *scorch* me. I've been teetering on the brink of hell ever since I laid eyes on you."

We-ell. That was an articulation I could do without. A reality check. More like a crash landing. A rundown of my defects and sins must not be far behind. Uh-uh. Didn't think so, thank you. Maybe it was time to run back to our corners, take stock, think how to go on from here.

I extracted my hair from his fascinated cosseting, rose to my knees, tucked my legs beneath me and started braiding it. His gaze on me was as effective as his hands, sweeping me, knowing where to pause, where to fondle, how to inflame and addict. I shuddered.

"I want you again."

My eyes dragged from his lust-filled ones downward, checking out his claim. No claim there. Fact, as solid as could be.

"And I want you." But after that hell comment… I mean, that hurt! No reason why he shouldn't share the torment. He reached for me and I pulled back. "Uh-uh. I wouldn't want to push you over the brink."

His shutters came down so hard I flinched. Without another word, he rose from his Roman-god-reclining-in-sexual-abandon pose. In seconds he was crammed in his pants, pulling on the rest of his clothes, regarding me with vacant eyes.

He'd turned off. Just like that. My comment had probably knocked his priorities back in place. Had snapped him out of the sexual fugue. It was over then.

As it should be.

I was fully dressed, too. I should get the hell out of here without another word. But I owed him, owed what we shared, better than that. Damn.

I opened my mouth, groping for a better way to conclude this, to leave the door ajar…

His next words slammed it, right over every vulnerable and exposed thing in me. "I want you to know I take full blame for this lapse." *Lapse?* "You were way beyond your endurance, were exhibiting classic posttraumatic stress—"

I cut him off. "And you what? Took advantage of me? Give me a break, Damian. I wanted you, and I took what I wanted. You did, too. And it was magnificent. Let's not start defiling it now. Let it stand there, a moment out of time, a healing outlet. Who knows, we could have defused our relationship. Maybe we can continue on better terms now."

His winged eyebrows rose in disdain. "And if you believe one word of that you need some serious psychological assessment to search for your misplaced insight!"

"No need to get offensive, mister. So we messed up. What do you suggest we do, keep at it, since it's already happened?"

God, I wanted him to say yes. To consent to our turning to each other whenever the hunger grew too large to contain. I wouldn't do it, but I wanted him to propose it, to want it...

I should be careful what I wanted. His golden eyes were still opaque but his words were transparent enough. "Yes, Calista. I want to keep at it, as you so delicately put it. And *at* it." My knees knocked once, my body readying itself for the pleasure it expected and was already addicted to it. It would turn on me when it realized I intended to deprive it. I had a withdrawal of the severest kind coming.

Damian spread his legs, eased the bulge in his pants. "But what I want doesn't matter. If we keep *at it*, we'd perpetually be either hungry or sated. It will take the edge off our every thought and action and we can't afford that now. But frustration can actually keep us sharp. We also need to be impartial."

"And if you believe that's what we'll be, whichever way we go now, you have some serious judgment repairs coming, too!"

His teeth did a nail-scratching-a-board number on me. "We can try. It isn't right in our conditions to get attached."

Hadn't he left it a bit late for that? The bastard. Or was he talking about his own detachment? Made him a bigger bastard. "Is that why you kept your lover right where you could have front-row seats to each other's maiming or death? Or is that the lesson you learned from her death?"

His eyes died. My heart kicked me so hard I almost stumbled. I sure deserved it. Why did I bring this up? How could I? Under any provocation? Apart from going crazy wanting to know the answer, some stuff should never be asked. Should never be exhumed.

Something that felt like another heart filled my throat as Damian took three loaded steps, bringing him within two inches of me.

When he talked his voice was soft, calm. Deadly. "I learned my lesson all right. I learned that I deserve every bit of suffering and self-loathing I live with, that I deserve anything at all that is still coming to me in this gruesome line of work. I hate no one more than I hate and despise myself. No one but you."

My heart tried to batter its way out of my chest.

That anguish. That stark revulsion...

I didn't mean—I never—I shouldn't have said...

How can I retract this, erase it?

Grief and remorse ricocheted inside me, a spear penetrating me back to front, shoving me on its point to throw myself at him, contain him, defuse his torment, atone for my unforgivable sin...

Was he waiting for me to beg or explain or extend a bridge? Was that a flicker of anticipation in the inanimate amber?

I was suffocating to oblige. I couldn't. I shouldn't.

It felt like the day he'd ended my career and cut me loose into the unknown multiplied by ten thousand, like amputating a limb without anesthesia. Yet it could be the only way out of this mess. A surgical excision, merciless, final.

I squared my shoulders, crushed the pain and the compulsions and looked up at him, sort of saying goodbye. "You hate me? Good! Hold that thought."

My heart drained, my legs numb, I turned away and walked out of the tent.

And right into Jake.

Chapter 16

"So—am I dreaming, or hallucinating, or are you really here?"

There was another possibility to the multiple choice he was proposing. I'd finally snapped. Lost it. Taken the leap over the edge. Common consensus had it that I was already crazy.

For proof, I'd gone and conjured up Jake's apparition!

I'd just lost the one passion I wanted, and I was summoning up the image of the only other I'd ever had.

The real Jake was somewhere deep in the mountains. We might never find him. Or if we did, might not get him out.

He couldn't be here.

He took another step toward me and my heart stuttered. No more air was left in the world to breathe.

But I'd never developed the ability to take refuge in wish-fulfillment phantasms. Would be too easy. I didn't get easy.

Jake was really here!

Didn't make sense. Didn't matter. He was real, here, standing before me under the stark light of the early morning sun. Alive. Unharmed.

And nothing like I remembered. Almost another man…

His metamorphosis was even more shocking than the fact that he was here. My Jake had rivaled Paul Newman in sheer good looks and Errol Flynn in panache. The man before me was more of a cross between Clint Eastwood and Steve McQueen. On a bad year.

But it *was* him.

"Jake!"

Without moving, I felt, I sailed across the three paces that separated us. Then I was all over him, sobbing his name in a refrain, as if it would solidify him, clear up the confusion.

I'd yearned for this. I'd prayed for one last look, one chance to scream "Forgive me." For two years. Two *years,* every day a new variation on the same despondency, chasing shadows and slamming against dead-ends until I was pulped. Until I gave up.

"You're real. And far more solid—not to mention even more demonstrative—than all of my imagined reunion, Calis."

His voice spread through a memory I no longer trusted, smooth and melodious. Had it deepened? Was the precise accent less pronounced? One thing I knew, the biting humor that had permeated it was gone. The words carried it, the tone didn't.

Something else had changed. My Jake had loved my impulsiveness, reciprocated it in devil-may-care abandon. He hadn't attempted to hug me back, his hands rigid at his sides.

Yeah, sure. As if he'd scoop me up and spin me in the air. As if these years of hell hadn't intervened in our lives. As if we weren't in the middle of hell now.

But how was this possible? Was it a dream after all? All of last night and up till now?

It would sure be one ingenious wish-fulfillment exercise, giving me all I craved. Thorough satisfaction with the object of all my simmering emotions and accumulated lust, saving me the emotional fallout with a brutal severance, then wrapping up by giving me the impossible, Jake delivered right up to me.

I squeezed him tighter and he groaned. This was no dream.

I unclamped him but kept my fingers digging into his arms. I wasn't taking the chance he might spiral away in a puff of smoke on me. "Oh, God, Jake—*how?*"

Elegant chestnut eyebrows rose. "How what exactly?"

"How *everything!* You're alive and here and I'm still unsure if *I'm* not the one hallucinating!"

My eyes clung to his, searching for something familiar. Their sky-blue-gray color was the only thing unchanged about him. There was nothing there. Nothing I could read. He just looked back at me. Then he shrugged. "I guess it's safe to say we're both sane—so to speak. There's probably tons of information we have to exchange before any of this makes sense. But for now, you're here, I'm here. It's enough."

It should be. It was. I tried to drag him to me again, and he stepped out of reach this time. "Maybe we should take this somewhere less public?" he said so formally it was almost funny.

Our surroundings zoomed back into focus. Damian was a few feet behind me. The rest of the camp and our teams were coming and going in the background.

But Jake's shadows were encroaching on us. Six militants, the closest less than two feet away.

And I'd sure given them a show!

No wonder Jake was stiff and acting so—weird. Like the refugees. No, not like them—his weirdness was different somehow.

He'd turned to the militants, was saying something. I didn't get it. The one who looked like the day leader nodded.

Jake turned back to me. "So where is 'somewhere less public' here?"

"They gave you permission?"

"Not for long. Is this your tent?" He pointed to Damian's tent, his eyes skimming Damian on the way back to my face. "Can we go in there for a while?"

Go in there? With all evidence of Damian's and my tempestuous night strewed all over the floor? I didn't think so!

"Uh, no, it's not mine." And I wasn't about to supply the need-to-know fact that it was Damian's. Speaking of Damian, he was coming forward. Must have considered it a good point to assert his presence. Wondered what he made of Jake's presence. Of my hysterical demonstration. Probably didn't like it after he'd established his claim on me to the militants. Sure made him look bad, me coming out of his tent and jumping on another man.

Damian's affiliation with GCA had come after Jake's time. Not the time to fill him in, but soon. For now I made the possible introductions. "Jake, meet Damian De Luna, our mission's logistician. Damian, Dr. Jacob Constantine."

Both men came into the same frame for the first time and my breath disappeared again. Boy, I had great taste.

Very inconsistent, too. I clearly didn't have a type. Two more different men didn't exist. Damian was night and Jake was day—uh, make that sunset. Damian had the all-around advantage physically, but Jake was mesmerizing. With his natural honey tan offsetting butterscotch hair and backlit eyes, that new harshness, the slow-burn maturity and the silver-brushed temples had augmented his looks about six hundred percent.

And his body. Another thing that had changed about him. I'd tortured myself imagining the atrocities befalling him, had wished he'd been killed and not tortured. But not only hadn't he been physically abused and degraded, he'd been upgraded.

My memory of him wasn't *that* defective. The muscles that had tensed beneath my digging fingers hadn't been there before. So how was that? Had they put him to hard labor? If they had, they must be feeding him really well, too.

My center-stage focus got a good yank as I noticed the way the two men looked at each other. A moment too long, both their faces and body language studies in emptiness and opacity, speaking volumes and oh-so-very transparent for it all. Then they shook hands, brief, formal.

There was instantaneous aversion for you.

Sour chemical reaction? Male territorialism? Over me? When one hated me, and the other barely remembered me?

I just had to giggle.

Both men turned on me, eyebrows raised. "Pardon me. Shock. And you have to admit, this is one black humor situation. Here I am, introducing you, the man I'd thought dead for eight years, to Damian just minutes after you materialized out of thin air as if you've been out shopping. But what takes the cake is you two shaking hands as if you were about to go in for a business lunch to be politely hateful to each other."

That won me my first shadow of a smile from Jake. And another delicious spanking look from Damian.

The militants chose this moment to call to Damian.

He stiffened even more. Tsk. Who'd believe the man had just spent the night getting all his tension thoroughly relieved? Clearly my effect was transient.

He gave Jake a reluctant nod, tried to pin me with an urgent gaze? Telling me something? Then he had to turn to the militants. They got a more amenable salute from him. The day's leader hooked his arm through Damian's and led him away.

Too bad. I would have really liked to see how this would have played.

My basic bitch was wagging her tail here. And could I blame her? There were the two men in my life, one hurling his hatred in my face, the other stiffening in my arms as if I had something horrifyingly infectious. Some sort of rooster fight would have been a much-needed appeasement right now.

Tangent alert. I was wandering. Jake. *Get answers.*

I looked at him, the man who used to be my smooth, outgoing lover. Hardened, harsh, his years in hell polluting his every line. A noise that wasn't a sound rose in my ears, a building pressure to snatch him away and run out of here. Back to safety.

Back to the man he used to be.

For now I took him back to my tent.

The militants followed us—no, more like guarded us, their guns at half-readiness. They usually weren't so vigilant. Did Jake warrant the increased level of care? Was he such a difficult prisoner?

At my tent, he addressed them again, and again the leader nodded. We were left to enter the tent on our own.

I turned to him, stunned all over again by his presence. It hadn't sunk in yet.

He was dressed like the militants, not exactly in uniform, but the same style and colors with black dominating. Suited him, augmented his new ruggedness and offset his superb coloring. He could pass for a PATS operative now, nothing like the pampered man and polished surgeon he'd been.

Oh, what the hell. I threw myself at him again. "Jake, Jake!" I tried his name on my tongue, savoring it, trying to remember how it had felt. "I can't believe it. I thought I'd lost it the moment I saw you."

Now that we were alone, his arms came around me. No statement there. No specific looseness indicating hesitation, no tightening hinting at agitation. Dammit, how did he feel about seeing me again? Was it good? Did he hate it? Was he just numb?

He drew away a bit, looked down on me. "You did look like you'd seen a—not a ghost, more of an apparition."

He'd taken one look at me and noticed the difference? A ghost was of someone believed dead. An apparition of something believed impossible. So that hadn't changed, that staggering perception of his. Was he now working out that I'd known he wasn't dead, just thought that it was impossible to see him?

I raised my face to him, to total opacity. So it was a one-way communication. "You certainly don't look shocked to see *me*. Contrary to your opening words."

"I already knew you were here."

"You did?" Seemed I should prepare myself for a barrage of shocks. What was going on here?

"I was told the aid mission to the camp was headed by a Dr. St. James. A beautiful woman with a long, thick, hundred-color braid. Couldn't get more specific than that. Still it's one thing to know you're here and another to see you for myself."

"Who told you that? The militants?"

"My escorts, you mean."

"Escorts?" I snorted.

"Some euphemism, isn't it? And do keep your voice down. They're very sensitive about being misunderstood and maligned."

Now *that* was definite humor. Oh, Jake. Maybe he wasn't totally lost to me.

"And why would your *escorts* tell you stuff like that?"

"They tell me everything. It's not as if I can use any knowledge to my advantage in any way. It's safe telling your prisoners whatever you want."

"So they tell you everything. Now *you* tell me. I'll burst if I don't understand everything right now."

"What's there to understand?" He shrugged, half turned, pointed to the mattress. I gestured for him to go ahead. He went down on it, sat with his back to the tent wall and his long legs extended and crossed at the ankle, looked at me. "You know most of it anyway. Our convoy was attacked and we were kidnapped. Almost a year later I think they were about to kill us. Then I happened to save one of their injured people and they decided to keep me as their medical aide."

Slave. That was what they'd made him. So this was why they treated him so well. He was useful. No. Knowing Jake, and the level of his almost magical medical and surgical prowess, he must be indispensable.

I sank to my knees before him. "Will you tell me what you're doing *here,* or do I have to scream first?"

He dropped his eyes. Not before their back draft of heat almost knocked me back. I did sag back on my heels.

Hel-lo. First sign of life. A whopper at that. Then he raised his gaze and those amazing translucent eyes lost any tinge of blue, radiating silver fire. Whoa. First no reaction, then a barrage. Then he made it far worse.

"I'd love to hear your screams, Cali," he whispered. "They've been in my head only for far too long."

And we both knew what he was talking about.

My body leaped, so recently and thoroughly awakened, so open and ready for more, for anything. So confused. Was it okay to react to Jake? it asked. His body had initiated it in the rites of pleasure. But the memory was so distant, and it now bore Damian's mark and taste. It had no idea if the heat sweeping it was just need for more intimacy and satisfaction, from Damian, or a reaction to Jake.

Was this how bigamists felt? Two-timers at least?

Nah. I bet they felt nothing of the sort, or they wouldn't have done it in the first place. But then I'd never thought I'd end up in a situation with two men at the same time.

I'd set myself up for this. I'd known I could end up finding Jake. I should have kept my hands off Damian until I did, so I'd be able to think, to *feel* clearly without having hormones gushing in my system, muddying everything.

Jake released my eyes. Probably thought it enough for now. He'd established his stance, made sure I'd registered it. He backed off, leaving me to sort my priorities, consider the ramifications and decide how to respond. Very systematic.

"Not that screaming is advisable." He smiled for real now. As if I needed more heartache and confusion. "It would bring the militants in to defend me."

I smiled back at him, tempted to laugh. "I can kill you in absolute silence, too, you know."

His smile widened, this time reaching his eyes. "I'm too

valuable to kill. Ask the militants. Who else has the expert opinion to answer your questions, to give you insight into the real situation around here? I'm sure you're dying to know."

I rose to my knees and bore down on him. "I again remind you that if I do, I won't die alone."

He suddenly looked like my Jake. He reached for my braid, taking its weight experimentally in his hand, making a satisfied sound. "God, Cali, I missed you. You haven't changed one bit."

I snorted. "With insight like that, who wants to rely on any of your expert opinions?"

"You mean you *have* changed?"

That was an open demand. *Have you changed beyond retrieval?* it said. *Have you moved beyond reach?*

I was stunned that he'd want me to be within reach. To do what with? From where he stood, I was just passing by his cell. Did he just need confirmation that I hadn't forgotten him?

I gave him the only answer I could. All I knew. "I have. I just don't know how much of the old me is left."

His gaze settled on me, and I felt as if I fell back into myself. I felt him joining me there, examining motivations, analyzing conflicting emotions, segregating lusts and irrationalities, reducing me to my basic components. It was bizarre, creepy even, but I felt as if he'd mapped a blueprint of my psyche. A blueprint I myself had no access to.

I inhaled sharply, shaking off the spooky moment. "Have you developed telepathy during the past eight years, Jake?"

He retracted his mental probes, ceased his distressing prodding, his full lips twisting. "That would have been convenient. I would have called to you if I had."

A fist battered its way out of my gut. I closed my eyes against the pain. "Oh, Jake, I can't even begin to imagine what it's been like for you all these years."

He threw his head back against the fabric wall, sighed. "I don't think I can describe it. Or that I should try. No reason to burden you."

My heart clenched again, my breathing going awry. A long, panting moment later, I whispered, "It's so easy to look at you, see how good you look, how stable you feel, and believe nothing really bad happened to you."

He sat up. Then he reached for me, his cold, dry hand feathering my hot, trembling cheek, a spear of longing and regret impaling me. I moaned and he drew me to him, pressed my head over his steady beating heart. "Then believe it, Cali."

He was taking pity on me.

Pity was one thing I never needed. I never had anything to be pitied for. Especially now. The shoe was so much on the other foot his pity should be outrageous. Unbelievable.

I could take anything. Only thing I couldn't handle was doubt, being in the dark. I pushed out of his gentle hold.

"I don't want to believe it, Jake. I'm not after solace here. I want truth. The only way I'd been able to go on was when I stopped going crazy with uncertainty and believed you dead. Now the uncertainty is back. If you want to unburden me, you'll tell me what really happened."

His eyes lost all expression again. He leaned back, drawing me beside him. My insides thrilled to the still ungrasped reality of his presence. Jake! He was really beside me!

He turned his head to me. "So—have you got eight years? For faithful real-time authenticity."

I pulled a face at him. "Don't go all British and wry on me, Jake!"

He pinched my cheek softly. His highest sign of appreciation. This was getting worse by the heartbeat. "Fine, from the start then. We were heading toward a refugee camp when military forces intercepted us with claims of security necessities. They arrested us with charges of supplying militants with drugs and medicines. Being the only Russian speaker I argued our case, gave them all they needed to establish our identities and connections and GCA's legitimacy.

"It took two weeks, but they finally escorted us back to the route we'd been traveling toward the refugee camp. Just hours afterward, the militants ambushed us.

"They accused us of going to refugee camps to poison the refugees, worse, to infect them with diseases they'd carry back when the federal forces pushed them back home, and cause an epidemic. We were just too stunned to answer. The machine guns in our faces also contributed to our lack of response or action.

"We were taken to one of their hideouts. What followed—till this day, I still find it hard to rationalize what they did to us…" He stopped at my indrawn breath, my frantic eyes over his face, looking closer for scars. "For some reason, they didn't touch our faces. I have many hidden souvenirs of the time. They just didn't go for crippling damage. They wanted to break us down, not kill us, or make us invalids. They went for the usual torture methods, excruciating pain, survivable injuries—and degradation."

Chapter 17

Excruciating Pain. Survivable injuries. Degradation.

The usual.

How brief. How nonchalant. How—comprehensive.

I didn't ask for an elaboration. I was agonizingly acquainted with all forms of human depravity. Through Dad. Through my work with GCA. Through my own crazy line of work.

I knew from extensive study, firsthand application, from direct observation about all levels of pain and injury a human body could sustain and still heal enough to keep on living, keep on functioning. I knew of every unimaginable thing a human being could invent to debase another, to make them beg for the mercy of a slow, agonizing death. What I didn't know, I'd been exposed to enough to make a very good guess.

I didn't need details to know what he'd suffered. What he'd endured. What he'd conquered, if he was sitting beside me, whole and strong now.

And I took it all back. Uncertainty was fine by me here. I'd take my morbid imaginings. His stiff upper lip dismissal made me certain of one thing.

The worst my mind could conjure up was far better than reality.

He'd taken my hand, seemed bent on examining my very fingerprints. I almost snatched it away. Mine had to be the worst kind of hands a woman could have. A surgeon's and a fighter's. Not pretty.

"They were after information we didn't have." He went on, his cultured, precise tones steady, droning. Hypnotic. "So they kept at it. And at it. I think it became a sport. Then they began showing signs that they'd either started to believe us, or got bored. I'm almost sure they'd decided to kill us on the day four of them were severely injured in an ambush by a rival faction. I was too damaged to do anything for them myself, but I coached their comrades in what to do, and three out of the four survived.

"It was a lightbulb moment for them. They made me an offer—to stop torturing us if we cooperated in another fashion, became their resident doctors. After a year of being subjected daily to their escalating and inventive brutalities, I was beyond broken. I'd been looking forward to my execution. Unable to wait for it. I would have latched on to any way out."

I gripped his hands in mine, a thousand questions crushing one another inside me. I couldn't form coherent enough words to ask them, couldn't make a sound. All I could do was cling to his hand, try to cling to my reason.

He sighed. "I was still naive enough to think that I could use their new leniency to investigate and plan ways to escape. I found out my mistake soon enough. Now that I was such a favorite, they guarded me with far more obsessive thoroughness.

"Not that I was incarcerated. Having the double advantage of being a surgeon and fluent in Russian, I was selected to escort the militants on their raids, dispensing my medical services

to their injured and all over the villages where they got their recruits. I was the spearhead of their campaign among the simple
people who couldn't make up their minds which side was the
worse devil. With me around, they became the devil that doles
death to those who don't side with it, and mercy to those who
do."

Now that was something I could have never deduced. Using
him for their political spread and rise. Ingenious. Seemed their
leader, or leaders, were formidable strategists.

He stared ahead, his gaze turned inwardly. "I began to actually accept my situation then. I joined GCA, in part, to reach people like those I was treating, those who never hoped to get real
medical attention, especially the sophisticated surgical variety.
For a long while I was insanely busy. I had hundred-patient
weeks, sometimes days. I set up quite the medical facility. Something close to your mobile surgical trailer, in a smaller vehicle.
The militants got me all the instruments and equipment I asked
for. I didn't ask where they got them."

I knew. From raiding convoys and hospitals. But I bet a big
part of their inventory came from smuggling stolen supplies or
mining the black market.

Wondered what Jake would say if he knew what I really did
with my life now. That we probably shared the same suppliers.

"Anyway, every now and then it surfaced in my mind that I
was still a prisoner, that I didn't have a life. That I couldn't go
back to you." Good thing I was young and strong. A weaker heart
would have burst right about now. I watched his lips twisting.
"So I tried to escape. They didn't punish me. As I said, I've become too valuable. They punished my friends. I didn't try again."

I didn't know I had that much control. That I'd developed it.
The old me would have gone out there right this second and
ended his enslavement at any cost.

Too bad the new me counted to ten. Counted costs.

He shifted, sat cross-legged, still playing with my braid.

Weird, his new fascination with it. "They moved their base to this region. Then the refugees settled here. After the first few months of skirmishes with the federal forces the land mines were planted."

So they were the ones who'd put them after all. It still didn't make sense to say they'd cleared them, to invite us only to blow us up. There was more to it. But Jake probably didn't know what that was.

"While it kept the federal forces away, it also cut the refugees off from the world. And I made a deal with my captors. That they let me come here, offer my services, when they didn't have need of me themselves, of course. They humored me, but didn't extend their indulgence to making use of their supplies. It was then that I fully realized the true affiliation of those people. The lack of it."

Could he have doubted it at all, bought for a moment their patriotic hyperbole? My old Jake had been a thorough cynic. Could he have been suffering from Stockholm Syndrome till then?

"I came here at every chance, did whatever I could without much supplies and instruments. Then something changed within their command. The positive effect I was having on their operations, along with their waking up to other militant groups in the world using media manipulation and exploitation to divide the world's sentiment and opinion against their so-called enemies, made them see the necessity of changing tacks. It was then they decided to let aid come to the refugee camp. When I first knew the aid mission was actually in the camp, for a moment there, I thought it could be my chance…"

Was this how people had heart attacks? Strokes? I couldn't feel my lips. My left side was burning, the rest of me buzzing with sick electricity. I found my voice at last. I had to, to tell him. "It *is*. Oh, Jake, we're getting you out of here!"

Something came into his eyes. Satisfaction? No—not exactly. Pity? For sounding like an overwrought fool, promising him nonsense I'd never be able to fulfill? Probably. He didn't know what we were capable of. He'd soon learn.

He finally shook his head. "No, you won't, Cali. And don't you dare petition for my release. If they suspect for a moment that you know I'm their prisoner, none of you will leave this camp alive.

"Uh, rewind and replay please?" I might be having a mental meltdown, but wasn't what he just said the biggest load of crap I'd ever heard? "*If* they suspect we know you are their prisoner? They must *know* we know!"

"How would they know that?"

"Because when you were kidnapped, it made headlines."

"When I *disappeared*. Kidnapping was one of the quickly discarded theories. There had been no claims of responsibility, no ransom or demands, no discernible reason. They have no reason to believe you know they kidnapped me."

Okay. I'd just dropped a hundred points off my IQ. "What else could we think you're doing here?"

"Working with them. In fact, the only reason you know they kidnapped me is because I told you."

It was starting to make a crazy sort of sense. Or maybe my mind was coming back online.

The militants had let us come here to report back to the world with a favorable testimony about them. They wouldn't risk us going back with one filled with long-kidnapped and tortured humanitarian operatives, undoing all their efforts.

They would far sooner explain our collective deaths in an alleged ambush by a rival faction than one confirmed tale of torture and imprisonment.

But in that case, why let Jake come here at all? Risking exposure? Never one to let my curiosity go unsatisfied, I asked.

He shrugged. He hadn't lost the elegance that pervaded his every move. In fact, he'd added something more to it, something

compelling, commanding. "As I told you, they—indulge me. I'm
now, as you saw, treated with utmost respect. They fear for every
hair on my head—like an irreplaceable golden-egg-laying goose.
And I do lay gold at their feet. I made adjustments to surgical
and diagnostic instruments and they sold the patents to legitimate manufacturers for royalty-paying fortunes. So when I
learned you were here, I told them that you must believe me
dead, and I had to see you to set you straight. They refused at
first, then suddenly today, they let me come."

I had a theory about why they suddenly did, why they'd been
prodding Damian into admitting to a blazing affair between us.
It removed me as a temptation for Jake. Now, the day after
they'd seen me racing Damian to his tent, they let Jake come
here.

"They just cautioned me," he said. "As if they needed to, that
if I cared for you, to explain my disappearance in a way that
wouldn't implicate them in any way. To convince you that working for them is advantageous beyond my wildest dreams, that I
married one of their women and am leading a happy life. And
this is exactly what you must say I told you, what you must be-
have as if you believe."

He really was resigned to his life. He did think he'd just take
a glimpse of me and go back to his prison. Thought that I'd leave
him there, leave him to his fate.

Would the old Calista he'd known have done that? Walked
away, consoling herself that there was nothing she could have
done about it?

Probably. I *had* been powerless then. I would have known any
act on my part wouldn't end in his salvation, but in both our
dooms. It had been knowing *that* that had driven me to never
again be powerless, or to use helplessness as an excuse.

How could I tell him that his imprisonment *was* coming to
an end? I had to tell him what I'd become first. No time now. I
had far more important things to ask him.

"Where do they keep you, Jake?"

He shrugged. "In the lap of luxury." I winced and he insisted. "I mean it. You wouldn't believe how equipped and luxurious their mountain hideaway is. Their dirty, rough-living look is just window-dressing, the self-sacrificing, heroic rebels living the hard life for their cause. They're actually warlords who make an obscene living."

Not surprising. But I didn't care *how* they lived. I wanted information to perfect how they died.

I heard sounds outside. They might have decided to end our interview, thought we'd had enough time to catch up on old times. I may have only seconds left. I fired questions at him. Better ones this time, more useful and specific. "About the militants, Jake. What kind of numbers are we talking about? What kind of security system and guard rotation? What level of firepower?"

"So you can launch an all-out attack and rescue me Rambo-style?" At my agitated, impatient grimace, he sobered. "Pardon me. You sounded so military-like, I couldn't resist. I know you must be curious."

He shifted, faced me fully. "About four hundred populate the base in shifts. Each set stays for a couple of weeks and rotates with the next. They come and go freely from Georgia. They chose the Georgian Military Highway so that no federal forces can attack them without invading another country's borders, while the Georgians let them be, since they have no quarrel with them. Security is lax, since there hasn't been traffic in the area for a long time now, and is mainly to guard against escapes, not against incursions. As for firepower, it's considerable. They're arms dealers after all."

That told me a lot. A few more questions would help crystallize our options and plans and we'd know when and how to strike with pinpoint accuracy.

I didn't have time for any more questions.

My tent's hard-wall door was flung open. I raised my eyes,

emptying them of animosity. And found no need to curb my hostility.

It was Damian. Striding in as if he were entitled. And daring to look angry!

I sprung to my feet. "Anything I can do for you, De Luna?"

"Not for me, *St. James.*" Stress enough here to bend a bar of steel. There was a not-even-bothering-to-be-subtle meaning for you. "It's eleven a.m. We have a huge schedule today."

I couldn't believe this. The militants putting an end to my time with Jake, I understood. But Damian? Had he lost his mind?

I crossed my arms on my chest. Mainly to stop myself ramming him out of my tent. "You can start without me," I hissed.

His glower deepened. "Our *leader* and head surgeon's presence is needed. If you can remember, we have thirteen casualties who need thorough post-op follow-ups. *If* you can bear tearing yourself away from this heartwarming reunion."

What the hell was this? Was he putting on a jealous act for the militants' benefit? If he was, it should have ended the moment he'd stormed inside the tent. Sour chemistry or not, he should have pounced on Jake with open arms, for all possible reasons.

So was he jealous for real? Oh, sure. It took a slip of my tongue, after I'd shared my body with him—and I didn't know how much more besides—for him to reveal what he really felt about me. I'd thought he'd never forgive me, resented desiring me when I thwarted him and got on his nerves. But never for a minute had I thought he hated me for real.

He'd put me straight on that. His hatred was real all right, tangible and staggering. If I were the type to let such blows shake me up. I wasn't.

So he couldn't be jealous. And even if he was, with some primitive male impulse, I wanted to kick his ass for it! He should be professional enough to control his smarting libido and inflamed ego.

I advanced on him, the intention of socking him if he didn't back off right now clear in my eye. "Matt is as good a surgeon as me and better, and he can follow-up our casualties."

"This sounds serious, Cali." Jake was getting up. Oh, no! Damian had guilted him away.

"You stay right there." He froze midmotion at my harsh order, amusement seeping into his eyes. "You'll leave only when your 'escorts' insist and not a second before!"

Damian bristled. Jake regarded me in total calm as he completed his rising motion. "I have three hours in the camp, then I have to run back to the base. I'd like to spend what remains of my time here tending to the refugees with you. Why don't you escort me to see your facilities and patients? I'll be an extra pair of hands for a while and free up one or two of your team to go tend other chores."

The only way to counteract the resolve in his eyes was to knock him down and sit on him. God, why where men so stupid?

I had to find out if all wasn't lost. "So we'll continue our conversation when you come here again?"

"I don't know if I will."

Oh, no! And the two morons were doing all they could to end this golden window of opportunity, each for his shortsighted, insignificant reasons. One was being territorial and the other feeling homesick for his cell! Could they both be so stupid?

"They're a bit tetchy with me at the moment," he explained. "My demand to visit you comes on the tail of a series of heavy-handed demands and in the middle of work they can't wait for me to finish. I'm afraid there's only so much I can get away with. On the way here they kept intimating that this was a one-off, that it was only for me to see you, that until you leave, the camp inmates have no need of me."

"Then they'd be wrong. As you said, I need every pair of hands. And when they're *your* miraculous hands, I can't wait to have them!"

Damian made a disgusted sound.

Jake pursed his lips, nodded thoughtfully. "I can argue that very point. You can add your own weight to the argument and ask for my help. Hmm, yes, it could work, since they are very open to impressing you with their goodwill. As long as you're careful, as we discussed…" Anxiety rose off Damian. Not that Jake noticed. "They won't deny us both."

"Great! Let's go set up your visiting schedule." I pushed Jake ahead of me. Let him put his familiarity with the militants to use. And his fluent Russian.

It was beginning to grate, being the only one around who didn't possess that effortless ability. I was learning two more languages on our return! *If* we returned.

Damian clamped my arm, stopping me from following Jake, his whisper fierce in my ear. "What did you tell him about us?"

Us? Or *us?* Whatever, the answer was one to both interpretations. "Nothing. I didn't have time."

"Thank God. *Don't* tell him anything."

I turned incredulous eyes on him and he shredded the words between clamped teeth. "Just—*trust* me."

All right. This was beyond weird. If not as beyond weird as the desperate look in his eyes and his hoarse…

"Please."

Chapter 18

It was that *please*.

It had a lot to answer for. I mean, Damian, pleading with me? How more unreal could we get? Was it any wonder it knocked me silent?

My logic was burning rubber, screeching at right angles trying to come up with plausible reasons for his plea. That contributed to the tangle inside my head and around my tongue.

Only knowing that Jake would be coming daily until our projected departure date arrived made not saying anything bearable. I would still get my chance to tell him everything.

When damn Damian released me from this ban of silence.

Just—*trust* me, he'd said.

I'd spent years wanting him, hating him, thinking of him whenever I had time to think at all. I owed him, huge debts of both gratitude and bitterness. I'd just had my life's defining erotic experience with him. But trust?

Sure, there was loads of that. Always had been. But my trust had been selective. I'd always thought it funny to trust him with my life but not with lesser things. Had to do with our wills locking horns from day one. Guess I never trusted him not to do anything to get his way. The only way, in his opinion.

The stunning part was, I trusted him now.

He'd said to trust him, and against every compulsion clawing inside me with the need to reassure Jake, I did.

Our approaches were still disparate, but more and more I realized we were both heading in the same direction. More than trusting him, I'd come to count on him. To believe in him.

Faith didn't come easy to me. Or at all. I didn't have faith in people, just in parts of them. No matter what they were to me. It was a biggie to have faith in almost all of him.

So, his hating me aside, I trusted the man. I still didn't appreciate the cloak-and-dagger stuff. Felt like wading in an oppressively vague movie, dubbed in colloquial Russian, no less.

I sure had issues with uncertainty. But then I also had issues with loss, oppression, exploitation, brutality, prejudice, fundamentalism… Hmm, seemed I had nothing *but* issues.

Only mitigating thing here was, Damian had truly had no opportunity to elaborate on his ban. We'd been separated since I'd gone to obtain the militants' approval for Jake's repeated visits and Damian had been whisked away by their leader to discuss a "pressing business matter."

Damian's last beseeching look as he went away haunted me.

Leave it. Focus. I had my hands literally full of bloody business now, removing the blood-soaked packs I'd stemmed my patient's retroperitoneal hemorrhage with.

And then there was the still unbelievable fact that Jake was sitting across the operating table, gowned and working with me on our patient, as if his being here and our operating together was an everyday occurrence.

He was now removing the packs that had stemmed our patient's liver hemorrhage so he could explore the extent of damage and implement definitive repairs. "Mm. The packs are a bit stuck." He flicked a calm look toward Ayesha. "More saline, please."

Ayesha at once complied, soaking the packs with saline so that he could remove them without yanking on the fragile tissues, causing renewed hemorrhage.

"Turn up the heat, please," I said without removing my eyes from his gloved fingers as they manipulated the gored organ with utmost delicacy. Lucia immediately pushed up the sliding dial of the electric blanket we had our patient on. "More heated packs," I added. "To the head and armpits—and raise IV fluid temperature to 108 degrees."

I couldn't do enough to make sure hypothermia didn't develop. Along with coagulation failure, hypothermia initiated the vicious circle of deterioration that caused death in multiple abdominal trauma casualties.

The scary thing was, it was aggressive fluid resuscitation that led to both. We referred to it as death by resuscitation.

To prevent that, I'd gone for infusing packed red blood cells and coagulation factors instead of fluids, before I'd rushed in with a damage-control surgery.

I'd lost little Goran last night during a similar surgery.

I wasn't losing *her*. No reason to now.

She'd lasted through the first stage of the surgery. She'd held up fine as I arrested her hemorrhage, prevented her deterioration, warmed and stabilized her for the second stage, the reoperation for definitive repairs a day or two later.

It had only been fifteen hours since her first surgery, but when we'd examined her, Jake had told me she was ready for the second stage now. I'd agreed. He'd said he'd like to help. I'd almost hauled him over my shoulder and ran with him to the surgery trailer in my eagerness.

"Incredible first-stage management, Cali!" Jake suddenly

said after we'd finished exploring the abdomen and pinpointing all the injuries we'd deal with. "I wouldn't have done better."

Now *that* was some over-the-top praise. I was good, but Jake had always been confident that no one could ever be as good as him. Not even close. Everyone had thought him an infuriating, condescending egomaniac.

I'd agreed that, to someone who hadn't known him, his behavior had been the essence of disparaging superiority. Normally, it would have annoyed me into kicking him into the next dimension. It hadn't. To my eyes, to the radical way my mind turned, to my extreme fascination with intense distinctiveness and eccentricity, his limitless intelligence and almost supernatural skill had not only excused anything he'd said but validated it. He'd had every right to feel superior.

He *was* superior. And then some.

Now you understand what it meant to have him praise my efforts. It elevated me into a new echelon of skill and achievement. I said something to that effect. Just a lot less eloquent. "Why, thank you kindly, sir. Coming from you, that's really something. You only ever had criticism for me."

His eyes, the only thing I could see of him beneath the surgical cap and mask, rose to me, their mind-probing feature full on. "You were starting out, your potential limitless but unformed, your basic skills being integrated into your intellect and senses. I was only correcting your direction before your abilities swerved on a permanently flawed and inferior tack."

He sure had. He'd been the one who'd implanted in me what colleagues called my uncanny diagnostic sense. He hadn't taught me for long, just a few months, but it hadn't been about time. It had only taken a couple of epiphanies under his clinical whip to shape me into the comprehensive-approach, precision physician I was now.

Weird how I'd had so many males influencing my life and being. Understandable though, starting so young, breaching only male-dominated arenas, looking like a helpless cutie. I'd been bound to stumble on patrons and mentors. I was no longer that young, or a cutie, and no arena was male-dominated anymore. I no longer needed patrons or mentors.

He examined a piece of stapled bowel. "But I can see you've fulfilled your potential. I always knew you would."

So much for not needing mentors. Guess you never got over the ones who'd taught you anything. I thrilled to his testimony. Not rational. Or commendable. Not over the open abdomen of a patient I had yet to save. "No satisfaction in my performance allowed until she's back on her feet," I said, more to myself than to him. "I lost a boy last night to similar injuries."

His assessing eyes turned to me once more. "Small, emaciated and had far more extensive injuries otherwise?"

Now how did he know that? "Yes." I gulped down the searing temptation to indulge in pity and pain.

"You have to accept it, Cali." His voice came as if from inside my head, persuasive, convincing. "We have to lose some to save most."

I raised my eyes to him, caught my breath. *He* had!

He'd accepted losing patients, had succeeded in shutting out the torment and defeat and rage. "How did you do it?"

He understood what I meant. Of course he would. He answered simply, "An epiphany, how else? And a lot of practice."

No kidding. Around here, he had all the epiphanies and practice he could possibly survive.

We fell silent as each of us worked on one of the woman's injuries. I handled the intestinal injuries, he took the spleen.

I was ready for anything, but was still stunned when he went for a splenorrhaphy, repairing the spleen, rather than the accepted, far easier and safer splenectomy and removing it.

"Always going for the hardest choice, huh?"

"I consider no other choice. There *is* no other choice."

All right. Some statement here.

He used to have the elements of that resolve. Impossible not to have it when hard had always been his easy, and hardest the first thing to start to challenge him. But his effortless achievement had been diluted by a why-bother attitude. Now, this new implacability... His ordeals had really boiled him down to his full potential. It made him awesome.

And here came the hardest and most delicate part of this particular surgery, the removal of the vascular shunt I'd place to bypass the inferior vena cava injury, and its repair.

"Medial rotation of the liver, Cali."

So he'd relegated me to his assistant's position, huh?

"Medially rotate it yourself" hovered on the tip of my tongue. I gagged on it for a second, then did as he asked, widely mobilizing the attachments of the liver to move it away so he could get to the IVC. Pride had no place here. He was the superior surgeon. If he was still anything like I remembered. I bet he was better now.

"Suction. And more exposure of the portal triad, please, Cali." His request was as tranquil as all the ones before it, his movements as he dissected the obscuring tissues and repaired the vessels a blur of fluency and assurance, the vein seeming to seal and reform under his hands.

This was the one thing I remembered with total clarity about him. Whenever Jake had entered the O.R., everyone had sagged with relief. Another patient saved for sure. No matter how bad their prognosis had been.

Long-forgotten sensations resurfaced, swelled. Awe, adulation, a touch of envy. The irresistible urge to reach out and touch those instruments performing such miracles. As I'd done the first time I'd seen him in action, setting all of this in motion. None of it would have happened if I hadn't touched him that day...

"Do you remember the first time we met, Cali?"

I dropped the needle I was suturing the rectus abdominus muscle with. Ayesha tutted and handed me another one. I glared at Jake. "Quit reading my mind, Jake. This is getting spooky!"

His eyebrows disappeared beneath his cap. "You used to love it when we thought the same thing simultaneously."

"Yeah, but now it's unilateral. I don't appreciate being a one-way, see-through mirror."

"Maybe I've sucked dry your ability, boosting mine." His eyes bore into me as he palmed an already threaded needle holder from Lucia, tinged by gauging, challenging humor.

"That would make you what? A mental vampire?" Lucia asked, only half joking. No need to guess what tinged her eyes as they flitted over Jake. Severe attraction. And intimidation.

I could see where the intimidation came from.

Before the authority he commanded in the O.R., she'd been there to see his weird influence over both militants and refugees. I could swear they held their breaths as he approached. He'd always had charisma, but it had been laid-back and exercised at will, which wasn't often. Now it seemed on all the time, at screaming pitch.

Witnessing his captors fidgeting under his steady power had been strange in a major way. They'd wanted to refuse him the demand to visit us. And couldn't. As for the refugees, I bet they wouldn't treat the messiah with more deference.

He took a drain from Ayesha with another gentlemanly nod, sutured it into place. She was the only other one who knew Jake from way back when. Her succinct reaction to the sweeping changes in him had been, "Lord. Jake under the effect of red Kryptonite."

She made another supernatural analogy now. "Jake probably is some sort of real vampire. Back when I worked at the same hospital with him, he never slept. Has to get his unlimited energy somewhere not quite kosher."

Haiku, who'd been almost dozing off after she'd worked her butt off on all our surgeries yesterday, perked up at hearing one of her favorite subjects. "It's the mystique of his apparent resurrection that makes him outstanding vampire material."

Jake cleared his throat. "*He* is right here."

Not registering his protest, Lucia, who was more than a little superstitious, said, only half joking, "But we've seen him in sunlight and with a lot of blood around and not a fang in sight."

The others laughed, and they launched into a discussion of what else he could be among the creatures of supernatural lore.

I continued working, listening, my mind taking in snatches of conversation, straying.

It had been drenched in sunlight and blood that I'd first seen him.

It was my second year in med school. They'd invited students interested in getting early hands-on surgical orientation to train under a few surgeons who'd agreed to have sophomores on their teams. I'd been picked for his.

Or as he'd told me later, *he'd* picked me. He'd seen me at sign-up and had demanded I be on his team, for very unprofessional reasons. To his regret. He hadn't realized how young I'd been.

At twenty-six he'd been nine years my senior, a prodigy himself and already not just a senior resident, but the only surgeon we'd ever seen who'd served in the Gulf War and who'd come back with his mythical reputation already formed.

I'd entered that sunlit room that he'd had transformed into an O.R. to him wading in the blood of catastrophic multiple injuries victim, preparing myself for a letdown. Surely no one could live up to all that hype?

He'd surpassed it. I'd been entranced by his performance. And it hadn't been because I'd been green.

After the surgery I'd ambushed him in the doctors' room, reached out for his hands. I wanted to see for myself, what they were made of, what energy ran through them. He'd let me turn them over, examine them phalanx by phalanx. Perfect hands, genius and symmetry and precision made flesh and bone. They'd finally taken both of mine in one, as the other cupped my cheek. Then he said, part aroused, part angry, part elated, "You'd better reach the age of consent quickly, Calista St. James."

As if it had been up to him!

Eighteen had come, and nineteen after it, and I'd continued our relationship platonically. Just about. I'd loved him, wanted him, with all the idiosyncrasies of an irrepressible, cocky and not a little narcissistic teenager. But I'd known my flaws, my emotional immaturity, been too eager to utilize my energies in other stuff. Sex would have taken my edge, a man my focus.

I'd turned to him for all-the-way sex and solace only after Clara. And it had been good. Not as can't-wait-to-devour-him-can't-get-enough as with Damian. Jake's attraction had been overwhelmingly intellectual, with healthy sexual overtones.

Then I'd left med school and joined GCA. I'd known there had been no way to continue a relationship with us so immersed in different pursuits, so divided by distance and purpose.

So he'd just followed me to the GCA. He'd proposed the day he had. I'd almost said yes, so overwhelmed, so guilty that he'd thrown away his rocketing career to be with me. So stunned that he had, that he'd felt that much for me.

But it hadn't been a reason to accept.

It had been almost a reason to refuse.

So I'd run to a middle ground, asked for a continuation of our status quo, for more time. He'd said he'd been mine since I'd taken his hand in mine. He'd give me all the time I needed.

There hadn't been any. He'd disappeared on his first assignment without me.

I'd touched his hand and sent him to hell.

Damian had said almost the same thing. Hard to believe. A more unlikely femme fatale never lived...

"Warm, stable. She's going to be fine."

Jake's assessment dragged my focus back to our patient. We

checked her vital signs one last time. Then Lucia and Ayesha took her I.C. and Jake and I headed for the soiled room.

He looked down at me as we stripped off our scrubs. "Did you ever imagine we'd finally work together this way?"

I huffed a laugh. "Until very recently I believed the only way I could work with you was in some afterlife O.R."

"I, on the other hand, have had highly detailed scenarios that we would, and just *how* we would."

"Telepathy to foretelling? Did you see how I'll head an aid mission complete with a surgical trailer and you'll descend from your mountain prison to join me—and to steal my thunder, too?"

His eyes mocked me back. "I admit I got a few details wrong. Yours. The two dozen extra pounds, the drastically cut and dye-tired hair, the 'character' lines."

I giggled. "How chauvinistic and superficial of you."

"Well, *I* have changed beyond recognition. I was trying to be fair to you in expecting that you have, too. Very unfair of *you* not to have changed, Cali."

Everything slammed into me, his bared desire, my rising confusion. *Keep it light.* "Aren't you too young for your eyesight to be going?" I walked out of the soiled room, escaping the crowding emotions, his overwhelming presence, passed the others as they cleaned up and prepared for another surgery on my way out of the trailer. "Or is it your memory?"

He jumped out first, handed me down. Ever the gentleman, huh? "My memory is an audio-video precision facility," he said softly and ooh, Mama! That heat better *not* be blushing! "On the outside, you only changed for the best. So tell me about the inner changes. What happened to bring them about?"

"Besides having my sister and later my lover dying on me through acts of criminal omission or commission, you mean?"

He just raised one eyebrow, expectant. I sighed. "If you need more reasons, how about my father finally going out there and eliminating forty serial rapists and killers who'd weaseled out of convictions on technicalities? That when he was caught he didn't even get the same leniency they'd given his 'victims'? That he has a life in prison to look forward to? That he's more in solitary confinement than not and before I came here I hadn't managed to hear his voice for three months? Oh, and that my mother went away two years ago? That I don't expect to ever see her or hear from her? So, enough for you?"

He studied me for a long moment. "It is, for you."

I chewed on this. He thought my losses—what? Trivial? Indulgently emotional? I doubted anyone could call them that. But compared to what he'd gone through and was still going through, *anything* would be.

"How's your father faring in prison?" he asked, low, solemn. "I should imagine a vigilante would not be popular in prison."

"You'd imagine wrong. He says he's not incarcerated with criminals, *they* are with him. He's become the kingpin of an octopoid vigilante operation set up from the inside, with his toll on crime in the last five years a thousand times that of his twenty years as a hyperactive cop on the streets."

Something leapt into Jake's eyes—raw, fierce. Surprise? Admiration? *Relief?* For Dad? No—something else… Not sure what…

"I always liked your father," he said, his aura once more placid, unreadable. And my father had liked him. Which still had me scratching my head. Such opposites in temperament should have had a hard time tolerating each other. "Now I know exactly why."

While I knew exactly nothing!

I wanted him to elaborate on that hundred-implication statement. I couldn't. His keepers were coming for him. With just a "See you tomorrow" and a last glance that penetrated my marrow, he turned and made his way through the militants, heading them back to their Jeeps.

Damian, who seemed to have been with the militants the whole time, walked up to me, his stormy expression almost a relief to witness after Jake's opacity. Not so welcome was the way my senses rioted at his approach.

Towering over me, body, anger and angst, he watched the Jeeps receding in the verdant horizon. "So, St. James, have you defied me?"

Defied him? And St. James, huh? Riiight. "Get over yourself, De Luna."

"You never got it, did you? It's never been about me. It's always been about you. And about you making me your accomplice."

Chapter 19

"What the hell are you talking about?"

What the hell was I asking? This had to be another blame blitz of some sort. Thanks, but I didn't think so. And he wasn't distracting me. "Don't bother answering that. I have better questions. Like what's this about not telling Jake anything? And what's that business the militants had with you?"

"I couldn't refuse to solve their logistical problems." He gave a short furious chuckle. "I've now made sure they have a smooth chain of supply plan in place."

"And my first and main question?"

For answer I got his hand clamping my arm and a ragged "We need to talk."

Talk? As in talk? Now? After six years? After telling me he hated me? I itched to knee him again.

Too bad I needed to hear what he had to say. If not what he probably wanted to say. Oh, what the hell! Let's get all dirty laundry lined once and for all. I knocked his hand off, led the way back to my tent. "Make it fast. I still have that packed schedule you so kindly reminded me of three hours ago."

The moment he entered behind me I turned on him, doing what Jake's presence here three hours ago had stopped me from doing. I rammed his chest hard with both open hands. I meant to hurt.

I did. Not that he showed it. Nor the slightest hint of surprise. He'd known this was coming, even when *I* hadn't. He'd been ready for it. No. Eager. His expression flooded with a give-me-all-you-got sensuality. Glad to oblige.

I rammed him again, needing to make contact, impact. Needing him to fight back, physically. He parried this time, one smooth knee bend dipping him to the side, letting one of my palms thrust air, the other glancing off his arm, expending my unspent momentum in a barely checked forward stumble.

Time for finesse. To make him an offer he couldn't refuse. We both really wanted, needed this.

I grappled with him, as if I was going for a *ko uchi gari,* my favorite *nage waza* judo throw, a minor inner reap sweeping one leg from the inside, while a frontal lunge took him down. He countered by widening his stance, pitching his upper body weight at me. Just what I was after, for the real throw I had in mind, a *ma sutemi waza,* the direct sacrifice judo technique.

I threw myself backward, clinging to him, bringing my leg up, my foot lodging in his midriff, the force of my fall, my leverage and his own pitched weight completing the *tomoe nage,* the circle throw. He flew over me in a full somersault, ended on his back. For about half a second. Always amazed me when he did one of those arms- and leverage-free elastic rebounds to his feet. Okay, so I could do it. He'd taught me, relentlessly. Then I'd perfected it. But I didn't tip the scales at two-hundred-plus pounds or have a six-foot-five frame!

He came after me in an *ô soto guruma,* a major outer wheel

designed to sweep both legs from beneath me by hitting the backs of my thighs, and slamming me on my back. I used his momentum first, did a *yoko otoshi,* a side sacrifice throw, my legs splitting open sideways, one intercepting his legs, tripping him, my dragging weight bringing his mass in a cartwheel flip over to my side. I loved judo. Maximum efficiency with minimum effort. Weight and size and strength mattered nothing here.

He rebounded again, his eyes blazing stimulation and lust.

This was what our rigorous training sessions had been like. Mind-emptying, senses-expanding, sharp, taxing, crucial. Thorough demand and satisfaction. Nothing better. Couldn't wait for the next attack. Especially since I was winning. And he wasn't *letting* me win. He never had. Never would.

I threw him again, twice, once with a hip technique, then with another side sacrifice one. He rose from the last throw, exhilaration setting his face on passionate fire. "Who's been honing her skills behind my back?"

His teasing kicked in my loins as he swung me up in a carrying-me-over-the-threshold hold. Showing me he could end it by simply picking me up? Nah. Damian wasn't into posturing. He knew if this were a real fight, he'd have a smashed face by now. He was indulging in this steam-venting exercise we'd wordlessly agreed on. This was the prelude to a throw. He'd just picked one that would give us both maximum pleasure first.

Next moment he completed the *ura nage,* the rear throw, hurling himself down in a sacrifice throw, flipping me over his shoulder and in a backward cartwheel.

I landed on my back. Ouch. So I hadn't thrown him on the mattress when I could have either. We ended up head to head. Then he tucked and flipped, arcing backward and landed on top of me. His mass impacted me, crushing, assuaging—necessary.

Then the real fight began. I took his tongue, fed him mine, ground my flesh into his. The time we'd been apart, all that we did when we weren't seeking, mingling, fell away, just necessary impurities in between pure living. This. Here. Now. In each other. Essential—on every profound and basic level…

What about Jake?

Oh, God, Jake! He stirred me, on so many levels, too, just poles apart in texture, whispering to different needs, satisfying my picky mind… But so did Damian, dammit!

Never thought I'd be in this position.

So damn flattering and oppressive and confusing.

My body wasn't confused. It sure knew its own mind, chose Damian, wept for him.

But Jake had had the disadvantage of being dead to me for the past eight years. Maybe given half the chance Damian…

"Damian!" An outburst of pleasure punched out of me. He was reacquainting with my still-sore yet open-to-anything breasts. Then he came up, caught every decibel and gasp and tremor, ravenous, dominant, supplicant.

Boy, could he *kiss!*

It didn't help any that his hands and teeth invented new erogenous zones wherever they landed, sure of their reception, their impact. Mine had wised up after last night's lessons, too. His growls told me every time I made inventions of my own.

His erection thrust a simulation through our clothes and I writhed to contain him, thrust back, imprisoning his hips in greedy legs, no more moral dilemma. I needed him inside me.

"Calista—I want to love every inch of you—I will—but first I need to feel you around me, *querida.*…"

I jerked. Hell—he wasn't supposed to say things like that. That way. And *querida*? That alone had me almost climaxing.

But it also made me remember. What he'd said, this morning and minutes ago. How all this had started.

My body screamed at me. *Remember later!*

And have him tell me afterward how much he hated me? Again?

God, I was tempted. To at least let him continue what he was doing, fondling where all my need converged, promising an off-the-Richter-scale release. I just needed to drink deeper of his taste, grind harder into his hand, let the wave crash on me…

I couldn't. Guess I didn't have it in me to take my pleasure and deal with the fallout later.

Last night, giving in to the long-awaited explosion of our simmering status quo had been unstoppable. Now there was Jake, and Damian had told me what he really felt about me and he'd been right saying this was all wrong. When his mind had done the talking.

Gasping and grunting, already cramping with deprivation, I shoved at him. He slid off me, didn't press his point.

We lay side by side, breathing hard, our flesh cooling fast. Thank God for the almost-zero temperature. Who needed a cold shower now? In two minutes we'd be talking hypothermia though.

I scrambled to pull my clothes back on. He straightened his far slower, unabated hunger coming off him in waves. I turned my eyes away, sat back on my heels redoing the braid he'd managed to undo at some point.

Suddenly he drawled, "I lied to you, Calista."

Huh?

"I said I hate you more than I hate myself," he explained. "That's a lie. I *tried* to hate you. It didn't work."

Then what did he feel? Did I want to know? Didn't I have enough on my hands dealing with how I felt?

"I loved Melissa. She was fun and strong and passionate—and she loved me."

Uh, was there a point to this cut-and-paste leap in logic?

"I thought it was the most I could feel. Then you walked into Sir Ashton's office, sat there, spitting fire at me, left me bloodied and bruised, and I no longer knew anything."

Him and me both! And he'd felt this way then, had hidden it that well? For that long?

"You asked why I had her on my team. She wasn't, even though she always wanted to be. Then you happened—and I took her on my team. My response to her waned every time I was exposed to you, and I felt so guilty I let her have her wish. I thought I might be cured if I had her with me all the time. I wasn't."

So that was why he hated himself. And me.

He jerked his head in a disgusted gesture. "But that wasn't why I hated myself and would have given anything to hate you."

I should give up even trying to come up with deductions. In emotional stuff it seemed beyond me to even hit the board.

He came to stand before me now, made sure I got first-row view of his revisited agony. "Want to know the real reason? That night in Darfur, she'd done her part and I'd sent her to safety. Then you hit me, ran off to get yourself killed and I could think of nothing but you in danger. I ordered them back, led the haphazard counteroffensive, knowing I was leading them to death. I sent her to die instead of you."

Oh. My. God.

This was what he lived with. What he believed he'd done.

"I still didn't hate myself fully then."

There was more?

I shouldn't be listening. I owed Jake and the others my stamina. This was horrifying, undermining. And history. I'd let it prey on me when the here and now took its dues.

He was bound on sharing his torment, whether I liked it or not. "I drove to her funeral after I testified against you, and all I could think of was that *you* had gone out of my life. I hated myself when I stood by her grave and mourned losing *you!*"

I recoiled, inside and out, images of the bubbly Melissa bombarding me. Gone, sacrificed for me, then not even mourned as she deserved. I hadn't mourned her enough, either.

No wonder he'd hated both of us. Now I did, too.

Only mitigation was that he'd always treated her with love and respect. I'd seen it. She'd died believing in his love.

I said so. And he just laughed, furious, scathing. "Really? A smart woman like her—*any* woman would have known how I felt."

"*I* didn't!"

"Didn't you?" His narrowing eyes forced a stark self-confrontation on me. Had I?

"I don't know." And I didn't. "I was too immersed in experiencing our conflict, in the currents between us, I just didn't put a definition to what was going on between us. Especially on your part. On my part, whatever I felt, you were someone else's and that was that."

He took a step closer, cupped my face in his large palm. A wave of unwilling longing rushed to meet his touch. "So we were commendably righteous. But didn't life surge into you, didn't everything and everyone fall out of focus—cease to matter even— the moment I was around? Didn't life dim when I wasn't?"

Yeah, all he said. Him, too? God, had we been obvious?

He clearly thought we had been. "I bet you Mel saw it all. Acting on it wasn't the issue, it was enough she *felt* who I really craved. I bet if I'd left her she would have felt rejected and betrayed, but she would have had the relief of hating me. Staying with her and wanting someone else, I only made her feel worthless while depriving her of that comfort."

Had I ever hated it that I couldn't read him? Why didn't I ever count my blessings? Here he was, throwing the whole open large-print book at me to read. And Lord—it hurt.

Something profound to mitigate his searing guilt was in order. "You must stop thinking you helped me kill Mel or the others." All right. Not so profound.

He gave my trembling efforts to absolve him the deserved ridicule, laughed. "Yes, ma'am. I'll stop right away."

"You must. You were right, before you had time to whip yourself over it all with survivor's guilt. Before you invented new versions of what happened. The blame *is* fully mine."

He shook his head, dismissing. I needed an eloquent closing argument. "And I never even noticed you looking at me funny."

So my eloquence had been swept away by the burst dam of revelations and realizations. Sue me.

"Funny, huh? And *never* noticed? Are you for real?"

"Don't underestimate your acting abilities, Damian. I do believe Mel didn't notice, either. I'd have known if she saw me as a rival. I'm not *that* vibe handicapped."

"I wonder. Because I looked—funny, and every other way. And I hungered. How I hungered for you, Calista—last night, just now? That's just the tip of the iceberg."

My own hunger thrashed inside the confines of my body, like a chained fire-breathing dragon clawing against the walls of its prison, roaring for its mate.

He came behind me, wrapped me in mighty, shaking arms. I pressed back into him. Necessary. The only word for him. He buried hot, ragged kisses in my neck and my pulse leaped to smother itself in his kiss. "I can no longer fight it—fight us, Calista. I won't. There's no point anymore. I'm already damned, and I want to be damned for taking it all."

I barely handled my quota of conflict and guilt without his compounding torment. Or his temptation to purge them by plunging into the very reason behind them and gorging on each other.

I pushed away. "You said it would jeopardize the mission...."

He clung to me, turned me, enveloped me. "I take it all back. We're professional enough not to let it. As for fearing for you and having that affecting my judgment, this will remain the same whether we're lovers or not."

"So we might as well be, huh?"

"Yes." The sexy hiss vibrated against my lips, spread all through me. Mmm—why was I resisting this again?

Ah, yes, just about a hundred reasons.

I bit his lip and he crushed me to him, deepened the kiss. I bit harder and he groaned and transferred his abused lips to my neck. "Presumptuous, aren't you?" I gasped, desire ripping through me. "You tell me it was just a night of solace and mind-blowing sex—and a mistake. Then you tell me it wasn't and you want it to be a regular thing."

"The word's *steady*. And it isn't a thing, and you know it."

"Do I?"

He put his hands on my shoulders, his eyes serious, pledging. Oh, wow. "Not for me. I don't go for *things*. It's either real or I don't have time for it. Hell, I don't have time or a place in my kind of life for *real* either. But you…"

"You'd make time and place for me, huh?"

"I don't have a choice here, Calista. I never needed anything or anybody. I need you."

So simple. So sledgehammer sincere. I had to stop letting him do this to me. Had to breathe. Crazy wanting, even loving were one thing. But need? We were taking another dimension here.

Could I afford need? Could he? Investing the biggest part of our beings and going nuts anticipating loss and devastation? Which brought me to the much-debated, never-satisfied question.

"What are you doing in this kind of life, Damian?"

He blinked, then burst into one of those displays of virile amusement. "Is this your way of telling me to take a hike?"

"You think I'd tell you to take a hike *indirectly?*"

He laughed again. "Touché. And good. Because I won't. Never again. So—why I'm in this life." He shrugged, mischief making him even more edible. "It's because my father was a Colombian drug lord. And before you search your database for it, De Luna is my mother's family name.

"She worked as an interpreter for his legit scam in the U.S. and had an affair with him. Then she found out the truth and reported him, and he fled the U.S. He abducted me when I was a year old, and I lived with him in Colombia until I was sixteen. Let's say I learned…a lot there. I managed to escape him then and returned to the States and my mother. All I wanted ever since was to be one of the people who put people like him out of business. Out of this world."

"You're kidding me, right?"

"Would I dare kid you?"

I stared at him. As enigmatic as ever, but it felt as if I suddenly possessed the key to his arcane code.

He was telling me the truth.

"Oh, man!" I was still unable to work the controls of my hanging open mouth. So that was his story?

Impossible to imagine, the difference between our first sixteen years. Mine had been idyllic. A model family, everything I ever wanted, safety, stability… While his—could we have had more different formative years? I shook my head. "You had to go have a life story to make mine look disgustingly dull, huh?"

"Yeah. It was all meant to top you." I poked him and he dragged me into his embrace, devoured me until I forgot everything. Again. Not good, these amnesia attacks.

I unfused our bodies. "And how did you stop being a SEAL?"

His hands ran down my buttocks, grinding me back into him, his lips twitching at my curiosity. I'd never displayed it and now it all but snapped insatiable jaws at him. "I left. I wanted to be a decision maker not just—pardon the pun—the executioner."

Made sense. All of it.

Now to wrap up… "So, this is why you went all out to punish me? For the feelings you can't control? The guilt?"

His tongue skimmed the imprints of my sensual abuse, pained pleasure transfiguring his face. I waited for the surge to abate, for him to justify the actions that had changed my life.

He shrugged. "Believe it or not, no. Not in the least. You had to be stopped then. You were out of control, drunk on your new-found power and fast becoming an extremist. I wasn't waiting until you ended up dead, mad or at best behind bars. Mel and the others or not, I would have tried my best to put you out of action until you found your brakes."

I believed him. That he believed in his cause, had acted in honest conviction. I had to be honest, too. "For what it's worth, I think you did achieve your goal. I don't know if you agree, but I hope I have the whatever-the-cost persona under control."

His eyes sobered. "It all depends, if you've told Constantine what we're here for."

Suspicion surfaced, crystallized in a heartbeat. "Does this 'talk' have anything to do with Jake's sudden appearance?"

I really should stop with the projections. I expected an instant denial. I got a sigh and an admission. "It did jolt me into doing this straightaway, instead of tomorrow."

Staking his claim first? Making sure I didn't sleep on the idea that he'd cut me loose and I was free to jump whichever way? Not sure I liked that.

Not sure what he'd meant by that accomplice shot, either. "So you say I create danger, you run to save me and the blood of those who end up dead is equally on your hands. What would make you my accomplice now?"

"If you tell Jake about us and our plans and he leaks info, we end up with a critical situation, I do anything to get you out of it in one piece, history repeats itself."

That was it? "I don't need you to get me out of anything. And Jake is anything but stupid. If he's in the know, he can provide us with invaluable insider information."

He set his teeth, hissed, "We don't need it."

"You don't need to know that there are about four hundred in there, that they rotate every two weeks and that the security is geared toward outbreaks not break-ins?"

"He told you all that? God, Calista how did you ask? If you let him suspect you're gauging status for a rescue op…"

"How could he, Damian? He knew me as a doctor working in an aid agency. He even joked about my questions, asked if I was asking to stage a Rambo-like rescue mission."

"It could mean he suspects—"

"It means he can't even begin to suspect."

"Even so, we don't need his info. Tonight we'll probably locate the militants' stronghold. Then it's a few more days of following their schedules and laying a plan of attack. What he has to offer isn't worth the risk of tipping them off. He may be the most intelligent man on Earth, but can you vouch for how someone in his situation may react to hope and anticipation?"

His point was getting clearer. Too clear. Damn. I still tried. "I just want to give him hope that his captivity is coming to an end."

"Are a few more days of the same old no hope on his side and no appeasement on yours too big a price for the mission's success?"

No price was too big. And Jake would probably suffer more knowing, going crazy wit anticipation, might even lose it, fulfilling Damian's prophecy.

Let's face it, Jake didn't need to know. *I* needed to tell him. I hated it when Damian was right. About me.

Was my mind so see-through?

"I need your word, Calista."

"I'll need to know what you'll do with it first."

"Calista!" He advanced on me and I started walking before he touched me again, snared me into more madness or heartache.

"Oh, you have it." I tossed over my shoulder. "Put it to good use. Now hop to it. I need five hundred X-ray plates."

It took control I didn't know I had not to answer his "Tonight, after the patrol" demand/command/plea with a resounding "Yes!" to stagger out of the tent, leaving him to resolve his huge dilemma.

Frigid air slapped through my lust-fogged mind. I couldn't believe it. I'd forgotten to ask! Why he was here at all!

Now I knew the facts, it was even weirder for him to be relinquishing his sought-after decision maker's role for an executioner's again. Did it have something to do with me? Again?

I might be deduction impaired where he was concerned, but whatever the truth was, I knew I wouldn't like it one bit.

Chapter 20

We found the militants' stronghold.

It took two nights, three close calls and one literal cliffhanger along the way. José ended up with a broken left forearm and Ari with a bone-deep calf gash. I got to play doctor a mile up with tempest-level winds almost tossing me about and into the abyss.

But it all went as predicted. Far better than predicted.

During our exploration of the base's perimeters to determine all possible routes of approach, attack and retreat, we discovered an ingeniously concealed opening into a new route that led all the way down the mountain.

It was gently sloping, wide and secure enough for a vehicle the size of our biggest trailer to make it all the way up there.

Sure enough, we found another grotto garage right on the other side of the exit, filled with high-end vehicles.

We tracked the route down until it forked. We split, each team following a tire-track-filled branch, mapping it out. The one my team followed circumvented the minefields and led onto a clear path into North Ossetia. The other branch was a round-about, highly disguised yet safe route to the camp.

And we hadn't been told about it.

Ed pointed out evidence that suggested that this route was new. A few weeks old at most. It still didn't explain why they hadn't told us about it. Not to mention how it had escaped PATS intelligence radar. A spectacular empty expression trans-mitted Damian's opinion on that. His own people had messed up bad. He wasn't happy. And neither would they be once he returned.

As for why the militants weren't using it, from the looks of the vehicle fleet in the garage, the high ranks had reserved it for themselves, either leaving the small fry militants who frequented the camp in the dark about its presence or denying them access to it. After all, why make their lives easier? Felt like something the treacherous head honchos would do.

The route's discovery meant that setting up our plan and ex-ecuting it would work far better than projected.

My team caught up with Damian's on the route back to the camp and we made it back at dawn after nine hours of grueling physical exertion, bushed but exhilarated by our new discovery.

This was going to work. I could taste it.

Then we headed for our tents and Damian caught up with me at mine and I was tasting him, his demand ragged against my lips. "Come to bed, Calista."

Shades of Pentothal-induced confessions! The way he said that! The same as that time in my condo when I'd hit him with the truth serum.

But after his unforced confessions a couple of days ago, and with Jake coming here in hours, I was spinning on one gigantic guilt merry-go-round, feeling like a slime bag all around.

I stepped away, escaping it all. He wouldn't let me. "We don't have to make love. Let me wrap around you as we sleep."

And I wanted him all around me, surrendering consciousness and care to our intimacy. But not make love, too? "Yeah, right!"

He licked smiling lips that said my skepticism was well-placed. "If you're worried about crucial sleeping time, I can promise swift satisfaction." I'd bet. Lightning swift, the way I was primed. He sobered, pressed me harder. "We've wasted enough time, Calista. Who knows how much more we have left?"

"Trying to make me desperate, Damian?"

"Is it working?"

And how. The idea of anything happening to him rated up there with having all my limbs snatched off. And my heart. I wasn't telling him that. I kissed him though, putting all my confusion in the fierce mingling of flesh. Then I pushed him away.

He let me this time. "Do you want me to stop pursuing you?"

"Would you?"

"The words *hell* and *freezing over* come to mind."

I laughed, pinched his cheek. "Hold that thought." I turned and dived into my tent. One more touch and I would have hauled him inside with me. Not a good idea when in four hours I had to be up and in surgery.

Not a good idea, period.

"Are you sure this is how they all died?"

The young man, my informant as the guys called him, nodded.

"I need more details. If it's a contagious disease, we can take steps toward stopping further contamination and spread."

Mishinko smoothed his long, lank blond hair from his eyes, blinked his hesitation at me. He really wanted to share his suspicions of how thousands of his fellow refugees had died.

His mouth opened. So did the door of the minor surgery compartment after a perfunctory knock. I immediately felt Jake's presence, saw its effect on Mishinko. The guy freaked out!

Mishinko jumped to his feet, blabbering something about being needed back in the camp's school. I barely held him back to finish wrapping his stitched forearm in gauze and jab him with antibiotic and tetanus booster shots. Then he streaked away.

I turned on Jake. "So good of you to scare off my patient."

Jake raised his immaculate eyebrows. "He behaved as if he was caught making lewd advances and was scared of being roughed up by the competition."

Mishinko had been making excuses to come here. This last injury could have been self-inflicted. Damian made him twitchy, too. If the truth was as ugly as I thought, he'd be right to be terrified if anyone overheard any of it.

"So, what's going on here?" Jake pulled off his gloves, threw them in the bin, picking up my list and scanning the cases I had for my afternoon. He'd been in the adjacent compartment performing minor surgeries all morning.

"You tell me. You've been coming here longer."

"I actually meant why you're working alone and I had three highly qualified nurses helping me."

Because Mishinko would only talk to me alone. "Oh, I didn't need anyone."

"And I did?"

Of course he didn't. "The ladies were just being helpful. And curious. Smitten, too, if I know anything."

He laughed. It felt so weird. He'd been coming for the last six days, from midday till sunset, working with me. And it felt so good. So natural. As if everything was okay. As if the past eight years hadn't happened. As if we'd go on like this forever.

As if tomorrow all hell wasn't breaking loose.

Jake touched the backs of two fingers to the side of my neck. "What about you? Curious and smitten yourself?"

My eyes closed, at his touch, at the intensity, in his all-seeing eyes, fueling his suddenly raw words.

There he went again, probing my feelings for him.

What did it matter to him what I felt if he believed, as he did, that in a few days he'd never see me again? Did he just need the comfort of knowing that I hadn't forgotten what we had, that if it were possible, if it were up to me, I'd be with him again?

If I thought I'd never see him again, I would have given him that comfort. But I was getting him out of here. I couldn't build up hopes that might never come to pass.

I prepared for the next patient, tried to concentrate on anything but his warping effect. The others, busy outside, the buzz of diagnostic equipment, the inflow of patients. The despondency of knowing it was all ending with so much left undone.

This was our last day here. We were not only running out of supplies, our plan was in place.

It had to be tomorrow, or never.

Jake wasn't taking evasions this time, coming up behind me. "I know I've been dead to you for too long." His voice was low, injected with a calm and terrible emotion. "That you've given up and moved on. I know you're confused. But you still feel a lot for me." He pulled me back against him, in a fierce, pleading embrace. "I'm not confused. I've loved you from the moment I saw you and every moment since. And here you are, the same yet so much more than the woman whose memory has kept me alive."

My heart did its best to uproot itself. At his admission, at his hands gripping my belly, his hard body seeking mine. I wanted to press back into him, offer him comfort and a declaration of equal weight. I wanted to bolt away. To weep.

He was everything I ever thought I wanted in a partner. With this new toughness and intensity to him, he was more so than ever. My once generous, appreciative lover. Could he be again, if I gave it a chance?

He was so right. I did feel a lot for him. But even without my feelings for Damian, could I really tell what I felt when awe and fascination, guilt and compassion, attraction and the sheer emotional burden of meaning so much to him were so mixed up?

This wasn't the time to deal with this. *Get him out first, get back home with Damian in one piece. Then worry about it.*

I couldn't struggle out of his arms though. I had to make him let me go. Before I could, he turned me around and took my lips. And I remembered everything I'd forgotten about him.

They deluged me, old memories, new discoveries. The same fresh connection and taste, a new proprietary, hypnotic feel. Something else, too. Having a woman here hadn't been a lie for my benefit. I could tell when a man had been practicing.

This somehow made it easier for me to kick to the surface of his drowning kiss. He loosened his hold on me, trailed hunger down my cheek and neck. "Are you afraid to kiss me back because you'll leave me again? Afraid to hurt me? You won't. I'm hoarding memories, Cali. Memories of a far lesser you have sustained me so far. Memories of the new you will fuel the rest of my life."

Now what could a woman say to that?

Was it a conspiracy? The two men voted least liable to be romantic and eloquent about it deluging me in soul-wrenching declarations? I was so flattered I was getting suspicious. Not to mention pissed. This was tantamount to emotional blackmail. I kicked blackmailer ass, always, just couldn't here…

I extricated myself and stood two steps away, panting, examining the brooding sensuality on his starkly handsome face. His gaze dissected my expression back. *Change the subject.*

He didn't give me the chance, spoke first. "If you have a choice, Cali, would you be mine again?"

"I was never exactly 'yours,' Jake."

"Is this feminist indignation? Extremely misplaced, since I was very much yours, Cali. I still am."

Oh, man. "Jake, this isn't the time…"

"Then when? When we're saying goodbye? I need to tell you how I feel *now*. I realize you may have formed new ties, new allegiances, that you may feel torn." Torn? Try shredded! "Under any other circumstances I would have given you, *us,* time, let our attraction, our shared knowledge and convictions work their magic, as they did before." He was pulling me back into him. I bolted this time. He spread his arms, looking so defeated. "But I don't have time."

Impending heart attack aside, this reminded me. *I* didn't have time. He'd interrupted my investigation, and whatever Damian said, I had to find out.

"Jake, I'm not trying to avoid this…" He raised one of these autocratic eyebrows and I burst out laughing. I was riding an emotional yo-yo gone crazy! "Okay, just a bit." I snorted at the understatement, thumped my forehead and hopefully my jittery brain back in place. "But I'm concerned about something bigger than you and me. The rocketing mortality rates in the camp in the last year."

He leaned against the exam table, folded his arms. "How do you know what they are? I know they keep no records."

"We made our own statistics. There's an estimated fifty-four thousand people here. That's down from sixty last year. Subtracting the births and the usual number of deaths expected in this situation, and that's almost nine thousand dead."

He got that spaced out look people had while mentally calculating. "That's almost a five deaths per ten thousand people a day average. The major catastrophe figure for refugee camps."

"That's right. And the spike in deaths seems to be caused by the same thing. And it all started after refugees started being 'taken away.' In fact, many of the estimated dead are people who just never came back. Those who did, came back only to die, with outbreaks of similar deaths following."

His gaze was unreadable. I really hated this. I was used to figuring out people, to handling all situations according to my pinpointed readings. With Jake, and to a great degree with Damian, I relied on guessing games. Inept ones.

Jake took my hand to his lips, pressed warmth and worry into my palm. "Tell me you haven't been conducting investigations overtly. Implicating the militants in something like this is even far worse than in my enslavement."

"Duh, Jake. But the only open communication I had from the refugees was that you're their hero, that you've been here for them to deal with mass emergencies."

He let go of my hand, sighed. "I tried. I did manage to get the militants to cough up supplies then, but I wasn't able to save most of them. I doubt any sophisticated medical measures would have done anything for an epidemic of viral encephalitis."

I mulled this. "Hmm. The symptoms did sound like an atypical strain, but of unheard of virulence. It takes about four days from onset of symptoms to death. I have no doubt that those people were infected on purpose. And I think children are now targeted. I have reason to believe they've been rounding them up for some sort of experiment. Probably still in the investigative phase, since none of them is sick yet."

Another long, silent moment, then Jake raised his head, looking at me, not seeing me. "I heard rumors of a multinational project somewhere in the region that's developing so-called nonlethal chemical and biological weapons."

"Do you mean you think it's them who've been experimenting on the refugees? Doesn't seem nonlethal from where those people are buried."

He shrugged. "Did you hear any tales related by the sick and now deceased refugees about their experiences? Did the refugees at least tell you who exactly took their people?"

"The sick refugees were beyond talking when they were returned. I also didn't ask who took them since it never occurred to me it could be someone else but the militants."

"Whatever happened, it has to be with their approval."

"So you think they have a deal with that project, importing guinea pigs to experiment on to their hearts' content?"

"In this world, anything's possible, Cali."

"Do you have any idea where that project is?"

"Damian probably does. Why don't you ask him?"

"Damian?"

"Terrorist bases and ultra-evil mass-destruction facilities are right up his alley, aren't they?"

"How would you like to die?"

Damian didn't turn. Matt and Ed, who were helping him, exchanged curious glances before raising their eyes to me. One look made them realize the gelatin plastic explosives they were making were far more stable than I was right now. They turned to kneading in flour and bicarbonate sodium into the antifreeze and guncotton mixture with extra diligence, lips twitching. Thought it was a lover's quarrel they were about to witness, huh? That earned them a barked "Out!"

Which only earned me cool defiance, even from the traitor Matt. Neither man made a move to conclude their work except after meeting Damian's eyes and getting his corroboration. Damned male-bonding!

I didn't wait for them to exit before coming up behind Damian and hissing, "Shall I shove you into the mixture?"

Making plastique with antifreeze and the crudely manufactured and self-igniting guncotton we'd made from cotton and nitric and sulfuric acid was a delicate procedure. Not in Damian's hands though. He was a true master of anarchy science.

He put everything down with assured care, turned his eyes to me. Their eruptive potential rivaled anything the explosives were capable of. "I did something to deserve more punishment?"

More? As in I was punishing him by not sleeping with him? "Capital punishment in my book—liar!"

Every erg of animation and passion was extinguished, his eyes gem-hardening. "Is this about Constantine?"

"He calls you *Damian.* As befitting two war buddies!"

"We aren't war buddies. We crossed paths during the Gulf War, serving in very different capacities."

"Why didn't you tell me you knew him?"

"It never came up."

"Never came up?" I'd introduced them!

"Listen, Calista, we had a couple of missions together, and we didn't mix well. I forgot all about him, then years later I heard he was missing and presumed dead. Then I met you." His eyes softened, melted. "Fell for you."

Oh. No. He. *Wasn't.* "Don't!"

He ignored my bare-toothed threat. "I fell for you, then found out that he of all people used to be your lover and my interest in him was piqued. So I took over PATS ongoing investigation into his disappearance. And here we are."

"And you didn't think any of this was important enough to *come up* at any time during the past four weeks?"

"We weren't on chatting terms for most of those weeks. Then we made love and among all the other stuff going on, telling you of my affiliation with Constantine was nowhere on my list."

My outrage entered the red zone. "Not even when you were trying to sell me on the idea of not telling him *what we are?*"

"Between wrestling with you and being out of my mind wanting you, it sure didn't seem like a priority."

"Really? Was your logic malfunctioning so badly that you pleaded with me not to tell him what we're here for, when you *knew* he'd know it *the minute he laid eyes on you?*"

His face was grim now. "I knew no such thing! He knew me in the war as a tactical liaison, with duties very much like my role in this aid mission. I was recovering from an injury, and I was not supposed to be there in the first place. I was only allowed to go in a tactical-support capacity."

"Are you saying he doesn't know what you are?"

"He doesn't."

That would have depressurized the steam building up inside my skull, except for the fact that, *"He does!"*

That silenced Damian's ready retorts. When he spoke, it was slow, ominous. "What did he tell you, exactly?"

"That you were the one I should ask about the top-secret biological-chemical weapons-producing installation around here, since you're the one keeping track of all terrorism and mass-destruction efforts around the globe."

I didn't scare easy. Or at all. I shuddered now. Someone I didn't know was glaring at me. Someone scary. Merciless. Inhuman. Then the moment passed and he exhaled and shook his head, his expression so mild, so self-deprecating I questioned my seconds-before observation, scoffed at my reaction.

"That man is a genius for real, isn't he? More even. I should have known. In the couple of missions we were on, a few days each, he ended up knowing as much as any of us about our own jobs just through observation and a few comments here and there. From evidence I thought negligible, he must have worked out my real job and why I wasn't on combat duty then."

Which, knowing Jake's ridiculous IQ, wasn't far-fetched. If he'd thought Damian a Special Forces fledgling then, it wasn't too wide a leap in his uncanny logic to calculate what the years' gap had made Damian or what he was doing here.

Everything fell in place. Fell flat.

A vacuum filled my head where suspicions and anger had been a minute ago. Seemed Damian considered the conversation closed, went back to preparing more explosives.

I watched him stuffing plastique into improvised pipe bombs made from the steel tubings we'd used to set up drinking posts and latrines for the refugees, joined in automatically.

We'd been making weapons every day. We couldn't have enough. Damian turned to making napalm now. He put foam crate fillers in gasoline, left it dissolving into the thickest gel, which would deliver the most flammability, and turned to get sugar. He melted that with Epson salts for smoke bombs.

I tossed Damian an oxygen mask, put mine on. I was going to make more hydrazine and it gave off toxic fumes. With ammonium nitrate it would produce my specialty explosive, astrolite. The two components had to be mixed in the field right before use due to the compound's high sensitivity.

It was even more powerful than nitroglycerine and TNT. But what made astrolite perfect for stealth attacks was that it got absorbed into the ground and remained detonable to up to four days, in any humidity conditions. We'd already soaked the ground around the militants' base in strategic spots. Igniting it would bring everything down on our enemies, killing or trapping them, stopping them from pursuing us.

During our repeated searches, no one could have doubted the presence of any of the chemical precursors of these explosive compounds. Both we and PATS had made detection impossible.

The searchers had only found allowed drugs, like INH, or isonicotinic acid hydrazide, an antituberculous drug of which we had loads and which we'd found a way to turn into its parent hydrazine. Other compounds needed for explosives manufacture were innocently hidden in our equipment. Ammonia ran in the ducts of our refrigerator units, protecting our supply of drugs and vaccines. Nitric acid sat in steel containers with the gallons of deionized water we needed for all the lab work we had to do. Sulfuric acid we got from our cars' spare battery fluid.

My team had made ammonium nitrate from ammonia and nitric acid, added it to fuel oil to make ANFO, a high explosive. We'd produced detonators in abundance from our spent cartridges and spare fuses. We even made acetone peroxide using Haiku's and Ishmael's supply of hair bleach and acetone.

There certainly was no end to deviousness and destructive potential if you know what you're doing.

Once I was done and we'd aired the trailer and taken off our oxygen masks, Damian spoke again. "It's a good thing we're making our move tomorrow. Constantine hasn't done anything to compromise us so far, but I'd rather not put it to the test. Just tell me you haven't told him specifics. Or that *you* are in on this."

I glared at him, found his expression carefully neutral. "Again?" I gritted.

"Knowing about me and a vague plan to storm the base is something, knowing exactly how we're going to pull it off and when is another. If he knows nothing specific, there's no chance of anything going wrong. Please, Calista, let's not debate this again."

I held his entreating gaze for a second and my breath left me. Heart discharging, I finally nodded and forced myself to continue working, thoughts more volatile than anything we were working with preying on me. Two thoughts. Convictions actually.

First conviction was, he was lying.

Everything he'd just said to me was logical, valid. But it was also a lie. My faith quotient nosedived, everything started unwinding, his every word ever coming under suspicion. I couldn't even begin to formulate theories why he'd lie to me.

But he was, directly and in great detail.

Second conviction was more of a decision. Nonnegotiable and final. Even if I was being a paranoid bitch, even if I thought he had a good enough reason for lying to me, that I should heed his warnings and demands, I wouldn't.

I had to tell Jake about our plans. I was going to. Down to the last detail.

I had my reasons.

Chapter 21

Our plan was simple.

No, not simple as in moronic. I hoped.

It was a hybrid of two plans actually. Damian's and mine. And let me tell you, making that marriage had been harder than making a real one!

Damian had been adamant that my and my team's part in this was over, that we'd done all that he could have hoped for, providing perfect camouflage, ingenious weapons and explosives, and invaluable combat and intelligence work. Now it was time to use all the data and weapons we'd made together, on their own. No matter how battle ready we were, the actual attack should be left to the pros. Him and his team.

His plan was to use all our knowledge of the structure of the base and activities of the militants to ambush their leaders on the roundabout route, injuring them, but leaving enough able to run back to the base. In the ensuing chaos, the attack would commence with some distant explosions. Those who came out to investigate would be picked off. Closer detonations and a few smoke bombs would convince the rest that the idea of hiding inside the base at that time was not a good one, bringing out more. Pop, pop.

Among chaos over their injured leaders and the explosions, surveillance of the hostages would be at its weakest. If they were brought out in the open, too, the rest was easy. If not, the frontal attack would begin. That consisted of napalm, screams, gunfire, smoke bombs and killing everyone right and left until they got to the hostages.

A margin of "acceptable losses" featured strongly in that plan. As you recall, I had issues with *acceptable* losses.

My plan was far less blitzkrieg-like. At least, the first part of it was. The second part, getting the hell out of there after securing the hostages, had a disturbing resemblance to Damian's. I could see no other way then but to let his tactics take over.

Problem in his opinion had been, my plan demanded my and my team's presence right there in the thick of things. That had been where we'd hit a wall.

Damian had wanted us safe, somewhere along our escape route, where he and the others would catch up with us after the mission was accomplished.

Since I couldn't pull rank on him during this phase, it had taken protracted debate, unrelenting pressure from every member of my team, and his own team's corroboration that my plan carried more probabilities of success and less projected losses on our and the hostages' side.

He hadn't been a happy man when he'd had to finally agree to my plan, which was actually a modification of his in one vital respect. He'd glared at me with a zillion pent-up frustrations when I'd patted him on the back, telling him he'd thank me later.

I mean, why invade the base when we could be invited?

It was time to put all the trust in our medical abilities that we'd garnered so far to use. I counted on that to get an open invitation to walk into the base with the militants' fervent blessings. To even make them run to us delivering the invitation, begging us to accept it.

Damian's plan had them injuring the leaders so little or so much they'd either be stabilized or die on arrival to the base. In either case, that would have freed their men to storm out looking for their attackers. That was where my twist came in.

I intended to make the leaders' conditions steadily if not too rapidly deteriorating, but so baffling the hostage doctors would be at a loss how to even begin treating them.

Guess who else the militants could turn to?

One snag here though. Jake. I knew whatever I used, Jake would figure it out. He'd take one look at the injured and mysteriously declining militant leaders, solve the puzzle and treat them, spoiling my plan.

I needed him not to interfere, to pretend he couldn't do anything for them, that their only hope was us, so that the militants would come to us for help, rattled enough they'd let us take charge, come en force, with our trailers along.

So I told him. Everything.

I'd never forget the look on his face when I did.

He looked—proud. Of me? I'd had no time to analyze this, for his next words had been a repetition of Damian's. Not to risk myself, to let Damian take care of it. I'd shut him up with a kiss and a promise to have him free before tomorrow's sunset.

And here we were, in the very first light of dawn, waiting for the scheduled arrival of the militants' high-ranking personnel convoy.

The plan was to ambush them, do our stuff, run back to the camp to wait for the militants to come running to us, demanding our urgent intervention. Said it was simple. Let's see how the execution goes. Figuratively and literally speaking.

In newly dyed black camouflage outfits and masks, we hid

behind strategic rock formations on both sides of the road. On my side, I was sandwiched between Matt and Damian as the awaited convoy made its appearance in the distance, heralded by flailing headlights.

I felt Damian's tension. Right now, I wasn't against seeing him burst with it all.

Hiding facts burdening you, darling? How about a confession to defuse you? Maybe a good whack on the head?

Too bad it wasn't the time to kick his butt over this. Not now, not during the hours leading us here. I'd had to force on my priority controls, to resign myself that explanations didn't feature in my near-future expectations.

And then we might all end up dead, and not even finding out that Damian and Jake were secretly married to each other would matter.

Yeah, some real twisted positive thinking going on here.

Damian's tension spiked, pummeling me. Enough already. My hiss rode the wind lamenting his way. "Relax, will you?"

His angst became vocal. "With you in this world? I doubt it. No tricks, Calista. Plan's solid. Let it play."

I didn't answer him. Tricks were reserved for absolute need situations. If those arose, he'd bet his gorgeous butt there'd be some fancy ones. I hoped there wouldn't have to be.

We let the ten-Jeep convoy pass by, then Damian, Ed, José and Suz did their thing. With the improvised mufflers secured to their rifles, they took out the first and last two Jeeps' tires. The convoy came to a staggering halt, Jeeps slamming into each other, two turning on their sides.

Still-on headlights illuminated a hoped for, and, hell yes, satisfying sight. The militants pouring out of their vehicles like ants escaping water, worsening their predicament.

Then we did.

The middle armored vehicles tried to pull out of the pileup, to escape. They met the same fate. Damian's team was unerring. Then they turned on the militants.

Damian exuded calm now, in his element, a true killing machine. In under three minutes I counted twenty-nine down. Dead for sure. What else when Damian and the others meant them to be?

The high ranks were in the two middle vehicles, eight of them. They hadn't come out. I could picture them screaming in their radios for backup. Would they be so scared if they knew we wanted them alive? Sort of? It was the others who were immediately expendable.

Nah. They'd probably envy those their luck, their quick demise. I tried to summon my guilt. I got negligible stirrings. There was this issue of nine thousand snuffed refugees messing up my mercy threshold.

There was some retaliatory fire. Haphazard. Ineffective. The high ranks still lay low, clinging to the safety of their bulletproof vehicles. We'd allowed for this possibility. Time to give them a new perspective on their safety levels.

A few pipe bombs thrown grenade style and four detonated Jeeps had them running out, too, yelling surrender, before it was their vehicles' turn.

Actually, it was Matt's and my turn. With the high ranks out in the open, Damian shouted at them to drop all their weapons and lie down on the ground. They promptly did.

We came out of hiding, me and Matt and Damian, ran toward them, with the others holding their stations, protecting our backs for any possible development. Damian covered the prone militants for us while we got our stuff out.

As soon as the first couple felt the needle jab their arms they instinctively struggled. Damian kicked them unconscious for us. It convinced the others to take the Valium alternative.

As I moved to the more insidious part of my plan, Damian and Matt rushed to strip the militants for me, making sure I saw nothing more than part of the buttock I was injecting.

A giggle burst out of me. "Protecting the little lady's modesty lest the sight of the genitals of the men she's killing soil her sensibilities, huh? The very genitals she'll be examining in a couple of hours if all goes to plan?" Damian's alarmed glare was one for the books. "Just some comic relief before you burst." His urgent gesture shouted for me to shut up. "Oh, they can't hear a thing. And even if they can, they won't be in any condition to tell on me. And it *is* true…" I injected the first one with a megadose of an ultra slow-release cocktail of drugs we'd concocted. "That much phenothiazines will give them, among far more scarier symptoms, priapism—that's sustained painful erection."

Damian maneuvered my next victim for me, hissed in my ear, "Yeah, you like to give men that."

I almost choked. "Ah, his sense of macabre humor resurfaces!"

Matt, who'd only heard the first part of the exchange, turned to his second victim. "Bet this spooks their underlings more than the rest of the neuroleptic malignant syndrome."

"That's a life-threatening derangement that affects multiple organ systems," I explained to Damian as he prepared my next victim. "Shooting fever, lead-pipe-like rigidity, severe tremors, stampeding heart, off-the-chart hypertension, incontinence, hallucinations…"

He huffed a dark laugh. "Merciless terminator here, feeling decidedly humane."

He would, wouldn't he? He'd said once that a healer made the best killer. No point arguing against it or feeling bad about it. Not when he was right.

And I *was* doing this, no pulling punches allowed. There was everything to lose if I didn't go all out, do what it took to scare the shit out of these monsters and their cronies.

Speaking of which, more confusion to the enemy was in order.

I turned to Matt. "How about we change the MO?"

"Give the other four a different set of symptoms?" Matt caught on at once. "Yeah, let's. What do you have in mind?"

"Toluene," I said and he grunted his approval as I got glue tubes out of my backpack and tossed him a couple.

"You're going to make them sniff glue?" Damian asked incredulously.

"We're going to feed it to them actually." Matt answered him, tossed me a nasogastric tube and proceeded to shove his down one militant's throat all the way down to his stomach.

"Most drugs we have cause overlapping symptoms with phenothiazines in toxic doses." I explained my change of strategy to Damian. "They also have similar antidotes. Not so toluene. On the off chance one of the doctors could figure it out, he'd still be at a loss about the toluene cases. I'm also counting on the contradictory clinical pictures paralyzing their thinking in the first place, stymieing them."

I paused to inject the glue down the nasogastric tube. "These guys won't even experience the first rush of euphoria and confusion that glue sniffers go for. Ingesting the glue will bypass the good part and go for the bad immediately. Cardiac arrhythmias, severe chest pain, groping for air, seizures, puking blood… I'm scaring you, am I not?"

"You always scare me, Calista." He made it sound like the most refined form of praise, feel like the most intimate caress he'd ever given me.

The familiar surge of longing almost made me forget he'd been fooling me, from the beginning. Seemed bent to keep on doing it, too. Almost. I beat it back.

Two minutes later, our insidious poisons delivered, Damian completed the picture the backup would encounter. He shot the leaders, wounds that would complicate their conditions by blood loss, but that would have them lingering long until they were found, until their doctors initiated resuscitation then gave up on the rest and called to us for help.

We hoped.

* * *

They did. Right on cue, too. We'd just arrived back in the camp when the militants, a group made up of the so-called day leaders, came for us.

Damian ran to us, pretended to be relaying the situation. We debated for a couple of minutes as the militants fidgeted. Damian went back to them with our needs, which they eagerly agreed to. We could have anything, bring anyone and everything along. And, according to plan, we did.

It took us two hours at a jarring sixty miles per hour in our trailers to make it all the way up there through the roundabout route. Seemed the day leaders were in the know about the alternative route and entrance.

And here we were, welcomed, almost carried into the militant base like the saviors that they thought we were.

"The doctor will examine the casualties first," Damian said to the militant in charge at the moment. "Then decide whether she needs to transfer them to our surgery trailer, or just get supplies from there. She also says she may need us to test everyone in the installation for blood donations as soon as we get blood samples from your leaders."

The man nodded, ran ahead of us, showing us the way. And let me tell you, Jake hadn't been joking. This place was a five-star facility. That emergency room we burst into was as polished and as equipped as any I'd ever seen in a GCA hospital.

And there lay the men I'd personally poisoned hours ago.

I noticed everything at once.

Generic emergency measures were applied. Sedated to control seizures. Wounds wrapped in pressure bandages. Fluid replacement underway. Ventilatory support with positive pressure ventilation. Nasogastric tubes decompressing the stomach and draining blood from the four with toluene poisoning. All hooked to cardiac monitors and pulse oximeters.

That had to be Jake's work. Doing enough to make it look

he'd done all he could, but not addressing their real problems in the least. He hadn't even initiated a blood transfusion. Good. I'd actually worried he'd get overzealous and go all out to save them, no matter what was at stake.

Me and my team flitted between the casualties, pretending to give the pseudo-exam all we had, converged at the end and put our heads together looking worried and exchanging huge medical terms at the height of apprehension.

Then I turned to Damian, pretended to tell him my findings and he turned to the militants.

"We need antidotes—yes, they've been poisoned. But we have the antidotes back in our trailers. We also need huge amounts of blood. We must exchange all of theirs with poison-free blood."

I intervened, more confident now of my Russian after the practice I've been getting in the past weeks. "My nurses are taking samples now and will cross match it. Then I need my paramedics to go perform a sweeping exam of everyone in the base for compatible blood donations. So please round up your men. I also need to operate on all of them. But we can handle only two at the same time. Which two do you prioritize?"

The man blinked at me. "The two most in danger?"

I shook my head. "They're all in equal danger. What I meant was, who are the ones you can't afford to lose?"

The man started. Seemed he thought the angels of mercy we were never thought in such a pragmatic, heartless way. I also knew I'd put him on the spot. Those eight were all commanders of equal status. He couldn't pick. And because he couldn't, I could say this and make it sound like his idea. "If we can't prioritize, then there's no way around it. We need help, *right now.* Round up all the doctors you have in the facility, Dr. Constantine and anyone else. We need *everyone.*"

The man gaped at me, as if I'd just asked him to flap his arms and fly. "But there's only Dr. Constantine!"

What?

All right. Stop, rewind and replay here. Breakdown of communication of the most profound kind in progress.

I took a deep breath, tried again, picking the clearest words I could. "Sir, I don't think you understood me. I need all the medical personnel you have in the facility."

I could swear the man said, "We don't *have* other medical personnel, only Dr. Constantine!"

Okay, I give up. Thankfully Damian intervened. He fired colloquial Russian at the man, who burst out on an elaboration now he didn't have to speak slow and clear for my benefit.

Damian took me to one side. "There *is* no one here but Constantine. And they won't bring him. You did your part, Calista, You got us inside, you've given us the means to round them up in one place and get rid of them. Now abide by the plan. Do what you would have done if all the hostages have been brought here. Tell them you'll take the leaders back to the surgery trailer and get out of here. I'll take care of Constantine. And everything else." He crushed my hand, his anxiety scorching my skin. "*Please,* Calista."

I nodded slowly, and he inhaled as if he hadn't been breathing at all till then. With a last fierce look, he turned and walked out with his team. I watched him, numb, dumb.

There were no hostages. Only Jake.

And one thing I was certain of now.

Damian had known it all along.

Chapter 22

There were no hostages.

Damian had lied to me, from day one, about everything concerning this mission. *About everything, period?*

Not important now. What he'd done. What I didn't understand. How I hurt. One thing mattered. He and his team were out there, implementing our plan… Which was what, exactly?

What was our mission then? What were we doing here?

The same we always intended, I smacked myself with the fierce thought. Whether there was only Jake or a hundred others, our plan remained the same. I'd figure this out when we were all safely out of here. When this base was brought down on top of everyone in it.

My team should be safe back in our trailers in minutes, while Damian got Jake out and brought the base down.

What if Damian didn't want to get Jake out?

Everything inside me screamed that I was being crazy. He'd

joined his body to mine, let me into his soul—*and lied all through it.* What if he'd lied about it all? I'd totally forgotten he was a master actor, a convoluted black-ops agent. Who knew what his real agenda was?

I had to allow for anything. I had to distrust every word he'd ever said. I wasn't counting on him anymore.

I had to get Jake out myself.

"Doctor, you must start the surgeries at once!" the man demanded. The man I might have to kill in a few minutes.

I had to try peaceful measures first. I only had Damian's word that they refused to get Jake. A word I would have staked my life on ten minutes ago. I wouldn't stake ten cents on it now. I turned fully to the man. "I'm afraid to move them."

He gave me an oh-God-she's-stupid look. "Then do it here? Use Dr. Constantine's things. They're good."

"Then I'll really need you to get him here to help me."

He shook his head. "We can't get him for you."

Which makes you redundant. Seemed it was down to getting Jake the hard way. I'd try to be humane about it first.

"Give me a minute with my team, to distribute chores." I beckoned and they joined me around one of the stricken men.

"Change of plan," I said. "I'll go fetch Jake myself."

Haiku's eyes widened. "Why? Damian will get him."

I couldn't bring myself to tell them of Damian's duplicity. Stupid, soft. Smitten. Not anymore. Still, when I explained I didn't implicate him. "With only one hostage to free and a hive of terrorists ripe for the picking, which would you handle first if you were a self-respecting antiterrorist agent?"

Ayesha nodded. "Might be an impossible choice for them. But how will you explain not joining us? Our head surgeon?"

"I'll say I need to work on the most serious case here."

Matt quirked his eyebrow at me. "You think we'll leave you here facing hundreds of militants alone and go wait in safety and for news of your death?"

"I'm not about to provoke a confrontation," I protested.

Ishmael shrugged. "There *will* be one. Together we stand a chance."

I tried again. "Jake is my concern…"

Ayesha actually smiled. "You're saying this to the people who've been here facing death daily for eight men we don't know? Who as it turned out, don't exist?"

God, I loved these guys. I smiled back my pride and thankfulness at them. "You're all crazy, do you know that?"

Haiku nodded. "Why else are we your friends and partners? So what do you need us to do?"

I had another very simple plan. What Damian would call a crazy, volatile trick that would only backfire. Whatever. I was pulling it. Seemed it was fine by my team, too.

I left Lucia and Haiku releasing the emergency trolleys' brakes and the others getting our prepared syringes out, turned to the man. "Before we start, we want blood samples from you."

Resentment rose off him. He really would rather let his superiors die. But he knew he'd be out of a lucrative business without the ones controlling the foreign bank accounts.

Grudgingly, he nodded to the other men who rolled up their sleeves. We had sixteen militants here. Two each. Sedate the first eight and we'd have an easier time dealing with the rest.

I kept them answering questions so they wouldn't notice we were injecting them with something before we drew blood. I injected my militant no problem. Then it all went wrong.

The day leader noticed, realized, thundered at us, to his men. My team instantaneously shoved the groggy militants out of the way, ramming the rest with the trolleys. The militants' cries echoed as their comatose leaders catapulted in the air, impacting them.

Everything slowed. As it always did under duress. As everything inside me sped up. The leader filled my focus, his red face distorting on hatred and rage, his gun materializing in his hand already discharging, straight at my heart.

No way was I going this way. I streaked out of range, heard Haiku's yelp, felt her go down behind me. *No!*

Stress hormones were a geyser now, pouring speed and honed skills and viciousness into my limbs. One *mawashi geri* roundhouse kick disarmed him. His wrist snapped, the sensation of shattering bones transmitting up mine. Outraged agony burst from him, transformed into blind violence.

He threw himself at me. My leg snapped out in a *kin geri* to the groin. He keeled, tried to throw himself after his gun. I straightened him with the same leg, never touching the ground in a *mae geri kokomi,* a vicious frontal thrust kick, ramming him in the chest, driving him to the wall behind him, pinning him there. His good hand snatched a gun from the hand of the man who rammed me. Time stretched with his macabre smile, stilled on the rising gun. Not in position to kick it. In position for much worse.

All right. He'd called it. I withdrew my leg, twisted, lashed it back full force in a *yoko geri kokomi,* a side thrust kick, with my foot sideways and my heel in his throat. I heard the crack this time. He fell like a sack of wet cement.

I snatched the gun from his limp hand, somersaulted over him for the other one, snapped it up, rolled with both pointed to defend my team. Heard another muffled gunshot.

Haiku. Her left arm covered in blood, she'd still managed to wrestle the gun from her militant, to shoot another who would have shot Doug in a heartbeat. The rest each ended his or her own confrontation, Matt terminally, with his bare hands.

"Hands over your heads," I shouted at the remaining four men. "Take the injections or we'll have to kill you all."

In seconds we had all but one unconscious, had Haiku dosed up on painkillers and her shoulder wound securely bandaged. We had to get her out of here. Had to grab Jake and get the hell out of here, all of us. Even in the sound-absorbent setting, the gunshots must have been heard. There could be hidden surveillance cameras. A deluge of minions could be on the way.

Had Damian done his part? Where was Jake, anyway?

Time to find out. I faced the vicious-looking militant I'd left awake. Incredulity, rage and fear trembled on his face. Mostly incredulity. Having a hard time reconciling the woman he'd ogled for weeks with the one who'd just crushed his superior's windpipe, huh? "Where is Dr. Constantine?"

He blinked. "I don't know."

I rammed my head into his nose. That had a martial arts name, too. *Jodan-tsukkomi.* First time I ever got to use it. He spluttered blood. "I'm telling the truth. He never stays in one place."

Oh, for God's sake. He didn't know. I nodded to Matt, who knocked him out.

"Next move?" Matt hooked a semiautomatic on his shoulder.

I took my jacket off, put it on Haiku, covering her bloody outfit. "Doug, get Haiku out of here fast. Say I sent you to get drugs. And let's get those leaders back on the trolleys. We may still bluff our way through more militants."

Haiku and Doug did, got out. We made it to the first sentry point within the base. Finding us alone and asking for Jake, one got uneasy and tried to contact their colleagues. It took the silence on the other side to clue them in.

They were five. We got rid of them in seconds. The one we kept awake didn't know where Jake was. We took him with us to show us the possible places Jake could be.

We were in the next passage when muted thunder resonated from the adjacent one. The sentries must have contacted more than our victims.

"Smoke bombs," I hissed. "Napalm. Keep to the ground. I'll take down the first ones, you follow through. Shoot high."

They rounded the corner, saw us hiding behind the trolleys. The thought *sure kill* wouldn't have had time to form. Lucia and Ayesha swung smoke bombs. They fell on them the same moment I crashed my trolley into them. The comatose leader flew in the air, his flaccid weight landing on them. Five stumbled under the impact and the spook factor. A domino effect followed.

I retreated to give the napalm bombs a wide berth. My head filled with the stench of burning flesh and screams.

But too many were still standing and more would come. No matter what, we'd end up with losses. All my fault. All Damian's fault. I wanted to beg my friends' forgiveness for dragging them through this, this kind of life. To berate them for letting me. To tell them to leave me to my insanity. Jake was *my* problem.

Gunshots popped from behind me. My friends. Telling me not to be silly? I just hoped they saw where they were firing.

Our out-of-control opponents retaliated, mainly got their leaders. They didn't care about killing them now to get to us. Good to know. It removed my last inhibition. I rolled on the floor, firing a dozen bullets. The smoke thickened. Then the militants did. More were pouring in, firing haphazardly, getting their colleagues. But bound to get us, too.

So this was it.

God's hand smote us all down. It was as if it took hold of the mountain and shook it like a kid would his rattle.

Earthquake!

No. Explosions. Oh, God no! *Damian.* The final phase. He'd initiated it. He didn't realize we were still inside! Had he gotten Jake? Did he care either way? The whole place would come down on us. It *was* coming down.

Boulders of false ceiling and mountain crashed down between me and our opponents. Telling me something? Like, run?

No such luck. The next falling boulder was coming straight for my head. I launched into the air, lodged myself in the space between the two levels of the emergency trolley. The bed almost caved under the impact, compacting me on the lower level, the storage box. Compared to crushed, compacted was good.

Now move. I pushed with my legs. The laden trolley creaked an inch. I pushed harder, started to make headway. More rocks fell on my shelter. On my legs.

Pain tried to shut me down. I only worried that my legs stay in one piece. I'd use them even if not. I shoved. Hard. Agony leaped through me, hot, blinding. Gashed. Bad. Still connected. I added my hands, crawling, clawing, pulling the increasing weight of my shelter-prison an inch. Then another. The possibility that I was in the process of being buried alive flashed in my mind. Didn't appeal. Still had to kick Damian's ass!

Smoke and dust filled my vision, distorted the moving shapes. My friends. Coming back for me. The morons! Thought I needed company in live burial, too? I screamed, *"Get out!"*

When did they ever listen to me? They didn't now. Ayesha's and Matt's shapes reached for me. "Get your arms out the front."

They were on both sides now. I did as she asked. Each latched on to one of my forearms and pulled. I really envied men for having no breasts to be sheared off in situations like this!

Everything happened at once. I was free, on my feet, running after my friends, one leg unfelt, the other on fire, and everything was collapsing behind us. And I realized.

The explosions had come, were still coming, from inside the base. That accounted for the outwardly expanding shock wave of damage. Seemed Damian had made changes of his own to the plan.

Then we were in daylight. Sky. I sagged to my knees. Not with pain or breathlessness. After that near-miss buried-alive experience, let's say I was beginning an open-air appreciation trend.

"The others?" I gasped, got nods from the doubled over Matt and Ayesha. Militants were shoving past us. And dropping like flies. My gaze swung up, knowing I wouldn't see Damian's men in their sniper positions. Cleanup duty, huh? Mission accomplished then. Time to rush back to our convoy. At least my team. I had unfinished business. Damian. Had to find him. Find out if he'd gotten Jake out. Find out what it was all about.

For once Matt and Ayesha didn't object to my order to leave without me. I had weapons and full coverage. Matt threw me his backpack, then I ran up the mountain.

I reached José. He'd seen me coming, still flinched. Had to be my exhumed look. "God, Cali! What were you doing in there?"

I kneeled beside him and bandaged my gushing leg wound. It would need stitches. "Where are Jake and Damian, José? Don't say you don't know or I swear I'll…"

"I don't know for real, Cali. After the first explosion Damian ran out and left us. I haven't seen him since."

I couldn't hear more. Damian had left his team behind. Where they could have been crushed. Set off more explosions…

I started running. From the horrifying suspicions.

Suddenly something impaled me from head to toe. Not realization. An invocation. I stumbled under the sickening sensations. The feeling got stronger. I was getting closer.

Then I heard it. A resounding bellow. Of pain. Jake's.

Inhuman strength and insupportable dread launched me over the rocks. *God no, please. Don't let it be—don't let it be…*

Another roar pinpointed his location. A hidden cavern a hundred and fifty feet from the outlet. Must have missed it before…

"…have enough. C'mon, you son of a bitch. Give me more excuses to make it an excruciating death. Yeah, that's it…"

A ghastly sound jolted through me. I knew it well. Flesh being pulped, bones caving in. Jake cried out again.

"Ow, what did I break now? Don't worry, your neck's turn is coming—just not for a long while."

Damian. Oh, God, Damian. His voice. The inhuman glee. The sheer pleasure. Killing Jake. A breath at a time. Loving every second. No paranoia could have taken me so far.

"She'll hate you for this…" Jake's gasp carried to me on the frigid air, tinged with amusement. *Amusement?*

"Who's going to tell her? You, from beyond the grave?"

"She'd work it out. She's too intelligent—for you, Damian. She's a—genius. Like me. That's—why we belong together."

"Over my dead body, bitch. No, let's make it over yours."

I had no idea what propelled me. I was pulped, paralyzed. Shock and horror had eaten through me. My soul wretched with betrayal. My heart—a jagged shard was embedded there, twisted with every word Damian uttered. So hearts *did* get torn to pieces. God—I let myself love him, believe in him…

I was at the cavern's mouth now and I saw the scene I'd already projected in my head. Seeing it made it real. Solidified the horror, made it tangible. A crippling blow.

Damian circled Jake, a big, vicious cat torturing its kill for kicks. Never thought he had it in him. To be cruel to those weaker than him. Thought the reverse. I knew nothing about him.

He prowled, let Jake drag himself to his feet, stagger away, throw himself on the ground again. At a gun. Damian let him pick it up, then launched in the air from a standstill, spun, his formidable leg cutting the freezing air in a swooshing arc, striking the side of Jake's head with another nauseating sound.

He'd pulled his kick. He could have snapped Jake's neck had he wanted to. He didn't. He still wanted to play.

Jake slammed to the ground in a heap, still groping for the gun. Damian let him pick it up again, then clamped his hand, made him shove the gun into his own jaw.

Damian smiled at him. "I'm giving you a way out. Go ahead."

Jake grimaced a wavering grin. "Go ahead yourself. Go back to her with my blood all over you. She'll know it's mine."

Damian twisted the gun out of Jake's hand, made sure it hurt a lot, threw it away. "I have a better idea." He hauled Jake up over his knee. "I'll break your back. This way you'll have a lot of time to despair and suffer here before you die."

I couldn't hear anymore. I burst into a run, launched in the air. Damian spun his head around, startled, dismayed, his eyes slamming an instant entreaty into mine. I landed with both feet in his back. He staggered forward, let go of Jake.

Jake crumpled to the ground, groaning, holding his ribs, his arm. Must be what Damian had broken.

I didn't stop there, somersaulted over both of them, landed on bent knees, snapped the gun up. Then I swung back to them.

"Calista…"

"Cali…"

"Shut up, both of you! Just *shut up* and start talking!"

Damian was on his feet. Jake was sitting up. Both reached out a hand to me. Men!

"Calista, this isn't what it looks like…" Damian started.

"You mean you weren't in the process of killing me?" Jake scoffed.

I stormed to them. "That's not the talking I want to hear." I took off my backpack. "I swear I'll knock you both out, tie you up and sit and wait until you both cough up the truth."

"You saw the truth, Cali." Jake's eyes, wounded, searched my face. "You saw for yourself what kind of monster Damian is!"

"Excuse me, establishing motives here! I don't believe even a monster would kill you just for fun, Jake. And not for me."

Damian reached for me. I knocked his hand with the gun. Hard. He grimaced, his eyes feverish on my face. "You'd be wrong there, Calista. I'd kill for you. I'd do anything. You know it."

I glared at Damian. "Are you telling me this is over me? You're eliminating the competition? Do I look stupid to you?"

"I told him you'd get it, Cali. He'll only continue misleading you. I'll tell you why he wants to kill me. Why he was after killing everyone in the base, hostages and all."

"There are no hostages!" I yelled.

"Who told you that? Damian?"

"The militants. They said…" That there were no other *medical personnel!*

Jake's eyes followed my thoughts, read them. "You were asking the wrong question. I'm the only one left of my team. They died one after the other. But there are two dozen others in the base, scientists, kidnapped, held hostage, too. And Damian is here, not to save us, but to eliminate us all."

I swung to Damian. I'd find his denial written all over him. I found confirmation. "But why?" I choked on my confusion.

It was Jake who answered. "Because it's what he does. When he's sent to treat an infected limb, he doesn't only tear the arm out, he puts a bullet in the patient's head."

"One more metaphor and I'll knock you out the hard way."

Damian approached me again, took another ram in the chest, spread his arms. "I won't trade accusations with that piece of slime, Calista. I want you to trust me. You know you can."

"Can I?" Until minutes ago, against all evidence, I'd still trusted him. Faith still demanded I gave in. I couldn't. "And trust you to do what? Kill Jake? Without asking why?"

"There's the best reason why, Calista."

"According to whom?"

His golden eyes flared his death intent. "According to the nine thousand refugees he's experimented on and killed."

I experienced something new. Nothingness. The logic and senses that made up my mind and being had stopped doing their job. Cessation seemed the only answer. The only sanity-saving outlet. Yet even through the vacuum, I still heard Damian.

"This base *is* the biological and chemical weapons facility in the region, Calista. And Jake is the mastermind behind it all. This is a search-and-destroy mission. PATS has given GCA manufactured proof of their operatives' survival so we can come this close under their legitimate cover. The rest you know."

"You've got to be kidding, right? I know *nothing!*"

"The only thing you don't know is that Jake and the scientists have sold out, and are actually working with the militants, who in turn are working for an international terrorist organization. The terrorists objected to the militants' bid for popularity, thought scrutiny might expose their real purpose before they were ready to strike. They replanted the minefields to stop them from carrying out their plans and to limit their movements. The bigwig militants found a safe route around it, no doubt under Jake's guidance."

"If Jake already knew what you were, why let us come?"

"He wanted you."

"You mean this is about me after all? Give me a break!"

Damian smiled. Indulgent? Now? "It *is*. But I'm also here to eradicate those men and their work. They were mere steps from perfecting new weapons like the world has never dreamed of."

I swung round to Jake. "*Is* this a biochemical weapons facility? The one experimenting on the refugees?"

He straightened with difficulty, nodded. "But the rest of his accusations are false. It's so like him, to mix just enough truth with fabrication to make it sound plausible and sincere."

I rolled my eyes. "Just how well do you know each other?"

Jake winced. "Well enough, wouldn't you say, Damian?"

"One more thing," I gritted. "Why didn't you tell me when I asked you about the refugees' death rates? Why did you say there was another installation here?"

"The same reason I didn't want you to reveal you knew I was a prisoner," Jake said, grimacing. "I wanted you out of here, safe. I knew you'd do something crazy to stop them if you knew."

I glowered at him. "So you *are* their accomplice."

"I'm not. And neither are the rest of the scientists. But we *are* privy to lethal knowledge. To Damian, we must be sacrificed with the guilty rather than risk future leakages."

Radical measures *were* right up Damian's alley. But I still had trouble believing he'd wipe out an innocent. In that brutal a way.

Point was, there was no way to prove either's words. Both
had lied to me. Both could be lying now. But if so, what was the
truth? Was there a truth, or as usual, just perspective?

Damian touched my shoulder, braving another ram. "I lied
to you because I was afraid of the depth of your feelings for Constantine, that they would blind you into taking his side, at least
letting him slip by. As you're doing now."

Which made sense. If Jake was guilty of what he'd accused
him of. But what else had he lied about? Had all his passion been
to secure me on his side, when I discovered his real agenda? To
have me willing to stand aside as he executed Jake?

Damian was going on. "I had no proof to offer you."

"And you still have none." Jake struggled to his feet.

"I have the proof of nine thousand dead refugees."

"I tried to save them. The militants let me struggle to, for
proof that their weapons were untreatable, unsurvivable."

Another plausible answer. To contribute to my impending
head burst. Jake's next words, so cool and quiet, did far worse
than that. They soiled my psyche. Where was catatonic shock
when a woman needed it?

"Anyway, why kill me now, Damian? If what you say is true,
why not take me back to be put on trial? I'll tell you why, Cali.
He has orders to sweep the whole thing under the rug. Which in-
cludes you and your team, now that you know the real danger
here. An unfortunate accident befalling you all would wrap it all
up."

The hell in Damian's eyes flared. Jake was a goner the moment I let my guard down. Then he turned those eyes on me, the
blast becoming love and entreaty. "Trust your heart, *querida*."

My heart? That shredded mess inside my rib cage?

Jake had his firm hold there, and point for point, plausibil-
ity-wise, he was winning. Still, it whimpered *Damian*....

Damian kicked me, in the abdomen, full force.

Telling me something? Like, I dropped my guard?

But I'm not guarding against you, I'm guarding Jake. Am I doomed to trusting you till you kill me, as Jake said you will?

Clinically, I observed his technique, how his kick plowed into me, folded me around his foot, lifted and hurled me backward. I wondered why I wasn't blacking out. Anyone would with that much force per inch impacting their solar plexus. Not to mention the anguish detonation. Then I slammed against the jagged cavern wall. Headfirst.

Darkness. Void. I surrendered to their onslaught, snatched at it. I didn't want to know.

One knowledge was forced on me. God was rattling us again. Another detonation. The cavern was shuddering and raining boulders. Right where I'd been standing a second ago. Where Damian was now, where his kick had displaced him. He was buried in a blink. Horror shoved aside pain and disorientation. I screamed it. *"Damian!"*

Another blow jarred me, knocking the gun away. What now?

Jake. Disarming me in case I turned on him? I had no time for him. Damian! Frantic, nothing counting but seeing him whole, all accounts frozen, I hauled rocks off him. More rocks could be coming down on me. So what? He moved, rolled more rocks off his chest.

A resounding boom jolted me. Damian jerked, too, his beautiful eyes seeking mine, uncomprehending, reproaching.

Then I saw it. The dark crimson blossoming on his chest.

Chapter 23

"I had to kill him."

Kill him. Kill him. *Kill him.*

Jake had killed Damian.

No!

He can't have. Damian isn't going to die. He isn't... He couldn't...

He will...

A bullet right in the chest—*in his heart*—his eyes fogging, leaving me, hurtling out of reach—oh God, oh God...

I pressed on his wound. His blood burnt my flailing hands, scorched my sanity. No knowledge left. All training erased. Heart flapping uselessly, imitating his, no blood pumping, everything receding...

No! *Save him. Do it! Now! Die later. Focus.* Focus!

I grabbed for my open backpack, groped in the debris of my shell-shocked mind for the forgotten emergency measures. ABC...

Yes, *yes*. Airway. Breathing. Circulation. Revive him, stabilize him… Reassure him! "Damian, I'm here…I'll take care of you, don't worry…I'll never let you go…help me…hang on…"

He opened his eyes and my heart ruptured. He was telling me something… Something important. Then I heard words. Jake's.

"He wouldn't have stopped until I was dead, Cali. Until we all were. Your use to him is over, and your danger is now…"

I was outside my body, watching it exploding in a violent backswing. The back of my fist impacted the side of Jake's head, sending him sprawling on the ground. Good thing for him it only packed a fraction of my horror and rage and despair. The full dose would have snapped his neck.

He fell, facedown. I forgot he existed.

Only Damian! *Save him.*

My heart stampeded, my breath fractured my lungs. My hands thrashed out of control. I still tipped his head back, suctioned blood out of his throat, placed the airway in his mouth so he wouldn't gag on his tongue and blood, started him on 100 percent oxygen. I fumbled for a saline bag, a line, a cannula, moves speeding up, blurring, set up fluid delivery, took his blood pressure. Oh, God, no, no… Like that night in Darfur, only so much worse—so much worse…

A movement behind me registered. Jake, staggering up. My focus dragged to him, long enough to see him wiping blood from his mouth. I forgot him as I looked on him, turned to Damian, kept the pressure on his wound, bathed in more of his blood.

"I understand your confusion, Cali." So damned reasonable and collected. "Damian is a master manipulator, and you think I'm the bad guy now. I won't even remind you that you interrupted him murdering me. But whatever you think, we have to run. His men must have heard this shot. Once we're in their power, it'll be all over. If we can reach your team, make a head start, we'd stand a chance. Come with me, Cali. I love you. We'll work this out."

Like I was listening to him after he'd killed Damian in cold blood... I gagged, wretched. *He can't die. He can't.* I forced myself to answer Jake without looking at him. "Give me the gun, Jake. If you really love me, don't force me to take you down."

"I'll need your promise first that you'll do as I ask, that we'll run together before they come."

"Damian was wrong to try to execute you." I had to admit that much. "And I won't let his men near you, either. You have nothing to fear. I guarantee it." Damian grunted something. It sounded like "Don't!" Another salvo of terror exploded in my gut. "That is, if Damian doesn't die. If he does, I'll kill you myself. So you'd better come here and help me save him."

"Unacceptable, Cali." Regret permeated his elegant tones, an acid drip on my exposed nerves. "I can't surrender my fate to your misconceptions. I would lift your confusion if I had the time. You of all people will understand why I'm doing all this."

All what? All Damian accused him of?

He went on. "You know how extreme measures are the only way to eradicate an insidious, devastating disease. Money is the narrow-minded motive a one-dimensional man like Damian can come up with. It's just a by-product and further means to an end, a higher cause. The *highest* cause."

His words hit me like a meteor shower. *He was confessing.*

"But you have freed me from my suffocating allies. And though this isn't how I planned it, I waited eight years for you and I can wait forever, if need be. I'll find you again one day, when you realize you've allied yourself with the wrong man. We will be together then, sharing it all." He retreated as he talked, those uncanny eyes crinkling in a smile that wasn't a smile. Then he was gone.

Icy shards skewered through me. How didn't I see it before? *He was insane!*

A mind of that caliber, deranged to that extent, was a major catastrophe.

A major catastrophe I didn't give a fig about. I had the only major catastrophe I cared about right here on my hands.

Damian had all signs of cardiac tamponade.

The bullet had a ripped a hole in his heart or his vena cava within the pericardial sac that covered his heart. Blood was accumulating there, preventing his heart from expanding properly to beat. His heart was being strangled into stopping!

"S-stop—him…"

Damian! Still conscious! He'd fumbled out the airway to rasp his plea. "I have to stop your deterioration first." A euphemism for *stop you dying*.

He would in minutes if I didn't evacuate the blood accumulating around his heart. Now. No time to transfer him to the surgery trailer, to run for help. I would have to aspirate the blood, blind, no way to monitor where my needle was going, or to record his progress or deterioration.

"I d-don't matter—he'll kill thousands more—cause wars…."

Damian's gasped words drenched me in agony and despair, went through my heart. In seconds I'd go through his. "I'm not that righteous, Damian, that I'd risk you to stop a war."

"Calista—please—g-get my team—g-go after him…."

"You first!" I struggled to take his jacket off, to raise his upper body up, drag a couple of flat-surfaced rocks, cover them with the folded jacket and lean him on it. He had to be reclining in a thirty- to sixty-degree position for this to work. "Now shut up and concentrate on slowing your heart. I'm sedating you so I can intubate you. I'm counting on your full cooperation here."

"Or else, huh?"

"You bet." I bent to his cold, twitching lips, took them in a fierce press, pledging. *I'm not letting you die.*

I performed rapid induction anesthesia and intubated him. Then it started.

I punctured his skin over his heart with a three-inch needle. I needed a longer one—his muscle mass—oh, Damian! Perfect, beautiful, cold—dying… *Focus. Fall apart later.*

Dread cut off air and blood. Introducing the catheter after the needle was the most harrowing thing I'd ever had to do. I could easily puncture his heart, finish him. "I'm not. I'm doing this right." A manic voice filled my ears. Mine.

I watched his distended neck veins compulsively as I withdrew blood into the 50 cc syringe. It filled over and over. I filled a blood bag with it, injected an anticoagulant in it and hooked it to his other cannula, dripped it back into him. There must be more blood around his heart, clotting by now—I had to get him to the surgery trailer and open his chest to remove the clot, control the injury—cut through his bones, expose his heart…

His distended veins began to collapse. Then I felt it. Something hitting the tip of the needle.

His heart.

I fell back, snatching the needle out, quaking, tears scorching my face, sobs shearing my lungs.

The catheter! Still in—still in… *Thank God.* Blood still coming through it. *Listen to his heart, take his pressure.*

Forcing myself back to my knees, I did. I only heard my crashing heartbeats and snatched breathing.

Get a grip. I must have done so. And what I heard drove my head to my knees, fetuslike, gulping down relief.

He was out of danger. For now.

I exploded to my feet, ran out of the cavern, almost bumped into Ed and José at its mouth.

"What happened?" Ed steadied me, his frantic glance roving over me. "You're not hurt. I heard a shot come from here. I had too much on my hands to come before."

Gibberish spilled out of me. It must have made some kind of sense. It had Ed and José streaking away.

What followed until they where back with a stretcher and

Matt and Ayesha, until we had Damian back in the trailer, until we'd performed the emergency surgery, cutting through Damian's sternum, exposing his heart and fixing what turned out to be a vena cava injury, was—indescribable. So *this* was despair.

An hour, all in all. Felt like a century.

But Damian was out of danger for real. I could breathe now. I could go after Jake. He wouldn't have gone far. I'd find him.

Damian had told me to take his people. If I did, it would be a hunt. Right or wrong, I couldn't do that. Jake didn't kill me when he had the chance. I owed him the same mercy.

But I had to stop him. I had to find him first.

To do that, I had to think like him.

How would a mad genius think? From what he'd said about his suffocating allies, he'd been counting on us getting him out. We had only up to a point. Now he had to improvise. To do that, he had to be privy to all the current facts. I had to be, too.

Ed told me what had happened. They'd disposed of dozens of militants, secured the scientists, then the first explosion rocked the base. *Before* they'd planted their explosives.

Jake.

He'd manufactured an illness to be excused from handling the injured leaders, no doubt managed to hide somewhere near the entrance of the base. According to the plan *I'd* told him about, my team and I should have been out of the base within minutes, leaving Damian's team deep inside the base.

Believing that, he'd set off the detonations to bury them inside, then planned to run to me so we could ride into the sunset together.

So many birds with one stone.

Then it all went wrong when Damian ran out to catch him.

Now Damian's people were making sure the base and militants were wiped out. I gave them one order. No executions of the scientists. Then I ran. I didn't tell anyone where I was going.

Jake couldn't be hiding, waiting for the dust to settle. He had nowhere to go without transportation. Which left him with one option. To go back to the camp.

He'd made sure the people he systematically killed thought him a hero. They'd shelter him, until he came up with another escape plan. No doubt he'd concoct one in no time. I bet he'd make an even more insidious deal with whomever entered the region now that the controlling militant group was decimated. Maybe even with the federal forces. From what I now realized, there was no limit to his potential damage.

He had to be on the Georgian Military Highway. He had quite a head start. And I was really battered. But so was he. Even had we both been perfectly fit, and no matter how physically upgraded he was, he was no match for me. I'd catch up.

I did. It took two hours. If anything the route looked far scarier by daylight. Not that I cared. Only bringing him back, finding a way to help him, to cure him, mattered.

I came around a steep bend and there he was. Walking as if on an afternoon stroll. I knew he'd felt my presence before I saw him. He turned, his left arm in a sling, the muted lights of the freezing afternoon accentuating his polished good looks. My heart clenched.

Jake, my first lover. I'd thought he'd overcome his ordeals by hardening, becoming more complex. I'd thought the physical changes were a manifestation of his inner changes.

They hadn't been changes. He'd been hurt too much. And he hadn't survived. They *had* killed him.

I was looking into a dead man's eyes.

I shuddered. He crooned, "Cold, my love?"

The chill spread. "Why, Jake?" I choked.

He sighed, cocked his head gracefully, leveled his gaze on me. "Because it's the only way. To beat evil you have to be even worse. Fighting the bad guys with the good guys' methods had never worked. You reached the same answer, Cali. You've adopted violence and anarchy. It's only then that you became effective."

He knew? How? "I don't kill innocents."

His smile was indulgent. Creepy. "There *are* no innocents. Those subjugated villages, that camp, they're filled with oppressed people who are biding their time to become oppressors, with women raising their children on dreams of genocide, with families breeding the next generation of terrorists. War leaves no innocents."

Oh, my! "And so you're killing them now, before they have the chance to become what you think they'll become?"

"It's not what *I* think, it's what they told me, what I heard them saying to one another. Being the underdog doesn't make them innocent. They just don't have the opportunity to manifest their evil. Sooner or later, they will."

"That's insane, treating evil by eradicating the victim."

"It's not only them I'm eradicating. In chronic conflict situations, all sides become diseased beyond redemption. Both so-called aggressor and victim have to be wiped out, so that others, untouched by madness, can start over. My weapons will be both a radical surgery that will uproot the disease, and an overwhelming disaster that will make the world come together, humbled and scared of being next. A lot will be sacrificed, but it will leave this world a saner place. For a while."

Some things were just too shocking, too atrocious, to be assimilated. No feeling did them justice. No reaction was enough. So I laughed. "Oh, Jake! I should have known you'd end up a mad scientist when you always rooted for Lex Luther."

He dared to look hurt. After the atrocities he'd committed, he was hurt that I called him mad? Right.

The flash of pain on his face was gone. He was again the beautiful, soulless monster that I now knew he was. And soulless wasn't an insult here, just a fact. All that remained of him was intellect, vast and brutal.

But he says he loves you. Maybe he still retains some spark of humanity. An Achilles' heel. I had to try. For that. For the memories. For the man he once was. "Jake, I want to help you."

"You can—as my partner. But you won't be, will you? Damian succeeded in turning you against me. He was supposed to die with my wardens. Then I would have brought you to my way of thinking slowly. I knew I'd never win you this abruptly."

"Just how *did* you plan this?" He'd brag. A genius always itched to flaunt the intricacies of his strategy.

"You're hoping I'll oblige the stereotype? The mad scientist ranting about his ingenuity when he should be securing his escape? Slowing me down until the PATS agents catch up?"

Dammit. Was his intelligence boundless? Or was he really a mind reader? "I don't need anyone to catch up, Jake."

"No, you don't, do you? You'd overpower five men twice your size. I'm so proud of what you've become, Cali. You've fulfilled your potential in a way even I couldn't have anticipated. You are what a doctor is meant to be—healer, defender, warrior."

Flattery? To soften me up? No. He really meant it. Had to make things more tangled and heart-wrenching, didn't he? "No one's coming, Jake. This is between you and me. I need to know."

His eyes melted. "Very well. I was physically incarcerated here, but I had access to the whole world through the Internet. I formed connections you cannot believe. Everybody has a price and I possess all forms of payments—information, problem-solving, money. I found out all there is to find out about you. I lost your trail, though, once you became too good at covering your tracks. I had to find you again, have you find me. So I planted this idea of popularizing the militant movement in my captors' minds, started the division with their parent terrorist organization. Then it was an easy matter of manipulating PATS and TOP to get all the players I wanted here."

"You wanted Damian here?"

"Of course not. But if I'd resisted his inclusion more than I did, he would have taken independent action. I couldn't have that. I settled for putting you as the thorn in his side, the harness that would limit his power and movements."

He was responsible for that? He had access to TOP's top people? This was getting more surreal by the second.

"Coming here, he already suspected my role in all this, just wasn't sure of its extent. Through the revealing conversations he had with my captors at my bidding, he formed the real picture. That was when he went after you to secure you on his side when sides had to be taken. You've been his team's real security ticket all through, up until I won you, of course."

Which could all be another truth-mingled lie. Or not. "But if he knew you worked with the militants, what made him think you wouldn't have him and his team killed, while sparing us?"

"He knew I wanted out, that I'd do everything to help even him to that end. I told him, after all. Why do you think he didn't want you to ask me for insider information? For the exact layout of the base? I'd already given it to him. We had a deal. He intended to double-cross me. I double-crossed him first."

I was way beyond being stunned. The sheer depths of duplicity of the two men I'd loved! Something must be wrong with me, to be attracted only to treacherous sons of bitches!

"All went according to plan, Damian's original plan, until you insisted on being part of the invasion of the base. It would have worked just as well, if it weren't for Damian acting quickly and finding me. Then for you finding us. Believing I was going to be dead in a minute, I called to you and you came. It complicated matters, but it did give me a second lease on life."

So he believed he had telepathic power over me, too. Wouldn't put it past him. I *had* felt a call. I shuddered again.

"Why didn't you escape before? Why didn't you get one of your powerful connections to spring you? Why didn't you manipulate your captors into letting you go?"

"Let's say I developed a phobia about physically trying to escape, after the first couple of years. My powerful connections had no way of storming the base without sacrificing me, but gave me the maps and knowledge of how to construct the access to the safe route as a preliminary to my escape plan. I had every confidence you'd find it. The militants thought I was presenting them with a way around the cordon their masters had put around them to limit their movements into Russian soil. As for manipulation, I did. You're here, aren't you?"

"And what do you intend to do now?"

"I have big plans. Some real powers can't wait to have me and my knowledge. What do *you* intend to do, Cali?

So. Moment of truth. "I intend to take you back. To help you. Please, Jake, let me. Give this up, come back with me."

"And what? We'll be lovers again? We'll work together? You'll forget what I did, protect me 24/7 from Damian's assassination attempts?"

"I *will* protect you. I'll help you see how wrong you've gone, come to terms with the reasons you did. You were hurt too much, experienced so many atrocities you've gone to insane lengths to put an end to them. You're too intelligent not to know that this is a pathological reaction."

"In whose opinion? In yours? Of course. You're not ready yet, Cali. I would have led you through the process slowly. This isn't how I planned it, and I am so sorry it had turned out this way. But when you start seeing my results, the better world I'll create, you'll believe. You'll come to me then. I said I'll wait forever. It won't be that long before we're together."

Then he simply turned and walked away.

I was tempted to let him go. God, how tempted.

What could a man without as much as a car, who was going

to take refuge in a miserable refugee camp cut off from the world by land mines, with nothing but godlike delusions do?

This is Jake you're talking about, a grieving voice inside me said.

He didn't only have divine delusions, he had satanic powers to back them up. A devil of the worst kind, the to-save-you-I-must-destroy-you-first variety.

A tear froze somewhere down my cheek. I raised my dart gun. "You're coming with me, Jake."

He answered without turning. "You won't stop me, Cali. Even if you throw me in prison, I'll carry on with my work."

Yeah, didn't I know that for a fact. Just look what he, and my father, had managed to do from their prisons. Capturing Jake was not the answer.

Only one thing was.

I still couldn't do it. I had to give him a chance. There still might be a way to reach him, to cure him…

He turned, his gun raised. "Not that I'll let you put me in prison again, Cali. Let's end this."

He pulled the trigger.

Chapter 24

I fired first. Got his exposed carotid artery. Threw myself on the ground. A bullet whizzed over my head, would have gotten my heart, had I stood still.

No time to load another dart. No need. He'd drop in seconds. He needed only one to shoot again, kill me. I tucked, rolled, unfolded and kicked the gun out of his hand.

He sagged, fell to his knees. I did, too. *I'd killed him.*

He'd be dead in minutes. He'd suffer first. Already he was flushed, trembling, gasping. I knew what he must be feeling as the overdose of phenothiazine coursed in his blood. Burning up, losing control of his every muscle, his heart firing, erratic, ineffective.

The heavenly color of his eyes brightened, his gaze filling with reproach, disappointment and oh, God—love… *So much love…*

I couldn't see this.

"Damn you, Jake! Damn you for making me do this!"

I staggered up, ran away, blind, shaking apart with misery and grief.

"Who died?"

The rasped question filtered through the interminable whup-whup-whup noise.

Had to be part of the dream. The mental seizure, more like. And I wasn't even asleep. I'd been in that state all the way back to the convoy, and all through the time while we crossed the border and had PATS and GCA helicopters come to pick us up, having their operatives replace us at the wheels of our convoy, driving it out of the region.

I'd been seeing and hearing snatches from my life's pre-chaos catalog, carefree moments, oblivious times. I'd been alert and tripping, my mind searching for safety valves.

A dry, warm touch feathered the wet-cold cheek I was leaning on the stretcher's railing. The seizure hadn't included anything tactile so far. So it had to be. Had to. Damian! Awake.

It was. I fumbled for his hand, pressed a trembling kiss to it between the cannula and the pulse oximeter. "You almost did."

"I didn't dare. You wouldn't let me." His voice was a thick rasp, an intimate caress. The man sure woke up all-systems go.

I rose, checked his monitors, his vitals. Everything steady, strong. Unbelievable, to see him so stable only twelve hours after being shot almost in the heart, after being opened wide and wired back together again. If only more of my patients were like that, powerhouses of stamina and resilience. And an indomitable will to survive.

"So—I hear you had my heart in your hands," he whispered.

"Literally this time. Yeah, I woke up once while you were gone."

My tension rushed out of me like water from a fast-draining sink. He'd resurfaced from deepest sedation, the most invasive surgery, alert and joking. Sorta. I'd dealt with enough trauma to know this was the best prognostic criterion. It would be a hard road back. But he was on it, and hard was what he was all about. He would be himself again. And not before long.

Now I could hate him.

I let anger resurface. It came in a gust that drowned even the din of the CH-47 Chinook helicopter's twin-engines and sixty-foot-span ceaselessly beating rotors. "Whatever it was I held in my hands, it was an uncanny imitation of the real thing."

He closed his eyes. Panic swamped me again. I'd developed phobic tendencies toward seeing his eyes closing. "You keep your eyes open, damn you!"

He complied. No defensiveness or guilt there. Just passion. "I told you why I lied to you, Calista. But I never lied about my feelings. If anything, I haven't told you the half of it."

It only made me more furious. "More evasions and omissions and half-truths, huh? If you'd told me from the start—"

"I *couldn't* tell you it was a search-and-destroy mission, because we would have lost GCA's backing. *You* would probably have led a kamikaze counter-rescue mission. We had no solid proof to offer you that the so-called hostages were willingly involved in biological-chemical weapons research and production."

"So what kind of proof did you have? Liquid?"

A surprised snort escaped him, a long groan following, his hand going to the focus of agony, his bandaged, sheared-open-and-wired-shut chest. I wagged an urgent finger at him, and he stopped short. "Don't make me laugh then." He sobered fully. "We had a couple of militants' accounts. Before they died."

We-ell. Convenient.

"And I was in the dark about Jake's plan. I thought he was only one of many. Then I had some revealing conversations with the militants during our business consultations, and I began to realize there was much more to him. Then you told me about the refugee deaths and that he knew what I was. I pieced it all together then. But if I'd told you then, would you have believed it of Jake? You saw and heard for yourself, and I bet you still can't believe it."

Which was a good point. Wondered if I'd ever believe it.

Still, Jake had given me a completely different version and set of motives for the same events. I bet Damian wouldn't tell me Jake had made a deal with him.

"Then he approached me." *When* would I stop making projections where he was concerned? "He told me he'd do anything to help us destroy the base in return for freedom and amnesty. His only condition was that you stay out of it, in every sense."

I chewed my tingling, stinging lip. "And you shook on it, intending to double-cross him. But he double-crossed you first."

"He was ready for us, knew when and how we'd attack."

"I told him." He gaped at me. I told him why I had.

He seemed to sag into the mattress. "So you didn't trust me even then."

"What's to trust? You lied to me from day one, you used me as protection…"

"I *never* did! I did everything I could to protect you, to stop you coming at all, then to limit your role. Both you and everyone else did everything you could to thwart me."

Which was another good point. Still… "I can understand, though not condone, that you lied at the beginning, when you had such a low opinion of my restraint and judgment, but later…"

"Later I was scared you'd take his word over mine. I saw you with him and felt I'd never mean half as much to you."

Which made him an insecure moron, of course.

But then again, he had a point. Emotional attachment wasn't all the blindingly passionate variety. Jake had had his vise around my being through the sheer weight of memories and guilt and compassion. More than ever now that I'd killed him.

Damian's gaze on me grew bleak. Thinking I wasn't buying his explanations, was drifting farther? Or was this another act?

I hated this. How could I ever trust him again? "You know the silliest part, Damian? All through our enmity, I trusted you. Implicitly. Now I love you and I wouldn't trust to…"

He jerked, startling me, all the stamina and power and uniqueness flaring back in his eyes. "You *love* me?" Wonder and elation made audible, that.

Had to burst his bubble. "Yeah. But so what? I said…"

"I'll never lie to you again, Calista."

"Really? Not even if you believe you're protecting me, from others or from my own recklessness? Or if you think you're looking out for my best interest, no matter what *I* believe it to be? Or if you don't think it's not a need-to-know for me?"

That dimmed his glowing eyes. He'd never thought of it this way, didn't know the answer to that one. I did. He'd do all that. Whatever lies and manipulation were called on, he'd use them, rationalize them.

"Calista, I love you…"

"As if that excuses everything—or anything. And just how do I even know that you do Damian? It's a case of crying wolf here. I can't pick and choose what to believe and what not to believe in your words. It could have all been part of a ruse, with Jake as its target and reason. It synchronized too well with all the stages of your plan."

His eyes went dead. He slumped. "And I'm continuing the 'ruse' just in case Jake resurfaces and tries to get to you? As long as he's out there, you'll never believe me?"

He didn't know? Which made his confession now genuine. It shouldn't make me want to somersault in the air. It did. It also didn't change a thing. "Jake can only resurface as a zombie now. If he does, he'd only get a stake in the heart."

"That's for killing vampires." He corrected me, so very serious. Then he exclaimed, "He's *dead?*"

A fountain of bile erupted into my throat. "I killed him."

He held my eyes, read my anguish. Then he closed his eyes. I snarled, "What did I tell you about closing your eyes?

He snapped them open. "Very confusing, feeling you worrying over me and wanting to strangle me at the same moment."

"Yeah, I'm full of surprises."

His large hand, with all the tubes hooked to it, like a cyborg in maintenance, caressed the hand that had snatched him back from death's snapping jaws. "Tell me about it. So—assuming I live, where do we go from here?"

"You'll live. You don't dare cross me. And back to square one, I guess."

"You expect to go on as if we aren't lovers?"

"We aren't. We just had one night together."

"*Just* one night?"

How dared the man look devastatingly sexy three-quarters dead? How could I lust after him now? How could I love him and not trust him?

The more I thought about it with hindsight as fuel, the more I realized there was so much more he was still hiding. Would keep on hiding. Not knowing… It was no way to have a relationship. Then again, what kind of relationship could two people like us have? I said so.

"I'll take anything, Calista. Anything at all with you."

"Anything? Such a broad term. From sporadic encounters to till death do us part."

He narrowed his eyes at me. "Sporadic encounters are out." Oh. *Oh!*

A diversion. One was in order.

The cosmic forces must owe some sort of break. I got one to order. Our retrieval posse, Sir Ashton and General Fitzpatrick, coming over from the back of the helicopter where they'd been conferencing with Ed and Matt, getting full reports.

"Good to see you awake, De Luna." Sir Ashton didn't sound at all pleased to see him alive even. "Quite the ruse you played on us. You're lucky any of you is still in one piece. And that the real threat is over. Thanks to Calista, of course."

Fitzpatrick puffed out his impressive chest. "I thought we'd agreed it had all been on a need-to-know basis, and that what Calista and her team went through and survived had been totally up to them. We would have gladly come here alone, with just a few papers from you saying we belonged to your GCA."

Sir Ashton sniffed. "Oh, yes, to kill our operatives based on the testimony of tortured-to-death militants."

Well, well. The plot congeals. Didn't hear anything about torture from Damian. The man was a compulsive omitter.

Fitzpatrick shrugged. "The intelligence was valid. And the *possibility* of those weapons being perfected and mass-produced warranted extreme action. We weren't about to let anyone with any information about them go free to possibly disseminate it."

"Whether they were guilty or innocent?" Sir Ashton seethed. He'd advocated that GCA change its tune. But not to an extremist anthem.

Okay. Enough. "Say, why don't you go back to your corner and continue bickering? Or do you actually have something to say to us? You interrogated the scientists. Any new info?"

Fitzpatrick inhaled a huge, irritated breath. "Just more details about Constantine's rise to power. They all think he went mad during his unendurable torture. Cynically, calculatingly, mercilessly mad. Then he put his superior skills and intelligence to use, turning the tide in his favor. When the militants asked him to use his medical expertise to make weapons he saw his opportunity. He contacted our captured scientists through the Internet, made sure each had the branch and level of expertise he needed and sent the militants after them."

"So they were kidnapped, too?" I asked.

"No. They were bought off."

"And what do you intend to do with them? Your original plan was eradication."

"And you went and changed my men's orders, so now we have a mess to deal with."

"You mean it's a mess to kill them now," I scoffed. "But not during the attack?"

He didn't answer me. I suspected some accident would befall them before they made it back to their various countries. I wasn't fighting this fight. Those people had betrayed science and humanity in the worst way. I wouldn't be their defender.

Seemed Fitzpatrick understood my silence, appreciated it. And me a bit more with it. Weird, that. This ruthless streak in me sure appealed to men, didn't it? Wondered what that said about them.

"They tutored him at first." Fitzpatrick continued his account. "He began with the rudimentaries of biological-chemical warfare knowledge, but in no time left them far behind."

Sir Ashton exhaled. "But even they became disturbed at the Armageddon potential of his research and discoveries. When they expressed concern, they were shut out, relegated to conventional venues. He experimented on the refugees, on low-rank militants, on his colleagues, yet still no one wised up to his true nature. Supernaturally cunning, that one. He sold some of his less diabolic weapons to the highest bidder, making millions for the rebels and himself."

It was all still unbelievable. Jake? "So he was keeping the *more* diabolic ones for an even more ambitious endeavor, huh? He'd told me money was just his means to the highest end."

"And what was that?" That was Damian, speaking for the first time since Sir Ashton and Fitzpatrick came over.

"Curing the planet's ills by eradicating the septic foci of chronic conflict. His theory is that there are no oppressed and oppressors, just evil that is manifesting now, and evil that will one day get strong enough to manifest. All sides in a conflict have to go, in his opinion."

"God save us from a madman with an ideology!" Sir Ashton huffed.

Fitzpatrick blinked. "Huh?"

"Ideology is social theory that rationalizes evil acts, twists them into good or even heroic acts, in his own and probably other's eyes," Sir Ashton clarified, long sufferingly.

"He was on his way to beating Hitler and Machiavelli, huh?"

Sir Ashton tutted at Fitzpatrick's comment. "Actually, Machiavelli never harmed a soul, and was much maligned and unfairly persecuted over his book *The Prince.* Maybe you should cite Lenin or Stalin with sixty million dead to their 'collectivization' and 'purges' or Mao's incalculable millions in his 'Great Leap Forward,' 'Cultural Revolution,' 'political purges,' 'reeducation' and his roles in Tibetan and Cambodian genocides. His ideology also caused the largest man-made disaster in recorded history, damaging agriculture and ending in twenty-five million starving to death. I *could* go on."

Fitzpatrick blinked again. Then again. I giggled. You'd think he'd know his military history better than that. Oh, well, Sir Ashton with the headmaster's rod to the rescue.

"Constantine sure had an edge on any historic totalitarian madman," Damian said slowly. "None of them possessed anything like his almost superhuman intellect, none had the access to lethal modern technology and medical science, either. Had he lived, gone unopposed, he would have caused far more devastation."

Sir Ashton nodded. "This superhuman intellect had to be why he believed he knew better, would take care of it all, how he came to see everyone as less, individual lives as worthless."

I couldn't add to their dissection of Jake's character, couldn't judge him. I wouldn't presume to imagine what he'd gone through that had destroyed the unique, balanced mind and the compassionate human being he used to be.

And now I'd never know, never have the chance to undo it.

No, I couldn't judge him. Not when I'd ultimately been the reason for it all. I'd started it. And I'd ended it.

As if to deprive me of my moment of piercing reminiscence and bleak self-flagellation, Damian said, "He might have shown you a different side of him, Calista, but you must remember he was an extremist in his beliefs, especially in his own mental superiority. But as he lived in a governed society, in a privileged and safe life, sort of moderated by being among peers he'd had his extremist tendencies under control. Then he was abducted, tortured, and his dark, life-despising side took over."

Maybe. Probably. But I *couldn't* judge him.

Yeah, funny that. I should have thought of that before I *executed* him.

Seriously, there was another reason why this was a raw and bleeding point with me.

Jake had been confident I could be brought to appreciate and embrace his nihilistic and annihilistic doctrines. And deep inside me, something, no matter how tiny, resonated with his views, awed and admiring of his macabre crusade, his larger-than-life-and-death goals.

And it scared the hell out of me.

I was truly my father's daughter. Damian had had every right to think I was a catastrophe waiting to happen.

Only good part here was I was aware, was scared. And was doing everything to bring my radical streak under control.

The conversation waned, and I told Sir Ashton and Fitzpatrick to move along. Damian, while looking impossibly vital after his near-death experience, wasn't exactly recovering from a tonsillectomy.

They moved away as Ayesha came over to help me with his periodic postoperative monitoring and measures, hanging another bag of plasma, administering the next dose of antibiotics and medications and checking his vitals.

I bent to kiss him before I sat back in my chair to continue my vigil. He caught me back as I withdrew. "I know you may not want to hear this under the circumstances, but I think you've only set him free from the festering hell he's been rotting in inside his own mind."

A sob-laugh tore through me. "Nice try, De Luna. I bet he'd beg to differ if he could. He seemed pretty comfortable within his mind."

"I don't think so. I really don't. Apart from that last isolated human island within him, the part that loved you, he was totally sick and tormented."

"Yeah, thanks very much. It's very comforting to know that I used that island as firm footing from where to shoot him to death."

"Don't. *Don't,* Calista. Don't let this fester inside you. You did what you had to do. What had to be done. As you always do."

I reached out, combed a lock of raven satin off his forehead. "And by your black-and-white standards, *if* they are really so…" He grimaced. I shrugged. "This is an all-objectives accomplished mission, isn't it? We destroyed a militant hive and an apocalyptic biochemical warfare project. We've opened the road to all international forces to reach the refugees and either set up a steady supply route or relocate them. And we brought the mastermind of this focus of insanity down."

"Well, yeah. All objectives accomplished." He smiled. Then his eyes grew puzzled, dimmed. My heart gave me the kick I deserved. *Good going, Calista. Save him only to talk him to death!* He was frowning now, as if he was looking for something he'd misplaced. "The mission—at least. What about us?"

"We'll see about us, Damian. Now rest, please."

"But you love me—still?" His eyes were defocusing, his voice slurring. I, too, began to lose coherence—until I realized. Ayesha had topped up his sedation. He wasn't deteriorating, just surrendering to artificial sleep.

Brutal relief rushed out, deflating me. He hung on until I said, "Yeah, I love you," then let go with a still uncertain smile.

Now *I* had to figure out what to do about that love.

And about the rest. My work, my vocation, my methods. My mind. The whole package, really. Reassessment and recalibration of self and path was good for the soul. For everything else. Every*one* else.

If one good thing had come out of this mess, besides the stuff I'd just recited, which was are-you-crazy-this-is-un-freaking-believable lot of good, it was that I saw an extreme vision of what doing good at any cost could lead to. I came face-to-face with my own judge-executioner tendencies, my need to walk this tightrope I chose for a life with constant awareness and control. Every day of my life.

Seemed like a plan.

* * * * *

Turn the page for a sneak preview of
Honeymoon with a Stranger
by Frances Housden.

Available from Intrigue
next month!

Honeymoon with a Stranger

by

Frances Housden

It was November in Paris, a bleak, damp month when the City of Lights turned petulant, more given to dampen a lover's shoulder with tears than blow a warm kiss, the way the capital would come spring.

The long nights and foggy weather suited Mac McBride's calling just fine, but then, Mac wasn't your typical American in Paris. As an agent for IBIS, the Intelligence Bureau for International Security on call 24/7, his days weren't anyone's idea of routine.

A snub-nosed pistol sat comfortably inside his left boot, and a 9 mm Glock, his favorite piece, was tucked neatly under the waistband in the back of his black jeans. Mac felt ready for anything.

His fingertips tingled with edgy anticipation as he fitted the PM53 Makarov pistol into his shoulder holster, knowing all his hard work was about to pay off.

The only important decision now was whether or not he

should keep on the gray tie with the black shirt? Did his outward appearance say Jeirgif Makjzajev, Chechen rebel, or did the slick oily sheen of the stuff he'd put on his hair yell Mafia lieutenant instead?

Mulling over the appointment ahead of him, he ditched the tie, then scraped his fingernails through this rough face stubble.

He drew his thick brown eyebrows into a frown that quickly disappeared once he was satisfied his reflection fitted the hard-ass look he'd intended.

The small break that took his nose off the straight and narrow became an asset on gigs like these. Though, he had to admit, he hadn't thought that at the time when he was training at Annapolis, but then life had been all about girls—women—and what attracted them. Now it was about terrorists.

His face hadn't seen a razor in more than six days, and the stubble looked darker where a dimple made a hollow in his chin.

Six days of dragging his heels on top of the month he'd already spent inveigling his way into the confidence of the slightly down-at-heel Algerian arms dealer he was setting up.

Meanwhile, his firm had made short work of any competitors without arousing suspicion.

He'd laughed when they told him he'd got this gig because of his razor-sharp cheekbones. Laughed to realize they thought he could pass for Chechen, and him with his true-blue American bloodline and a family history spanning 250-odd years since the first McBride set foot in America.

What the hell, he was more than willing to be involved in one of the craziest operations he'd yet encountered. And it helped that he spoke fluent Russian.

Though the Algerian didn't, so the odd curse word was enough to fool him.

Luckily, Mac's ability to finesse a deal speaking French was every bit as effortless as working in English, Russian or any of the other languages he'd picked up while his father's career took the McBrides to U.S. embassies around the world.

Mac was shrugging his broad shoulders into the soft well-worn creases and shoulder-hugging cut of his black leather bomber jacket, almost ready to leave, when the phone rang.

Without looking, he shot out an arm, snagging the receiver, thankful it no longer took a guessing game to locate things he needed in the Le Sentier apartment. Reciting his number, he heard, "Zukah is on his way up to the apartment."

The voice was Thierry's, one of the other IBIS agents—French—working with Mac. "Damn, how far away?"

The importance IBIS placed on this case showed in the amount of money they were willing to commit. Thierry's assignment was to tail the Algerian and his men; he and three others covered that end, but only Thierry was a master at disguise.

"They entered the building as I punched in your number, three of them. Want me to follow them up?" he asked.

"No, wait. Pick up their trail again when they leave. Zukah probably thinks there's safety in numbers, but three shouldn't be a problem now I've been warned."

Mac only stated the facts as he knew them. The word *arrogance* didn't raise a ripple on his conscience.

After focusing most of his adult life training to be the best, able to kill with his bare hands if need be, he now took those abilities for granted.

Roxanne Kincaid looked back over her shoulder, wondering if it was the last time she would see the little Renault.

She hadn't worried about the car when she'd stolen a heart-racing gap in the traffic from under the wheels of the one along-side her, or while she swerved into the corner to cross the Seine at the Pont Neuf, but parking in Le Sentier?

This dark, dank *quartier* of Paris was the contrast that proved the rule when they spoke of the City of Lights. It would be just her luck to find the wheels missing when she returned.

She looked along the sidewalk, saw three men walking ahead of her and slowed her pace.

Earlier that evening the couturier Charles Fortier had caught her eye as he spun his bright glance round the avenue Montaigne workroom, and before he could say *"Bon soir, Roxie,"* she'd known he had a special job for her.

One she couldn't refuse.

And now here she was, outside a six-story apartment building that hadn't been on her agenda for this evening's entertainment.

Gathering the upstanding collar of her charcoal-colored coat closer to her ears, she cast a baleful frown up at the persistent drizzle, sniffing air that had long since lost the dusty scent of autumn.

Everyone said winter had come early this year, but what it meant to Roxie was that all the straightening lotion in Paris wasn't going stop her hair curling.

Standing under the dismal street lamp, she checked the washed-out number painted on pitted plaster as she swayed against a gust of wind that funneled through the narrow streets. This *quartier* really hadn't changed much over the years.

She found it hard to imagine her grandmother growing up not a two-minute walk from this very doorway. Grandmère's neat Dorset cottage, where Roxie grew up, had been a far cry from the dark, sightless windows crowding the narrow cobbled streets.

Though, if Grandmère were alive to see her now, she wouldn't be delighted to see Roxie visiting her old haunts.

No, Anastasia Perdieu Kincaid hadn't been the type of woman who minced words or called a spade a shovel.

A quick twist of the wrist and Mac checked the time on the flashy gold watch—Russian—and checked it against the plain clock, the only piece of decor on his apartment walls. The transient feeling of the place was exactly what he'd had in mind.

The Algerian was thirty minutes early, but if he'd thought to surprise Mac…?

As far as he'd discovered, Ahmed Zukah had only lately begun playing out of his league. Until now the worst crimes listed on the Algerian's rap sheet were shady arms deals.

But this one was bigger, much bigger, a deal deadly enough to be brought to the attention of the IBIS.

Though Zukah acted as front man and had two Frenchmen working for him, none of them had the cojones to put this together, but the IBIS had still to discover who was running the Algerian.

Mac wondered if tonight would bring him any closer to the man he really wanted to lay hands on, the fourth man. These others were small potatoes compared to the brain behind the scheme.

Right on time, a fist hammered on the door of the third-floor apartment. Mac sniffed; they could wait.

The wooden door received three more poundings while he finished pulling his shirt collar over the neck of his jacket.

His dark gold eyes narrowed, fierce lights burning in them, sparked from his resentment of the impatient demand on his door.

It was a look those who knew him had come to dread, but then, the bad guys outside the door didn't know that.

Yet.

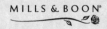

MILLS & BOON

Classic novels by
bestselling authors for
you to enjoy!

PASSIONATE
PARTNERS

2-in-1
FOR ONLY
£4.99

Featuring
The Heart Beneath
by Lindsay McKenna
&
Ride the Thunder
by Lindsay McKenna

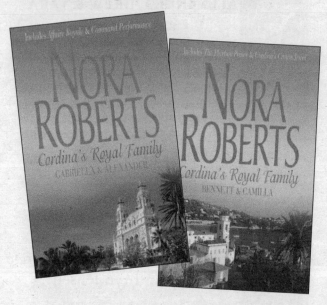

"When the bullets finally ceased, the bodies lay in a coiled embrace on the lifeboat."

The sinking of a cargo ship and the slaughter of its crew seemed a senseless act of violence. But Clea Rice knows the truth and is determined to expose the culprits.

When Jordan Tavistock is asked to steal the indiscreet letters of a friend, he reluctantly obliges, only to be caught red-handed—by another burglar. The burglar is Clea, who is looking for something else entirely.

Only together can Jordan and Clea find the answers to the sinister questions surrounding the sinking of the ship. Answers that some are prepared to kill for to keep buried.

20th April 2007

MIRA

FREE

4 BOOKS AND A SURPRISE GIFT!

We would like to take this opportunity to thank you for reading this Mills & Boon® book by offering you the chance to take FOUR more specially selected titles from the Intrigue™ series absolutely FREE! We're also making this offer to introduce you to the benefits of the Mills & Boon® Reader Service™—

★ **FREE home delivery**
★ **FREE gifts and competitions**
★ **FREE monthly Newsletter**
★ **Books available before they're in the shops**
★ **Exclusive Reader Service offers**

Accepting these FREE books and gift places you under no obligation to buy; you may cancel at any time, even after receiving your free shipment. Simply complete your details below and return the entire page to the address below. You don't even need a stamp!

YES! Please send me 4 free Intrigue books and a surprise gift. I understand that unless you hear from me, I will receive 6 superb new titles every month for just £3.10 each, postage and packing free. I am under no obligation to purchase any books and may cancel my subscription at any time. The free books and gift will be mine to keep in any case.

I7ZEE

Ms/Mrs/Miss/Mr..Initials ....
                                                                    BLOCK CAPITALS PLEASE
Surname ....

Address ....

....

....Postcode ....

Send this whole page to:
The Reader Service, FREEPOST CN81, Croydon, CR9 3WZ